Praise for Leona Karr
and her novels

LEONA KARR
Hero in Disguise
&
Hidden Blessing

Steeple Hill®

Published by Steeple Hill Books™

STEEPLE HILL BOOKS

Steeple Hill®

ISBN-13: 978-0-373-65263-1
ISBN-10:   0-373-65263-1

HERO IN DISGUISE AND HIDDEN BLESSING

HERO IN DISGUISE
Copyright © 2002 by Leona Karr

HIDDEN BLESSING
Copyright © 2002 by Leona Karr

www.SteepleHill.com

Printed in U.S.A.

TABLE OF CONTENTS

Books by Leona Karr

Love Inspired

Rocky Mountain Miracle #131
Hero in Disguise #171
Hidden Blessing #194

A native of Colorado, Leona (Lee) Karr is the
author of nearly forty books. Her favorite genres are
romantic suspense and inspirational romance. After
graduating from the University of Colorado with a
B.A. and the University of Northern Colorado with an
M.A., she taught as a reading specialist until her first
book was published. She is a presenter at numerous
writing conferences and has taught college courses
in creative writing.

HERO IN DISGUISE

Call unto me and I will answer you,
and will tell you great and hidden things
which you have not known.
—*Jeremiah* 33:3

With thanks to Paul Fanshane,
a very special and delightful friend

Chapter One

Let me say and do the right thing, Melissa Chanley prayed as she entered the Colorado State Capital.

It wasn't going to be easy, no matter how she approached David Ardell. The contents of the folded note in her purse were going to shake up the handsome young attorney's life the minute he laid his eyes on it.

How would he react? She'd never met him personally, but she'd seen his picture in the newspaper with the governor, and on television. He was in his early thirties, had wavy hair almost the color of old gold and dark brown eyes. In public he was poised, articulate and successful—but what kind of person lay under that successful political veneer? Was there a compassionate nature that she could appeal to?

As she opened the door to the outer office, Melissa hoped she wasn't embarking on a fool's errand. A middle-aged secretary with graying hair sat behind a computer. A wooden desk placard identified her as

Elsie Shaw. She gave Melissa a practiced smile and an enquiring raise of her eyebrows. Curiosity was evident as her frank gaze assessed Melissa.

"May I help you?"

"I'm Melissa Chanley. I have a two o'clock appointment."

When Melissa made the appointment, the secretary had enquired as to the reason for the meeting, but Melissa had sidestepped the question. In her capacity as freelance writer for Colorado's *Women of the West* magazine, Melissa had learned to save explanations for the person she was interviewing, and even though her appointment had nothing to do with her professional occupation, she wasn't about to share that with his secretary.

"Oh, yes, Ms. Chanley. I'll let him know you're here." She spoke briskly into the intercom, listened a moment and then nodded. Turning to Melissa, she said, "He'll see you now, but only for a few minutes. Mr. Ardell has a busy schedule this afternoon." She left her desk, opened an adjoining office door, motioned Melissa inside and then quietly closed the door behind her.

Melissa hesitated just inside the office as her sweeping gaze quickly assessed the room, which was crowded with more furniture than any decent interior decorator would allow. Large windows were banked by bookcases and a collection of scenic western oil paintings was mounted on the opposite wall. A ring of chairs took up space in the center of the room as if left by a previous meeting, and a large executive desk was loaded with books and papers. The leather office chair behind it was empty.

"Please, come in, Ms. Chanley." The masculine voice edged with a hint of impatience startled her.

She saw then that the lawyer was sitting on a dark leather couch in a far corner of the room. As he stood up, he put down some folders on an already loaded coffee table. His eyes traveled over her as she walked toward him.

"I'm David Ardell." He introduced himself as if he wasn't certain that she had come to the right office.

"Yes, I know." She felt a smile hover on her lips. He was definitely more attractive in person than on television, even though a slight frown marred his handsome features. "Thank you for seeing me."

What now? David thought. At any other time, he might have enjoyed the interruption of an attractive dark-haired woman, but the governor was waiting for a report that was only half finished, and he had to attend a committee meeting in a few minutes. He caught the waver of a smile and the confident lift of her head as she came toward him. Who was she, anyway? Some socialite wanting him to serve on a community committee as representative of the governor? Then he remembered his secretary had told him that she was a reporter for a local woman's magazine. Great, he thought wryly.

"How can I help you?" he asked, already forming a routine dodge for handling the matter, whatever it was.

"I'm sorry to bother you, Mr. Ardell, but this is important."

That didn't surprise him. Heaven knows, half of what crossed his desk was stuff *somebody* at the capital thought was urgent and needed his immediate attention. Sometimes he felt like a firefighter with a dozen fires to put out. "Yes, Ms. Chanley?"

From his tone Melissa knew that he was ready to get rid of her as quickly as possible. Only the dire necessity of her visit stiffened her resolve to take as much time as she needed to make him understand the situation.

"I'm here at the request of someone else," she said evenly. "And when you know who, I'm sure you'll agree that my mission is important enough to take up a few minutes of your time."

Something in her tone warned David that his intention to dismiss her in short order might be premature. For a moment he let himself appreciate the way she held her slender shoulders and kept her unbelievable pansy-blue eyes locked on his face. Even the trim summer suit couldn't hide feminine curves or lovely long legs showing under a modest-length skirt as she stood in front of him, her head high, her eyes fixed directly on his as if she was the one in control of the situation.

"May I ask who sent you?" David's involvement in the political world had made him appreciate a worthy adversary. He sensed that in some fashion Melissa Chanley was here to challenge him.

"This will take a few minutes," she said smoothly. "Shall we sit down?"

"Of course. I'm sorry." He chuckled to himself at how deftly she'd taken charge of the interview by that simple request. Maybe this was going to be interesting, after all. Her firm yet gracious manner was fresh and appealing, and in spite of himself he was intrigued with the reason for her visit. He couldn't ever remember meeting her at any of the political fund-raisers or rallies, and he was certain he would not forget a woman as attractive as she.

"Please, sit down." He motioned her to the leather couch and he eased down into a chair opposite her. Moving a few things around on the coffee table, he said, "As you can see I'm trying to dig out from under some paperwork that the governor's office unloaded on me. I'm sorry I don't have time to offer you some coffee. Unfortunately, I have a meeting in a few minutes. Perhaps you'd rather make an appointment on another day when I have more time?"

"No. I'm afraid this can't wait." Melissa's heart began to race. *Speak into my words, Lord. Give me the wisdom I need.*

"All right, Ms. Chanley." He raised a questioning dark brown eyebrow. "I understand that you're a writer for *Women of the West* magazine?" He allowed himself a smile. "I really can't see that I have anything to offer in the way of material for your publication."

"I'm not here in my professional capacity," Melissa explained as she reached into her white leather bag and took out a piece of paper. "I have a message for you from Jolene McCombre."

Jolene McCombre.

He stiffened and for one startling moment he wondered if he'd heard the name correctly, but something

in the way Melissa Chanley was looking at him said
that there had been no mistake. Just hearing the name
jerked the scab off a wound that had never quite
healed. Until that moment, he'd thought that he had
successfully buried everything having to do with his
high school sweetheart.

They had planned to marry as soon as he finished
law school, but Jolene had jilted him a month before
their wedding, disappeared from his life and married
a serviceman who was home on leave. David had
never gotten over Jolene's cruel betrayal, and even
though some protective instinct warned him not to
open that door again, he knew better than to lie about
knowing the woman who had left him at the altar.

"You have a message for me from Jolene," he repeated in a tight voice. "What kind of message?"

Melissa fingered the letter in her hand, unsure how
she should prepare him for the contents. His expression had become a closed mask, and hardness flickered
in the depths of his brown eyes. She knew that the
success of her mission depended upon how well she
handled the next few minutes. "Before I give you the
letter, I want to explain how I got it."

David gave her a noncommittal nod and remained
silent. Better not to say anything until he knew exactly
why this woman was here and what her intent was.
She was a writer, after all. Had Melissa Chanley stum-
bled into this juicy tidbit of his past and planned to
use it for some nefarious purpose of her own? Busy
with his life and career, he had lost all track of Jolene
through the years. Why would she be sending him a
letter through this stranger? A flicker of intuition

warned that this meeting was going to challenge his determination to leave the past buried.

"My magazine does profiles on women, past and present, who have shown strength and dedication in a lifetime of helping others," Melissa explained. "I was doing an article on May Bowers who founded the Denver Christian Shelter for homeless women and children. While spending time with May and collecting information for my article, I made friends with some of the women in the shelter, and they shared their stories of abandonment and poverty with me." Melissa drew a firming breath. "Jolene was one of them."

His eyes widened in disbelief. "She was one of the women at the shelter?"

Melissa nodded. "Yes. Penniless and homeless with two little boys. Apparently, the father of the boys died when they were two and three years old, and she raised them by herself until last year when she married a man who took her for everything she had. The scoundrel ended up in prison for fraud, and left her with huge bills and no money. She came to Denver, hoping to find a job and start again, but she became ill before she could find work and ended up at the shelter. I befriended her two little boys, Richie and Eric, and when Jolene was taken to the hospital she asked me to take care of them instead of leaving them at the shelter."

"Is Jolene there now? In the hospital?" When she shook her head, he said, "Oh, I see. You took her home with you." Now, he understood. Ms. Chanley was here to get money from him for Jolene and her kids.

"No, I'm afraid Jolene never made it out of the hospital."

He swallowed hard. "She died?"

"Yes, I'm sorry. She gave me this letter in the hospital, and asked me to read and deliver it if she didn't make it." She handed him the folded sheet of paper.

David's stomach took a sickening plunge as he focused on the familiar handwriting. Jolene had written him every week while he was in law school, and there was no doubt that she had penned this letter. For a moment he wanted to hand the note back without reading it. Then he took himself in hand. He was not the same person he'd been ten years ago.

Melissa watched as David read the letter written by a mother who knew she was dying. Jolene had simply reminded David Ardell of the love they had once shared and asked him to look after her sons now that she was no longer able to care for them. Her greatest fear was that they would end up in foster homes, and she begged David to use his resources to assure their care and happiness.

Melissa searched David's expression as he read it, but his thoughts were hidden from her. Only his long fingers tightening slightly on the letter hinted at an inner turmoil. He was good at hiding his emotions, she thought. Jolene had not shared much about their past relationship, and Melissa only knew what was in the letter.

Slowly he folded the letter, and when he raised his dark eyes and looked at her, his gaze was guarded and his mouth set in a firm line. "I'll have to check this out, of course."

"Please do. May Bowers and St. Joseph's Hospital can verify everything I've told you. I'm sorry to be the messenger in this situation," she said sincerely, sensing a deep concern beneath his professional demeanor. She suspected that he tried to keep his personal hurts hidden from everyone.

"It isn't that I doubt your integrity," he assured her.

"I understand. Anyone in your prominent position has to be careful. You can check out the handwriting with May."

"That won't be necessary, but there are some other things that I want to verify. Where are the boys now?"

"They are still with me."

"And how old are they?"

"Eric is six, and Richie is almost five. They're very bright little boys." She smiled. "Most of the time, they're pretty easy to handle."

"Unfortunately, it may take a little time to track down any relatives who could take them, but I'll put an investigator on it right away." David had recovered from his initial shock, and his agile mind had begun to search for ways to handle the situation with impersonal dispatch. If things were exactly as she had told him, he didn't have much choice but to get involved, temporarily at least.

"I hope we can find someone soon. We need to get the boys settled as soon as possible."

"I know that Jolene's parents passed away some years ago—and I know nothing about the father's relatives," he added with a hard edge in his tone, referring to the man Jolene had chosen to marry. "Did she make any mention of family while she was at the shelter?"

"No, and I doubt that she would have been there with her children if she'd had any family to go to," Melissa said. "I took the boys because there was no one else she could ask."

"I see, and you're willing to keep them until some other arrangements have been made?" He used a professional lawyer tone, as if he were taking a deposition instead of handling a very personal matter. He did not want to meet the children that under different circumstances might have been his.

"No, I'm afraid not. I'm not in any position to keep Eric and Richie at my place," she said firmly. Where was a sign of compassion for the woman he had once intended to marry?

"If it's a matter of monetary compensation, I'm sure we can come to some satisfactory arrangement. I'm willing to assume the expenses of the children's care while you have them."

"How generous of you," she said with gravel in her voice. Obviously, his checkbook was as close as he intended to get to the sweet little boys who could use a caring man in their lives right now.

"You should be compensated in some fashion for their care," he said, well aware of the sarcasm in her tone. A flash of anger in her lovely blue eyes startled him. She looked ready to light into him. What was the matter? His offer seemed reasonable enough. Was she after more money than just expenses for keeping the boys? "Did you have some specific arrangement in mind?"

"Although I would love to keep Eric and Richie, I can't. And it isn't a matter of compensation." She didn't want him to think she was trying to fleece him out of any money for keeping them. "I live in a studio basement apartment with a fold-down bed. We've been playing camping with sleeping bags. I've managed to keep Eric and Richie fairly entertained in the small space, but some other accommodations have to be made." She eyed him frankly. "What kind of living space do you have?"

He knew the question was rhetorical. From the thrust of her chin, he could tell that she already knew from reading the society pages that he lived in Denver's fashionable Cherry Creek district in a spacious family home, which was his residence now that his parents had retired and moved to Florida. He decided to deliberately sidestep the inference that he had a home large enough to comfortably house the two boys.

"Frankly, I'm not quite sure what Jolene expected me to do in this situation." There was no way that he was going to become personally responsible for the care of Jolene's two boys. He'd do his best to find a relative to take them, and he'd foot the bill for their care until then. That was it.

"I think it's pretty clear that she wanted you to look after them, Mr. Ardell."

"It's David," he said, brushing away her formality. "And I will do my best to get them placed."

Melissa looked at him with a warning in her large eyes. If he suggested they call Children's Services to take the children, she was ready to challenge that decision. "We need to do what's best for the children."

"Yes, of course, but we have to consider what would be better for them in the long run. Don't we, Melissa?"

"The long run," she echoed in disbelief. "You and I have the responsibility of deciding what should happen to them right now, today. We have two little boys that have just lost their mother. Sadly enough, their lives have been in a state of upheaval almost since the day they were born." What they need is someone to love and take care of them now!

"What options do we have?" David didn't like the feeling that she was personally attacking him. None of this was of his making. He sympathized with the homeless little boys and regretted that Jolene had made such a mess of her life, but the responsibility for the situation was not his. "My taking on the personal care of two youngsters is impossible."

"Surely you know a nice family with children who would take Eric and Richie until a relative can be located," Melissa insisted, knowing she had lost the first round. He wasn't going to get personally involved.

"Honestly, I don't." He brushed back a forelock of dark blond hair and frowned. "My single life doesn't include anyone close enough that I can call up and dump two strange kids on them. If you could just keep them temporarily—"

"I told you I don't have the space. I wish I did, but I don't. This afternoon I had to leave Eric and Richie with my landlady, whose apartment is almost as small as mine." She refrained from telling him that the past two weeks had been an almost impossible challenge—trying to meet her deadlines at the various magazines she wrote for, while cooped up in a basement apartment scarcely big enough for one adult, let alone two rambunctious little boys. She fell silent, waiting for him to decide what he was going to do about Jolene's request—if anything.

He was silent for a moment, then he asked, "And what about time?"

She looked puzzled. "What do you mean?"

"Have you had the time to care for them?"

"I've made the time," she said flatly. "Since I'm a freelance writer, I can set my own work hours. That's the only way I've been able to spend days at the park with the boys, and compose at night with my laptop computer on the kitchen table."

"I see." He surprised her by suddenly getting up from his chair and easing down beside her on the couch. "Well, Melissa, we may have a solution, after all."

She caught a whiff of spicy men's cologne as she steadied herself against his nearness. *Careful,* she warned herself. David Ardell's ability to deftly manage people was evident in the disarming smile he gave her.

"Let's look at the problem this way. You have the time to care for the children but not the space. I have the space but no one to care for the children. Doesn't the answer seem obvious?" He raised a questioning eyebrow.

"What are you suggesting?"

"A businesslike solution. While I hire an investigator to find the boys' relatives, you could move into my house temporarily to care for them."

"I couldn't do that," she said quickly. "Move in with you, like that. It wouldn't be proper."

"You wouldn't be moving in with me." David was amused by the indignant spark in her eyes. Her reaction told him a great deal about her moral fiber, and he hastened to reassure her that his offer was strictly based on the children's welfare. "This arrangement would have nothing to do with me, no more than if I hired you as a live-in nanny for the children. And I'm willing to do that, make it purely a business arrangement. Just consider it a temporary job until this thing is settled. You can still keep up your obligations at the magazines. I think it's a perfect solution all around."

"I don't know. It seems very...irregular."

He saw a flicker of indecision in her eyes. "You don't have to be afraid that you'll have to suffer my company," he assured her. "I'm rarely at home. Believe me, we would scarcely see each other."

When she remained silent, obviously weighing what he was saying, he stressed the point that the arrangement would be a good one for Eric and Richie. "The place is large enough for you and the boys to be perfectly comfortable staying there. There's a lovely fenced-in backyard with plenty of grass for running and jumping. You could even set up your work on the covered patio while the boys are playing."

Melissa found the idea of living in a place that must be ten times bigger than any place she'd ever had, to be a little frightening. "And we would be alone in the house, except when you're there?"

"No, I have a wonderful couple, Inga and Hans Erickson, who take care of the cooking and house-keeping. They've been with my family since I was in grade school, and they'll be delighted to have some youngsters in the house." Inga was always lamenting the fact that David wasn't married and raising his own children by now. "You'll like them. And I'll bet they'll like you."

Melissa hesitated. The offer was unconventional, to say the least. She had hoped that David would respond to Jolene's request and see to the boys' care, but she hadn't expected to be part of the package.

Was this the answer she had been praying for? Would it be the best arrangement for Eric and Richie? She had already grown so fond of them. She knew she couldn't have the boys permanently, but turning them over to strangers pulled at her heartstrings. The pos-sibility of keeping them in her life a little longer was tempting.

"Well, what do you think?" David asked, surprised at how much he wanted her to say yes.

"How long do you think it will be before we find the right place for the boys? And will the authorities let us keep them until we do?"

"I can take care of all the legal matters. That's no problem. We'll just have to wait and see what an in-vestigator turns up and then decide our next step." He smiled. "Maybe I ought to give you time to think about it."

"I don't see any better solution at the moment," she said honestly. Eric and Richie deserved to live in a nice place for a change. Some of things they said about being hungry and cold when they were homeless made her grateful that they'd have the chance to live in a nice home and play outside in the beautiful Colorado summer weather.

"All right." She was taking a leap of faith that she was doing the right thing. "We'll consider it a nanny job with no pay except board and room for the three of us," she said firmly. She'd spent one summer as a hired companion to a disabled little girl, and this situation wouldn't be much different—if David Ardell kept his distance as promised. "I'll stay at your house with the children until your investigator locates some relatives and we find a proper home for them."

"Good. It's a deal," he said. "When do you want to move in?"

"Tomorrow morning. I'll need the rest of the day to make arrangements for the move."

"Fine." He suddenly realized that having her around would be a definite boost to his lonely life— then he caught himself. He'd promised her that he would make himself scarce if she moved into the house. Now, as he looked into her soft blue eyes and at her appealing smile, he realized that it might be the hardest promise he'd ever had to keep.

Chapter Two

Melissa's heart sank as she viewed the spacious white brick mansion and beautifully landscaped grounds set back from the road. What business did she and two rambunctious youngsters have living in a place like that?

"Are we lost?" Eric asked with childish anxiety as he sat stiffly beside her in the front seat. The large brown eyes in his thin, pinched face were filled with apprehension. He was a small-boned child and terribly underweight. Wiry sandy hair hung longish over his ears and narrow forehead, and freckles dotted his slender nose.

"No, we're not lost," she quickly assured him as she turned into the curved driveway that led to the front of the house. The upheavals of Eric's young life had already left its mark. He had just begun to trust Melissa and was opening up a little to her. Guarded and solemn, the young boy was the protector of his little brother, who was sitting in the back seat happily munching a fruit bar.

"This is Mr. Ardell's house. It's pretty, isn't it?" she said brightly as she braked in front of marble steps leading up to a terraced veranda and double wooden doors with etched glass windows.

"Are we going to stay here a long time?"

A long time? She knew what Eric was really asking. *Is this home?* She hated to think about how many times the small boys had moved around before they ended up at the homeless shelter.

"We're going to stay here until we find someone in your mommy's or daddy's family who want you two lovely boys to come and live with them," she said brightly. "Then you won't have to move anymore."

"What if we don't find anybody?"

"We will. You wait and see." *Ask and it shall be given, seek and ye shall find.* Never had the scripture seemed more reassuring than it did in this situation. The grandmother who had raised Melissa had lived by that promise, and her faith in God's guidance had been instilled in Melissa from an early age.

"But what if they don't like us?" Eric insisted with childish pugnaciousness. "Some people don't like kids."

"Maybe not, but I know they would love you and Richie." Impulsively, Melissa gave him a quick hug, and was rewarded with a weak smile. "Now, let's unload our stuff and see what the inside of this place looks like. I bet you guys won't have to sleep on the floor anymore. How about that?"

"Goody," Richie said with a four-year-old's enthusiasm. He had a mop of dark brown hair, a bone structure that was heavier than his sandy-haired brother's and the same large dark eyes. "I want a bed—a big, big bed." Then he giggled as if a thought tickled him. "And I'm going to jump up and down on it lots."

"No, you're not," Melissa corrected quickly, trying to blot out a picture of two playful boys turning some elegant bed into a trampoline. "There'll be a nice backyard for you to play in. Now, let's get out of the car and take a look at this place."

She hoped they couldn't see her nervousness as they unloaded the trunk and set the luggage on the front step. The pile included only two small suitcases, her laptop computer and a brown sack containing a book and old baseball that Eric wouldn't let out of his sight.

The boys had few clothes, and they were wearing the one new outfit of jeans and summer shirts that Melissa had bought them. She'd return to her place to pick up things for herself if their stay lasted more than a week.

When she'd talked to David last night and arranged to arrive about ten o'clock in the morning, he told her that Inga and Hans Erickson would help them settle in. He also assured her that an excellent investigator in Denver had agreed to conduct a search. The man expected to have something to report within ten days.

Ten days.

As they stood at the elegant front door and waited for someone to answer the bell, Melissa had the feeling that ten days could be a lifetime.

"Maybe nobody's home," Eric said with his usual worried expression. Before Melissa could stop Richie, he reached up and pushed the button a half-dozen times.

"Don't, Richie." She pulled his hand away, just as the door swung open. David stood there, a slight frown on his handsome face.

"The doorbell works," he said wryly.

"I'm sorry, Richie got carried away," she apologized. Great, she thought. Off to a great start. David was obviously on his way out, in a beige business suit that did great things for his dark blond hair and tanned complexion.

"Usually Inga answers the door, but she's busy in the kitchen and I was just leaving," he explained. "Come on in. Hans will bring your luggage." He opened the door wide and stepped back.

Melissa motioned the boys to go in ahead of her. Richie bounced through the door with his usual childish eagerness, and Eric followed more slowly, hugging a brown paper sack as if it were his only anchor in a threatening world.

"Say hello to Mr. Ardell, boys," Melissa prompted, but when neither responded, she said quickly, "This is Eric."

David smiled at him. "I'm glad to meet you, Eric." The solemn-faced little boy only nodded slightly.

"Richie, say hello to Mr. Ardell," Melissa said, but a black glass fountain in the middle of the spacious foyer had already caught the little boy's attention.

Ignoring everyone, Richie bounding over to it, squatted down and stared into the pool of water. Then he looked up at David with a frown. "No fish?"

"No fish," David echoed.

"Did you already eat them?"

The humor in the innocent question was tempered by the child's honest bewilderment, and David held back a laugh as he shook his head. "No. I don't think real fish would like a little pond like that."

"Not like a big, big lake," Richie agreed solemnly, and then, before Melissa could react, his little hand picked up one of the colorful pebbles decorating the fountain display. He threw the rock so hard that it made a resounding splash in the water against the glass bottom.

"Richie!" Melissa gasped.

Dear God, no. They had been in the house less than five minutes, and already...disaster.

David grabbed Richie's arm before he could pick up another pebble. He jerked the boy back from the fountain and said harshly, "No! Don't throw rocks. Understand?"

Richie let out a frightened whimper, and Eric's normal passiveness shattered. Fiery color rose in his freckled face, and he threw himself at David. His little fists pounded David. "Let my brother go!"

"Eric! Eric, stop it." Melissa pulled him back and held his arms firmly. "No one's going to hurt Richie."

At that moment, she felt cold water easing into her open-toed summer sandals and knew her worst fear was realized. The rock had cracked the glass pool, and water was leaking out on the foyer floor.

She heard someone in the doorway behind her draw in a breath. Melissa turned and saw a large-boned woman with a round face, yellow hair braided in a coronet around the top of her head and blue eyes wid-

ened in disbelief. "What is going on?" she demanded
with a slight Swedish accent.

Richie wiggled away from David and ran to Melissa. She stood there with both boys hugging her, not
knowing what to say to David or the housekeeper.

"The fountain is leaking," David said shortly. "Get
Hans."

The woman nodded, gave one last look at the growing pool of water in the middle of the foyer, turned
on her heel and left, muttering something under her
breath.

"I am so sorry," Melissa said. "Richie didn't mean
any harm."

David started to say something, but seeing her
standing there, defensive and ready to meet his anger
with the protectiveness of a mother bear defending her
cubs, and two boys glaring at him as if he were some
kind of ogre, he couldn't find the right words. He
swallowed back the urge to launch into a lecture about
proper behavior while under his roof. At the moment,
he would rather have addressed a belligerent jury than
his houseguests. He finally settled for a brisk, "We'll
talk tonight."

Melissa nodded, and her hands tightened on the
boys' shoulders in a reassuring squeeze. She could feel
the tremors in their little bodies as they hugged her
sides.

"Inga will help you get settled. She's prepared two
adjoining bedrooms on the second floor, and there's a
small lady's parlor off the breakfast room that you can
use as a working office. If the arrangements are not

satisfactory, let me know and we'll work out something else."

"I'm sure they'll be fine," she answered in the same businesslike tone, trying to ignore the widening spread of water about to reach his expensive, polished shoes.

"Well, then, I have to get to the office." He glanced once more at the draining pool, wondering how many more catastrophes two little boys could create in the space of a few days.

Melissa saw his frown. "I'll keep a close rein on the boys," she promised.

As he nodded and turned toward the door, his shoes squeaked wetly with each step, and she wondered if the governor's counselor was going to work with damp socks. Melissa put a hand up to her mouth and suppressed a giggle.

When Inga returned with Hans and his mopping equipment, she indicated that they were to follow her, and led the way into a spacious front hall. It was obvious that the house was a decorator's dream, a fact that Inga didn't hesitate to point out. "This house is filled with nice things. *Very* nice things."

"It is lovely," Melissa agreed as she glimpsed beautifully furnished rooms opening off the main corridor. She felt as if she were someone viewing a showcase home, instead of someone who was about to be a resident in such luxurious surroundings.

Holding tightly to the boys' hands, she followed the housekeeper up a wide central staircase. A massive grandfather clock on the landing chimed the hour just as they passed it. Startled, both Eric and Richie missed the next step, stopped and stared at the clock in wonder.

Melissa smiled at their wide, rounded eyes. Obviously the boys had never heard anything like the resonant Westminster chimes. They begged to wait and hear the clock again, but Melissa shook her head, promising that it would chime many more times while they were there.

"Mr. David said to put you in the front bedrooms," Inga said in a tone that indicated it wouldn't have been her choice for the temporary houseguests.

Nor mine, Melissa thought as they accompanied Inga down the hall to the front of the house. The size and fashionable decor of the two front bedrooms made ready for her and the boys was unbelievable. Her room alone had more living space than her small studio apartment, and the boys' bedroom was only slightly smaller. Even Eric and Richie were subdued by surroundings that were completely alien to their experience. Both boys stayed close to Melissa as if she were some kind of life preserver, as they walked through the bedrooms and peeked into the large adjoining bathroom.

"Very nice," Melissa said, nodding her approval. She wasn't about to show any uneasiness or awkwardness, but she knew that Inga was wondering why a temporary nanny was being given one of the best rooms in the house. Melissa couldn't help but wonder the same thing. She would have been much more comfortable with accommodations in line with those of Inga and Hans.

The housekeeper's manners had softened when she

realized the little boys weren't going to turn into hooligans. "Mr. David said you are to use his mother's sitting room for your work," Inga told Melissa. "He didn't say what kind of work."

"I'm a writer for a magazine, and I can set up my small computer anywhere. I really don't need a special room." She glanced around the bedroom and failed to see anything that might serve as a desk, but she wasn't about to ask Inga or Hans to start moving in furniture. "Thank you, Mrs. Erickson, for your help—"

"Inga," she corrected.

Melissa held out her hand. "Nice to meet you, Inga. And I'm Melissa."

A softness touched the woman's blue eyes. "Melissa. Pretty name. Mr. David says it is a nice thing you are doing, taking care of the children. You are a good lady." Then she eyed Richie and Eric. "And they are good boys, ya?"

"Yes, they are very good boys," Melissa echoed, smiling at the obvious combination of question and warning in Inga's tone.

Just then, her husband came in with the small suitcases and Melissa's computer. Hans Erickson was a broad-faced man with huge shoulders, thick arms and brown hair lightly highlighted with gray. He just nodded at Melissa when she thanked him for bringing up the luggage.

"I'm sorry about the fountain," she told him. "It was just an accident. Richie didn't mean to break it."

"I know. He's a good boy. I can tell that." He smiled down at Richie. "Mr. David give you a bad time? You ask him about throwing a rock through the kitchen window, eh?'' He winked at Melissa and then walked out of the room, chuckling.

"Boys," Inga said with undisguised fondness in her smile. "They never grow up."

Melissa laughed, suddenly feeling that Hans and Inga had given them a pardon for the fountain incident. Maybe David would have second thoughts about the whole thing, and they could start again on a harmonious footing.

It took all of ten minutes to ''settle in.'' The beds in the boys' room were twins. Eric seemed satisfied, but Richie ignored the beds and immediately scrambled up in the middle of Melissa's queen size bed.

"No jumping," she warned him. From the sparkle in his eyes, she suspected the first time she turned her back, he'd get on his knees and bounce.

Her stomach tightened. How could she keep them corralled in this fashion-plate house? There wasn't anything in the two bedrooms that would keep the boys occupied and happy, and the few things she'd brought like crayons and coloring books wouldn't last for very long.

Somehow, in some way, she had to make the next few days a comforting and healing time for the boys.

"No doubt about it, you're the governor's fair-haired boy," Stella Day told David with a pleased smile as they lunched at Denver's fashionable Cherry Creek Country Club. "We all know he's schooling you for big things. If you keep focused, you've got a wonderful future ahead of you, David."

He was pleased with this optimistic projection from

the governor's executive assistant, but he knew he had a long way to go. "Right now, I'm just learning the ins and outs of government."

"Well, your father and mother are going to be very proud of you one of these elections when you run for Colorado's attorney general."

David knew that his parents held high expectations of him. He was used to the pressure they'd put on him as he was growing up. As their only child, there was never any question about David following in their footsteps. His father had been a state senator until he retired, and his mother had been a political activist. It was clearly due to their influence that the governor was promoting David's legal career, and they were expecting him to make his mark in politics.

"It's a little premature to think anything like that," he answered evenly, and turned the conversation back to the business that had brought them together. David was used to these working lunches. In fact, he couldn't remember very many meals when he wasn't conducting some kind of business for the governor.

Stella had an appointment waiting for her right after lunch, so she didn't tarry. After she drove away in her car, David sat for a moment in his luxurious sedan, trying to make a decision about whether to drop by his house since he was so close, or head back to his office downtown.

He hated to admit it, but he hadn't been able to put the morning's fiasco out of his mind. A nagging sense of guilt plagued him when he remembered Richie's frightened face and Melissa's eyes sparking fire.

Better mend some fences, he decided as he drove

out of the parking lot. Even though he'd probably be a little late for his afternoon appointments, he wanted to swing by the house for a few minutes and try to set things right. He didn't want Melissa Chanley upset with him. Something about her steady, totally feminine, and yet uncompromising personality challenged him. Even dressed as she had been that morning in jeans and a simple white pullover, she could hold her own with any of the stylishly dressed women who had lunched at the club. She intrigued him, and he knew that if the boys didn't accept him, it wasn't likely that she would, either.

He parked his car at the house and was about to enter a side door, when squeals and laughter coming from the backyard stopped him. Curious, he walked down the narrow sidewalk, opened the gate and came around the back of the house.

Then he stopped short. "What in the world?"

Both boys and Melissa were on the ground, rolling over and over down a grassy incline that led away from a terraced patio. When they reached the bottom of the slope, they ran back to the top and, shouting and giggling, started rolling down again.

The boys always beat Melissa to the bottom and sat up, squealing, "You lose. You lose."

Melissa laughed as she pulled dry grass from her tousled hair. "All right. I give up." Then she glanced up and saw David standing a few feet away. The expression on his face was one of incredulity.

As she got to her feet, her first impulse was to give in to total embarrassment. Instead, she managed a smile and gave him an airy wave of her hand. "Hi, there. Would you like to enter our contest? The Best Roller Down the Hill?''

At first, he didn't answer, then he surprised Melissa by returning her smile. ''I might. What are the prizes?''

''There aren't any,'' Eric said flatly. Both boys had moved to Melissa's side and were glaring at him as if he had no right to intrude upon their fun.

''Well, I guess I'll pass, then,'' David said. ''Maybe I'll join you in a different game sometime.''

''Nothing else to play.'' Richie scowled at him.

''He doesn't have kids' stuff because he doesn't like them,'' Eric told his brother with his usual solemnity.

Melissa didn't look at David's face, and held back from saying anything. She hadn't found anything in the house that would keep two lively boys happy and occupied. Now she sensed an instant tightening in David's body as he stood beside her, but it wasn't her place to correct the boys. Maybe Eric told the truth. Maybe David didn't like kids. It was hard to tell about things like that, and his beautiful home and lifestyle didn't give a clue. In fact, she hadn't seen any evidence during her earlier tour of the house that the young boy he had once been had ever lived here.

''Maybe we can find some stuff for you, boys,'' David said, ignoring the remark about his not liking kids. He'd been too busy in the world of lawyers and politicians to know whether the remark was closer to the truth than he was willing to admit.

''That would be nice, wouldn't it, boys?'' Melissa said, but their expressions didn't change.

''Sorry, I have to run. I just dropped by to see if

Inga and Hans were being helpful,'' he lied. He knew
the Swedish couple would rally to the cause, no matter
how much extra work it created.

"Oh, yes, they're wonderful. Inga fixed us a nice
lunch, and the boys ate every bit of it.''

"Good. And you've found working space?''

"The small sitting room will be fine. It's lovely
with the windows overlooking the garden.'' She knew
the sitting room had been his mother's, and Melissa
was curious about the woman who had raised such a
purposeful, solitary son.

"I have a late meeting tonight so I'll have dinner
in town. If you need to reach me, tell Inga and she'll
pass the message along.'' He turned to say something
to the boys, but his usually articulate tongue failed
him. All he could come up with was a quick "So long.
See you guys later.''

Later that afternoon, the boys were down for a nap
when the delivery truck arrived with a bright red swing
set, jungle gym and small merry-go-round.

Melissa was working in the sitting room when she
saw Hans and another man setting up the playground
equipment in the backyard. Who would believe it? David must have stopped at a store on his way back to
the office, bought everything and paid extra to have it
delivered that very afternoon.

She was delighted, and totally surprised. Maybe he
was bent on hiding from everyone what a softy he
really was.

She remembered how he'd smiled at her as she sat
on the ground with blades of grass caught in her hair.
Why had he come back to the house? He'd warned

her that he would hardly ever be around, but he had been here when they arrived this morning and he had shown up again after lunch. Even though she was pleased by his attention, she wasn't comfortable with it. Maybe this whole arrangement had been a big mistake, she thought—until she reminded herself that this was the perfect place for the boys until the right home was found for them. She knew that Eric and Richie would be ecstatic with the playground equipment, and she was relieved that the boys could play outside, while she worked and kept an eye on them through the sitting room windows. The only sad part about the gift was that it would never replace the male companionship David could have given them.

Chapter Three

"**B**urning the midnight oil, are you?" David teased later that evening as he leaned up against the door frame of the sitting room and smiled at her.

"Just a little." She saw that his tie hung loosely, his white shirt was wrinkled, and he was carrying his summer jacket. "You look as if you've had a full day."

"It's been a long one. How did things go with you? Did the play stuff get here?" He walked over to the back window and squinted out into the night. Decorative patio floodlights spilled out into the yard, and she could tell that he was satisfied by what he saw.

"Yes, they're great. The boys loved everything. Especially the jungle gym. You should have seen them. They looked like a couple of monkeys, climbing and swinging—and scaring the daylights out of me." She laughed. "They're working up some tricks to show you."

The tired lines in his face eased. "Really? I mean, after that little episode this morning I thought I rated number one Grinch."

"Children are very adaptive and forgiving, if you give them a chance." She almost added that they were great teachers, too. She suspected that David could learn a lot about himself if he spent a little time with Eric and Richie while they were here.

"I'm sorry I reacted so strongly about the fountain. It's just that it was one of the things that my mother prized, and I felt protective of it."

"I understand. You have a lovely house, and the boys need to respect that. Thank you for taking them in while we find someone who will give them a good home." She got up from the desk. "Well, I think I'll call it a day. How about you?"

He sighed. "I have some briefs to look over, and I'd best get started. Of course, you could agree to try some of my famous hot chocolate and give me an excuse to procrastinate a little longer."

An automatic refusal was on her lips. "No telling how early the boys will be up and about. I really should get to bed."

He nodded, as if he had expected her refusal. "Yes, of course. Good night, then."

Somehow she sensed that his brisk tone was protective and a cover-up for lonely feelings he didn't want her to see. His obvious need to talk with someone touched her.

"Come to think of it, a warm drink does sound good," she mused. "Maybe I'll change my mind.

That's a woman's prerogative, you know.'' She laughed and met his steady dark eyes.

"So I've been told." David smiled. He liked the way she was able to change her mind without any long drawn-out justification. She seemed to be perfectly at ease with herself, and he realized that there was no need for him to play a role or keep his guard up when he was with her. "Come on, then. We'll mess up Inga's kitchen and get bawled out for it in the morning.''

He led the way into the kitchen, and Melissa perched on a high stool at the breakfast counter while he prepared the cocoa. A shock of hair drifted across his forehead, and his rumpled appearance made him seem less formidable than usual. She wondered if he ever relaxed enough to wear something comfortable, like jeans and knit shirts.

She was surprised at how efficient he was in the kitchen. He had two steaming cups of hot chocolate ready in no time, and sat on the stool beside her as they sipped the hot drink.

"Mmm, delicious. You're a man of many talents, I see.''

"Hot chocolate is about the peak of my culinary art," he admitted. "And now that I've revealed my hidden expertise in the kitchen, it's your turn. What secret talents are you hiding from the world?''

She laughed. "No secrets. My life is an open book, but that's not the one I want to write." She hadn't intended to talk about the goal she had set for herself, but the way he was looking at her invited an explanation. "Since I've been writing for the magazine,

I've run into some wonderful accounts of strong, spiritual women who helped settle the Rocky Mountain west. I'm trying to organize their stories in a book. I started it before my grandmother died, almost three years ago. She was the one who raised me after my parents died in a car accident when I was eight years old. She told me true stories about courageous women who held on to Christian values while they raised families in wild, frontier towns. I was fascinated by their devotion to family values and faith in God, and I decided to write a book about them."

"Well, if you believe in something, I guess you should do it," he said. It wasn't an enthusiastic endorsement.

His tone left Melissa wondering why she was sharing her passion with this man who probably thought she was some dewy-eyed female, wasting her talents on a book that would have limited marketing appeal. "I don't expect to make a lot of money at it."

"And are you happy writing for your magazines?"

She nodded, a little piqued that he had been less than encouraging about her book. "Are you happy working for the governor?"

"Sometimes. On the whole, he's a pretty good boss."

The way he said it, she knew that professional ethics would keep him from discussing his real feelings. Anyway, it wasn't any of her business. "Do you like being an attorney?"

"Most of the time, but trying to find a way through all the legal mazes isn't always rewarding. Sometimes I think law is like looking for a black cat in a dark room." He smiled wryly. "You know it's there, but you can't find it."

"If you weren't an attorney, what would you be?"

He shrugged. "Frankly, I've never given that possibility a thought."

"Not even when you were a little boy?"

"Truthfully, I can't remember back that far. It seems to me that my name was submitted to the University of Denver Law School when I was born." He laughed but there was no mirth in it.

Melissa resisted the temptation to ask about his parents and his boyhood. Prying into his personal life was out of order. He'd made it clear that he was willing to offer the use of his house for a few days, but that didn't include delving into his personal history.

She quickly finished her drink and slipped off the stool. "Thanks for the cocoa. I'm ready to hit the pillow and get prepared for my cherubs tomorrow. Thanks again for the playground equipment. It will make the next few days much easier."

He walked with her to the kitchen door. "I'll call Mr. Weiss, the investigator, tomorrow. Maybe he's turned up something and we can get the boys placed in quick order. Then things will get back to normal."

"We'll try to keep out of your way," she said firmly. His tone had made it clear that he was ready to have them gone as soon as possible. "With luck, we won't overstay our welcome."

"I just meant that it can't be easy for you or the children to be in limbo like this," he added quickly, apparently recognizing he'd said the wrong thing.

"I agree it's important that we get the children settled as soon as possible."

He wanted to tell her how much he'd enjoyed her company this evening. Her candor and natural manner were refreshing. There was nothing pretentious or false about her, and she allowed him to drop the mask he wore most of the time. If he hadn't promised to stay his distance from her, he would have confessed that he was looking forward to more of her company.

"Let me know if there's anything else that will make your stay more comfortable. I'm going to be gone for a couple days. The governor is scheduled for several events in eastern Colorado and wants me to go along. We'll fly out tomorrow. The Ericksons know how to get in touch with me if something comes up. Just make yourselves at home, please."

She knew that he was doing his best to make things go as smoothly as possible for her and the boys. Having two kids like Eric and Richie running riot in a beautiful home like this would test anyone's Christian charity.

"We'll behave like guests whether you are here or not," she assured him. "Don't worry. Everything will be in one piece when you get back, I promise. Have a safe trip."

He smiled at her. "Thank you. I can't remember the last time someone said that to me."

She turned away quickly, sensing something in the situation that could pull them across the line they'd drawn between them.

David left early the next day, and while he was gone the boys settled into a routine of outdoor play, naps and quiet time. Melissa finished two articles and put them in the mail to her magazine editor. She liked to write two months ahead on her assignments, which gave her some leeway to research her book. There were moments when the uncertainty of the boys' future worried her, but she firmly lectured herself: "Let go and let God." Everything was in His hands. *Lord, give me patience,* she prayed, and then added with a chuckle, "And, please, give it to me right now."

Inga seemed happy to have her company when she popped in the kitchen for a cup of tea. The housekeeper liked to chat, and Melissa's curiosity was satisfied by some of the stories Inga told her about David, his parents and their hope that he would be governor someday.

David leaned back in his seat as the governor's private plane climbed into the air and headed northeast. They were scheduled to arrive in Denver about four o'clock, and the cabin was filled with tired members of the governor's staff. They had been on the go for two days, and David had a briefcase filled with more work when he got back. Not tonight, he thought, anticipating getting home before dark for a change.

"David, I'm handling the reservations for next week's fund-raiser," Stella Day said as she stopped beside his seat with a pencil and pad in her hand. "We need to know how many tables to reserve for the governor's staff. I'm putting you down for two places."

"Two?" David raised an eyebrow, but he knew what was coming. His unattached status was never overlooked when it came to these political affairs.

''The governor wants you to escort the daughter of one of the speakers. Not bad-looking, I hear. Should be more of a pleasure than a chore,'' Stella promised.

''Sorry, I've already asked someone,'' he lied, deciding that when he showed up alone, he could say the lady had been indisposed. ''You'll have to find another escort to do the honors.''

''Who is she?''

''You don't know her.''

Stella studied him. ''You're lying, David.''

''Am I?'' he asked with a challenging smile.

She let out an exasperated breath. ''You know how important these contacts are. An eligible bachelor like you should venture out of that shell you've put around yourself and start dating. I could give you a list of charming eligible women a mile long. Why don't you let yourself go? Get out and do some socializing?''

''I don't have time,'' David said flatly.

''Make time,'' Stella told him, and walked away sighing.

He knew he'd have to attend the elegant affair, which was to be held at one of Denver's fashionable hotels. Stella was right: it wouldn't sit well if he showed up alone when the governor wanted him to escort another lady. David didn't know when the idea struck him to ask Melissa to be his date, but almost immediately he dismissed it. Of course she'd refuse. She'd hesitated even to move into his house until he'd made it clear that he would hardly be around. Still, the prospect of spending an evening with her kept nagging at him. He didn't doubt for a moment that she would be a delightful dinner partner and could hold her own conversationally with anyone at the table.

By the time the plane landed and he drove home, he had decided to wait a few days before mentioning the social affair. In the meantime, he'd try to get more involved with the boys, a sure way to win her approval.

His good intentions were almost immediately reduced to ashes, when he came into a small utility room off the garage and nearly tripped over a mangy, flea-bitten, stray dog. The mutt was as startled as David. He lurched up on skinny legs, peered at him with round dark eyes through a tangle of dirty brown hair, and backed away from David, barking and growling.

Eric and Richie came bursting through a door that led to the back hall. "Scruffy! Scruffy!" Falling to their knees beside the straggly, long-haired dog, they engulfed him in a protective hug and glared up at David.

As Melissa hurried into the room, David demanded in a sharp tone, "Explain this, please."

She moistened her lips. "I'll try. Boys, go outside with the dog for a little while."

"He's ours," Richie yelled at David.

"We adopted him," Eric added fervently. "He's like us. He ain't got a home."

Melissa didn't look at David as she scooted the boys and the dog into the backyard. She knew that her weakness over the stray dog was going to create friction all the way around. Obviously, David was going to put his foot down about keeping the mutt, and the boys didn't need one more heartbreak in their young lives. She silently prayed for the right words as she went back inside the house to face a glowering David.

He was in the kitchen with Inga, and she was talking to him about dinner. "I baked some stuffed pork chops and potatoes, just in case you made it home in time to eat. The kind of meals you have at those political junkets of yours don't fill up a man the way they should."

"Actually I'm not all that hungry," he said, allowing a wave of weariness to sweep over him. It had been an exhausting trip and all he wanted was to come home to some peace and quiet. He had already decided to put off the confrontation about the dog until later when his nerves weren't so raw. He liked to handle problems in a detached way, and he felt anything but detached about keeping a mangy stray dog—boys, or no boys!

"Why don't you go upstairs and freshen up," Inga coaxed like a mother hen. "I can set the dining room table for you and Melissa, and feed Eric and Richie in the kitchen. Both of you look as if you could use some quiet time. And you need to settle this dog thing, ya?"

David allowed himself a weak smile. "Ya."

"Good. Now, out of my kitchen, both of you. Dinner in half an hour."

David and Melissa exchanged smiles as Inga banished them from her kitchen.

When David came downstairs, he was surprised to see Melissa already seated at the dining room table. She had changed into a simple pink dress revealing her tanned arms and shoulders, and her raven-dark hair glistened in the soft light from an overhead chandelier. She looked lovely. Pleasure sluiced through him and his evening took a brighter turn as he looked at her.

"Sorry to keep you waiting," he said quickly, taking a chair opposite her.

"You didn't. I was trying to get the boys settled in the kitchen, and Inga ordered me out." Melissa laughed.

"Inga insisted they eat with her and Hans tonight. She put Hans at the table between them, so I guess everything's under control."

"We can always hope," he said dryly, and then quickly changed the subject. He wasn't ready to spoil the evening so soon. The subject of the dog could wait a while, but there was no "question" in his mind about it—the dog had to go.

"How is the writing coming?" he asked politely.

As they talked for a few minutes about her current assignment, she realized what a polished dinner companion he was. He kept the conversation moving, asking questions and listening to her answers with a soft smile on his face.

As he leaned toward her, his slightly damp hair was burnished by the light's glow into shades of golden brown. He wore tailored brown slacks and an expensive chambray shirt open at the neck.

"I decided to go freelance because I felt called to write my women's book," she told him as she reached for a crystal water glass and took a sip.

"'Called'?" He raised a skeptical eyebrow. "That's an interesting word."

"Yes, I believe that there is a divine pattern in our

lives. If we will only let go and let God, surprising things will happen. Haven't you ever felt that a coincidence is not that at all?''

Inga's entrance with a loaded tray saved him from getting into any discussion of her naive beliefs. As he looked at her, Melissa's eyes were sparkling with such sincerity, he didn't have the heart to argue that it was up to an individual to make things happen in his or her life, not some far-off deity.

As expected, the meal was delicious, perfectly prepared, and the beautiful dining room with its richly paneled walls lent a kind of magic to the whole evening. Melissa had trouble believing that she was sitting there in the company of a handsome and entertaining host who took all this elegance for granted. She hid a secret smile as she imagined him sitting at her marred Formica table on chairs that were losing their stuffing.

Once in a while she could hear Eric's and Richie's childish voices in the kitchen, and, although she missed them, she was grateful for the reprieve from their less-than-polished eating habits.

By the time they had finished their deep-dish apple pie and their after-dinner coffee, they had grown more comfortable in each other's presence. Once again the idea came to David to ask Melissa to be his companion for the fund-raiser. He knew she'd be a perfect companion for the evening. Undoubtedly it would be a different experience for her, with all the handshaking and back-slapping, but she would charm them with her lovely eyes and sweet smile. And if tonight was any test, for a change he would finally enjoy himself at one of these political affairs.

He wondered why he suddenly felt more self-conscious asking her to go with him than he would have approaching a formidable dignitary. "I would like to ask a favor of you, Melissa."

Melissa waited, wondering why he suddenly seemed ill at ease. This private time together had gone well, hadn't it? Had she missed something? Was he going to ask her and the boys to move out of the house?

"Please, feel free to say no. There's an important political fund-raiser next weekend. It's a reception, banquet, and a national dinner speaker. I have to go." He cleared his throat. "And I'm expected to take someone with me. I was wondering—hoping, really, that you might consider going as my dinner partner. The food will be lousy, I can promise you that, but you might find the political circus entertaining."

She had to smile at his not very persuasive presentation. "It sounds interesting, but I wouldn't be comfortable at that kind of thing. Sorry."

"As a writer, I would have thought you'd be open to new experiences." Her flat refusal didn't surprise him but he wasn't about to accept it without an argument.

"My life is already full of new experiences," she countered. Sitting here in this elegant dining room with him was one of them. She pretended interest in her coffee as she took another sip. She knew it wasn't the challenge of spending an evening with Denver's rich and influential that was making her say no. It was the idea of going out with the esteemed David Ardell as his date that brought an instant refusal. He moved in elite social circles. The society pages were filled with the kind of women and social events that were a part of his life. She didn't belong in that kind of society whirl, now or ever.

"Thank you for the invitation." She shook her head. "I'm sorry."

"I'm sorry, too." He could tell from the finality in her tone that further discussion was pointless. "All right, then, I guess we'd better move on to the problem at hand. The dog."

She met his eyes. "Yes, let's talk about the dog. I want to explain what happened."

He leaned back in his chair. "Please do. Never in my life have I seen a more disreputable creature. It is really beyond me why you would allow the boys to have anything to do with it."

"I really didn't have much choice. The boys were playing in the backyard, and I was keeping an eye on them through the window. Inga set out a plate of sandwiches and some drinks on the patio table, and I intended to join them as soon as I finished what I was working on. The next time I looked out, I saw Eric and Richie on the grass with this dog, feeding him their sandwiches." She drew in a deep breath. "Apparently he came to the gate, whined and wanted in. You can guess the rest. The poor thing was starved."

"Why not feed him and then call Animal Control?"

"How could I? Before I knew it, the boys were pouring love on the stray as if they'd found something to make their lives less bleak. I told them the dog was the scruffiest-looking thing I'd ever seen, and they started calling him Scruffy. I think they identify with him because they've been hungry and alone. I just couldn't take the dog away from them.''

''Well, I can,'' David said firmly. He'd never had a dog. Never wanted one. His mother had said they were nothing but nuisances and he agreed. ''No dogs.''

''We could keep him in the backyard and utility room. With a bath and trim, he might even look presentable,'' she argued.

''Be sensible about this, Melissa,'' he said as gently as his irritation would allow. ''We've got two children to place, and so far, the investigator hasn't come up with any relative who might take them. As long as the children are here, there'll be no dog.''

She looked at him with a stubborn set to her chin. ''Let's make a deal. I'll go with you to the fund-raiser if you'll let the boys keep the dog.''

He wanted to laugh. The idea that he would even be open to such an absurd bargain was ridiculous, and he couldn't believe that he didn't flatly reject the offer. ''What kind of a deal is that?''

''A good one, don't you think? You get what you want, and the boys get what they want.''

''And what do you get?'' he asked with a teasing smile.

She grinned. ''A chance to wear the new dress I just bought.''

As his gaze swept over her animated, smiling face, he knew that, dog or no dog, he wasn't about to turn down the trade she'd offered. ''It's a deal. Shall we shake on it?''

"Is that how you lawyers seal important deals like this one?" she asked.

"Absolutely." As she slipped her hand in his, he was tempted to let his fingers lightly stroke her soft smooth skin but he knew better. She wasn't the kind to engage in any casual dalliance, and he wasn't going to jeopardize the chance to spend an evening with Melissa instead of some boring debutante.

He couldn't quite figure out why she intrigued him so much, but he suspected that once the boys were placed, there was little chance their paths would cross again.

Chapter Four

$\sim$

The next morning when Melissa and the boys went down for breakfast, the dog was gone.

"Gone?" Melissa said in disbelief when Scruffy was nowhere to be seen. The boys began to wail loudly.

"You lied!" Eric clenched his little fists. "You said we could keep him."

Richie's dark eyes suddenly filled with tears. "I liked Scruffy. He was a neat dog. Why did you let someone take him away?"

"I'm sure there must be some mistake," Melissa soothed, trying to keep her own anger under control. She'd heard David's car leave early, so he must have decided to dispose of the dog before the boys got up. He'd skipped out of the house before the ax could fall. She couldn't believe that he'd gone back on the deal they'd made. Apparently he'd decided her company at the fund-raiser wasn't worth the hassle of putting up with a scrawny mutt for a few days.

Inga came into the breakfast room with a puzzled look on her face. "What's all the fuss about?"

Melissa tried to keep her voice even. Nothing would be gained by lighting into the housekeeper. "What did David do with the dog, Inga?"

"Oh, he told Hans to take him to some dog place."

"The dog pound?" Melissa asked, almost choking on the words.

"No, not the pound. You know, one of those place where they give dogs baths and trim them up nice. Hans was supposed to take the dog to the vet for some shots, too."

As a surge of relief swept over Melissa, she was surprised at her own quick reaction to think the worst. In fact, she was a little ashamed. David had been more than gracious to put up with this invasion of his home and privacy, and he had every right to protest keeping the dog. Melissa felt guilty about the way she had judged him, when, instead, he was spending money on the dog for grooming and shots. She was as bad as the boys.

"What happened to Scruffy?" Eric demanded, not understanding Inga's explanation and looking as worried as ever.

"It's all right, boys," Melissa assured them. She explained where Hans had taken the dog and why. She joked that they might have to change Scruffy's name to fit his new looks. "David just wanted to make sure the dog was all nice and clean and healthy."

"He must like Scruffy," Eric said, suddenly happy, his lips curving in a soft smile.

"David's a good guy," Richie agreed, in an instant change of heart.

Inga just shook her head. "Wonders never cease. A dog in the house. Heaven help us. I don't know what's gotten into David to allow it." Her clear eyes held a knowing glint as she looked at Melissa and added, "And then again, maybe I do."

The way the housekeeper was looking at her made Melissa stiffen. Surely the housekeeper didn't think that there was anything personal in allowing the boys to keep the dog. While she was trying to decide how to respond, Inga gave a teasing laugh.

"David spoke to me about keeping the boys on Friday night while you two go out," she said. "He wants his tux put in order and his silver cuff links polished. My, my, such a to-do." Inga's eyes held a merry sparkle as she asked solemnly, "Will you be needing my help getting ready for the special occasion? Your dating the governor's counselor will raise a few eyebrows."

All of a sudden Melissa wondered what she'd let herself in for by agreeing to accompany David to this political affair. She'd be on display as his companion. What in the world had she been thinking of? Maybe she should back out now before she embarrassed them both.

"It's really not a date," she corrected the housekeeper.

"Of course not," Inga agreed much too readily to be sincere. "David explained that you were just helping him out. He's always getting pressured to take someone—many times a woman he doesn't know—to these affairs. It's nice that you're willing to go along with him.''

Melissa sighed. ''I don't know if he'll think so when I get all tongue-tied with some of his fancy friends, or say the wrong thing. Reading the society page is as close as I've ever gotten to this kind of shindig.''

''David wouldn't be taking you if he had any doubts about you. Just keep your head high and show them that pretty smile of yours, ya?''

''Ya,'' Melissa agreed with a chuckle.

Hans came back with the dog, who was all bathed and clipped. Scruffy still looked like a skinny, long-haired mutt, but the boys thought he was absolutely handsome. Now that Scruffy had had a bath, his coat was more caramel-colored than dirty brown. He couldn't have been more than two years old, and looked as if he might grow another head taller. His mixed heritage gave him long legs, a stubby body and long ears, but his friendliness made up for his ungainly appearance.

As the boys tumbled in the grass with him, Melissa prayed that a family could be found for the boys that would also include an affectionate young dog. Every time she started to worry about what was going to happen to Richie and Eric if a relative couldn't be found to take them, she reminded herself, *Let go and let God.*

Melissa made a quick trip back to her apartment while the boys were down for their naps. She needed other things that she hadn't brought with her the first time. Certainly, attending a fancy function hadn't been in her thoughts when she packed her clothes for a few days' stay at the Ardell home.

With some misgivings, she drew her new summer dress from the closet. Somehow, it didn't look as chic as Melissa had remembered. At least she had two pieces of her grandmother's jewelry to wear with the lilac, floor-length dress. The amethyst necklace and earrings were as lovely as any offered in the modern stores. She touched them lovingly and murmured, "Granny, I'm going out on the town."

Go get 'em, girl.

Melissa could almost hear her beloved grandmother's voice as clearly as her own breath. Even after her death, the loving woman who had raised her never seemed far away, and her strength of faith and her courage were still guiding forces in Melissa's life. She knew that her grandmother would approve of the steps she'd taken to find a home for Eric and Richie. And even though her grandmother might not totally approve of David Ardell and his worldly lifestyle, Melissa knew that she would have applauded his willingness to suffer the presence of two playful children and an energetic dog in his home.

"What's this I hear about you making reservations for two at the fund-raiser?" Stella asked, breezing into David's office with a smile on her face. "Don't tell me you broke down and invited some lucky lady to go with you?"

"I don't know whether *lucky* is the right word," David countered, amused at Stella's open curiosity.

"But yes, I've invited someone to attend the affair with me," he admitted, and then purposefully let his eyes drop back to the paper he held in his hand, as if the subject was closed.

"Well, who is she?" Stella demanded, not the least bit put-off by his dismissive manner. "Did you finally ask Senator Wainwright's daughter? It's plain to anyone with eyes in his head that Pamela's been giving you the green light every time you're in the same room together. She's the perfect one for—"

"It's not Pamela Wainwright." David cut off her monologue of the attractive young woman's virtues. He was well aware that everyone, including the governor, had decided that Pamela Wainwright would be good for his political future. Her father had been in state politics for years, and Pamela was at ease in the fast-paced climate of elections and candidates. But David had found her company rather tiring and shallow. He'd avoided spending any more time with her than was necessary, and had resisted pressure to make them a twosome.

Stella raised an eyebrow. "Who, then? Do I sense some reluctance in your choice?"

"Not at all." David met her eyes directly. "I'm very pleased that she has consented to go with me."

"Well, do I know her?" Impatiently, Stella settled her hands on her hips. "Really, David, I don't understand what's going on here. Are you planning on making a grand entrance with some famous supporter on your arm? Is some movie star coming that I don't know about?" Her eyes sparkled. "That would be just like you—waltzing in with Hollywood's latest diva."

David silently groaned. He should have been open about taking Melissa and avoided all this unnecessary speculation. Now he would have to bring Stella up-to-date on the arrangement he'd made to keep two little boys and their temporary nanny.

"Have a seat, Stella," he said reluctantly. "I have some personal business that I suppose you ought to know about."

She listened without interruption as he explained how he had become responsible for finding a home for Jolene McCombre's two children. "The boys are staying at my house in the care of a young woman, Melissa Chanley, while an investigator searches for a relative to take them in. I talked with him this morning. Unfortunately, so far he's come up empty searching for relatives on the mother's side, but he is hopeful that something positive will break on the father's side."

"And what if it doesn't?" Stella asked bluntly. "Really, David, I think you've let yourself be drawn into a situation that's exploiting your good intentions. This Melissa Chanley sounds manipulative to me."

"Really? Well, I guess you'll have a chance to decide for yourself. She's the one I'm bringing to the fund-raiser."

Stella lost her voice for a moment and then sputtered, "You...you have to be kidding. How did this woman manage to get you to agree to such a thing?"

"You wouldn't believe it if I told you," David said, laughing.

"Don't you know how important it is for you to be

seen with the right people, David? What is everyone going to think when you walk in with this woman?''

"They'll probably think that she's the most poised and beautiful woman in the room. Trust me, Stella, I won't have to make any apologies for Melissa Chanley, but I'm not sure how the rest of the company will measure up in her eyes." He frowned. "I don't think all the superficial folderol will impress her in the least."

Stella rose. "Let's just hope she doesn't make the kind of fool of herself that hits the papers."

Even though Melissa had covered some of Denver's social events when she was just out of college with her journalist degree and working briefly for one of the local newspapers, she'd never been a guest at any of the governor's affairs. Not in her most fanciful dreams had she pictured herself walking into a sparkling banquet hall with an escort as polished and suave as David Ardell.

As Melissa dressed for the important evening, she was filled with misgivings, and her hands trembled as she applied light makeup. What if she made some terrible faux pas? She couldn't bear to think that she might embarrass David in some way. When she was ready, she was almost afraid to go downstairs.

The boys were in the Erickson's apartment, playing a game with Hans while Inga was preparing dinner. Inga had promised to get them to bed early, and Melissa hoped they wouldn't give her a bad time before settling down.

As she walked down the stairs and across the foyer

to the front parlor where he was surely waiting, she hoped he wouldn't be able to tell how rapidly her heart was beating. This was worse than going on a first date, she thought, but she put a smile on her lips and went on.

At the sound of her high heels on the marble floor, David turned and watched her move gracefully across the room. The soft folds of her dress fell in graceful swirls about her lithe figure. A necklace of small amethyst stone circled her neck, and matching earrings highlighted the smoothness of her lovely face and the upward sweep of shiny dark hair in a coil upon her head. As his eyes took in her loveliness, an undefined rush of emotion made him speechless.

"Is something the matter?" she asked anxiously, uncertain why his eyes were fixed so widely on her.

He was impeccably dressed in evening clothes, and had the air of someone who could wear a tuxedo, black tie and ruffled white shirt with the same ease that most fellows wear faded jeans and sweats. She despaired that she had been presumptuous enough to think she could fit into his high-class life, if only for one evening.

"Do I look all right?" she asked anxiously.

His dark eyes softened. "You look lovely, Melissa. Stunning, in fact."

"Are you sure? I mean, I'll understand if you want to change your mind. It might be better all around if—"

"Oh, no, you don't." He shook his head. "You're not going to back out now. We have a deal, remember? I can't promise you the most exciting evening in your life, but I'll do my best to keep you from being bored.''

"Bored?" She laughed. "I doubt that very much."

"Good." Smiling, he made a mock bow. "Well, then, Ms. Chanley, shall we go have dinner with the governor and a few hundred others?"

"I'd be delighted," she said in the same playful tone.

Suppressed excitement radiating from her youthful spirit was infectious, and he found himself really looking forward to spending the evening with her. In the past two years, he'd attended so many state dinners, political rallies and fancy receptions that these affairs were now something to be endured—but not tonight. Her presence would cast a glow over the tedious proceedings.

They drove up to the posh hotel's entrance in David's deluxe black sedan, and a young valet in a smart uniform instantly hurried forward to greet them. Melissa suppressed a smile, wondering how the officious valet would react if he had to park her ten-year-old, secondhand car with its uncertain paint job.

Once inside the glittering lobby, Melissa was grateful for David's guiding hand as he led her to an elevator. They emerged on the second floor, where a cluster of fashionably attired men and women were already filing into a huge banquet hall.

David began nodding and smiling, but Melissa sensed there was little warmth in the exchange of polite greetings. She felt questioning eyes upon her, but no one gave her more than a polite nod, until an attractive gray-haired woman in a silver lamé gown approached them.

"David, I believe you and your guest are at my table," she said with a bright smile, and as her sharp eyes locked on Melissa's face, she held out a long, slender hand. "Stella Day. I'm pleased to meet you, Ms. Chanley."

"Thank you, my pleasure," Melissa responded, wondering if the attractive woman knew more about her than just her name. The way Ms. Day's sharp eyes were traveling over her gave Melissa the impression that the woman was more than just casually interested in her. How much had David told Ms. Day about the boys? Was she aware of the fact that he was bringing a "nanny" to this gala event?

"Stella is an executive assistant to the governor," David explained. "She keeps us all in line."

She gave a self-depreciating wave of her hand. "I just try to guide David as best I can, but I'm not always successful." Stella smiled at him, her tone clearly indicating that this might be one of those times.

"You must have a fascinating and rewarding job." Melissa smiled, steadily meeting the woman's eyes. "I can't even imagine the challenges that go with that kind of responsibility. It must be overwhelming sometimes."

"Yes, it is," Stella answered, her expression softening.

David suppressed a grin. Good girl, Melissa, he thought. A flattering interest worked every time, even with a seasoned veteran like Stella.

"If you'll follow me, I'll show you to our table," Stella said. "I checked the place cards earlier."

"And moved them around to your satisfaction?" David chided, skeptical that they had ended up at the same table by chance.

"You could say that," she admitted with a smile.

Melissa was grateful for David's hand in hers as they followed Stella to the front of the banquet hall near the speaker's platform. Melissa was nervous, and David must have felt the sweat beading on her palm, because he squeezed her hand and whispered, "You're the most charming woman here. Relax and enjoy yourself."

"I'll try," she said, but she wondered how she could do credit to the five-hundred-dollar-a-plate dinner. Magnificent chandeliers hung from a high ceiling, and individual candles were placed on the tables along with the flowers, sparkling crystal goblets and silver tableware.

When they met several state congressmen and their wives, who were also taking their places at various tables, David hastened to introduce Melissa. He was delighted at the ease with which she handled the barrage of names.

As Stella led them to a round table with eight other people, David silently fumed. Two of them were Senator Wainwright and his daughter, Pamela. He knew that the seating was a deliberate ploy on Stella's part. She avoided looking at him as she quickly sat down at her place.

David introduced Melissa to the other dinner guests, and she was well aware of the curious exchange of

glances among them. Obviously they were wondering
who she was, and there was particular interest from a
very attractive blonde seated directly across from David. The blonde was introduced as Pamela Wainwright, the senator's daughter, and Melissa's own curiosity was aroused when she intercepted a questioning
look the young woman sent David. She couldn't help
but wonder if David had been expected to take the
woman to this affair. Had they been dating?

All during the meal, he seemed to pointedly ignore
Pamela, even when Stella tried to draw the two of
them into a conversation about a mutual friend. Most
of the table conversation revolved around people and
issues that had little meaning for Melissa. When personal questions were directed to her, she answered
them honestly, explaining that she was a freelance
writer and doing research for a book.

The fact that she could hold her own in a company
that was alien to her background impressed David. He
was enjoying the evening's political hype more than
he had expected. Since he had been brought up with
the never-ending political speeches and party "hurrah," he couldn't imagine a different kind of life for
himself. As the evening ended, he hoped that maybe,
just maybe, he might persuade Melissa to accompany
him again to one of these affairs.

On the ride home, he noticed that her earlier bubbling eagerness had given way to quiet contemplation.
"Tired?" he asked.

She nodded. "A little."

"I'm sorry the speeches were so long. I've never
met a politician yet who ran out of words before he

put his audience to sleep. What did you think of the governor?''

"He seems very energetic and popular. Quite a shrewd politician, I gather." She glanced at David's handsome profile. "Stella told me in confidence that he's grooming you for big things." Melissa didn't add that Stella had added that David couldn't afford to offend people like Senator Wainwright.

David wondered what else Melissa had heard about the party's plans for his political future. "I was hoping we might go somewhere and talk for a little while."

She shook her head. "I don't think so. I'm ready to call it a night." Even though she had enjoyed being with David, the superficial, charged atmosphere of the evening was not to her liking. Her values were too different from those of the people she'd met that evening who were playing roles and trying to impress guests they thought were more important. She firmly believed that individual worth came from within, and not from the opinions held by others in this competitive, often unloving world.

"Does this mean you're tired of my company?" he challenged. "I really was hoping that we might do this again sometime."

She ignored the question in his voice. The evening had been an interesting experience, but her glimpse into his social life made it clear that he'd been brought up in a lifestyle that was completely foreign to her. In truth, she felt as if she'd lost something important by going out with him. It would have been better to confine their contact to the house and the boys' welfare.

She had no desire to hear any more about his political ambitions.

"I think I'd better be checking on the boys. They could have turned your house upside down by now," she said lightly.

He got her message loud and clear. She was going to keep their relationship on an impersonal level. "I'm sure Inga was able to handle them."

"I really appreciate your patience with them. Hopefully, we'll be out of your hair before long." She asked him about Mr. Weiss's search, and he brought her up-to-date on the investigator's progress, or lack of it.

"If he reaches a dead end trying to locate a relative, we'll have to look at other options," he warned her.

She knew what he meant, but she wasn't about to consider the idea that Eric and Richie would have to be turned over to foster parents. Stubbornly she held to her faith that they would find the right home and loving care for them.

"Everything is moving in divine order," she said with a stubborn lift to her chin. "We just have to be patient. If you feel that you no longer want to continue with our arrangement, I'll try to find some other accommodations for the boys and me."

His temper flared. "I wasn't asking you to move out. You're welcome to stay as long as is necessary, but I think you need to be realistic about this situation."

"I am realistic." She smiled at him sweetly. "Just look how nicely things have gone so far. The boys have a nice place to stay, and now they even have a dog.''

He couldn't help but laugh. "You're point is made.''

After they parked the car and quietly slipped into the house, Melissa thanked him again for the evening. He just nodded and said, "Thank you for going with me.''

She quickly turned away, leaving him in the kitchen as she raced upstairs.

She was hurrying through her bedroom to check on the boys in the adjoining room, when she saw a little figure sleeping in the middle of her bed.

She thought it was Richie who had taken advantage of the situation to try out her queen-size bed, and she smiled, but as she came closer, she saw Eric curled up and hugging one of the soft pillows. Unbidden tears came to her eyes as she looked down at his tender, innocent face. There must be a loving home waiting for him and Richie somewhere.

Some inner voice chided her for running away from David earlier. Was she afraid to spend a few minutes of quiet time with him? Was she afraid that she'd lose her perspective? The answer to both questions seemed to be yes.

Chapter Five

When Melissa and the boys came down to breakfast on Sunday, all dressed for church, they found David getting ready to go play golf.

"I'll probably eat at the club," he told Inga. "We've got a foursome set up for eighteen holes. The governor wants me to see if I can smooth out some rough spots in a new bill these fellows are proposing."

"Business, always business. Better you be going to church."

David smiled. "I've told you before, Inga, I'm putting my church-going in your name."

Inga turned to Melissa. "I give up. The only time he sees the inside of a church is when someone is buried or married."

"You're welcome to come with me and the boys," Melissa invited, knowing before he shook his head that he was going to refuse. Keeping the sabbath holy was not on David Ardell's agenda.

Melissa took the boys with her to a small church that she and her grandmother had attended. Located on the western edge of the city in the shadow of the nearby Rocky Mountains, the tranquil setting always made the sabbath especially renewing for her. Melissa had taken Eric and Richie twice before while they were in her care, and the small congregation had warmly welcomed them.

"They're bright little boys," the Sunday School teacher told Melissa. "Eric doesn't say much, but Richie takes it all in and isn't shy about telling you what he thinks."

Melissa nodded in agreement. She never knew what Richie was going to say. When a kind, elderly lady fussed over the boys, saying sadly, "I'm so sorry that you've lost your mother," Richie spoke up with indignation, "My mama's not lost. She's in heaven."

Melissa hid a smile and thanked the lady for her concern. She felt the support of the church family, and an elderly minister assured her that the children's names were on the prayer list and reminded her, "Trust in the Lord, and he will direct your paths."

On Monday morning that assurance seemed to be fulfilled when David called from his office and told Melissa that he was bringing Sidney Weiss home for lunch. "Will you ask Inga to prepare something simple, and we'll eat on the patio? I have to be back to the office for another appointment at two."

"Does the investigator have some good news?" Melissa asked anxiously, her heart suddenly beating in double time.

"I'm not sure. Don't get your hopes up too high," he warned. "Sidney will explain everything at lunch."

The morning crept by with agonizing slowness. Melissa couldn't keep her mind on work, and the boys seemed to be especially trying, fussing over the same swing, or arguing about whose turn it was on the jungle gym. Inga was irritable about the unexpected guest for lunch, so Melissa volunteered to make some sandwiches for the boys and feed them early. She had them settled down with coloring books in the sitting room, when David and the investigator arrived.

Sidney Weiss was a small, full-faced man with smiling eyes behind brown-rimmed glasses. He was somewhere in his late forties, and Melissa liked him at once. She tried to control her impatience to know why David had brought him home, but as they took their places around the glass-topped table on the patio, Melissa realized that nothing was going to be said to enlighten her about his visit until after they had enjoyed the seafood salad and fruit cobbler that Inga had prepared.

She forced herself to smile and contribute to the general conversation as if there was nothing on her mind but being an entertaining hostess, but an exciting quivering in her stomach affected her appetite. She was relieved when Inga served coffee and David leaned forward in his chair, signaling that the time for business had arrived.

"We appreciate your taking the time to personally bring us up-to-date in your investigation. I thought Melissa should hear directly what you have to say."

"My pleasure." Sidney reached into his jacket

pocket and brought out a small notebook. "I'm sorry that even after using our considerable resources for tracking down people, I failed to find close members of the McCombre family who might be suitable to adopt two small boys. As you know—" he nodded at David "—Jolene was an only child of middle-aged parents who passed away several years ago. We found two of her cousins, but unfortunately one of them is engulfed in an ugly divorce and the other has extreme financial problems. I can provide you with their names and addresses."

"The children need a stable, secure environment," Melissa said quickly. "They've already suffered too much upheaval in their young lives."

"What about the father's family?" David asked briskly. "Any better luck?"

"A little." Sidney's expression brightened slightly as he flipped a page in his notebook. "We located an aunt of the boy's father. Her name is Paula Bateman. She is single, never married, and is in her late forties."

Melissa's heart fell. "I'm not sure that she'd want to tackle the raising of two small boys at her age."

"What about her finances?" David asked, cutting to the essentials as he saw them.

Sidney checked his notes. "She's financially independent from the sale of land that was homesteaded by her grandparents. Our reports indicate that Paula Bateman is a very respected member of the small community of Wolfton, Montana." He handed David a piece of paper. "This is her address and telephone number."

"Well, what do you think, Melissa?" David asked, searching her face.

She couldn't bring herself to answer. She'd been praying for a young couple to take the boys, not a middle-aged, single woman. Surely, this wasn't the answer for Eric and Richie. "Are you sure there's no one else?"

"I'm afraid not. We've investigated comprehensive family trees on both the mother's and father's sides, and Paula Bateman is the only relative in the picture who could possibly offer to take them in."

David watched Melissa's crestfallen expression replace the hopeful eagerness that had been there a moment before. "It wouldn't hurt to give her a call, Melissa."

"I suppose not," she agreed reluctantly.

David knew she had expected Sidney to come up with the perfect solution to their problem, but this aunt might be the boys' only hope.

"I think you should call her," Sidney said. "After talking with her, you may have a better feel for whether putting the boys in her care would be feasible. After all, she may flatly refuse to have anything to do with them—and that will be that."

David agreed. He knew Melissa was dead set against any foster care, and he didn't like the idea much either—if they had another choice.

"I'm sorry," the investigator said, preparing to leave. "I wanted to explore every possibility before completing my report. Of course, you're free to hire someone else, but I'm confident that we have turned over every bit of ground in our search."

David shook hands with him and thanked him for his services. After he'd gone, David turned to Melissa and asked gently, "Do you want to make the call, or shall I?"

She was tempted to say, *You do it,* but she took a deep breath and replied, "Maybe I'd better talk with her, but I'm not sure I'll be able to tell much about her on the phone."

"Just explain the situation and see how she reacts." He gave her a wry grin as he teased, "You're good at that. Remember how deftly you dumped all of this in my lap?"

She smiled back at him, and as their eyes held, an unbidden sense of intimacy sparked between them. Even though he made no move to touch her, she felt a tender caress in his eyes. She looked away quickly, trying to ignore a sudden warmth that eased into her cheeks.

"I want to think about what I'm going to say before I call her."

"I bet you're as persuasive over the phone as you are in person," he encouraged.

"But what if this isn't the right home for Eric and Richie?"

"But what if it is?"

"I guess there's only one way to find out." She looked at the paper that had Paula's number on it. "Do you want to listen in on the call?"

He glanced at his watch. "No, I've got to rush. I'll be in conference all afternoon but I'll try to get home early enough tonight so you can fill me in." He gave her shoulder a light squeeze as they walked into the house. "Good luck."

Melissa waited until the boys were down for a nap before she sat down at her desk and dialed the number the investigator had given her. She cleared her voice several times as the phone was ringing, and was about to conclude that no one was home, when the receiver was picked up.

"Hello." The woman sounded a little out of breath.

"Paula Bateman?"

"That's me. Look, will you hold a minute? I ran in from outside and didn't get the screen door shut tight. Those pesky squirrels will follow me in to see what's in my cupboard if I let them." She gave a short laugh, followed by a clatter of the receiver and the muffled sound of a door slamming. "There, that's better. Sorry to keep you waiting."

"That's all right," Melissa assured her, caught off-guard by the woman's breezy manner, which made her own rehearsed speech seem much too stiff and formal. "My grandmother had a couple of squirrels that were determined to make a home in the porch roof. We finally gave up and let them raise three litters there."

"Just be glad they weren't skunks." Paula laughed, a nice full, robust laugh, and Melissa's spirits began to rise.

"Ms. Bateman, I—"

"It's Paula. We use first names around here."

"I'm Melissa Chanley, calling from Denver," Melissa explained. "Your name was given to me as Edward McCombre's aunt." She tried to keep her voice light and friendly. "Do I have the right party?"

"Land sakes, Eddie was my nephew, all right. There were never any close ties between us, but when I heard about his dying young like that, it was sad."

"Did you know his wife, Jolene?"

"Never met her. Last I heard, he left her with a couple of babies."

"Well, those babies are now wonderful little boys, four and six years old. Their names are Eric and Richie. I'm sorry to tell you that their mother, Jolene, recently passed away." She waited until Paula had made sympathetic sounds and then added, "I'm a friend who is looking after the boys until we can find a permanent home for them. And that's why I'm calling you. We want very much to place Eric and Richie with a relative who will love and care for them."

"Oh, I sure hope you find someone, but I can't think of anyone on Eddie's side of the family who could take the youngsters and raise them."

"What about…you?"

Paula's answer was booming laughter so loud that Melissa had to hold the receiver away from her. "Me, raising two young'uns, that's a hoot!" she bellowed. "Now, if you were talking about an abandoned colt or an orphaned fawn, that would be something different, but I don't know nothing about raising kids."

"They just need the same kind of love as any of God's creatures," Melissa offered. "And they're very good teachers, believe me."

"Land sakes, I'm on the downside of forty. Too old to be saddling myself with that kind of responsibility. There's no way on God's green earth that I would agree to take on Eddie's kids."

Melissa swallowed back her disappointment. "Won't you take some time to think about it?"

"It turned out that the good Lord didn't see fit to give me a family of my own, and it's too late in life for me to be raising someone else's kids."

There was such finality in her voice that Melissa didn't know what else she could say. "I understand. Thank you for being honest." If the aunt didn't want the boys, they didn't belong with her.

"I wouldn't mind seeing the little fellows." Paula softened her tone. "For a visit, that is. Nothing more. Of course, if you've got someone else to take them right away...?"

"No, we haven't," Melissa answered as evenly as her disappointment would allow. "Our plans for the boys are up in the air."

"Good, then why don't you bring them around for a nice visit? My house is a big old thing, built by my parents on the side of a mountain. Real pretty country, too. Ever been to Montana?"

"No, but I don't think it's feasible to take the boys on a trip right now."

"Too bad. I'd really like to see Eddie's kids sometime."

"I'll pass the word along to whomever takes the boys," Melissa promised, trying to keep her voice positive.

Well, that's that, she thought after she thanked the aunt and hung up.

When David came home that evening, the boys had already gone to bed and Melissa was working at her computer in the sitting room. From the half-hearted smile that Melissa gave him, he suspected that the telephone call to Paula Bateman had not gone well.

"Long day?" she asked, as he dropped down onto a comfortable floral sofa and stretched his long legs out in front of him.

He nodded. "How about you?"

"Longer than usual." She faced him, clasping her hands on the desk and meeting his questioning eyes. "Paula Bateman won't take the boys."

"I can't say that I'm surprised," he admitted. "It was a long shot at best."

"I know, but she's the only lead we have. The sad thing is, I think she'd be good with them." Melissa repeated the telephone conversation as best she could. "Obviously she has a good heart. She said she'd love to have the boys come for a visit but adamantly refused to consider taking them permanently."

"She said they could come for a visit?" He perked up.

"Yes, but I told her that it wasn't possible because everything is too unsettled."

David frowned thoughtfully. "Maybe a visit is not a bad idea."

"Are you serious?"

"Sure, why not? Let her get acquainted with Eric and Richie. There's a chance she might get hooked and want to keep them. Of course, there's just as good a chance that she'll be happy to send them on their way," he added wryly, "but it's worth a try, don't you agree?"

She just stared at him. "You think I should take the

boys all the way to Montana to visit an aunt who doesn't want them?'' There was a dull ache in her chest. Was David so anxious to have them out of his house that he was willing to bet on the long shot that the aunt would change her mind and absolve him of any more responsibility?

''You said she invited them for a visit. Why not accept and see how things go?''

''And just how would we get there?'' Melissa said tersely. ''Drive my vintage car?'' She was lucky to make it across town without something breaking down.

''You're not afraid of flying, are you? I could look into some possible flights to Wolfton, Montana, if you decide to go.''

''It seems to me that you've already decided,'' she said, more sharply than she had intended.

Her barb had hit its mark. His mouth tightened. ''No, I haven't decided anything. I'm just going on what you've said—that Paula Bateman might change her mind if she had the chance to know the boys. It's your decision, Melissa. I'll finance the trip and make the arrangements, if you want me to.''

''Let me think about it.''

He didn't know what else to say. Turning the boys over to a state agency was not to his liking, either, but Sidney's exhaustive search had not turned up any other relative. Paula Bateman was their only hope for placing the boys with family.

''I'm sorry if I've upset you, Melissa. I just feel that if there's a chance that Paula might change her mind, we ought to take it—don't you?''

Melissa got up from her chair and walked over to the window. She stared at the purple night sky, weighing David's suggestion. She had to admit that there was some merit in letting Paula get acquainted with the boys. Even if their great-aunt couldn't take them permanently, she would be aware of their existence, and that could work to their advantage whatever happened.

"I'm only trying to figure out the best course to take," David said, defending himself. He knew that he'd cast himself in a bad light. "I wasn't trying to get rid of you by suggesting that you take the boys to visit their aunt. I just think saying no over the phone is a lot easier than doing it in person."

He was surprised when she walked over to the small sofa and sat down beside him. Her nearness made him aware of her appealing femininity. Her pink knit top and soft white slacks nicely molded to her slender figure, and her dark hair was pulled back by a pink ribbon into a ponytail. As he felt the sweet length of her warm body sitting so close to his, he boldly let one arm rest casually behind her shoulders as she talked.

"I think you may be right," she admitted. "If Paula has a chance to know and love the boys, it could only be a plus in their lives. Taking them to visit her is a gamble, I know, and it's very generous of you to suggest the trip. You really don't have to do this. It's enough that you've turned your whole house over to us."

"There are compensations," he said, enjoying the sudden closeness that they were sharing. She had relaxed against the curve of his arm, and he could feel

a sudden excitement in her replacing the initial disappointment. At that moment, he wondered why he'd
been such a fool as to suggest that she take off for
Montana and leave him with an empty house echoing
with loneliness.

She felt his arm tightening around her shoulder, and
for a moment she didn't know what to do. The easy
companionship they'd been experiencing was suddenly gone, and something deeper and more intimate
was threatening to take its place. She knew that if she
turned and looked at him, she would invite his kiss.
Her feelings threatened to spin out of control, and it
frightened her.

"I'll call Paula in the morning and make sure she
meant the invitation," she said, easing to her feet. The
timing was right for a change of scenery, she thought.
And maybe none too soon.

He was already gone the next morning, when Melissa made the telephone call to Paula and accepted
her invitation to bring the boys for a visit.

Melissa was too excited to wait until evening to tell
David. Impulsively, she called his office. His secretary
answered, about to run interference on his calls until
Melissa said her name.

"Oh yes, Ms. Chanley," Elsie said so sweetly that
Melissa guessed the gossip about her "date" with David had made the rounds.

She had never called him before, and when he heard
her voice, he asked anxiously, "Is something wrong?"

"No, not at all. In fact, I have good news," she
reassured him, and explained that she'd organized the

visit with Paula. "I thought you might want to start making plans."

"I'll get right on it, and tell you tonight what I've arranged." He wanted to keep her on the line longer, but as usual he was pressed for time. Feeling that when he'd held her close last night he'd overstepped the bounds they'd set, he wasn't sure how to apologize. Certainly trying to say anything over the phone wasn't a good idea. "I'll check and see what's the best way we can fly you and the boys to Wolfton, Montana."

When he reported to her that evening, it turned out that there wasn't a best way. In fact, making airline connections to Wolfton proved nearly impossible. Wolfton was miles from any commercial airport. Only small puddle-jumper airplanes fly anywhere close to the town, and none of their schedules matched.

"You'd make better time driving instead of taking small hit-and-miss charter flights," David told Melissa, exasperated. "You'll need a car once you get to that mountain town, anyway."

"How long a drive is it?"

"You can make it in two days if you do some hard driving." As he saw the flicker of apprehension in her eyes, he added quickly, "Of course, you could spend two or three nights out if you decided to take it slow. You'll have to drive all across the state of Wyoming and into Montana. Think you can do it?"

"Of course I can do it." Her eyes snapped at the fact he'd dared to question her driving ability.

He chuckled at her feisty response. "Good. I've got some maps of Wyoming and Montana. We'll mark out the best route."

"Are you loaning us your car?" she asked boldly. If they weren't going to fly, they'd have to have something decent to drive.

"I'll see about a rental. Any car preference?"

"One big enough to hold two boys and a dog."

"You're taking the dog?" His eyes rounded in disbelief. "Are you out of your mind?"

"Probably, but I don't have a choice."

"Of course you do," he argued. "It's going to be a long drive at best. Why saddle yourself with the added stress of taking a dog?"

"Because the boys will have a fit if I leave Scruffy here. They love that dog too much to part with," she said frankly. "Besides, if our little plan works and the boys remain with Paula, I'll feel better about leaving them if they have the dog with them."

"Are you going to be all right driving back alone?"

She just smiled. "Don't worry, I'll bring the car and myself back in one piece."

He wasn't entirely comfortable with the idea of Melissa traveling by herself, but he knew better than to argue the point.

They spread the maps out on the desk, and almost immediately David realized that she wasn't going to take his suggestions about which route to take. She listened politely to what he had to say and then pointed out a different route that was a little longer, but would take them through one corner of Yellowstone National Park.

"You can't make any time going through Yellowstone," he said with macho authority.

"I know, but the boys would love seeing some of

the wildlife and so would I. They say that deer and buffalo wander right down the highway.'' Her eyes sparkled. ''And I've always wanted to see Old Faithful geyser. It seems a shame to go right by the park and not take a little time to see some of it.''

''If you go that way, you'll lose half a day's traveling.''

''Or gain half a day's pleasure? It depends on how you look at it, doesn't it?''

He gave up. Obviously she wasn't going to follow his advice about making the trip as speedily as possible. If she wanted to dally with two kids and an overgrown dog, the choice was hers. He'd make sure she had enough travelers' checks to take care of expenses, and that was the end of his responsibility. Wasn't it? She'd never made the slightest suggestion that he might go with them, and even if he wanted to, his commitments made it virtually impossible to drop everything and leave town.

When Melissa saw his frown and the weary lines around his mouth, she said with her usual candor, ''You look tired. Maybe things will be easier for you with us gone.''

''Easier?'' he echoed. ''That isn't the word I would have chosen.'' He was going to miss the brief contacts he had had with her while she'd been in the house. When he came home late and tired, the place was no longer empty, and there was a different feel to it. Even scattered toys were somehow reassuring. He knew that she was critical of his lifestyle and lack of spiritual convictions, but he regretted that she was ready and eager to put an end to the arrangement they'd made for the boys. "You're welcome to stay as long as necessary."

"That's generous of you, but you don't need us around to complicate your life. If things don't work out with Paula, it's time to look for a different answer."

"And what would that be?"

"I don't know, but I'm certain Someone does. There's a divine pattern here, but we just can't see it."

He silently scoffed at her naive belief, but kept his skepticism to himself. If she wanted to delude herself that an answer was going to fall from the sky, it was her choice. He knew that hard facts about the children's future would have to be faced soon enough.

David tried to distance himself from preparations for the trip, but he was concerned about any unforeseen problems that might arise. He decided not to trust a rental car, but let her have his Lexus so he could quit being anxious about having the car break down in the middle of nowhere. How would he ever forgive himself if there was an accident?

He was *determined* not to get any more involved. So no one was more surprised than he was when what started as a nagging in his mind became, over the course of the next few days, a decision, full-blown and definite. The mountain of work remained. His tight schedule included appointments with important people like the Lieutenant Governor.

But one day he called his secretary into his office and said, "I'm going to be out of town for a few days. I have to make a trip to Montana."

Chapter Six

David had wanted to get an early start on the trip, but it was mid-morning before they finally got on the road. The boys were in the back with Scruffy, who was taking up most of the seat between them. While Melissa endeavored to keep them busy with quiet activities, David concentrated on making up as much time as the speed limit would allow. He finally began to relax when they left Colorado and crossed the Wyoming border, but his satisfaction was short-lived.

A few miles out of Cheyenne, Richie announced loudly, "I gotta go."

"Me, too," Eric added.

When Melissa saw David's jaw tighten, she asked, "I don't suppose we need gas or anything?"

"We've only covered a hundred miles," he answered shortly. He was used to getting behind the wheel and thinking about business as the hours went by. He couldn't believe that they were making a stop even before the trip really got started.

"There's a rest stop ahead," Melissa said. "It'll only take a quick minute."

Somehow the quick minute turned into more than fifteen. Scruffy had to be leashed and allowed to explore the dog run. He seemed more interested in bounding about than in anything else, and Melissa knew the energetic young dog wasn't going to take to hours of inactivity in the back seat of a car. Even though she had been delighted when David decided to drive them, she wondered now if it had been a good idea. Obviously the "stop and go" of his young passengers was not his idea of travel.

She had to give him credit for trying to accommodate the needs of his young travelers. "I take it you've never been on a trip with youngsters before."

He shook his head. "I was an only child. When my family traveled, we held to a rigid timetable. In fact, we'd just get to our destination and my father would set an itinerary for leaving."

"Not much fun for a kid," she said. No wonder he wasn't very spontaneous.

"What now?" he asked in disbelief, when Melissa and the boys disappeared into a curio shop adjoining a gas station, while he waited impatiently outside with the dog. He kept glancing at his watch, wondering if he should have made arrangements to be gone for a fourteen-day trip instead of three.

"Look what we got," Richie said excitedly, drawing some plastic dinosaurs out of a sack. "Melissa said they used to live around here."

"I got cowboys," Eric said solemnly. "Wyoming's full of cowboys."

David swallowed back his impatience and forced a smile. "What? Nothing for Scruffy and me?"

"Would you like us to go back and see if we can find something?" Melissa asked with an amused glint in her eyes.

"Maybe at the next stop," he answered. "Ten minutes from now."

The Wyoming highway ran north through rolling hills of mustard-colored grass with unrelieved vistas in every direction. As they traveled across the open country, Melissa realized how sparse the population was and how far apart the towns were. She breathed a prayerful thanks that she wasn't out on this barren road alone with the boys. She had been utterly astounded when David told her he'd arranged to drive her. He told her that depending on what happened with Paula and the boys, he'd make arrangements for her to get back to Denver.

Melissa had called her editor to explain that she'd be out of town for a short time. She was totally surprised when the woman told her that an editor's job was going to open at another magazine. She asked if Melissa would be interested.

"Would I ever," Melissa had exclaimed. A steady salary instead of depending upon freelance articles would ease her tight budget considerably.

"Good. We'll talk about it when you get back."

Melissa wanted to tell David about the offer, but held back. Somehow she felt that her little milestone wouldn't impress anyone else very much, especially someone whose career goals were set as high as David's.

"How far are we going to go tonight?" she asked, as the sun slipped out of sight on the flat horizon.

"Not as far as I planned," he said reluctantly. There was no way they would make it to the town he had picked on the map to have dinner and spend the night. "Let's look for a place to stop in the next hour."

When they spied a rustic motel stretched along the Platte River, David decided to check it out.

"The cabins are small," he reported back. "You and the boys could have one, and I'll take the dog with me in the other one."

"What about dinner?"

"Well, that depends," he said, winking at her. "They have a small fishing pond set up for kids with trout swimming around in it. Do you suppose Eric and Richie might want to try catching our supper? The motel's got someone who'll cook the trout for us. How does that sound?"

An excited clamor in the back seat was his answer. Melissa was amazed at this spontaneous adjustment on his part to the situation. Maybe there was hope for him yet.

After they checked in, a lanky, soft-spoken fellow who owned the motel gave the boys fishing poles and a can of worms.

"Ugh," Eric said, looking at the slimy bait. Then he looked wistfully at David. "You show me how?"

Melissa secretly smiled when David ended up baiting both the hooks. With his trousers rumpled from kneeling on the ground and his hair hanging over his forehead, he didn't look like the governor's efficient counselor. The feeling that welled in her on seeing him in this new light created a peculiar tightening in her chest, warning that she was treading on dangerous ground. Because she had grown up alone with her grandmother, she had not experienced the joy and fullness of family life. More than any personal success, she wanted a husband, children and a marriage blessed with God's goodness. As she watched David with the boys, she knew that his interest was only temporary. He'd made it clear where his true commitment lay. There was no room in his life for anything but his driving ambition.

The fact that the hungry fish practically jumped out of the water to be caught didn't diminish the boys' excitement in landing four beautiful rainbow trout. They proudly handed them to the owner's wife, and were eagerly ready to eat them when she brought the meal out of the kitchen.

Eric wanted to take some of his fish to Scruffy, who'd been left in the cabin, but he was finally persuaded that the dry dog food they'd brought along was a better choice.

"Do you think there's any chance we could get an earlier start tomorrow?" David asked hopefully, as they were finishing a dessert of cherry cobbler and rich cream. "I'd like to drive into Wolfton before dark tomorrow, and if we spend any time in Yellowstone, it's going to be a push."

"How early is early?"

"Six o'clock," he said, hoping for seven.

"I'd best get these guys to bed, then."

He started to say something, but the insistent ring of a cell phone in his jacket pocket stopped him. "Ex-

cuse me.'' He got up from the table and walked away
to take the call.

As he stood in the doorway of the hall, Melissa
watched his expression change. Whatever was being
said deepened lines in his forehead and shifted his
easy, relaxed posture into one of rigid tenseness. When
he returned to the table, the governor's counselor was
back.

''I'll see you and the boys to your cabin,'' he said
briskly. ''Something's come up that needs my attention.''

''Tonight?''

He gave a brisk nod. ''The governor has appointed
me to an important committee with influential people
who could be an asset to my future. I have to get some
thoughts down on paper right away. Fortunately, I
brought my laptop along, just in case.''

''Maybe you shouldn't have come prepared to
work,'' she said, disturbed by the power that one telephone call had over him. All signs of the boyish fisherman were gone, and she could tell that his mind was
already back on business. It both saddened her and
made her angry that he was willing to sacrifice all
personal enjoyment for the sake of his political ambitions.

*Where your treasure is, there will be your heart,
also.* She knew very well where David Ardell's heart
lay. A few glimpses into a different side of him didn't
change his basic nature. She knew he was anxious to
get the trip over with so he could get back to Denver
as soon as possible.

She had trouble sleeping, and was aware that the

light in his cabin stayed on late into the night. As she turned restlessly in her bed, she tried to sort out the tangle of her own emotions where he was concerned. She'd never felt like this before. Several times she had dated rather seriously, but there never had been anyone to set her emotions on edge the way David did. If the boys' future had not been involved, she would have walked away from him in a minute. Obviously, he was not the man to give her the kind of spiritual life and Christian home that she desired. She wanted a soul mate. Someone to pray with her, attend church with her, and read God's word as a daily ritual. She wanted someone beside her who was strong enough in his own faith to meet the challenges of life. David Ardell was not that man. She knew that. She also knew that getting her feelings muddled over him would lead her down a path that would be disastrous for both of them.

The next morning after a fitful sleep, she awoke just as dawn was breaking. After quietly dressing, she sat on her bed, reading her Bible and spending time in meditation. The daily scripture was Ephesians 1:18. ''I pray that your hearts will be flooded with light so that you can see something of the future he had called you to share.'' She found reassurance in the promise that her future was in His hands, and that her heart would make the right decisions.

At six, she woke the boys and left them to finish dressing while she walked over to David's cabin. She knocked on his door with smug satisfaction that he couldn't complain about them oversleeping.

No one answered.

She wondered if he'd worked until early morning

and was sleeping too soundly to hear the knocking. Better not disturb him. Scruffy would wake him up soon enough, she decided, and she started to turn away.

"Melissa."

She swung around and saw that David and Scruffy were a short distance away, heading toward the river. He waved for her to come along, and as she hurried toward them she suddenly felt wonderfully alive. The morning air was brisk. A brilliant orange sun was rising on the horizon and touching the hills with gold.

As she fell in step beside him, he said, "I thought we ought to let the hound have a run before we coop him up in the car again."

"How did you two get along?"

"He snores," David said, smiling. Tired lines around his eyes hinted at a sleepless night, but there was an energetic pace to his steps, as Scruffy bounded ahead of them.

She was surprised when he reached out and took her hand as they walked. He'd never made that kind of gesture before, and she didn't know quite what to do, but the sound of the river flowing smoothly over polished rocks and lapping gently against the bank was in harmony with an unexpected companionship between them.

"Are you a morning person?" he asked.

"I guess so." She chuckled. "My grandmother was always quoting, 'Early to bed, early to rise, makes a gal healthy, wealthy and wise.' It's a habit with me now."

He had suddenly realized how little he knew about

her, even though she seemed able to fill up the empty places in his life without any effort. After a few minutes of asking questions about her personal life, he saw color sweep up into her cheeks when he said bluntly, "I don't understand why you're not married. I mean, you love children, that's obvious, and from the way the fellows at the fund-raiser were looking at you, I'd say you could attract about any man you wanted."

"I guess that's your answer." She lightly tossed her head. "I haven't found one that I wanted."

"That picky, huh?" His grin teased her.

"Very." She disagreed with people who said you should compromise with life. Her faith wouldn't let her willingly make a bad decision and throw away the future by marrying the wrong man.

"What about you? Stella told me that there were plenty of eligible women who would be very happy to be Mrs. David Ardell."

"But you're not one of them," he said lightly, as if teasing her.

The conversation was beginning to make Melissa uncomfortable. She pulled her hand from his.

They walked a little farther along the bank, but their earlier harmony was lost. "I think we should get back to the boys before they decide to come looking for us."

David nodded and called Scruffy back from his sniffing explorations.

They had a quick breakfast and were on the road again within an hour. Melissa doubted that the boys would be at their best when they met their aunt for the first time later that night. Tired, and probably cranky from the long day's travel, it wasn't likely they'd make the best impression. If David hadn't been along, she would have taken an extra day, but she knew he was anxious to deliver them and head back to Denver.

She tried to entertain the boys as best she could by pointing out windmills, some Black Angus cattle, spotted horses and a small flock of sheep grazing on one of the grassy hills. They made a game of seeing who could "I Spy" something different out the window.

David was the one who surprised them when he slowed the car and pointed to a herd of tan-and-white animals, smaller than deer, on a nearby hill. "Antelope."

"I've never seen one before," Melissa said, craning her neck for a better view.

Much to her surprise, David stopped the car on a pull-out where an access road led across the flat ground in the direction where the herd was grazing. "There must be thirty of them."

The boys were scrambling over each other and the dog in the back seat, trying to see out the back window, when Richie had a better idea. "I go look," he said, and reached for the door lock and handle.

"No! Don't open the—" Melissa cried too late, as the back door swung open, Scruffy beat Richie out of the car.

The dog jumping from the parked car alerted the animals, and in a split second the antelope were on the run—with Scruffy in pursuit.

"Scruffy! Scruffy! Get back here!"

The dog ignored their frantic cries as if some lingering strain of heredity had fired his determination to round up the fleeing animals.

Even as they watched dumbfounded, the herd of antelope and Scruffy disappeared out of sight over the next rolling hill.

"Scruffy's gone. Scruffy's gone," the boys wailed loudly. "Come back, Scruffy. Come back."

"Blasted dog," David muttered. Why on earth had he stopped the car in the first place? In a weak moment, he'd given in to a stupid impulse to show the boys some antelope, and look what had happened.

"What'll we do?" Melissa asked, not having the faintest idea how far or how long the dog would chase the antelope before giving up.

"Well, there's no way he can catch up with the herd, that's for sure," David answered shortly. "Antelope are fast and can outrun almost anything. If the dog has any sense he'll give up in short order."

"I guess we'll just have to wait for him to come back," Melissa said.

David didn't answer, and she knew there was a limit to the time he'd be willing to spend waiting for the dog to reappear.

"He's lost," wailed Richie.

Nearly an hour went by, and still there was no Scruffy.

"We got to go find him." Eric set his little chin and glared at David.

"Maybe we should hike a little ways in that direction,'' Melissa suggested. Anything would be better than just sitting and waiting for the dog to show up.

''All right, but we're not going to put in the whole morning hiking up and down these hills.''

They all got out of the car and calling the dog's name as loudly as they could, they walked in the direction that the dog had disappeared.

No sign of Scruffy.

As the midday sun beat down on them, their eyes began to blur from the strain of staring at the surrounding hills for some sign of the pet.

''This is ridiculous,'' David said, wiping his brow. ''No telling how long he kept up the chase.''

''Why don't we go back to the car, and just drive a few miles down the road. Maybe we'll meet him coming back.''

He looked at her as if she couldn't be that naive, but he nodded. ''All right. But if we don't find him in the next hour, we're going to leave him. Agreed?''

The boys howled a protest, but Melissa reluctantly nodded. Even though she hated to think about abandoning Scruffy, she didn't know what else they could do. She knew they could spend the whole day waiting and looking but never find him in these wide open spaces.

David drove slowly down the narrow road that ran along the bottom of the hill where the antelope had been grazing, before they disappeared with Scruffy in pursuit. The terrain was one rolling hill after another, and when David stopped the car, Melissa feared that he was going to give up and turn the car around, but instead he craned his neck and stared upward.

''What is it?''

''See that bunch of rocks on top?'' He pointed to a high plateau. ''Maybe we can see something from there. Let's hike up and take a look.'' He turned to the dejected little boys. ''I'm sorry fellows, but if I don't see some sign of the dog from the top of that hill, we're leaving. Understand?''

They nodded, but both of them held their little mouths in stubborn lines. They all piled out of the car, and the boys bounded up the slope of the hill like mountain goats, while Melissa and David climbed after them at a slower pace.

When they reached the outcropping of rock on the highest point, a panorama of rolling treeless hills and wild grassy plains spread out in every direction. Melissa's breath caught at the spectacular view of vast uninhabited space that stretched to the horizon. Nothing relieved the seemingly endless grasslands and occasional rock formations. No farms, ranches or houses.

They shaded their eyes with their hands and searched the landscape. Nothing. No movement of any kind.

''Where's Scruffy?'' Eric demanded with childish impatience, as if he'd expected to find Scruffy at the top of the hill, ready to jump on them with wet kisses.

Melissa moistened her dusty lips but couldn't find any words to reassure him. Her silent prayers to find the dog had gone unanswered. David moved off the rock on which he'd been standing, and she expected him to admit the search was at an end, but he didn't.

''I'm going to check something out,'' he told her. ''I want all of you to stay here. I mean it! Don't be wandering off. I sure don't want to spend the rest of the day hunting for one of you.''

"What is it?"

"Probably nothing."

He started walking in a diagonal direction down the hill. With every dusty step, he chided himself for being foolish enough to prolong the inevitable. He wanted to find the dog so badly that he was giving in to hallucinations. A moment before, when he'd let his eyes play over flickering patterns of light and dark below them, he'd thought he glimpsed a moving form. The impression was so quick and nebulous that it was gone before he could focus on it. It was probably a trick of his own vision or a moving cloud's shadow upon the ground, but he knew he'd never forgive himself if he didn't investigate.

As he came down the hill to the spot that had caught his attention, he could see some flat boulders in a jumbled heap. Even before he reached the rocks, he was ready to admit that his imagination had provided an illusion of movement, but as he came closer, a muffled sound reached his ears.

He stopped. Listened. Tried to identify the sound. Cautiously, he approached the rocks that were piled up in a way that provided meager shade. He stiffened as he saw something move, and was ready to jump back quickly. Then he saw two familiar, sorrowful eyes looking at him from the protective shade of a leaning rock. Utterly collapsed and panting heavily, Scruffy lifted his head wearily and then let it drop again. His tail barely flickered in recognition.

"You stupid hound," David said in a tone that was

both affection and exasperation. He knelt down beside Scruffy. "Come on, get up! Let's get out of here. You've cost us half a day already."

Repeatedly he tried to urge the dog to his feet, but Scruffy wasn't having any of it. There wasn't an ounce of energy left in the dog's body, and his chest heaved with labored panting. When David eased him out from under the rocks, he just went limp.

"It's all right, boy." David stroked him. There was no doubt that Scruffy was in bad shape. The dog had almost run himself to death. Undoubtedly his whole body was dehydrated, and David knew that he'd never make it on his own up the hill and down the other side to the car. Unless they wanted to abandon him, there was only one answer.

David groaned just thinking about it.

Melissa had tried to keep track of David as he made his way down the hill, but when his lone figure blended into the landscape, she lost sight of him.

The boys kept up a steady chorus of questions about Scruffy and David's whereabouts.

She gave them cryptic answers as she kept scanning the hillside below. When David finally came into view again, she realized that her fingernails were biting into hands because they were clenched so tightly.

"Oh, no," she breathed in disappointment. There was no sign of a dog following at his heels as he slowly climbed the hill toward them.

His bulky figure looked strange and his walk was labored. At first her mind didn't register the truth. Then a cry burst from her chest when it hit her. He was carrying Scruffy on his back, the limp dog's legs draped over his shoulders.

When he reached them, instead of running forward, Eric and Richie backed away, terror in their eyes as they stared at the limp dog.

Melissa chest tightened. *Please, dear Lord, don't let him be dead.*

David dropped to his knees and eased the dog from his shoulders. Scruffy made an effort to get up and then collapsed, lying motionless with his legs stretched out flat like a bear rug.

"What's the matter with him?" Melissa asked anxiously. Her relief that the dog wasn't dead was suddenly overshadowed by fear over his alarming condition.

"He just about ran himself to death. The mutt must have chased the antelope herd until he collapsed. Then he managed to crawl under the shade of some rocks. It's pretty likely he would have died of exhaustion and dehydration, if by some miracle I hadn't caught a glimpse of him."

She closed her eyes in thankfulness. Although David would never admit they had been led to this very spot, she knew better.

"What's the matter with Scruffy?" Eric demanded as he eased forward with Richie peeking around him.

"He's just tired. Once he gets some water and some rest, he'll be fine. David found him in time." She smiled at him, her eyes filled with grateful tears. Then she leaned over and impulsively kissed his dusty cheek. "Thank you."

"I just didn't want to spend the rest of the trip listening to a lot of weeping and wailing," he said gruffly, trying to deny the pleasure her happiness and kiss gave him.

"We found Scruffy. We found Scruffy." The boys began chanting, hopping around in glee.

"We'll get him back to the car and get him some water." Then David eyed the sky. "Looks like an afternoon storm is brewing north of us. Just what we need to make this a perfect traveling day!"

"It's a happy day," she corrected him. "You were right. It was a miracle that we found him."

Chapter Seven

David's hopes to make up time once they got back on the main highway quickly faded. They had to stop at the first place they could, to get water for Scruffy and fill a bottle to take with them. Although the tired dog's thirst began to be satisfied, he required additional stops because of drinking all that water.

The boys were fussy and irritable. Tired from the trek up and down the hills, and uncomfortable crowded in the back seat with the sprawling dog, what they really needed were naps. Melissa tried putting Richie in the front seat while she sat in the back with Eric and the dog, but that didn't work. They were just as fussy as ever. Her own reserve of calm composure was depleted after the ordeal Scruffy had put them through, and when she started seeing billboards advertising places to stay in the next large town, she decided that all of them had had enough for one day.

Even though there were several hours of daylight

left, she leaned forward and told David in a firm voice, "I think it's time to stop for the night. There's no sense going on when we're all exhausted. We can have an early dinner and then hit the sack. Frankly, I'm not in the mood to put up with two fussy kids any longer than I have to."

He tightened his jaw. "I wanted to get as close to Yellowstone as we could so we could drive in early tomorrow, spend a few hours and head on to Wolfton." He didn't add that he'd have to turn around and head right back to Denver the next morning in order to make an important appointment with the Senate chairman. What a fool he'd been to think he could get away for even a couple of days.

"We could skip going into the park," she said, wishing that she'd never planned the extra excursion.

"It's too late to change our route now. We'd have to backtrack to go around Yellowstone." He glanced in the mirror, and when he saw the pained expression on her face he felt guilty. Just because he was under pressure to get the trip over with, didn't mean that she and the kids should suffer. No one had forced him to come along. The fiasco with Scruffy wouldn't have happened if he hadn't stopped the car. "All right. We'll find some accommodations and call it a day."

Melissa would have settled for an economy motel, but David pulled into a luxurious resort with a swimming pool and landscaped gardens bordering a golf course. An attendant took Scruffy to an enclosed area, with his own doghouse and patch of lawn. The boys might have made a fuss about leaving him if the dog hadn't plopped down beside bowls of water and food, and gone to sleep.

A bellhop escorted them to two deluxe rooms on the second floor with wrought-iron balconies overlooking an inner courtyard. Each room had two double beds, a sitting area and glass doors leading out on the balcony. Melissa was grateful for the iron railings when the boys bounded about like scouts checking out new territory.

David said he'd meet them downstairs in half an hour, and disappeared into his room. Melissa maneuvered the boys in and out of the shower, and grabbed a quick one for herself. In fresh clothes, revived and hungry, they joined David in the elegant dining room.

As they waited to be shown to David's table, Melissa was glad that she'd changed into a blue linen summer dress and matching sandals, and had caught her dark hair in a twist at her nape. She'd even touched her lips with a soft pink gloss. She was a little amused because she almost felt as if she were on a date, even though she was holding hands with two coltish boys.

Eric's and Richie's faces were clean and shiny, and their rebellious hair neatly combed. They wore clean knit shirts and shorts, and Melissa had wiped off the dust from their only pairs of shoes.

David stood up as they came across the room toward him. His hair was still damp, and dark blond strands lay softly on his forehead as he smiled at them.

"You guys clean up pretty good," he teased as he held out chairs for all of them.

The boys were amazed by the spacious dining room. David suspected that they had never eaten in such a place in all their young lives, and they looked small and vulnerable sitting in the dining chairs. Both of them stared openly at the formally dressed waiter who hovered around them, and when David asked what they wanted to eat, they were suddenly mute.

Melissa ordered baked chicken and French fries for the boys because they'd enjoyed that when Inga had fixed it. She was pleased that even in such a short time, regular meals had put some meat on their bones and fleshed out their shallow cheeks. She was sure that with good nutrition, Richie would probably be a stocky child, while Eric's slender body structure would always carry less weight. Her heart swelled with affection as she looked at them.

David saw the tender softness in her eyes and a spurt of protectiveness surprised him. He didn't want to see her hurt. Clearly her emotions ran deep in her quest to find a home for the boys, and he feared that she was heading for heartache. It was a long shot that Paula Bateman could be persuaded to take two active kids to raise, even though they were blood relatives. He sighed inwardly, knowing that the boys probably should have been turned over to Social Services in the beginning. He wanted to honor Jolene's wishes, and he'd do his best to make certain that the children didn't lack for anything, but he and Melissa might have no choice but to go through government channels to place them. Just delaying the inevitable wasn't good for anyone.

Melissa had made it clear that she was in no position to raise them alone. Apparently there was no man in her life who offered her the kind of marriage she wanted. Obviously she had no intention of keeping up any contact with David once the boys were placed— and it was just as well, David told himself. He'd had his heart broken once. He wasn't open to inviting that kind of hurt again.

Melissa caught smiling glances from other diners at nearby tables who seemed approving of the young family they appeared to be. How easy to give the wrong impression, she thought. She knew David's mind really wasn't on the polite conversation they had during dinner, and that he'd probably be up half the night working again. It wasn't any of her concern, but she couldn't help but resent the fact that he couldn't get away for even a couple of days without demands being made on him. She wanted to challenge the mad merry-go-round that left no time or space in his life for anything but worldly pursuits, but she knew he would just mock her naiveté.

As they left the dining room, they passed an expensive gift shop, and the boys stopped short when they saw some colorful children's cowboy hats and boots. Melissa knew the prices would be exorbitant and tried to pull them past the window, but Richie hung back, staring longingly at a pair of rust-colored boots about his size.

David glanced down at the old shoes that the boys were wearing. Their mother had probably picked them up at a thrift store, he thought. He hadn't paid much attention to Richie's and Eric's clothes, but he suddenly realized that Melissa must have bought some of them at her own expense. He was mad at himself for not noticing, and irritated with her for not saying something.

He jerked his head toward the shop's door. "Come on, fellows. Let's see if they have a couple of pairs of cowboy boots your size."

Melissa nearly swooned over the price tags, but by the time they left the shop, the boys were outfitted in cowboy boots, hats and fringed leather vests. Melissa thought David seemed as pleased with the purchases as the boys, as they strutted in their new duds down the hall ahead of them. Maybe men always remained little boys at heart, she mused, pleased to catch a glimpse of this side of the usually staid David.

"What time are we heading out tomorrow?" she asked him as they paused at her door. She knew that he'd be pushing hard to cover as much distance as possible.

He frowned, obviously mentally calculating the trip that lay ahead of them. "How about a six o'clock wake-up call, and we can get away by seven?"

"Fine," she agreed, knowing that if he were alone, he'd have hit the road hard and steady, but the handicap of two kids and a dog had tossed his timetable to the wind. "I really appreciate what you're doing."

"What *I'm* doing? You're the one." His voice was suddenly husky. "You're a very special person, Melissa. I've never known anyone quite like you." He searched the deep calmness of her ocean-blue eyes. "Don't you ever think about what you want out of life and go after it?"

"Of course I do. And sometimes I want things to be the way I want them, *right now,*" she admitted with a sheepish chuckle. "Then I soon find out that the timing was all wrong, and I wish I'd had more patience and trust."

He just shook his head. "I don't believe that anything is accomplished by waiting around. If you don't work hard and stay on top, you never win."

"It depends upon what prize you're after," she said. With a deep sense of sadness, she knew that they were miles apart when it came to understanding each other.

After the boys were tucked into bed, prayers said and one short story told, Melissa quietly slipped out on the balcony to try to unwind from the day's activities. She could hear the ringing of David's telephone next door, and she knew that she was right in her earlier assumption.

The evening air was cool, and she hugged her robe tightly around her as she leaned against the balcony railing. The indigo night sky was speckled with stars, and there was only a sliver of a new moon. She spent several minutes in quiet meditation, as she drew on a sense of oneness with the magnificent heavens and the divine Creator.

David's light was still on when she slipped back into the room and went to bed. In spite of her unwillingness to think about him, she couldn't stop wishing that things were different. Her confession to him about being too impatient to wait for something had been an honest one. More than once, she had ignored intuitive warnings and bolted ahead, only to reap the fruits of her impulsiveness. Never one to lie to herself, she admitted that her feelings for David had deepened. The more she was with him, the more she wished he might have been the one to share her life. Maybe taking this trip together had been a mistake, she thought as she tried to ignore a deep sense of loneliness that she hadn't felt before.

The next morning, they had two grumpy little boys on their hands. Waking them up early enough to fit David's schedule did little to ensure the right mood for a long day in the car. Scruffy was rested and ready for something aside from sleep, but neither Eric nor Richie would put up with his licking and tugging. They fussed at the dog and at each other.

"Eric's on my side!"

"The dog won't get off me."

"Tell Richie to move over!"

David shot them a quick look over his shoulder. "Simmer down, cowboys."

"Melissa," one of the boys wailed, but she didn't say anything or turn around. She'd already tried gentle persuasion to get them interested in something other than fighting, but without any success. She was curious to see how David would handle the situation. The boys were quiet for a few miles, and then the squabbling began again.

Melissa swallowed back a snicker when David raised his voice in a thick western drawl. "I reckon I'd better be letting you drive, Melissa, so I can join them two cowpokes in the back seat. Sounds like they be riding for a fall."

There was a weighted silence in the back.

"How about it, partners? You want some help figuring out what the trouble is?" David looked into the rear mirror at two wide-eyed little boys who were shaking their heads. He winked at Melissa as the low murmur of boyish voices replaced their earlier squabbling.

Late in the morning, the bright sunny weather gave way to dark clouds gathering on the northern horizon. As gusts raced across the open prairie, David tightened his hands on the steering wheel to keep the car steady against the wind's battering.

"Wow, when the wind blows around here, you'd better batten down the hatches," Melissa exclaimed as she watched prairie tumbleweeds race over fields and across the highway. Wire fences were already clogged with the prickly dry weeds.

A brown haze rose from nearby plowed fields, and David said, "Looks like some of the farmers are losing their topsoil." As the wind-driven sand clouds grew thicker, they could hear a steady peppering against the exterior of the car.

"Do you think we'll drive out of it?" Melissa asked, as visibility steadily deteriorated. She'd been caught in white-out blizzards in the mountains when the wind drove snow in blinding sheets across the ground, but a sandstorm was something she'd only read about.

He nodded—but there hadn't been any oncoming traffic for miles and he wondered if that meant conditions were worse ahead. He had turned on his headlights, and hoped that any cars coming in his direction had done the same.

Slowing his speed and hunching over the wheel, he kept his eyes fastened on the yellow line of the highway as it appeared and disappeared in dirt clouds rolling in front of the car. A high-pitched shrieking wind and the constant sandblasting against the car frayed their nerves.

Scruffy started whining and moving restlessly from the seat to the floor.

"I can't see out the window," Eric complained in an anxious little voice, perceptive enough to sense the tension in the adults.

"It's just a windstorm," Melissa said as casually as she could. "The wind is picking up dirt and making clouds out of it. Some people call them sandstorms."

"I don't like them," Eric said.

"Me, neither," Richie chimed in. He was sitting quite close to his older brother instead of on his own side of the seat, and was even using the middle seat belt, as if disputes over seat territory didn't count when things got rough. Melissa didn't blame him. She found herself leaning a little closer to David as the wind and sand battered the car. She was glad that she'd risen early enough for her usual morning prayers for guidance and protection.

Any kind of traffic on the road would have been reassuring, but mile after mile they seemed to be alone in the vast emptiness of Wyoming. Melissa had never seen so much open space in her life.

At one point the wind slackened and they saw that they had left the cultivated area behind. No more plowed fields should mean less loose dirt waiting to be whipped into the air.

"Maybe we're out of the worst of it," David said hopefully. His eyes burned from concentrating so intently on the highway markings, and a pain in his neck and shoulders protested his hunched position over the steering wheel. He didn't want to think about how much time they'd lost during the past couple of hours, creeping along at a snail's pace.

Instead of driving out of the storm, they found themselves engulfed in a blinding brown-out; miles and miles of barren land offered no resistance to gale-force winds sweeping across open ground. The highway disappeared in clouds of sand just as a blast of wind hit the car with a tremendous impact.

David tried to compensate for the car's movement sideways, but couldn't. The heavy car began to slide as its tires lost traction in the moving sand.

The ground fell away.

Melissa cried out as the car dropped off the road and plunged downward. All of them were flung forward against their seat belts, and when the car came to an abrupt stop, it pitched to one side.

There was stunned silence, not because anyone was hurt but because of the suddenness of what had happened. Then Eric and Richie began to cry.

"It's all right. It's all right," Melissa soothed as she quickly unfastened her seat belt and climbed over the seat into the back. She let out a prayerful breath when she saw they were safely fastened in. Scruffy was the one who looked a little dazed; he had been thrown off the seat onto the floor.

"Anyone hurt?" David asked anxiously as his gaze traveled over Melissa and the children.

"No. Just scared," she assured him as she unfastened the seat belts and gathered the sobbing boys in her arms. "You're okay. You're okay. Everything's going to be fine. Just fine," she murmured as her worried eyes held David's.

What are we going to do?

He looked away quickly, not wanting to let her see how stunned he was. His relief that no one had been injured instantly faded as the realization of their perilous position hit him.

The wailing of the wind and the relentless barrage of sand against the car was even louder now that he'd turned off the engine. Trying to see anything out of the windows through the thick brown haze was impossible. The pitch of the car indicated that they had slid into a ditch, but he didn't know how deep, or how far off the road, the car had plunged. Venturing outside too soon would be suicide.

His cell phone wasn't any good under the circumstances. It wasn't strong enough to transmit at this distance and in these conditions. Around town it was fine, and he'd never expected to need it in an emergency like this one. He ran a hand agitatedly through his hair as he analyzed the situation.

"What are you thinking?" Melissa asked, needing to share whatever thoughts he was having, even if they weren't the most reassuring.

He kept his voice as even and steady as he could. "As soon as the wind settles down, we'll be able to see how to drive out of here, or I'll go for help."

Go where? Melissa silently asked. They both knew that the closest highway facilities were still miles away, because they had checked the map when they made plans where to stop for lunch. Plans that were now a mockery. As a quiver of panic threatened to overcome her, Melissa reminded herself, My protection comes from on high. She began to mentally draw on all the scripture verses promising that God's grace was always with her.

As the torturous minutes ticked by, the wind kept up its fierce attack. David became anxious that if the winds didn't abate pretty soon, blowing sand could bury the car and make it impossible to get the doors open. As he listened to Melissa's efforts to counter the boys' fears with stories, songs and prayers, he wondered if she fully realized the danger facing them.

It didn't help to know that *he'd* put their lives in jeopardy. He should have stopped before the winds got so fierce, but he had stubbornly stuck to the decision he'd made on how far they would get by nightfall. Now, all of that seemed insignificant. What did a few extra hours or even a day really matter? It hadn't been worth the risk. He knew that anyone but Melissa would have been berating him for his stupidity. At all cost he had to get her and the boys out of here safely.

For hours they remained trapped in the car, waiting, listening and watching for any sign that the dust storm was over. When Eric and Richie finally fell asleep in the back seat, Melissa climbed into the front seat with David.

He avoided looking at her. Admitting his mistakes had never come easily for him. All his life he'd tried to live up to his parents' expectations, fearful of losing their love. Now, he was sure that he'd destroyed any positive feelings Melissa might have had for him.

"Quit blaming yourself," she said with insight. Impulsively she took his hand and gave it a reassuring squeeze. Then she leaned back against the seat, closed her eyes and kept her hand in his as the minutes ticked by with excruciating slowness.

David kept glancing at his watch. The afternoon was nearly gone when the sound of whipping wind lessened and the brown haze outside the windows grew thinner. Were they going to be trapped here all night? Would the car be almost buried by morning?

David was afraid that his senses might be betraying him, but when Melissa sat up and raised a questioning eyebrow, he knew that she had noticed the subtle difference in the wind, too.

"I think it's letting up," she said softly.

He nodded and took the first breath of relief he'd had in hours. The responsibility for getting them into this mess rested heavily on his conscience, and he was ready to do anything to make sure that they came out of the experience safely.

At first, they couldn't see clearly through the windshield, but gradually it became apparent that the car rested at the bottom of a ravine. David felt his chest tighten, knowing that it would be impossible to drive the car back up that kind of steep slope. And the chances were infinitesimal of anyone seeing the car at the bottom, covered with sand.

"I'll have to get back to the highway and stop someone."

"We'll all go."

"No," he said firmly. "It's still bad out there. You and the boys are better off here."

She knew he was right, but just sitting there waiting

wasn't going to be easy. No telling how long he'd be gone.

"I'll have to tie something over my nose to keep the sand out."

"Here, take this." She pulled off the soft scarf that she had used to tie back her hair. Quickly, she put it over his nose and mouth and knotted it at the back of his head. "There. You look like a highwayman," she said lightly, trying not to let him see how vulnerable she felt as he prepared to leave her alone in the car.

He pulled her into his arms, gave her a long hug and said in a muffled whisper through the scarf, "Don't worry. I'll be back with help."

When he tried to open the door on the driver's side, he discovered that the car was snugged up tightly against a bank of dirt and rocks and the door would open only a crack. Even before he could get it closed again, a gust of wind sent sand flying into the car.

Melissa tried the passenger door and it opened more easily, but it took David's strength to move the sand piled against it and open it wide enough for him to slip out.

As the blast of air invaded the car, Scruffy gave a *woof,* leaped over the front seat, and was out the door before David could slam it closed again. When David turned and disappeared through the thick haze, Melissa couldn't even tell if the dog was at his heels.

As she felt a trembling rising within her, she closed her eyes and repeated the ninety-first psalm until the words brought her a calming assurance. "...because you have made the Lord your refuge...no evil will befall you...for He will give his angels charge of you to guard you in all your ways."

Chapter Eight

The air was thick with sand whipped by a lingering wind. Fortunately David's dark glasses protected his eyes enough to keep them open. Melissa's scarf protected his nose and mouth. As he lowered his head and started up the ravine's rocky slope, Scruffy darted around David's legs, nearly tripping him.

"Down, down," David ordered in a voice muffled by the folds of the scarf. He couldn't believe it! That's all he needed: to try to keep track of a dog. He knew that the winds could build up again at any moment, and he couldn't afford the time to get Scruffy back in the car. He had no choice. He had to make use of the small window of partial visibility, and get up to the highway. The dog was on his own. Why on earth had he ever agreed to bring the mutt along in the first place?

In some places, David had to climb upward on all fours. Wild coarse grass and sticky weeds cut into his hands. Drawing air through the layer of cloth over his nose and mouth made his breathing labored. Despite the glasses, his eyes were scratchy from dirt getting under his eyelids. The car had dropped so quickly, he couldn't judge how far it was to the top. A sporadic wind was still creating a brown fog all around him.

Scruffy bounded recklessly at David's side, repeatedly bumping against him as he tried to rub his face against David's arms and legs to clear his dust-filled eyes. Sometimes the dog pushed so hard that he almost caused David to lose his balance on the sliding rocks and earth.

"No, no," David ordered.

When the dog suddenly left him, David felt both a sense of relief and worry. Because his focus had been on the ground under his hands and feet, he had no idea whether the dog had dropped back or gone ahead.

David let out a muffled "Scruffy."

No response. Maybe he'd gone back to the car. Was Scruffy smart enough to scratch on the door for Melissa to let him in? In any case, trying to locate him in the murky fog was impossible.

David shoved concern for the dog behind the compelling need to get help for Melissa and the children before the storm's reprieve was over.

As David continued to struggle upward, a frightening thought made him stop in his tracks. He paused, squinted upward, but couldn't tell what lay beyond a scattering of wild bushes. Panic overtook him. Had he been moving sideways on the hill instead of straight up to the highway?

David stood there, frozen, trying to make some

sense out of the terrain, when suddenly he heard Scruffy's insistent bark. What now? thought David in exasperation. Was the dog lost on the hillside? Needing rescuing again? His irritation began to lessen when he realized that the barking was coming from somewhere above. Could it be that Scruffy had already reached the top of the hill and the highway?

Guided by the dog's barking, David scrambled over jagged rocks, climbing upward until he pushed through scratchy bushes and suddenly found himself on the shoulder of the highway.

Scruffy jumped on him with a welcoming yelp, and David hugged him. "Good dog. Good dog. Thanks, fellow."

With Scruffy bounding at his heels, David walked out in the middle of the highway and looked in both directions. The road was still shrouded in brown fog. His heart sank. No sign of any car lights. The only sound was the wailing wind. He knew that anyone used to this kind of dust storm would know better than to venture out on the road when the visibility was so poor.

What to do now?

He told himself that if the winds continued to abate, there was bound to be some traffic eventually. But how long would that take? When he thought about Melissa and the boys cooped up in the car, hungry and frightened, he clenched his fists in anger at his helplessness.

He walked a little way in one direction with Scruffy at his heels, and then in the opposite direction. He couldn't see any sign of human habitation on either side of the road. Even though visibility was improving, he was careful not to leave the place where the car had gone off the road. There was nothing around to serve as a marker. No trees. No signs. How would he ever find the exact spot again? He had no choice but to stay in the same place until help came.

He paced and paced, and when a faint white spot finally appeared in the distance he jerked off his dark glasses, not knowing what he was seeing. Then, as a vehicle took shape, he let out a shout that set Scruffy barking.

A highway patrol car.

David raced to the middle of the road and stood there, waving and shouting. As the patrolman braked to a stop, David ran over to him and started shouting, even before the man had a chance to roll down the window.

"My car," he shouted. "It's down there. I've got people inside."

"Calm down," the middle-aged patrolman ordered. "Get in the car, and take that thing off your mouth so I can understand what you're saying."

Melissa heard voices and David's shouts even before his face appeared at the dusty window. She had put the boys in the front seat with her, and let them take turns behind the steering wheel. They made up a game of pretending where they were going, and the children were enjoying the fantasy. She was the one who had to deal with reality as the minutes passed.

In her mind's eye she tried to visualize what was happening, but finally gave up and kept her focus on believing in answered prayer. When the long vigil came to an end and she opened the door to David and a man in a trooper's uniform, grateful tears spilled down her cheeks. *Thank you, Lord. Thank you.*

David stiffened when he saw the tears. "Are you all right? The boys?" he asked anxiously.

She wiped away the happy tears and assured him, "We're fine."

"Where's Scruffy?" Eric demanded in an accusing tone. David's return obviously wasn't his highest priority.

At the sound of his name, the dog jumped into the car and began laying sloppy kisses on the two giggling boys and Melissa.

"Come on. We've got a climb to make," David warned.

Clearly, the patrol officer had expected to find a tense situation, and he looked a little bewildered by the high spirits and laughter inside the car.

As Melissa, the boys and dog climbed out of the car, David said, "This is Officer Mackey. He's got a patrol car waiting to take us into the next town."

"I can be calling for an ambulance if you'll be needing one," he said.

"No, there's no need," Melissa said quickly. "You're an answer to our prayers, Officer."

His eyes crinkled in a responding smile. "I'm thinking you've had more than a little blessing today."

"I guess we gave the Lord a workout, for sure," she agreed.

The wind had diminished to a light breeze, the air was clearing, and the position of the car at the ravine was clearly visible. Officer Mackey surveyed the hillside where the car had slid off the highway. "It's hard to believe that the car didn't turn over on the way down." He shook his head. "No way a wrecker can get this baby back up that steep slope."

Until that moment, David hadn't given any thought to how they were going to get the car out of the gully. His attention had been on getting help. Now the impact of the situation hit him. "You mean, there's no way to recover the car?"

"I didn't say that," Officer Mackey said as he let his brown eyes rove up and down the gully in both directions. "Could be there's a way to bring a wrecker in from the other side. There's a county road that runs along this ravine a little ways back. Might be they could come in that way." He eyed David. "Going to cost you some, though. They'll have to remove some rocks and clear a track. A lot cheaper than letting this baby turn to rust."

David nodded. "That's for sure. How long would something like that take?"

The patrolman shrugged his broad shoulders. "Hard to tell. If Tom Yates Towing can get right on it—no more than a day, I'd say."

David's stomach took a sickening plunge. What was the governor going to say? Another extra day could risk the appointment that had been promised him. "How far is it to the next town?"

"About fifty miles. You're lucky my run this afternoon brought me in this direction. We always get a bunch of stranded travelers in dust storms like this, but usually there's nothing to do but wait out the storm on the side of the road.'' He looked as if he was ready to give David some advice, and then thought better of it. ''Well, I'd better be checking in before they send another unit to follow up on my call.'' He gave Eric and Richie an appraising look. ''You fellows good at climbing?''

''We're real good!'' Richie boasted.

''We climbed a big, big hill when Scruffy was lost,'' Eric said.

The patrolman's eyes twinkled. ''Sounds as if you've had yourselves an exciting trip.''

Before the boys could start relating Scruffy's escapade, Melissa told them to get what they needed out of the back seat. The first things they grabbed were their cowboy hats. There was no way they could carry all the suitcases, so they chose a couple of overnight bags, and Melissa and David strapped on a couple of backpacks. David took the heaviest overnight bag, and Officer Mackey took the other one.

Now that the skies had cleared and a late-afternoon sun bathed the earth, they could see the easiest path up the hill to the highway. They made the climb in half the time it had taken David.

The patrolman placed a small red cone on the shoulder of the highway to mark the place where the car had gone off. ''We'll check the odometer on the way back to get the exact mileage,'' he told David.

Settled in the back seat of the patrolman's car with the boys, Melissa drew a deep, relaxing breath. David sat in the front seat, and Officer Mackey called ahead and reserved a couple of rooms for them in the Homestead Hotel. The officer said it was the only place he knew that allowed pets.

"Right downtown, it is," he assured them. "Nothing fancy. Rents out rooms by the night, week and month. Nice little café just around the corner. You and the missus should be real comfy there."

Melissa waited for David to correct him, but he didn't. She decided that either David didn't think it was important to set the record straight, or he was getting used to people jumping to the wrong conclusion. She secretly liked the idea of giving the impression that they were a family. If there were a way their relationship could become more permanent, she would welcome him into her life, but the truth of the situation was undeniable. All of David's energy was focused on the vision he had for his career. She'd glimpsed the world in which he lived and knew that she didn't belong in it. Not now. Not ever. And one thing seemed certain: he wasn't going to change. She had tried to bring up any discussion of spiritual beliefs several times on the trip, but he sidestepped them with all the finesse of a successful lawyer.

Now he looked tired and preoccupied. No doubt he was wondering what else could go wrong. They should have been in Wolfton by now. They would have to call Paula and explain the delay.

Melissa sighed. Her grandmother had taught her to believe in divine right timing, but at the moment she saw nothing good coming out of this forced delay. Her weariness was bone deep, and she looked forward to a nice warm bath that would soak the rigid muscles in her neck and back.

David was relieved to see that the small town was more than just a wide spot in the road. Three stoplights controlled the traffic on a busy main street that stretched five or six blocks long. When a familiar fast-food restaurant came into view, both boys put up a howl.

"I'm hungry."

"I want a burger."

"Scruffy wants one, too."

With a deep laugh, the patrolman turned into the drive-in. "Well, now, I can't have a couple of starving young'uns on my conscience, can I."

Melissa's own stomach contracted with emptiness as they picked up their two-sack order and promised the boys that they'd eat as soon as they got to the hotel.

"Here we are," Officer Mackey said a few minutes later, as he pulled up in front of a two-story stone building. "You folks make yourselves comfortable now. Just ask the Henshaws for anything you need." He turned to David. "Tom Yates Towing is two blocks down. I'll stop and give him the details, but you'd best be giving him a call yourself. Tom will have to hire some extra help to get the job done."

David nodded. "As soon as we get settled, I'll walk down and talk with him."

As the boys got out of the car with Scruffy pulling at his leash, the officer told Melissa, "There isn't much to do around here to pass the time, but we've got a city park with a nice playground. I'm betting you'll find some friendly kids and dogs running around there. You've got a couple of live wires there."

Melissa laughingly agreed and thanked him for all he'd done for them.

The Homestead Hotel was well named. The weathered stone building looked as if it had stood in the same spot since Wyoming was a territory. Numerous renovations had only added to its Old West look. The rustic lobby was paneled in knotty pine and furnished more like someone's homey living room than a commercial hotel. The furniture was worn, and several older gentlemen stopped their chatter long enough to give the new arrivals the once-over.

There was a small registration counter in one corner, and a hefty man with graying hair and a close-clipped beard and mustache watched them as they crossed the lobby. His broad mouth spread in a welcoming smile as he greeted them.

"You're the folks that Officer Mackey called about. The wind can sure kick up a fuss around here. Guess you've had yourself a time, all right." He wore small round glasses that perched low on his nose, and his eyes fairly danced, as if he could hardly wait to hear all about it. "Ran off the road, did ya?"

"Yes, we did," David responded without elaborating. "You have a couple of rooms for us?"

"Nothing right together. We only have a few rooms to let. Most of our guests are residential. I've got rooms 4 and 9." He peered at them, raising his salt-and-pepper eyebrows. "Hate to break up a family but that's the best I can do."

"That'll be fine," David said, and indicated he was ready to sign the register. He put both rooms in his name as he had done the two nights before.

"There's a fenced yard in the back where you can let the dog out. No barking, though."

"No barking," David repeated, as if there were no question about Scruffy's manners.

The rooms were at both ends of the hall, but they were spacious with high ceilings and tall narrow windows. One had a double bed and the other twin beds. Their earlier arrangement of Melissa having the children in her room wasn't going to work. They were going to have to split up the boys. One of them would have to be with David.

Melissa explained. She expected a big to-do, and was surprised when Eric volunteered to make the change. Then the truth came out.

"I'll keep Scruffy company," Eric said happily, knowing that the dog had stayed in David's room during the trip.

David winked at Melissa. "I guess that tells it like it is. Which room do you want?"

"You take the twin beds. Richie and I will do fine in the double bed."

David glanced at his watch, and his jaw tensed. "I'd better talk to the towing people right away. If the patrolman's idea of reaching the car isn't feasible, we'll have to look at some other options."

She knew that he was tired, drained and functioning on pure willpower. Impulsively she touched his face, murmuring reassurances that everything was going to work out. She was startled when he turned his head and pressed a kiss into the palm of her hand. The soft and gentle touch of his lips brought a warmth to her cheeks.

For a long moment they didn't move, as if some strange chemistry was humming between them, and then Melissa drew away. She was startled by the unexpected physical attraction, and knew that their frightening ordeal had made them both vulnerable.

"You better eat your burger before you go," she said as evenly as she could, avoiding looking at him.

When she wouldn't meet his eyes, he regretted that he had added a new constraint between them. He wanted to explain that he'd given in to an affectionate impulse to show her how very special she was. He hadn't known many people like Melissa who "walked the talk," and any doubts he'd had about the strength of her religious faith had been dispelled by the way she handled herself and the boys during their ordeal.

Even though he had never been drawn to a woman on so many levels, he knew that the hope of developing any lasting personal relationship with Melissa was just wishful thinking. She would never accept his cynical attitude. She'd made it clear that she believed in God's intervention and credited Him with keeping them from harm until they could be rescued. He wanted to argue that all of the happenings could just as easily be explained as coincidences or blind luck. His trained mind wouldn't let him accept what his mother used to call "delusional fantasies."

"I'll be back as soon as I can. I'll take my burger with me. You'll be all right, won't you? Is there anything you need?"

She shook her head. "I'm pretty sure there's one change of clothes around in overnight bags and back-

packs. If we don't get our luggage tomorrow, we may
have to do some shopping.''

He nodded and left, but she knew he was frustrated
by his lack of control in the situation.

After eating and bathing, they took Scruffy outside.
Melissa was pleasantly surprised. The backyard turned
out to be a spacious lot, and the boys and dog took
off at a run toward a tire swing hanging from a sturdy
oak tree.

A brick fence enclosed a broad lawn and planting
of wildflowers that bordered a flagstone path leading
to a charming old gazebo. Melissa felt as if she'd
stepped back in time as she sat on a bench, watching
the children and the dog play. Her love of pioneer
history was stirred as she gazed upon the old stone
hotel, suspecting that a hundred stories were waiting
to be told about the women who had passed by this
very spot. If they were stuck here for a couple of days,
she'd do a little research.

Eventually, Melissa began to wonder if something
had gone wrong at the towing company, and was relieved when David came into view. He spied her sitting in the gazebo, gave her a wave and walked toward
her with that long stride of his.

Scruffy bounded over and threatened to trip him
with his exuberant welcome. Whether David cared or
not, Scruffy liked him, and Melissa was happy to see
him laugh at the dog's antics.

''Sorry to be so long,'' David said as he dropped
down on the bench beside Melissa. ''Mackey had already contacted the towing company, but the owner,
Tom Yates, wasn't convinced that the patrolman's

idea about how to reach the car was viable. He called in a couple of the guys that work for him, and they spent nearly an hour hashing the whole thing over before they decided to try Mackey's idea. They'll go out first thing in the morning, but there are no guarantees.''

"The patrolman seemed to think it could be done."

"Well, I offered a good monetary incentive. If they can get the car out of the ravine early enough in the day, we can be on our way before nightfall.'' He brushed back a shock of hair. "Of course, that's assuming that the car isn't damaged in any way. The engine was still running fine when I turned it off."

"Well, there's nothing more you can do about it tonight," she said. "What do you want to do about dinner? I don't think the boys will be very hungry after eating so late in the afternoon."

"I don't feel much like eating, myself," he confessed. "There's a small café a few doors down the street. I'll watch the boys, if you want to get something."

She shook her head. "Right now, I'd like to call it a day—or maybe a day-and-a-half," she added with a wry smile.

"It does seem like ages since this morning. Time is really relative, isn't it?'' His eyes fastened thoughtfully on her face.

"Yes, it's hard to grasp sometimes."

"I can't believe there's a time when I didn't know you. How has it happened, Melissa Chanley, that you've become so much a part of my life in such a short time?"

"I'll have to think about it," she answered with an evasive smile. He wasn't being flippant or flirtatious, and his sincerity momentarily threw her off balance.

Just then, Eric and Richie raised a fuss about who was taking the longest turn on the swing. "Time to put them to bed," she said.

David agreed. "I'm going to hit the shower and then the sack myself. Any advice about tending Eric?"

"I think he'll be fine. You'll probably be awake before he is in the morning. Bring him down to my room if you want to leave early."

She helped Eric gathered up his night things, gave him a good-night kiss and told him to take care of Scruffy. He nodded and held Scruffy's leash tightly as he followed David down the hall to the other room.

David wasn't quite sure how to handle the "getting ready for bed" routine. He was relieved when the boy seemed used to looking after himself. By the time David was out of the shower, Eric was already in his pajamas and in bed, with the dog at his feet.

"All set?" David asked as he sat down on his twin bed and prepared to turn out the light.

"Don't you do prayers?"

"Do prayers?"

Eric nodded. "You can go first."

David had been backed into a corner more than once in his professional career, but never by a kid. "That's okay," he said. "You go ahead."

"God likes you just to talk to him. Melissa says so," Eric explained a little defensively. "But you don't have to do it out loud."

"I understand." David nodded, wondering how to

play the part suddenly thrust on him. ''Doing prayers'' had never been a part of his upbringing, and as an adult he'd never joined a church or made worship a part of his life.

He watched as Eric closed his eyes, clasped his hands and moved his little lips in a silent prayer. When he was finished, he turned to David. ''Now, a story.''

''It's getting pretty late. I think we'd better forget about any story tonight.''

He frowned. ''Don't you know any?''

''Sure, I do, but—''

''Melissa always tells us a story,'' he complained. ''She knows lots of them. I like 'Baby Moses in the Basket' best. He needed a new home, just like me and Richie. Do you know that one?''

''I'm not sure,'' David said slowly. ''Why don't you tell it to me?''

''Okay,'' he said with his shy smile, obviously pleased to know something that David didn't. The way he told the story, the baby's trip down the river in a basket was pretty exciting. David had to question whether some of the extra details that he put in were even in the Bible, but the message was clear. God had found a neat place for Moses to live.

''That's a good story, and you told it very well,'' David said, smiling. ''I guess I can turn out the light now.''

Eric frowned. ''Don't you do 'good-night kisses,' either?''

''I guess I have a lot to learn about this bedtime business.'' David chuckled as he bent over Eric's bed and kissed the boy's freckled cheek. "Good night. Sweet dreams."

Eric beamed. "That's what Melissa always says."

David lay awake for a long time, trying to remember a time when his mother or father had kissed him goodnight and wished him "sweet dreams." They were usually gone somewhere, leaving hired help to watch him. He'd never known the gentle sweetness that Melissa showered on the two children who weren't even her own. She believed in a God of love, and maybe what he had said to Eric about having a lot to learn was true. He felt a little foolish wishing that someone would kiss him goodnight and wish him "sweet dreams."

Chapter Nine

"Will you watch the boys for a few hours this morning?" Melissa asked, as they sat at a table in the crowded café, enjoying a home-style breakfast of sausage, hash brown potatoes and pancakes. "I'd like to spend a little time at the local library. There may be some interesting stories about women in this area that I could work into my book." She saw the flicker of a frown cross his face. "Did you have something else to do?"

"I just need to make some phone calls and check in at the office, but I can do that later today," he said quickly, unable to turn her down. After all that had happened, she deserved a little time to herself. He marveled that there was no sign of yesterday's trauma in her manner or easy smile. She continued to amaze him with her ability to adjust and accept a situation that would have thrown most women into a tailspin. "Checking out the library sounds like a good idea."

"Are you sure? I know you're feeling a lot of pressure over the delay."

"I'll get a handle on it," he reassured her, even as he thought of the work piling up on his desk. His secretary would be having a fit, trying to reschedule appointments and fielding all kinds of questions that only he could answer. As soon as they towed the car into town and checked it out, he wanted to get on the road again. He'd leave Melissa and the boys, and head back to Denver as soon as possible.

"Why don't you take advantage of the situation?" Melissa asked him, seeing the tense set of his jaw.

He looked puzzled. "What do you mean?"

"Nobody knows where you are. You could sneak in some free time before they catch up with you."

He smiled and responded to the teasing glint in her eyes. "You're a bad influence, you know that?"

"I know. But haven't you ever had a secret desire to leave everything behind? Run away and join the circus?"

"Me?" He shook his head and laughed. "Never."

"Circus?" Eric's head jerked up from his pancakes. "We saw a circus on television, didn't we, Richie?"

His brother nodded eagerly. "Can we join one, Melissa?"

"Not today," Melissa answered smoothly, as if the question were reasonable enough. "But I'm sure David will find something fun for you to do."

"Thanks a lot," David chided Melissa. With that kind of promise, what choice did he have but to live up to their expectations? "All right, you go do your thing at the library, and the boys and I will see what this little town has to offer three fellows on the loose.''

They left the café and went back to the hotel to feed Scruffy and put him on a leash. ''Shall we meet back here at lunchtime?'' she asked.

David nodded. ''Okay, buckeroos, let's hit the trial.''

Melissa couldn't help but chuckle as she watched him head down the street with a dog and two boys clumping along beside him in cowboy boots and hats. The scene brought a rush of tenderness to her heart and tears to her eyes.

The time Melissa spent at the library turned out to be wasted. Even though she found the early history of the town interesting, she failed to find any reference to a pioneer woman who might have left an imprint on the local history because of her strength of character or convictions. She needed the account of a truly courageous woman as a lead on her book. Discouraged, she began to question the whole idea of writing a book about pioneer women of faith. Maybe it wasn't worth continuing. Even as doubts crossed her mind, she remembered a favorite saying of her grandmother's, when Melissa would predict failure about something. *If you name it, you claim it.*

The memory reminded her that if she decided that the project wasn't worthwhile, it wouldn't be. She'd doom it to failure because of her own disbelief. Deep down, she felt that she was supposed to write this book, and as she left the library she renewed her commitment to keep searching for the right material.

Melissa glanced at her watch. Nearly noon. She wondered how David had made out as a baby-sitter. Eric had proudly confided in her that he had told David the bedtime story of Baby Moses. Even though she was happy to see that Eric was opening up and beginning to trust David, she was also worried about how the sensitive boy would react when David disappeared from his life the way his mother and father had.

When she returned to the hotel, she found two excited boys who each wanted to talk at once. It took her a few garbled moments to get the story. David had found a pony ride for kids. Broad smiles and sparkling eyes lit up their little faces.

"You should have been there," Eric told her.

"My horse went fast," Richie bragged.

"Mine was the biggest."

"He couldn't catch up with mine."

"Yes, he could."

"Okay, fellows," David said in a tone that put an end to the mine's-better-than-yours argument. "You both did a good job."

"You let them ride real horses?" Melissa couldn't quite believe what she was hearing.

"Yep." David winked at her. "And if they hadn't been going around a circle in that corral, they would have been streaking across the prairie like real cowboys after a runaway steer. Right, guys?"

Eric and Richie waved their cowboys hats and yelled, "Hip! Hip! Hooray!"

"You didn't think I was up to this kid-watching business, did you?" David said, grinning.

"You set a pretty high standard," Melissa admitted, laughing and shaking her head. "I'm afraid taking them to the park this afternoon is going to be a let-down."

"The park?" Both boys looked at David and whined, "You promised. You promised."

"Promised what?" Melissa asked, afraid to hear the answer. At this point, she didn't know what to expect. David was suddenly full of surprises.

He gave her an apologetic look. "I guess I promised that you'd take them to a movie this afternoon."

"Can we go, Melissa? Please?"

Relieved that the promise was one that she could keep, she said, "Sounds like a good idea."

Before they left the hotel, Melissa called Paula's number, and a recording machine clicked on. Melissa left a message that they hoped to arrive tomorrow afternoon, and they'd call again if plans changed.

After putting Scruffy on a leash in the backyard with water and food, they had a quick lunch at the café. David planned to return to the hotel to work while Melissa took the boys to the movies, but as they left the restaurant she decided to see if she could change his mind.

"I think you ought to come with us. When was the last time you slipped off to an afternoon movie?"

"Well, not recently," he answered smoothly, when the truth was that he couldn't remember when, if ever, he'd neglected work or school to go to a movie.

"Maybe it's time," she said. "You might like it."

He had opened his mouth to tell her he couldn't, when a little hand crept into his. Eric smiled and gently pulled at him like someone urging him to join in a game. "You come, too."

Melissa held her breath. This kind of reaching out to someone was totally unlike Eric, and she feared that any kind of rejection could send the boy back into his shell. Would David realize the fragility of the moment and surrender to the little boy's need?

With great effort, David swallowed back all the well-worn excuses that had supported his work-centered life. The feel of a child's hand in his, and a hopeful smile on a grinning freckled face completely disarmed him. He knew it was idiotic for him to spend precious time watching a kid's show when important matters were waiting for his attention. He couldn't believe it when he let himself be pulled along by two joyful kids and a smiling dark-haired woman whose lovely eyes did something to the rhythm of his heartbeat.

A little later, loaded down with popcorn and soft drinks, they sat in the small theater with a crowd of squealing kids and watched the children's movie. At first, David couldn't adjust to the bedlam and the behavior of the uninhibited audience. The clapping, laughing and yelling drowned out the movie's dialogue, but nobody else seemed to pay any attention to the added noise. Everything was in constant motion, and he lost count of the number of times the kids in his row scrambled in and out of their seats.

He sat next to Melissa, with Richie on her side and Eric on his. When he let his arm slip over the back of her seat to lie softly on her shoulders, she didn't seem to mind, and he laughed at himself for feeling like an adolescent again, taking his girl to a Friday night movie.

Melissa was concerned that he wouldn't be able to relax and enjoy himself. A children's matinee was not comparable to a performance of the Denver Civic Orchestra or Ballet Company but as she caught glimpses of his relaxed face and ready smile, she grinned smugly to herself. Maybe there was hope of softening the governor's counselor, after all.

As she leaned closer into the curve of his arm and shoulder, she teased herself with the illusion that the real world would not be waiting for them when they walked out the theater doors.

"We're close enough to walk over to the towing garage and see what's happening with the car," David said, after the film ended. The owner had told him it would be late afternoon at the earliest. He had warned David that he wasn't sure their plan to reach the car was even feasible. It all depended on whether they were able to find a way into the ravine that would allow them to tow the car back to the road. If not, he said, David might as well forget the whole thing and count the loss.

As they approached the garage, David's pulse quickened. The Lexus was already parked outside the garage. "Look. There it is! Maybe we can get out of here today, after all."

The magic of the movie's fantasy faded abruptly when Melissa saw the instant change in David. Smile lines around his mouth and eyes disappeared, and she could tell from his expression that he was already focused on making up for lost time.

The boys hung back, staring at the dirt-covered car with apprehension. Melissa had the same reaction. Just seeing it brought back vivid memories of the hours they'd spent hearing the lashing wind and blasting sand.

As David started toward the door of the garage, Melissa said, "We'll see you at the hotel."

"All right. I'll call you if I'm going to be delayed." He gave them a wave as he disappeared inside the building.

How quickly his holiday was over, she thought sadly. He was already looking ahead to resuming the frantic pace he'd set for himself. She wondered if he would recall the afternoon he'd spent at the movies with fondness—or guilt. As she walked back to the hotel between the two boys, Eric tugged at her hand.

"Can't we stay in this place?" he asked, looking up at her with an old-man worried expression. "I like it here."

"Me, too," Richie added.

Their innocence tugged at her heart. Only children could see life in such simple terms, she thought, and her voice was husky as she tried to explain that they hadn't finished their trip yet. "If the car is okay, we'll have to leave here in the morning."

She'd already decided that there was no way they were going to push and drive anywhere this late in the day. They all needed a good night's sleep for the last day's journey through Yellowstone and the final hundred miles to Wolfton. When they reached the hotel, she let the boys play with Scruffy in the yard for a few minutes before she put them down for a late nap.

Taking her daily meditation book out to the gazebo, she sat in quiet contemplation, praying for guidance and giving thanks for the Lord's protection.

The boys slept for about an hour, and woke up hungry. Just as she was wondering how much longer David would be gone, he joined her and the boys in her room, carrying two large carryout sacks.

"I thought eating in would be easier than going out somewhere. We've got a full day tomorrow, so we'll need to get the kids down early."

"I take it that the car's in working condition."

"You bet," he said happily. "It's hard to believe, but the slide down that rocky hillside didn't damage a thing. After the guys carefully checked the car all over and gave it a wash and wax job, you'd never know it had been buried in a gully. I guess we were lucky all around."

David could call it luck if he wanted to. She'd never believe it was luck that had kept them safe and brought them help.

They left the hotel and were on the road early the next morning. It was only fifty miles to Yellowstone, and Melissa could tell that David wasn't going to spend any more time than was necessary to satisfy her. He was probably thinking that if she hadn't insisted on going through Yellowstone in the first place, they would have taken a different road and would have avoided the sandstorm altogether. But she didn't see any point in letting the unfortunate accident spoil this part of the trip.

"We are going to see a lot of real animals," she told the boys. "Not just pictures."

"Bears?" Richie asked, his eyes wide.

"Maybe not bears," Melissa admitted. "But I bet we see some deer and buffalo, and maybe even a bull elk with antlers this big." She held out her hands to show the wide span of a full-grown elk.

"What are antlers?" Eric asked, frowning.

David suppressed a smile. He couldn't fault Melissa for wanting to educate the boys, but reaching them on their level might be a bit of a challenge. She patiently tried to answer their questions, and he was wondering why she hadn't pursued a teaching career. He wasn't at all convinced that she should be spending her time working on a book that had limited commercial value, but he knew better than to question her decision. She seemed as set on her vision of what she wanted out of life as he was on his.

He had mapped out their trip so they would take the east entrance into the park, make a circle trip to get a view of the lake, Old Faithful geyser and some of the wildlife, and then exit at the west entrance.

Melissa was in awe of God's magnificence as they traveled deep into the natural setting of forests, cliffs and rushing waters. The beautiful color of Yellowstone Lake was almost indigo, she thought as she stood on the bank and watched it rippling toward the shore.

"Are there fish in there?" Eric asked David, peering intently into the water.

"Probably lots of lake trout."

"Can we catch some?"

He laughed. "Not today."

"But sometime?" Eric persisted.

"Maybe," he said, avoiding Melissa's frown. They both knew that there was little chance of repeating the fun the boys had had fishing for their dinner.

David kept a tight leash on Scruffy. Loose pets were not allowed in the park. When they stopped a little later to view a herd of elk resting in a meadow close to the road, they made certain that Scruffy didn't pull his usual trick of bolting out of the car while the door was open.

Melissa insisted that they take the boys on the boardwalk that overlooked the thermal springs steaming out of the earth.

"They look like Inga's teakettle," Richie said excitedly, pointing to the hot white clouds of steam.

Melissa laughed and winked at David. "You're exactly right, Richie. Steam is coming out of the earth the same way that it comes out of a teakettle."

They had lunch in a lodge that had been built near Old Faithful. They sat on benches that circled the area, and when white foaming water blasted hundreds of feet into the air, Melissa jumped up and squealed, "See, see, there it goes."

David laughed and circled her waist to keep her earthbound during the few minutes of the spectacular display. Eric and Richie watched quietly. Apparently bigger wasn't better as far as the boys were concerned. They were a lot more enthusiastic about the steaming "teakettles" and "bubbling mud pots."

David looked at his watch after the geyser had disappeared, and said firmly, "It's time we headed north if we're going to get to Wolfton this afternoon."

"I know," she said regretfully. "Thanks for being so patient and sharing this beautiful park with me." She knew she would store the memory in her heart for a long time. She'd never forget the beautiful scenery, but part of that cherished remembrance would be the warmth of the man and the children who had briefly been a part of her life for this wonderful day.

They reached Wolfton about three o'clock in the afternoon and were surprised at the size of the mountain town. A welcoming sign at the city limits informed them that it was the county seat.

There was a western charm about Main Street that gave it the ambience of a small community, while it showed every sign of being a bustling little city. Paula had given Melissa simple directions about how to reach her place, and on the way, she caught glimpses of houses scattered along the steep slopes of the mountain and thick stands of evergreen trees. She was disappointed that Paula's home was so isolated.

Richie and Eric were unusually quiet, and when she glanced in the back seat she could tell they were fearful of another change in their young lives.

"It's going to be all right," she assured them with a bright smile. "Your aunt Paula is going to love you."

"What if she doesn't?" Eric asked with his usual bluntness. "Do we have to stay?"

"No, of course not," Melissa said, as if they had

some choice in the matter. "But we're going to have a nice visit."

A brightly colored mailbox with a carved wooden blue jay on top stood at the bottom of a curved driveway.

"Nice place," David said as he parked at the bottom of a flight of stairs leading up to the log house's redwood deck. He gave a couple of toots on his horn, but nothing happened.

"Maybe she didn't hear us," Melissa said, wondering why she was so nervous.

"Well, let's announce ourselves." He gratefully stretched his long legs and walked around the car to open the doors for Melissa and the boys.

Scruffy bounded out of the car with his usual exuberance, and for a change, nobody yelled at him. The dog seemed to be the only one filled with enthusiasm about having finally arrived at their destination. Eric and Richie hung behind Melissa and David as they walked to the house, acting more like victims than two little boys coming to visit their aunt.

David didn't see a doorbell, and when he opened the screen door to knock, he saw a note taped to it: "Gone for a walk. Come in and make yourselves at home. Paula."

"I guess she got tired of waiting for us," David said as he tried the front door. When it opened easily, he turned to Melissa. "I say we take her at her word."

Scruffy didn't wait for any further discussion; he slipped past David into the house. As if the boys were waiting for that kind of reassurance that everything was okay, they darted in after him.

Melissa laughed as she slipped her arm through David's. "I guess we've arrived, ready or not."

Chapter Ten

"I feel funny about coming in when she's not home," Melissa said in a hushed voice, as if someone was around to hear them invading. Even the boys were nervous as they looked around, and stayed close to Melissa. Scruffy seemed to be the only one totally at ease. He began sniffing his way around the place, as if he were in charge of deciding whether they should stay or not.

"Let's wait to unload the car until she gets here," David said. "In the meantime, we'll be polite guests and not disturb anything—right, boys?"

Richie whispered anxiously, "Does she have a potty?"

"I think we can find one." Melissa motioned for him to follow her down the hall to a small bathroom opposite the staircase. Wide-planked floors and a beamed ceiling stained a rich walnut color harmonized with a colorful Indian and western decor in furniture and wall hangings. A staircase mounted the wall at one end of the room, and a center hall led to a roomy kitchen and back patio that overlooked the valley below and surrounding mountains. Everything about the home was warm and inviting.

Eric was the one who discovered a pan of cookies sitting on the stove. Melissa decided the aunt must have baked them as a welcome for the boys, so she let each of them have one.

The boys were happily playing with their cowboy figures in front of the fireplace, when the sun began to fade behind the nearby peaks. There was still no Paula, and David and Melissa exchanged questioning looks. The note had said "a little while," and they had been there a couple of hours.

When the telephone rang, David quickly picked it up. "Hello, Bateman residence."

"Who's this?" a man's gruff voice demanded. "I was wanting Paula."

"I'm sorry, she's not here. We're waiting for her."

"Are you the one bringing the kids?"

"Yes, I'm David Ardell. I'm here with Melissa Chanley and the two boys. May I ask who this is?"

"Jim. Jim Becker. Let me talk to Paula."

"She's not here, but she left a note on the door saying that she'd gone for a walk and would be back shortly."

"What?" He gasped. "You mean, Paula hasn't come home yet?"

"No, not yet. We've been here a couple of hours."

"That note was on the door yesterday when I dropped by to check on things."

"Maybe she posted the note again when she went for another walk this afternoon."

Silence. "Is there a pan of cookies still out on the stove?"

"Yes," David said. He felt a sudden cold ripple up his spine.

"She hasn't been back." He slammed down the phone.

David slowly replaced the receiver and stared at it.

"Who was that?" Melissa asked, puzzled. She didn't understand why David had hung up without even saying goodbye.

"It was Jim Becker, asking for Paula."

"I heard you tell him that she'd gone for a walk. Is something wrong?"

"I don't know," he answered as he walked over to the front windows. *She hasn't been back.* The man's words kept repeating themselves in his head like the harsh clang of a warning bell. If Paula had left yesterday afternoon for a walk, where was she now?

Melissa came up beside him, searching his tense profile. "What is it? What's wrong?"

He quietly repeated the conversation he'd had with Jim Becker. "There could be a hundred explanations for the note still being on the door. Maybe she didn't take it down yesterday or she put it back up this afternoon."

As she searched his face, her chest suddenly tightened. Had Paula been gone over twenty-four hours? "Where could she be? What could have happened?"

"At this point, everything's a guess. No good jumping to conclusions until we have more to go on. She could have stopped off to visit with a friend and let the time get away from her.''

''I suppose so,'' Melissa said without conviction.

Melissa swallowed hard as an uneasiness rose to the surface. ''It's almost dark, and the note said she'd be back in a little while. What do you think we should do? Should we alert someone, like the police?''

David knew that a person had to be missing twenty-four hours to be put on a missing person's alert, but if what this Becker guy said was true, Paula had been gone since yesterday afternoon.

''I think that this Becker will call in her disappearance,'' David said. ''He seemed really worried. Let's just stay put and see what happens.''

A few minutes later a flash of car lights hit the front window. Both David and Melissa breathed a sigh of relief. ''Someone's here,'' he said.

The front door flew open and a young man burst into the house. He had dark hair caught in a ponytail and was dressed in jeans and a plaid shirt.

''She come in yet?'' he demanded with obvious agitation.

Both David and Melissa shook their heads.

''I dropped by yesterday morning when she was baking. When I came by the house in the afternoon, she wasn't here.'' He waved the note in his hand. ''This is the same one that was on the door yesterday afternoon.'' There was an edge of accusation in his worried tone.

David said quietly, ''We had no way of knowing that she hadn't put it there just a little while before we got here. There was no reason for us to be concerned. We thought she'd be back momentarily.''

"Yes, of course.'' Jim took a deep breath. ''How would you know the note has been on the door since yesterday?''

David held out his hand. ''I'm David Ardell, and this is Melissa Chanley.''

"I'm Jim Becker.'' He introduced himself as if he'd forgotten he'd already given his name on the phone. ''I was a lodger with Paula until about six months ago, when I got on the fire department and had to move into town. Then I married Nancy and haven't been paying as much attention to Paula as I should have.''

After making certain that there had been no change in the kitchen since the day before, he called 911 and reported her missing.

Eric and Richie were still sitting on a rug with their toys, not saying anything and watching with big eyes.

"These her two nephews?''

"Yes, this is Eric and Richie.'' Melissa smiled reassuringly at them. ''Eric is six years old, and Richie is almost five.''

"Paula was pretty excited about them coming for a visit. That's all she's been talking about. She knew you were arriving today, didn't she?'' he asked.

Melissa replied, ''She expected us yesterday afternoon, but I called and left a message that we'd been delayed and would be here today.''

Jim swung on his heels. ''Her answering machine is on her bedroom phone.'' He turned and bounded up the stairs.

David and Melissa followed him into a large front

room that was obviously a combination lady's bed-room and sitting room. A small lady's desk flanked by bookshelves stood in front of a picture window over-looking the small town below. The telephone answer-ing machine on the desk was blinking.

Jim pushed a green button and a mechanical voice said, "You have one message."

When Melissa heard her voice on the recording, her stomach took a sickening plunge. *Paula had not picked up yesterday's message.*

"She must have already been gone from the house," Jim said in a worried tone. "What time did you call?"

"About twelve-thirty, when I got back to the hotel from the library. Maybe she just didn't erase the mes-sage," Melissa offered in the hope there was some simple explanation.

"Why would Paula put the note on the door yes-terday afternoon if she hadn't been expecting you then?" Jim countered with a frown.

They reasoned that Paula had probably already left the house before Melissa tried to telephone to advise her that they were going to be delayed a day. That meant she had left the house before twelve-thirty yes-terday.

Jim glanced out the windows, where darkening shadows were beginning to creep across the landscape, warning them that the sun was already sinking behind the high mountain peaks.

"They'll be rounding up a search party, but we can't do much more than check the area around the house tonight."

"Where else would she go?" Melissa asked, utterly bewildered by the sudden crisis. She couldn't believe that they had been comfortably passing the time waiting for Paula, when she might be in some kind of danger.

"Hard to say. Paula loves hiking. She's been traipsing all over these mountains since she was a child. I've been hard put to keep up with her when we've been out together. If she took a walk, you can be sure it was more like a hike." His forehead wrinkled in concern. "Some kind of trouble found her or she'd be here, spunky as ever."

"Does Wolfton have an adequate police force?" David asked. How efficient could the law enforcement be in a town this size?

"Paula's house is in the county. It'll be the sheriff and his deputy in charge."

David didn't find this news very reassuring. He knew from experience that county law officers were overworked, with too much jurisdiction to do the best job.

"There's a mountain rescue unit in town. I'll notify them and call in some help on my own," Jim said, sitting down at the desk and starting to dial.

David and Melissa went back downstairs and found Eric and Richie waiting at the bottom of the stairs. Melissa knew she had to explain the situation to them—but how?

Before she could collect her thoughts, Eric said angrily, "She ran away, didn't she. She doesn't want us and that's why she ran away."

"No, it's not that at all," Melissa said, taken aback

by his vehement tone. She hadn't realized that such a fiery rage seethed under the surface of his quiet manner.

"We don't like her even if she makes good cookies," Richie added pugnaciously, taking his cue from his older brother. "We want to take Scruffy and go."

"Your aunt did not run away because you came to see her," David said firmly, and Melissa gave him a grateful look. "Come and sit down, and we'll explain."

"Why do we have to stay here?" Eric demanded as the boys trailed David across the room.

"For now, we all have to stay here," he answered, knowing that he was included. His plans to leave in the morning would have to be put on hold by this latest development. "Your aunt is missing."

"Like the lady at the church said my mother was missing?" Eric asked. "Is Aunt Paula in heaven, too?"

"What?" David asked, looking totally puzzled.

"I'll explain later," Melissa told him as she sat on the sofa with the boys beside her and tried to explain. She wondered how her voice could sound so positive when inside she was reeling from the sudden nightmare that had such tragic possibilities.

While they talked, Jim came downstairs and started pacing the living room floor. When a car pulled up in front of the house, he dashed to the door and jerked it open to let two men into the house.

"You've got to get a search party going right away, Sheriff," Jim said without preamble.

Both men were dressed in tan uniforms. The sheriff

was a sandy-haired man, fortyish, with thick shoulders and a large-boned frame. The deputy was a young man with a stocky build and muscular arms. They both had tense and unsmiling expressions.

The sheriff's sharp eyes fastened on Jim's face. "The report said Paula's been missing since yesterday. How do you know that?"

Jim thrust the note into his large hand and repeated his story about having seen it pinned to the door the day before. Then he nodded at Melissa and David. "She was expecting these folks yesterday, but they got delayed. They found this note still on the door. That means—"

"You're sure it's the same note?"

"Yes," Jim said firmly. "It was fastened on the door the same way, in the same spot—"

"All right," the sheriff conceded. "Maybe she left the note on the door two days."

"What about the kitchen and the cookies? Nothing's been changed since yesterday morning. She hasn't been here, I tell you." Jim's voice rose, and the sheriff put a firm hand on his shoulder.

"Calm down. It won't do anybody any good to panic." He turned to David and Melissa, and let his sharp gaze slide over the boys. "You're Paula's kinfolk?"

"The boys are," David said. He introduced himself and Melissa. "What can we do to help?"

"Not a heck of a lot right now. I've got a call out for a search party. As soon as they get here, we'll check out some of Paula's favorite spots." Even as he spoke, another car pulled up in front of the house.

"It's Judge Daniels," the deputy said, peering out the window.

"That figures. Zackary Daniels has been sweet on Paula as long as I can remember. I wouldn't be surprised if he didn't close up court the minute he got whiff that she was missing."

Judge Daniels was a well-built man with pleasantly balanced features and a beard and mustache. When Jim let him in, he asked anxiously, "Is it true, Jim? There's a missing report out on Paula?"

Jim nodded and explained that she'd probably been gone since the day before.

"How in the blazes did that happen and nobody knew?" he demanded almost angrily.

"Easy, Zach," the sheriff said in a warning tone. "We'll figure this thing out. You know how Paula is. No telling what she got in her head to do before company got here."

The judge's worried eyes swept over David and Melissa, and settled on the boys. He forced a smile. "These little fellows must be the kinfolk Paula was telling me about. Richie and Eric, I believe she said their names were."

Melissa nodded, surprised when he introduced himself as Zackary Daniels, omitting his title. "Most everyone calls me Zach."

There was an obvious touch of affection whenever he said Paula's name, and the sheriff's remark about Judge Zackary Daniels being sweet on her seemed to be the truth. Obviously not willing to let another minute go by without deciding on some course of action, he turned to the sheriff and demanded, "What's the plan, Sheriff?"

"We'll have to wait until daylight to make any kind of a thorough search. The foothill behind the house is about all we can safely do this time of day. In another hour, you won't be able to determine what's a rock and what's a tree, let alone anything else."

"We should check out Chimney Rock tonight," Zach insisted. "That's one of her favorite hikes and it's not far from the house."

Three more men arrived with an attractive woman with curly blond hair who looked to be in her thirties. She wore a sloppy pullover and faded jeans, and had a bounce to her steps as she came right over to Melissa and the boys, greeting them with a broad smile that showed a dimple on her round face.

"I'm Carol Carlson, the reverend's wife. Paula told me all about your upcoming visit." She beamed at Eric and Richie. "What sweet boys. I have two little girls about your ages who would just love playing with you."

"That would be nice," Melissa said quickly, trying to make up for the boys' scowls and turned-down mouths as they glared at the woman.

"Shall we go in the kitchen while the men get themselves organized?" she said in a way that told Melissa that Carol Carlson had probably taken charge in this kind of tense situation more than once. "I brought a little something for a quick supper so you don't have to fix anything."

"That's very thoughtful of you," Melissa said gratefully. Her own stomach was so tight she hadn't thought about eating, but she'd bet the boys were more than ready for supper.

Carol directed Melissa toward the right cupboard to get the plates and glasses. "I know Paula planned to use her good china, but under the circumstances I think the everyday service would be better."

For the first time, Melissa heard a falter in her voice, and sensed the strain she must be under to keep everything upbeat and positive. "You and Paula are good friends, aren't you?"

She nodded. "When my husband, Skip, and I came to Wolfton, neither of us knew anything about serving a church. I would have been lost if Paula hadn't befriended me."

"Do you know where she might have gone yesterday afternoon?"

Carol was silent as she began to uncover her casserole dishes. One was a baked chicken potpie with a golden crust and the other a deep-dish apple cobbler. "I talked to Paula yesterday morning, and she didn't say a thing about going anywhere. She was all excited about getting the boys' room ready for them. Do they like the cowboy bedspreads?"

"We haven't been up to the bedrooms yet. We were waiting to unload the car until she got back." Melissa worried her lower lip. "We kept thinking she'd be back any minute. We didn't know she'd been gone since yesterday."

They heard the men leaving, and a moment later David came into the kitchen. He had hung back, listening to the men, wanting to offer to join them but knowing that he'd be more of a liability than a help.

They didn't need someone stumbling around blindly on the side of a hill while they looked for Paula. "I feel like a fifth wheel in this situation. I'm afraid a paper-pushing lawyer isn't much good in a crisis."

"Sometimes we just don't know what our role is," Carol told him, smiling. She glanced at him and then at Melissa as if wondering about their relationship.

"David was a friend of the boys' mother," Melissa said, and then explained how her connection with Eric and Richie had developed through the homeless shelter. "The two of us have been working together to find a new home for the boys."

"I see." Carol nodded her approval. "Well, sit down. We'll thank the Lord for our blessings and put Paula in his care."

"Amen," Melissa said softly, and was startled when both Eric and Richie chimed in "Amen, amen, amen," as if they had decided that if one "amen" was good, a few more were even better.

Neither David nor Melissa did justice to the delicious meal, and both were unusually quiet, but Carol didn't seem to notice. She paid a lot of attention to Scruffy and listened attentively as Eric and Richie talked at once, telling her about the dog running away after the antelope.

When it was time to clear the table, Carol said, "I'll just pop the leftovers in the frig. There's coffee, toast and cereal for breakfast. Paula probably intended to make fresh biscuits and sausage gravy, her favorite," Carol said with an obvious catch in her throat.

"What do you think has happened to her?" David asked as kindly as he could. It was obvious there was a close tie between the two women. As a lawyer, he knew the value of listening and asking questions.

"I think Paula took one of her hikes and got into trouble. What kind, I don't know."

"Could she have gotten lost?"

"No, not Paula. She knows these mountains like the proverbial back of her hand."

"Then, something unexpected must have happened. A fall? A wild animal?"

"I don't know," she said, "but I believe in angels, and I know one of them is watching over her right now."

Melissa nodded at Carol. "'He will give his angels charge over thee'," she quoted. "We'll keep Paula in our prayers and the Lord will bring her home safely."

David managed a smile but disbelief was in his eyes.

"I'm sorry I can't stay," Carol said, after the kitchen was in order. "I'd better get home and collect my daughters from the neighbors. Skip can catch a ride home with someone."

David walked out to the car with her. They stood for a moment, searching the darkness of the hill behind the house. Lights like giant fireflies flitted among the trees as the searchers made their way upward.

"How will they ever find her on a mountain as big as that one?" David asked quietly.

"There's an outcropping of rocks about halfway to the crest where Paula likes to sit and view the valley below," Carol explained. "It's a hard climb for someone not in condition, but I know she's hiked a lot farther than that many times. If the note said she'd be back in a little while, I don't think she planned on going too far.''

''Is she impulsive?''

''Sometimes,'' Carol admitted. ''More now than she used to be. But you'll like her, I know you will.'' On that positive note Carol got in her car and gave David a friendly wave as she drove away.

He began to unload the Lexus. He knew that there was no way he could head back to Denver as planned. A trip that had seemed simple in Denver had turned into a complicated snarl. The hope of persuading Paula to keep the boys seemed farther away than ever, and what was worse, they might have pulled Eric and Richie into another heartbreaking situation. The kids had already been tossed about from pillar to post, and he was less than optimistic that Melissa and he had done them any favors bringing them here.

There were three bedrooms on the second floor aside from Paula's. Cowboy-patterned bedspreads on twin beds identified the boys' room, and their missing hostess had obviously furnished the other two bedrooms for guests or lodgers like Jim.

Melissa was grateful for David's help as they got the boys settled in for the night. She was surprised when he even stayed around for a short story and the boys' bedtime prayers.

Without any prompting, Eric added to his usual prayer, ''Please bless Aunt Paula.''

Richie's prayer was a little more direct. ''Please find Aunt Paula and make her like us.''

Leaving a small light on in the room, Melissa and David went back downstairs with Scruffy trotting at their heels. The emotional drain of the past few hours had taken its toll on both of them. They sat down on the couch together, Scruffy at their feet.

"I wish there was something we could do," she said wearily as she looked around the living room. The missing woman's presence was everywhere. Her creative touch was on the decorated pillows, colorful knitted afghans, gaily mounted pictures and rows of delicate potted plants that provided evidence of Paula's loving care. A book lay open on one of the end tables as if she'd put it down in haste. Melissa blinked back a sudden wash of tears. *Where are you? Why aren't you here in your lovely home?*

"Steady now," David said softly as he drew her close and she rested against his chest. She felt small and fragile nestled against him, and as he stroked her soft hair with one hand, he felt her tremble.

"I can't believe this is happening. I keep thinking there's some simple explanation that we're missing."

"I know," he said, letting one finger lightly traced the soft curve of one ear. "Everything has happened too fast. There's nothing we can do but wait it out."

She closed her eyes, feeling the rise and fall of his breathing, and comforted by the soothing touch of his hands on her skin. His gentle stroking calmed her nerves and relaxed her tense muscles. She didn't realize how close she was to falling asleep until he placed a soft kiss on her forehead and whispered, "Time for bed."

She reluctantly lifted her head and moved away from him.

"You won't do anybody any good if you don't get

some rest,'' he said gently as he eased her to her feet. ''Go on to bed.''

''What are you going to do?''

''Take Scruffy out for a walk.''

''Don't you go wandering off,'' she ordered. ''You're not thinking about joining the searchers, are you?''

''Not *tonight*.''

The way he said it, she knew then that he had no intention of being left out of the search if Paula was still missing in the morning.

''Good night, then.'' She leaned up and impulsively kissed him on the lips. His arms suddenly tightened around her and his mouth captured hers in a breathless kiss that sent a wild spiral of warmth through her. When he released her, she couldn't meet his eyes, bewildered at how a simple good-night kiss in the midst of such upset could turn into something so wonderful.

Chapter Eleven

Melissa awoke with a start, just as the first ray of gray light lined the edges of the bedroom drapes.

Men's voices.

She sat up, straining her ears. Were some of them just coming back from their all-night search? Or were they leaving again?

She dressed quickly and hurried out into the hall, as David came out of his room. His hair was tousled from sleep, and he was still fastening the buttons on his shirt as he came toward her.

"Do you think they found her?" she asked anxiously.

"They gave up the search about midnight," he said as they hurried downstairs together. "Jim said they'd be back here about dawn with a full-scale search party. I guess they've arrived."

She was surprised when David stopped her at the top of the stairs. Putting his hands on her shoulders, he searched her face. "Are you going to be all right?"

She was warmed by the concern in his eyes. "Yes, I'll be fine."

"This waiting isn't going to be easy."

"I know. Waiting never is." She sighed. "I'd much rather be hiking all over the mountain and using up my nervous energy. I guess I'll just have to find some way to keep the boys and me busy."

"Don't go off somewhere on your own. I want to know that you're all safe and sound inside this house."

"Don't worry. We're not going anywhere."

"Keep a tight leash on Scruffy. There will be search dogs running around, and I don't want him taking off to parts unknown."

She felt the corners of her lips curve in amusement. The way he was firing orders at her revealed more than casual feelings for her, the boys and the dog. He almost sounded like a husband and father.

The smell of coffee teased their nostrils as they entered the crowded kitchen. Several men were huddled over a relief map spread out on the table, marking out sectors for several groups of searchers. When Jim saw David and Melissa come in, he reached for the coffee percolator and filled two cups for them. It was obvious that he felt at home in the kitchen, and came and went as he pleased. Deep worry lines in his face showed how much he cared about the missing woman.

"Jim, what can we do to help?" Melissa asked quietly.

"I don't know. Mr. Shornberger from the Mountain Rescue Service is taking charge." He nodded toward a robust man with a ruddy complexion, dressed for mountain climbing.

David moved closer to the table, and after listening to the exchange of ideas between Mr. Shornberger, the sheriff, Zach and the others, he decided that the search was in good hands.

"We'll have to sweep both sides of Prospect Point," the sheriff said. "Paula's been known to hike all the way down to Beaver Lake."

"She's a fool about taking pictures of wildlife down there," someone agreed.

Zach grumbled. "Last week she was climbing all over the place trying to get some snapshots of a couple of eagles. I warned her that she could take a fall—but did she listen to me?" He gave a sheepish grin. "The only authority I have around here is in the court-room."

As they continued to mark out the map, fear was almost palatable in the kitchen. They went over every possibility of what might have happened to keep Paula away from her home all this time.

When Carol came in with her minister husband, Melissa was surprised and pleased to meet him. She never would have taken Skip Carlson for a man of the cloth. He was tall, had the graceful movements of an athlete, and was dressed more like a lumberjack than a preacher with his heavy pants, checkered shirt and hiking boots. He gave David and Melissa a slow, friendly smile that immediately dispelled any worries they might have had about treating him differently than anyone else.

"This is terrible, isn't it," he said, shaking his head.

"Paula's known for doing her own thing. But who would have thought she'd have the whole town worried about her?"

He chatted with them for a couple of minutes until the sheriff told Shornberger, "There're about a dozen men milling around in the front yard, waiting to be told what to do. I think we've got a good team."

"All right, let's see how many patrols we need," Shornberger said, rolling up the map. "We'll cover the area as best we can."

Before he left the room, David approached him. "I don't know the terrain, Mr. Shornberger, but I'd like to help."

"You that city guy Paula's been expecting?" His sharp eyes traveled over David's expensive chambray shirt and tailored slacks, and down to his brown leather oxfords. "Some kind of a lawyer, aren't ya?"

David nodded. "I work at the Colorado State Capital for the governor."

"Well, fancy lawyering isn't going to do us much good about now," he answered shortly. "And we don't have time to spend watching out for someone who could get lost himself."

"Of course not," David answered evenly, refusing to let the man's dismissive attitude get to him. "But there must be some details of the search that have to be handled from this end. An extra pair of hands and legs ought to be of some use, wouldn't you think?"

Shornberger's ruddy face crinkled in a slight smile. "You're a lawyer, all right. Okay, there are about a half-dozen houses like this one that are perched on the side of this mountain close to Paula's. We contacted as many as we could last night. You can help by hiking up those private roads and chatting with the people who live in these mountain homes. Maybe Paula mentioned something to one of them that will give us a clue as to where she might have gone or remember something that will help. With luck, someone might have seen her before she took off. We haven't had time yet to really get the news out to everyone in the valley, and we need to talk with as many people as we can." Then he added briskly, "It'll free another man if you take over this job."

"I think I can handle it," David said, refusing to take offense at the man's attitude. He knew that everyone was tense and under pressure.

The search party formed into groups, and when they were ready to leave, Skip Carlson held up his hand and immediately the gathering fell silent. They bowed their heads as the minister uttered a simple prayer of thanksgiving for God's presence and guidance. Skip asked for heavenly protection for all those who were giving of themselves in this moment of need, and prayed for a successful ending to their search. "Thank you, Lord. Amen."

Then Shornberger waved his hand, and the men moved forward in their assigned patterns and began their search for any sign of the missing woman in the rugged terrain of trees, rocks and thickets.

"Can you stay with Melissa?" David asked Carol, as she stood on the front deck with Melissa. "I don't think she should be here alone all day."

Melissa started to protest, but Carol cut her off. "I agree. As soon as the girls wake up, my neighbor will bring them here. The phone will probably start ringing off the wall once the news gets out. I promise you, we'll have more company and food than we need." Her eyes twinkled. "Our church ladies just wait for a chance to compete with each other when it comes to showing off their cooking skills."

"What are you going to do?" Melissa asked David, when it became obvious that he didn't intend to stay at the house with her and the boys.

"You'd better hurry if you're going to join one of the groups," Carol warned him.

"I'm not." David gave a rueful laugh. "My offer got turned down. Shornberger gave me another job. He wants me to check the houses on this side of the mountain and see if Paula might have said something to any of the residents that would help find her."

"Sounds like a good idea. I warn you, though," Carol said with a teasing grin, "some of the women will talk your leg off just to keep a handsome guy like yourself around for a little while."

"He's used to having women make a fuss over him," Melissa said. "We went to a fancy state dinner, and David was the most eligible bachelor in the whole crowd. You should have seen the way the women looked at him."

"Not true," he said, a slight flush rising in his cheeks. He'd never been able to take teasing very well; his upbringing had always demanded a sensible, no-nonsense attitude. But something had changed. *He'd* changed. And he'd laughed more since Melissa and the boys had come into his life than he ever had before. The way she was smiling at him made him want to land a kiss on those full tempting lips, and give Carol something to tease about.

"I'll reserve judgment," Carol said, as if she'd caught the way he was looking at Melissa. "In any case, watch out for Madelyn Delange. She's the second house up the hill, and would love to tell you all about her reign ten years ago as Big Sky Beauty Queen. She's a divorcée and sets a mean trap, so watch out."

"Warning noted," David said, smiling. "Would she be likely to know anything about Paula's activities?"

"She might. Paula gets along well with her neighbors," Carol told him. "There are several scattered houses on this side of the mountain besides Paula's. When you see a mailbox and a driveway, you know there's a house in the trees somewhere high on the side of the mountain. There are some other side roads that were left years ago by loggers, but they're pretty much grown over."

"Don't get lost," Melissa said, trying to deny an insidious feeling of uneasiness about his going off alone. In the past few days he had become an integral part of her, his comforting presence giving her a sense of well-being. She was tempted to ask Carol to watch the boys so she could go with him, but after what Carol had said about the women making a fuss over him, she'd just sound jealous if she indicated wanting to tag along.

David saw flickering apprehension in Melissa's forced smile. He surprised her by giving her a light kiss on the forehead. "I should be back in a couple of hours," he reassured her. "Don't worry."

Carol eyed the Lexus and said, "You'd better take Paula's Jeep. There are some pretty steep driveways leading up to some of the houses. Almost everyone around here uses four-wheel-drive vehicles."

"What about keys?"

"Oh, Paula always leaves them in the ignition. She claims it's easier than hunting all over the house for them."

David just shook his head. This must be the only place remaining in the world where people left their house unlocked and keys in the car. He waved to them after he backed the Jeep out of the garage, then headed up a climbing narrow gravel road that led to other scattered homes on the mountainside.

Carol looked at Melissa with unabashed curiosity as they went back in the house. "Are you two...?"

Melissa laughed. "A couple? An item?" She shook her head. "No, we don't have that kind of personal relationship."

"Really?" Carol said in surprise. "You could have fooled me. I thought I saw a lot of personal feelings mixed in with what you were saying, and not saying, to each other."

"It's complicated."

"Love always is."

Melissa frowned.

"Oh, I forgot," said Carol. "We're not talking about love. Or anything personal like that."

"Would you like to hear the whole story?" Melissa asked. She might as well satisfy Carol's curiosity right up front. In a way she was grateful to be able to share her feelings with someone. How had her desire to help two little boys turned out to be so complicated for her emotionally?

"I'll whip up eggs and toast, and we can have some breakfast before your boys get up," Carol said as they went into the kitchen. "I bet Paula laid in a good supply of everything for your visit."

There was a poignant silence, and then Melissa said prayerfully, "God willing, I look forward to meeting her."

As they ate, Carol listened attentively to Melissa's account of the unusual circumstances that had brought Eric and David into her life and into David's home.

"I could love David, maybe I already do love him," she confessed. "But I can't see a future for us together. The fact that we're not spiritually compatible is a big obstacle."

"How does he feel about it?"

"About what?"

"A future together. Don't you talk to each other?"

"Not about feelings or spiritual things."

"Maybe you should. I was an unbeliever until Skip got hold of me. Then the Lord took the blinders off my eyes—and here I am, a preacher's wife!" Carol laughed. "Talk about God working in mysterious ways!"

Their quiet breakfast was cut short when they heard Scruffy barking upstairs. "I guess the boys are up," Melissa said, pushing away from the table. "I'd better get upstairs before they need a referee."

"And I'd better check on my girls," Carol said, heading for the telephone. "I'll have my neighbor bring them over so they can play with Eric and Richie.

They're all about the same age. Holly just turned six, and Sarah is four.''

Melissa tried to prepare the boys for the arrival of their new playmates, but her enthusiasm fell on deaf ears. Both boys gave her a disgusted look. "Girls!"

She couldn't help but laugh. In a few years, they'd be knocking themselves out to get noticed by "girls."

Holly and Sarah were diminutive copies of their mother: blond curly hair, lively blue eyes and boundless energy. They completely snowed the boys in the first five minutes. Carol sent Melissa a triumphant smile as the four children settled on the front room rug to play games.

"Let's slip out and have a second cup of coffee on the deck."

They settled in a couple of patio chairs, and Melissa explained that she earned her living as a writer and about her current project.

Carol looked impressed. "Now, that's amazing."

"What is?"

"You've come to the exact place to find the kind of story you're looking for. Paula's great-grandmother! She came west at the turn of the century with her doctor husband. Emma Bateman was a trained nurse and rode horseback with her husband to every isolated cabin in the valley. They were strong in their Christian belief, and when Dr. Bateman died of pneumonia, Emma continued to go anywhere she was needed to nurse the sick. She even managed to raise a son, Paula's father, all by herself. There are families all over this area whose lives were touched by her dedication. 'An angel on horseback,' they called her.''

Carol cocked her pretty head to one side. "How's that for a story?"

Melissa looked at her in awe. She felt like a treasure hunter who had just come upon a lode of gold. "It's perfect. Exactly the kind of story I needed as a beginning chapter for my book. Thank you, thank you."

"Don't thank me. What is it the Bible says? 'Trust in me and I will direct your paths'?"

"Come on, I'll show some pictures and things that Paula has from her grandmother. She won't mind. I think she even has a diary or daily log somewhere. We'll ask her when she gets here," Carol added, as if there was no question in her mind that Paula would soon be home.

David was glad that Carol had suggested his taking the Jeep. A narrow twisting driveway branched off the main road and abruptly mounted upward. Set high on the mountainside was a two-story log home that overlooked the valley. David sat in the car for a minute before getting out. The magnificent panorama was unbelievable as an early morning sun touched high peaks with a crimson glow and lent a velvet patina to green carpets of trees lining the surrounding hills.

David couldn't put the sensation into words, but he felt a stirring deep inside, as if a hidden part of him had suddenly come to life. He wished that Melissa had been there with him. She would have understood. The silence held an enveloping peace that startled him.

As he slowly got out of the car, the front door of the house opened and an elderly man walked down

toward him. The mailbox at the bottom of the driveway had read, The Finleys.

David quickly explained to Mr. Finley why he was
there, and from the man's reaction David knew that
the news about Paula had not reached her neighbors.
The older man was obviously shaken up, hearing
about her disappearance, but he couldn't offer any help
in finding her. David took his leave as quickly as he
could and headed along the side of the mountain to
the next home. Driving slowly, he watched on both
sides of the road for mailboxes and private driveways
cutting through the trees. He was glad that Carol had
warned him about Madelyn Delange.

When she answered the door of her spacious Swiss
chalet-style home, she was wearing tight white pants
and an off-the-shoulder blouse, and her blond hair
looked as if she'd just come from the salon. She gave
him a welcoming smile even before David introduced
himself as a friend of Paula's. She immediately invited
him to come inside, but he refused and quickly explained the reason for his call.

When David told her about Paula's disappearance,
she raised plucked eyebrows, her eyes widened, and
she lifted a manicured hand to her mouth. "Oh, my
goodness. Whatever could have happened? You don't
think she was kidnapped or anything?" She gasped as
if that worry were not foreign to her. "She doesn't
have any money."

"Have you seen or talked with her recently?"

She shook her head. "I like Paula a lot, but we're
not real close neighbors—you know what I mean? She
goes with an older crowd," she added pointedly.

Before David could stop her, she launched into a recital of how busy she was, implying that being the town's social queen was very demanding. She was obviously not concerned about Paula's disappearance but was more worried about a situation that might put her personally in some kind of jeopardy.

David thanked her for her time, refused her invitation to come inside for a cup of coffee and quickly made his escape back to the Jeep. No one was home at several of the houses. Other neighbors were friendly and concerned when he told them the reason for his visit. They had been contacted the night before and wanted to help. But his talks with them ended with the same disappointing results. No one had any information that would help locate the missing Paula.

Discouraged, he turned around in a cul-de-sac where the mountain road ended and headed back toward Paula's house. He hated to see Melissa's disappointment when he told her that he'd learned nothing that would help. His promise to the governor to be back in the office in a couple of days weighed heavily on him. How could he leave her and the boys at a time like this?

He was nearly back to Paula's house when he glimpsed a weather-beaten roof lower than the road and nearly hidden by a bank of rocks and trees. Had he missed seeing a driveway and mailbox?

He braked the car, got out and started walking down the hill toward the weathered roof. As he broke through the trees, he saw a dilapidated old log cabin facing downhill toward the river. Obviously the place had been abandoned. If there had ever been a road leading down to the cabin, there was no sign of one now. Windows gaped crookedly in its sagging sides and the whole place looked ready to fall in on itself. Relieved that he hadn't missed a house in his enquiries, he turned around and started to hike back up to the road.

At that moment, the unmistakable sound of a whimper reached his ears. He looked around. An animal?

The sound came again. He retraced his steps. He was almost to the front door of the cabin, when the truth hit him.

The sound was human, and it was coming from under a pile of fallen beams just inside the cabin.

"Who's there?" David called as he moved cautiously through the gaping door frame and peered into the darkening shadows of the abandoned cabin. Splinters of lights came through holes in the roof, and as his eyes adjusted to the gloomy interior, he saw that the whole structure was ready to collapse. It wouldn't take much for the leaning wall joists to give way and bring the roof tumbling down.

He heard the whimper again, as he moved farther into the cabin. Then his breath caught. A woman's hand protruded from under a heap of tumbled boards.

"Paula?"

Chapter Twelve

As quickly and as carefully as David could, he began to move the smallest timbers off the pile. When he could see the dazed woman's face and the part of her body that wasn't pinned under the heaviest timbers, he knew she was barely conscious.

"Paula. Paula." He stroked her face and tried to rouse her, but a pitiful moan from her open mouth was her only response. "It's going to be all right. You hold on. I'm going after help." He cursed himself for leaving his cell phone in the Lexus.

As he turned away, his foot got tangled in some kind of strap. He picked it up and saw that it was attached to a camera. What on earth was Paula doing taking pictures in a place like this?

As fast as he could, he climbed back to the road where he'd left the Jeep. He couldn't believe how close he'd come to driving right by the spot. If he hadn't glanced in that direction when he had, he never would have seen the old cabin through the trees.

He drove at a mad speed back to the house, slamming on the brakes and bounding out of the car. He raced up the front steps and burst through the door, yelling, "I found her! I found her!"

Melissa and Carol were sitting in the living room reading a story to the children. They stared at him in shock and then jumped to their feet.

"You found Paula?"

"Where?"

"She's in that old cabin. About a half-mile down the road. I don't know how badly she'd hurt, but she's alive."

"Thank you, Lord." Melissa closed her eyes a moment in prayerful thanks.

"That's the old McGuire place," Carol said in disbelief. "I can't imagine why Paula would go there."

"She had a camera with her," David said as he grabbed up the telephone.

"Tell them they can reach the cabin from the dirt road along the river," Carol quickly told him as he dialed 911. "It will be faster."

As David made the call, Melissa and Carol hugged each other in prayerful joy. A moment ago they had been reading a scripture that promised "Call unto me, and I will answer." Melissa smiled to herself. Even though David would never admit it, in answer to their prayers he had been an instrument in God's hands.

"They're sending paramedics and alerting the search parties," David said as he hung up the phone.

"You go with him, Melissa," Carol said. "I'll watch the kids, and alert the men when they get back."

Melissa didn't argue. David reached out and grabbed her hand, and they raced out of the house together.

"Keep your eyes open for a glimpse of the cabin through those trees," he said as he headed the Jeep back the way he'd come. "I'm not exactly sure where it is. It was a miracle that I saw it at all."

Yes, a miracle, Melissa silently agreed.

Because they were going in the opposite direction, they weren't able to see down the hill clearly. They almost passed the place where David had left the road and hiked down to the cabin.

"I think this is it," he said, and made a sharp U-turn in the road to park the car. "Yes, there it is."

Melissa strained to see where he was pointing. The logs of the weathered cabin blended in so completely with the wooded hillside that it was incredible he had even noticed it. Just thinking that Paula had been lying there for almost three days made Melissa shiver.

They bounded out of the car and scrambled down the hillside, slipping and sliding on rocks and loose dirt and pushing through thick wild undergrowth. Melissa couldn't believe her eyes when they got close to the cabin; she was completely unprepared for its dilapidated condition. Half of the roof had already fallen in, and the rest of the building looked as if a strong wind would easily flatten it.

"What on earth was she doing here?" Melissa asked.

"She must have been taking pictures when she got trapped by some falling timbers."

Cautiously, they eased step by step into the darkened cabin. David had warned her not to touch any of the sagging walls. The boards under their feet creaked a warning as they put their combined weight on them, and Melissa held her breath that they wouldn't give way.

"She's over there." David pointed to the heap of fallen timbers that had been too heavy for him to move. He listened for a whimpering sound, but deadly silence met his ears. "Paula. Paula, we're here," he said, as they knelt down beside her.

Melissa swallowed hard, horrified by what Paula must be going through. How could anyone survive this long, trapped under the weight of those collapsed boards? As Melissa put her fingertips on the wrist of the hand lying free of the boards, she felt a faint pulse. Paula was still alive.

Almost immediately the shrill sound of a siren alerted them that the ambulance was coming up on a river road below the cabin. Melissa stayed with Paula, and David hurried out to explain everything to the two young male paramedics and their older driver.

"She's trapped inside under some fallen rafters," David told them. "And there's danger that the rest of the roof could go anytime."

The paramedics ordered Melissa out of the cabin, and quickly and efficiently assessed the situation. One of them admitted, "We can't do much for her until we can examine her and see what condition she's in. We'll have to radio for more help."

"The four of us should be able to move all the heavy timbers," David argued. "Why wait?"

"It could be risky," warned the driver. "What do you think, Smithy?" he asked the other man.

He thought a minute and then said, "If this here fellow's willing to give it a try, I say let's do it." He turned to the driver. "Call it in. We may need some backup help."

Melissa stood by, helpless, as the men disappeared inside the cabin. She could hear voices, and the scraping and shifting of boards. Her ears strained to hear any signs that the listing roof and walls were about to cave in on the men. She drew on her faith that God would not have brought them this far without his protection.

When the paramedics appeared for the stretcher that they had left outside, she knew they had successfully freed Paula. They were ready to bring her out! Tears of relief flowed down her cheeks as she waited, for what seemed like an eternity.

They finally appeared with Paula on the stretcher, covered with blankets and motionless. Melissa wished there was something she could do or say, but she had to be content just watching the men load her listless body into the ambulance. A minute later the doors slammed shut, and the ambulance was gone with the sound of the wailing siren.

When David turned to her, his face smudged with dirt and his hands scratched and bruised, she was so overcome with emotion that she couldn't speak. He had willingly jeopardized his life to save a woman he didn't even know. God's goodness ran through him, deep and true.

Why couldn't he see that there might be a greater purpose to life than following a path that the world put before him?

When Melissa and David arrived at the modern, sixty-bed hospital, Paula was still in the emergency room. They were told that her condition was stable and she was undergoing a battery of tests to determine the extent of her injuries.

While they waited, they went to a small chapel, and Melissa knelt and prayed while David sat in the pew beside her. He closed his eyes and let a quiet peace flow through him.

The adrenaline rush of the rescue had taken its toll. He felt as if he'd been running full speed. He'd used every ounce of energy to get Paula safely out of the cabin before it totally collapsed. Every time they had removed a piece of timber, the whole structure vibrated. At the time he hadn't thought so much about his own life being in danger. He'd been worried that Paula might be closer to dying with every strangled breath.

He lowered his head and covered his eyes with his hands. Was Melissa right? The idea of his being a tool of a God in whom he really didn't believe was ludicrous and a little scary. He couldn't deny that this whole trip had been one of contradictions. His plans for a quick, easy trip to Wolfton and back had been thwarted at every turn. Would all this happen without design? The question made him uncomfortable. He had been drawn into a family unit with Melissa and the boys that he had never expected, and, in truth, didn't know how to handle. He'd never been this close to anyone, not even his own parents. If he didn't get back to Denver soon, he would lose his perspective and do something extremely foolish…like admitting that he had fallen in love with her. She'd made it clear what kind of husband and life she wanted. Even if he asked her to marry him, she'd never accept—despite the fact that marrying him would provide the home she wanted for Eric and Richie.

When she eased back on the seat, light coming through a stained-glass skylight bathed her face in a luminous light. She smiled at him and squeezed his hand. He had never seen a woman so beautiful. All lines of worry were gone from her face, as if she'd received a message of reassurance and peace.

When they returned to the E.R., they were given the good news. Paula had suffered no internal injuries. Only one rib was cracked and one bone broken in her right leg. She was suffering from shock and dehydration, but was already responding to treatment.

"No visitors for the time being," the doctor told them. "She needs rest for a day or two. Paula's one fortunate lady. From what the paramedics said, any one of those heavy timbers could have crushed her."

They were just about to leave the hospital, when Jim arrived breathless and anxious with Nancy. "We got here as fast as we could when we heard the news. How is she? Is she seriously hurt? What was she doing in a place like that?"

Nancy laid a soothing hand on his arm. "Easy, honey. Get hold of yourself."

He nodded. "Sorry. I just can't believe all of this."

David and Melissa tried to answer the flood of questions in a calm manner. Obviously Jim cared deeply for Paula and so did Nancy. They seemed like a caring couple who would have done anything for Paula.

When Melissa and David got back to the house, they were engulfed by a jubilant crowd of returning searchers.

"Hooray. Hooray for the man of the hour!" The men clapped David on the back.

Zach gave him a bear hug that almost squeezed the breath out of him. "Thank you, thank you. We'll never forget what you did this day." Tears filled the honorable judge's eyes as he hurried from the house and headed for the hospital, determined to see Paula even though he knew no visitors were allowed.

The sheriff shook David's hand. "Good man. I heard you risked your neck getting her out. You're made of good stuff. We're mighty grateful."

Even Mr. Shornberger was complimentary about David's success in finding the missing woman. There was just a tinge of surprise in his tone. Obviously, he had given David the chore of checking out the neighbors, thinking he wouldn't turn up much information.

Melissa could tell that David was embarrassed by all the fuss they were making over him. He seemed almost stunned by this outpouring of goodwill. She left him to enjoy his popularity and went in the kitchen to help Carol.

A half-dozen women crowded in the kitchen, busily setting out food and drink on the deck. Paula's picnic table was loaded down, and Eric, Richie and the Carlson girls were already sitting on the deck steps enjoying their full plates.

Carol hugged her. "Praise God."

"Amen," Melissa breathed, and they just held each other for a moment. Then the women began crowding around Melissa, introducing themselves. Their names escaped her but their warm smiles and kind words were a genuine welcome.

Everyone seemed to know that she'd brought Paula's nephews to visit, but nothing was said about the possibility of her keeping them. Apparently Paula had meant it when she refused to consider the responsibility of raising them. Now there seemed little hope that their visit would persuade Paula otherwise, but Melissa pushed away such thoughts. This was a time for thanksgiving. The lost had been found.

As each group of searchers returned to the house, the celebration swung into a greater expression of joy and gratitude. There were songs, laughter and prayers of thanksgiving. Neither David nor Melissa had experienced anything like it. The crowd kept getting bigger and bigger, spilling out into the yard as cars arrived with more of Paula's friends.

Melissa kept her eyes on the boys and made sure that Scruffy stayed close through all the comings and goings. Jim and Nancy returned to the house, and Melissa was pleased to see that they were reassured by their trip to the hospital. They shared with everyone what the doctor had said about Paula's condition.

The sun had set and most of the food was gone by the time people began to drift away with promises to keep in touch. Finally, when the Carlsons were the only family left, David and Melissa began to realize how exhausted they were. They had been caught in a roller coaster of emotions since early morning.

"We'd love to have you come to church with us in the morning, and stay for Sunday dinner, too." Skip invited them with a nodding agreement from his wife.

"Sunday?" Melissa said blankly. "Tomorrow's Sunday?" She gave an embarrassed laugh. "I guess I've lost track of the days."

Both Carol and Skip looked a little surprised. In their world, Sunday was never forgotten.

"We were delayed getting here," David said without going into any further explanation. He wasn't proud of the way he'd stubbornly headed into the sandstorm with nearly tragic results. "I had planned on being back in Denver two days ago."

"What a blessing that you weren't," Skip said solemnly. "You certainly were in the right place at the right time, as far as we're concerned."

"I'm glad that things turned out the way they did," he admitted. "But I'm afraid I have no choice but to head back as early in the morning as I can get away. It's important that I get back to Denver as soon as possible."

"But you and the boys will be staying on, won't you, Melissa?" Carol asked. "I know Paula would be brokenhearted if she missed your visit. Besides, it would be a blessing to have someone in the house with Paula when she comes home. She's an independent soul, but this ordeal is bound to take a lot out of her."

"Our plans were for me to remain with the boys until Paula had a chance to get acquainted with them,"

Melissa answered easily. "I've made arrangements to send in my magazine articles from here."

"Good, I know Paula will be eager to tell you stories about her grandmother that you may be able to use." Carol laughed. "See how wonderfully bad things can be turned into good for everyone?"

Melissa tried to respond in an upbeat fashion, but the fact that David would be leaving in the morning sent her spirits in a downhill slide. She knew it was foolish to think that anything had changed. In spite of all the time they'd spent together, and the closeness that had been developing between them, he was still the same goal-oriented, success-driven man he'd always been.

After the Carlsons left, Melissa had little to say to him. She wanted to grumble that the state of Colorado ought to be able to do without him for a couple more days without falling off the face of the earth. Why couldn't he take charge of his life for once, and quit being a puppet on a political string? She knew she was being childish and selfish, but she didn't care. Her feelings for him had grown beyond a superficial friendship. It wasn't his fault, it was hers, but that didn't help her deal with the emptiness he'd leave behind.

When he offered to help put the boys down for the night, she refused. "Thanks, but you'd better get your own self to bed. Morning comes early. You won't want to waste any time getting on the road. You won't have us along to hold you back. You can drive as long and fast as you like."

Her crisp tone startled him. "I have to go, Melissa," he said apologetically. "Please understand."

"Oh, I understand. The governor's office would collapse if you were away another day or two."

He saw her lip quiver and he said gently, "It's not the governor's office I'm worried about. It's my career. If I'm not there to fulfill an important assignment, they'll give it to someone else. I can't afford to turn my back on opportunities that may not come again."

"No, of course not."

He sighed. "I thought you realized how important my work is to me."

"I guess I forgot. It's a good thing you reminded me."

"Melissa—" He reached out to her, but she turned away into Eric and Richie's bedroom. She heard him go into his room and shut the door. There was a finality about it that brought an ache to her heart.

She tried to hide her sinking spirits as she put the boys to bed, heard their prayers and tucked them in.

Eric wasn't fooled. "Aren't you glad David found Aunt Paula?"

"Of course I'm glad. Why do you ask that?"

"Because your eyes don't smile anymore."

"Maybe she's mad at us," Richie volunteered. "We beat those girls real good in every game." An overtone of pride canceled out his concern that they'd done the wrong thing.

"Maybe they were just being nice and let you win," Melissa suggested with a smile.

Richie frowned. "Why would they do that?"

"Sometimes it's better to make other people happy, even if you have to lose to do it."

"Nobody likes to lose," Eric said.

"No, I guess not, but there's joy in doing the right thing, even if it's hard sometimes. I'm glad you had a good time and made some new friends." She hesitated, then said, "David will be going back to Denver in the morning, but we're staying here for a little while."

"Why can't he stay, too?" Eric frowned. "I thought he liked us." The slight quiver in his voice revealed a frightened little boy who had lost too many people in his young life.

Melissa hugged him. "Of course he likes you, but he has to get back to Denver. He has an important job and lots of people depend upon him."

"He bought us boots and everything," Richie said, as if that were reason enough for David not to go.

"Maybe we ought to go back, too?" Eric's eyes suddenly took on a hopeful shine. "Scruffy likes Denver better—don't you, Scruffy?"

The dog was stretched out on the foot of the bed, and at the sound of his name, he lifted his head and gave a responding "Woof."

"See!" Eric said. "He wants to go home, too."

Home? Not for a minute had she intended for the boys to consider David Ardell's house as *home*. She felt as if someone had landed a fist in her stomach. *Dear Lord, what have I done?*

Melissa tried to recover as best she could by changing the subject and talking about what a wonderful visit they were going to have staying here with Aunt Paula and all her friends.

When she left the bedroom, she went into her room and sat on the bed, staring at the floor. She'd never been one to lie to herself and she couldn't do that now. No man had ever created such an agonizing need in her to be a part of his life as David.

Surely, true love couldn't come like this.

She couldn't fall in love with a man whose goals in life would always be at odds with her deepest convictions. Why had God brought him into her life? Was the Lord testing her? Where was the deep sense of divine guidance that had always been her assurance?

Reaching for her Bible, she read Jeremiah 29:11: "For I know the plans I have for you, says the Lord, plans for good and not for evil, to give you a future and a hope." When she closed the book, she felt a sense of peace returning. *Let go. Let God.*

Early the next morning, when she heard David loading the car for his departure, she drew in a deep breath and lifted her chin. Then she went downstairs and waited for him to come back into the house after putting his suitcases in the Lexus.

When he saw her waiting for him in the living room, a frown flickered across his face, and as he walked toward her he seemed to brace his shoulders for another sharp rebuke about his leaving.

"I'm sorry," she said quickly, looking him squarely in the eyes. "I shouldn't have spoken to you the way I did. I was wrong. Of course you have to honor your commitments. I guess I was feeling off balance from everything that has happened."

"I know. You don't have to apologize," he said, obviously relieved. "I'm just terribly sorry that I can't stay until things get settled."

"The boys and I will be fine here, really. Hopefully things will work out for Paula to keep the boys. If not, something else will. I have the feeling that this is a better place to find them a home than Denver, and I'll stay as long as I need to in order to get them settled."

"And what about you, and your writing?"

"I may have found a golden lode," she said, and quickly explained about Paula's grandmother. "So everything is working out well."

He reached out and let one finger play with a wayward curl falling on her cheek. "Is it?" His searching and questioning gaze was filled with a sudden longing. "I'm not so sure."

She fought against yielding to his touch, as he let his hands slip down to rest on her waist. She knew this was no time to give in to the deep feelings that he created in her. The moment he returned to Denver, he would be swept up in his frantic world and their paths would not cross again. Even as she told herself that she should purposefully walk away, she lifted her lips to meet his and leaned into his embrace.

He had kissed her lightly several times before, with a brush of his lips against her cheek or forehead, but this kiss was like the one that had sent her emotions reeling. There was a heat to his mouth pressed against hers. His hands molded the soft curves of her back, soothing and caressing.

"We can't let this go," he whispered. He didn't know how it had happened, but he'd found the woman he wanted. She was lovely, intelligent, gentle and loving. "This is so right...so right. You can't deny it."

She turned her head to avoid the warm, demanding pressure of his kisses and said breathlessly, "No, no it isn't right. It's wrong. All wrong."

"What is so wrong with us being in love? I want to marry you and build a life together."

She swallowed hard. "There's something very special between us, David, but it's not a foundation for marriage."

"Why not? We could keep the boys and start a family of our own. I'd learn to be a pretty good father, given a chance. And I'll make you proud of me. You might even end up as the First Lady of Colorado someday."

He said it with such pride that she wanted to cry. Didn't he realize that he had used the very argument that made any commitment to him impossible? Married to him, she would have to live in a political fishbowl. Her life would never be her own. She'd spend her time constantly trying to meet social demands and compromising her own integrity so she wouldn't embarrass him.

"I can't marry you, David."

"You don't have to give me an answer now," he said, as if she had just hesitated instead of giving him a flat rejection. "We'll keep in close touch by phone while you're here, and we can talk things out."

"There's nothing to talk out."

Her bluntness brought a flash of color to his cheeks. "You don't even want to think about it?"

"I have been thinking about it," she admitted. If he

only knew how many hours she had agonized over the growing feelings she had for him. "I'm afraid my decision is final."

"I see. Well, I guess that settles that." He tried for a light laugh but failed. "I'd forgotten how stubborn you can be."

"David, you're a wonderful person and I don't know why God brought you into my life, but I'll be forever grateful. You'll always be very special to me."

"But not special enough to marry, I gather."

"I'm not the one for you, David," she said kindly, even as she felt a growing ache in her heart. She believed she was being sensible to voice her deep feelings now. He'd already been deeply hurt by one woman, and she couldn't bear to do that to him again. "I could never handle the pressures that go along with the kind of lifestyle you've chosen. In a way, you're already married to your career. Neither of us would be happy with the kind of compromises both of us would have to make."

"I'm sorry you feel that way." He'd never felt so much like a loser in his whole life, but he knew that further argument was useless. He cupped her sweet chin with his hand and allowed himself another brief kiss on her warm lips, before he turned away, firming a resolution to accept her rejection and put her out of his life and thoughts.

Chapter Thirteen

When Carol came by to pick up Melissa and the boys for Sunday School and church, she poked her head in the door and called, "Anybody home?"

"We're almost ready," Melissa called back as she came out of the kitchen. "The boys are finishing up their breakfast."

Although she knew she was in need of some spiritual recharging, Melissa wished she could just hide out for the day. She didn't feel like facing a bunch of new people.

Carol took one look at her listless expression and said, "Let me guess. David left?"

Melissa nodded. "About four o'clock. He likes to get an early start when he's traveling." An unbidden memory of their early morning walk by the river threatened a wash of emotion that she struggled to hide. "I wouldn't be surprised if he drove straight through to Denver."

"And you wish you'd gone with him?" Carol asked.

Melissa shook her head. "No, my place is here for the moment."

"You don't look very happy about it," Carol commented with her usual frankness. "If I didn't know better I'd guess that you two had a fight. I know it's none of my business, but if you need an ear, I'm your gal."

Melissa was used to handling problems on her own, and she'd never had a really close friend, someone to share things that were bothering her. She couldn't believe it when she heard herself saying, "David asked me to marry him, and I turned him down."

"I see. And you're having second thoughts?" Carol asked with a concerned frown.

"No. I made the right decision," Melissa said firmly. She had gone over all the things they had said to each other. Even if she'd taken time to think about his proposal as he suggested, she would have refused. It wouldn't be fair to him or to her to settle for a marriage that wasn't supportive for either of them.

"You don't love him?" Carol asked with an edge of skepticism.

Melissa managed a weak smile. "I love him so much, I feel as if someone has planted a dagger in my chest."

"Then, why…"

As succinctly as she could, Melissa tried to explain the situation to Carol.

Carol took her hand and squeezed it. "Sometimes we don't see how the sun is ever going to come out and shine again, but it always does. There's a rhythm to God's blessings if we'll just keep the faith and let the good times roll around again.'' She grinned. ''How about that for a good affirmation to start every day? Let the good times roll. After all, the Lord promised blessings pressed down and overflowing.''

The way Carol mixed the Holy with the vernacular was delightful. How could anyone be despondent when she was around? Melissa chuckled. ''Let the good times roll.''

''I think we're kindred spirits,'' Carol said, winking at her.

Melissa felt at home almost immediately in the small, simple sanctuary with stained-glass windows depicting Bible stories, and wooden pews polished to a golden hue. It was exactly the kind of church her grandmother would have loved.

Skip Carlson looked strange to her in his clerical robe and polished black shoes. In her mind's eye, she kept seeing him as he was dressed yesterday, in faded blue jeans, western shirt and boots. Carol boldly winked at him when she caught his eye. He seemed perfectly at ease behind the lectern, and spoke in an easy, personal way that made his sermon seemed like a friendly chat with each member of the congregation. Melissa silently added her own petitions for understanding and a willingness to accept the future as it unfolded.

After church the sincere concern some of the parishioners extended to Melissa eased some of the discomfort she felt, living in a strange house, in unfamiliar surroundings and waiting for a woman whom she'd never met to come home. She refused all the invitations except the one from Skip.

"You'll come to our house for Sunday dinner, won't you?" the minister asked as he stood at the door, shaking hands after the service. "Carol put in a roast this morning with plenty of vegetables, and I spied a couple of apple pies that she made last night."

Melissa accepted without hesitation. "And thanks for the message this morning. I needed to be reminded about keeping an 'attitude of gratitude.'"

"We all tend to forget what we already have, and dwell on what we want," he agreed.

"Not me," Carol said, overhearing his words as she joined them with the children. "When I forget to count my blessings, Skip reminds me. Don't you, honey?" she teased.

He grinned at her, and Melissa saw a tender look of love pass between them. "Just doing my job."

Carol slipped her arm through his. "Come on, Preacher, let's go home."

The afternoon spent at their house was a healing one for Melissa. The Carlson home celebrated a joyful acceptance of the Lord's presence and constant blessing. Peace radiated in the midst of normal family chaos. It reinforced her determination to hold out for the kind of marriage and family life she wanted.

David had been on the road nearly eighteen hours when he finally checked into a motel. The long drive across Wyoming had been filled with constant reminders of Melissa and the boys. He tried to close his mind to memories that were only a mockery, in light of the way the whole business had ended. How in the world had he allowed himself to get into this fiasco in the first place?

He went over in his mind everything that had happened. He had just wanted to honor Jolene's wishes, and each step of the way seemed innocent enough. How could he have known that he was going to fall head over heels in love with a woman who despised everything that was important in his life? And how had two kids and an ugly dog gotten under his skin the way they had?

He glanced at his watch. Six o'clock. The kids' suppertime. No doubt, Melissa would have plenty of offers to eat out. He thought about the celebration gathering, and all the friendly people who had brought food and drink. He was sure they'd look after her and the boys. They'd be fine.

He stared at the bedside phone. It wouldn't hurt to check. Before he could change his mind, he found Paula's number and called the house. After four rings, the answering machine clicked on and he listened to Melissa's sweet voice on the recorded message.

She sounded confident and upbeat.

Slowly he replaced the receiver without leaving a message, chiding himself for thinking she might feel as empty on the inside as he did.

Melissa checked the answering machine when she came in from the boys' picnic. There were two calls, from a neighbor and from someone else who had not left a message. The phone rang several times during the evening and each time she held her breath, hoping to hear David's strong resonant voice—but it was always one of Paula's well-wishers.

Well, what did she expect, she asked herself as she dealt with the disappointment. The truth was, there was little more to be said between them. He was as strong-willed as she was, and there was little ground for compromise. She wouldn't give up her strong Christian family values. The only bond between them was the welfare of the boys. Once they were placed, she'd probably never see the illustrious David Ardell, except in the newspapers or on TV.

That night she read her Bible, said her prayers and went to sleep on a tear-stained pillow.

Carol and Skip brought Paula home two days later. Melissa and the boys were on the front porch waiting to greet her as the car drove up.

Paula's hazel eyes were bright and clear as she stepped out of the car with Skip's help. One arm was in a cast, and she moved gingerly, but her full mouth spread in a welcoming grin when she saw the welcoming party coming down the steps toward her. She was a small woman, about four feet eleven inches tall. Her face was round, framed by brown hair cut short for easy care.

"Well, here I am. You must think I have a screw loose," she said, smiling and looking slightly embarrassed. "I was wanting to make an impression—and I guess I did."

"Always going for the dramatic," Carol teased. "You really outdid yourself this time, sweetheart."

"Let's not have any encores." Skip grinned fondly at her. "It's time you met these two handsome nephews of yours." He motioned for the boys to come closer, and he playfully ruffled their hair as he introduced them. "This is Eric. He's six years old and has a lot of smart questions popping around in that head of his. And this bright fellow is Richie, and he has more energy than a pack of monkeys."

"I'm very happy to meet you both," Paula said warmly. "I'm very glad you came to see me." She didn't rush at them with any hugs and kisses, but Melissa thought she caught a glimpse of moisture in Paula's eyes as she looked at them.

"And this is Melissa," Carol said, pulling her forward.

"You're as pretty in person as you sounded on the phone. I'm sorry about the delayed welcome."

Impulsively Melissa kissed her cheek. "This is the best welcome we could have."

"What were you doing poking around in the old cabin, anyway? I would have thought you had better sense than that," Skip chided her with affection.

Paula answered with spirit. "While I was waiting for the boys to arrive, I thought I'd walk down to the river and take a few photos. On the way down the hill, I saw this prissy mother raccoon with four darling little ones just outside the cabin. I thought they would make some cute pictures to show the boys, so when they disappeared into the cabin, I decided to slip inside and snap a few. I guess just the weight of my body caused something to shift. All of a sudden, the whole place seemed to be falling down on me."

Her voice wavered, and Carol quickly put an arm around Paula's waist. ''You are home, and that's all that matters.''

Once inside the house, Paula looked around slowly as if she had never expected to see it again. Obviously, all those hours of being helplessly trapped had left their mark, and Melissa knew that Paula would need some emotional healing along with the physical.

Carol and Skip were wonderful with Paula, and Melissa and the boys stayed in the background as they settled her on the living room sofa.

When the boys brought Scruffy inside, Melissa held her breath. Obviously the verdict was still out on the boys' acceptance of Aunt Paula, pending her attitude toward the dog. It was obvious, in their childish reasoning, that if Scruffy wasn't welcome, neither were they. Wagging his scrawny tail, he greeted Carol and Skip and then danced over to the sofa to sniff at the newcomer, while Eric and his brother told her about Scruffy's escapades.

Melissa's spirits took wing as she looked at the boys' grinning faces and the tenderness in Paula's eyes. A bond of affection was already evident between them, and Melissa began to relax. It was going to be all right.

The next few days just about convinced Melissa that they'd found the perfect place for the boys. Even with her injuries, Paula was not content to sit idly by and twiddle her thumbs. She had shoeboxes full of pictures that she'd taken of deer, elk and about every other animal that had ever shown up on the mountains around Wolfton.

"How about making some nice posters?" she asked the boys. "You can paste the pictures you like on a large piece of cardboard and hang them on the wall in your room."

"Neat." She had shown Eric a bunch of horse pictures, and he was all for it.

Richie decided on bears for his poster. He was still a little disgruntled that they hadn't seen any in Yellowstone.

While Melissa took care of house chores and smiled secretly to herself, Paula entertained the boys with stories of her childhood growing up in this mountain valley. More and more, Melissa became convinced that once Paula recovered physically from her ordeal, she might be reluctant to turn down the chance to keep them. She was almost positive that Paula would not want Eric and Richie to be turned over to strangers to raise. But forcing her too soon into making a decision about keeping the boys was not a good idea. Although she was eager to talk about the boys' future, she forced herself to be patient.

She waited for a couple of days before mentioning her own interest in Paula's family and background. When she told her that she was collecting material for a book about courageous pioneer women of faith, Paula's eyes sparkled. "Let me tell you about my great-grandmother."

"Please do," Melissa said eagerly, and then confessed that Carol had already mentioned Paula's grandmother as a perfect subject for her book. "I can't help but believe that the Lord brought me here so that I can tell her story."

Melissa was completely overwhelmed by the wealth of material that Paula shared with her: journals, old photographs and personal accounts of this courageous lady who had ridden horseback through all kinds of weather, night and day, to nurse the sick.

"That's her Bible," Paula said, pointing to a weathered, leather-bound volume lying on a nearby shelf. "She always took it in the saddlebag with her. Sometimes when I open it, I can almost hear her sweet voice reading me some of her favorite passages."

Melissa listened attentively, as Paula shared wonderful stories that had been handed down by families in the valley who had experienced her great-grandmother's unselfish dedication.

Paula's eyes misted when she said, "I'm so proud that you are going to tell her story."

Paula had quite a few people dropping in to see her, but Judge Daniels was the most frequent visitor. Melissa tried to make sure the boys didn't raise any ruckus while he was there, but after a couple of visits she began to relax. He was more than cordial to her and insisted that she call him Zach, instead of Judge.

"That's a fine young man of yours," he told her. "He showed lots of courage and foresight. I bet he's a darn good lawyer."

"The governor of Colorado thinks so," Melissa said, agreeing with his last statement and ignoring his implication that David was her young man. "David is his legal counsel."

"Is that right?" The judge looked duly impressed before he sauntered outside. They could hear him laughing with Eric and Richie as they played catch.

"He's good with kids," Paula said with an approving nod.

When Melissa teased Paula about his attentions, she just smiled sheepishly. "It's kinda nice having him around."

"Why haven't you ever married him?"

"You know, while I was lying there, almost dead, I kept asking myself the same question. I just may say yes, the next time he asks me."

Melissa hoped Paula didn't see the leap of joy that surged through her. Paula and Zach! Perfect. The boys would have a wonderful male role model and the tender care of an aunt who loved them.

Although Paula fussed about having to go to the doctor for a checkup after a week had passed, Melissa left the boys with Carol and drove her there in the Jeep.

While she was having an X ray made, the doctor asked Melissa if she'd be staying with Paula for an extended time.

Melissa explained that she had brought Paula's nephews for a visit. "We're hoping that she will be willing to give them a home," she added.

"You mean, take them to raise?" he asked sharply. When she nodded, he shook his head. "No, that's impossible."

Melissa's mouth went dry. "Why?"

"Paula's medical condition is such that she needs to cut back on her activities, not take on the responsibility of raising two young boys. She didn't agree to keep them, did she?"

"No," Melissa said, her chest suddenly tight. "We just thought that—"

"Well, you thought wrong." The doctor leveled stern eyes on her. "It's a miracle this last fiasco of hers didn't kill her. Paula is one brave lady, but I don't think even she would be foolish enough to consider taking on the responsibility of an adopted family." He gave Melissa a warning look. "Paula has a medical condition that is under control but could be exacerbated by stress. You'll have to find someone else to raise those boys."

Chapter Fourteen

David returned to the office, worn out from the hard drive from Montana, and instantly was caught up in a never-ending maze of demands. He couldn't believe the backlog of work waiting for his attention. The list of calls to be returned looked like a telephone directory. He'd never felt so swamped by work in his life, or less like doing any of it.

His secretary eyed him frankly. "Your little vacation certainly didn't do you a lot of good."

"It wasn't a vacation," he responded shortly. "Personal business."

"Did you get rid of those kids who've been living at your house?" Elsie asked, ignoring the "no trespassing" tone of his voice.

"We think we've found a place for Eric and Richie," he answered without elaborating. He wasn't about to grease the gossip mill with any comments about his trip. At that moment, he was trying to sort out all the drama and trauma that had left his emotions in a muddle. His thoughts kept centering on what was happening with Melissa and the boys. How soon would she be coming back to Denver? Would she let him know? Probably not, he thought with painful resignation. She couldn't have been much clearer about not wanting him in her life.

"What about Ms. Chanley? Did she come back with you?" Elsie asked, as if reading his thoughts.

"No. She stayed," he said shortly, and then asked abruptly, "What meetings have been rescheduled?"

She gave him an updated calendar and suggested that he call Stella Day for confirmation. He did so.

"So you're back," Stella said in a relieved voice. When she had told him that the governor had held the important committee appointment open for him, he breathed a sigh of relief.

"You're one lucky guy," she told him. "There are a half-dozen guys who would kill to be on that committee. A word of warning, though. I don't think the governor will go for any more disappearing acts. I'd stay pretty close to home if I were you."

"Don't worry, I'm not going anywhere," he reassured her.

"There's a reception at the governor's mansion this weekend. Better send your tux out to the cleaners and get your hair trimmed."

"Yes, Mother," he mocked. "Anything else?"

"Don't get derailed, David, or you'll get left at the political starting gate."

He had little time to think about anything but fulfilling his obligations, as he prepared reports, met with the governor's staff and attended a marathon of meetings. Even after spending ten to twelve hours at the office, he brought work home with him. Sometimes he didn't turn off the light in his den until after midnight, but even then the house closed in on him with its emptiness.

Sometimes he wandered into the kitchen, tired but not wanting to go to bed. When he saw Scruffy's water dish still sitting on the floor, he suppressed a peculiar wrench in the pit of his stomach. He'd never been one to be sentimental or nostalgic about things or people, but the kitchen echoed with the memory of the children's loud voices and Melissa's laughter, and he felt a poignant sense of loss.

He wasn't the only one who found the house much too empty and quiet. Both Inga and Hans had bombarded him with questions about the boys, and Paula's rescue. He left out the drama of his part in the rescue, and simply said they found her in an old cabin with some minor injuries. "I'm sure she's back home now, enjoying Melissa and the boys."

"You don't know for sure?" Inga asked with her usual directness. "They don't have telephones in Montana?"

"I called once. Melissa said everything was fine," he hedged. He'd been tempted a hundred times since he'd been back to pick up the phone and call her, but usually the impulse came at an inopportune moment at work or late at night. And what was there to say? *I miss you. I love you. Why won't you marry me?* He knew that nothing he said was going to change her

mind. Melissa had been right about their not being
suited to each other.

"You call." Inga shook her finger in a scolding
fashion. "I'm not blind. I saw what was happening
when Melissa and the boys were here. You were
happy and smiling and enjoying yourself. Now you
are the same old David, buried in work."

Daniel smiled at her motherly chastising. All the
time he was growing up, it was Inga that he ran to
with his problems, not his mother. "All right. You
win. I'll call her tomorrow."

"Good. And you tell her that we *all* miss her."

Melissa and Paula were out on the deck with the
boys having lunch, when the telephone rang.

"Let the machine pick it up," Paula said. "I don't
feel like shooting the breeze with anyone right now."

"It might be Carol. I thought I might run over and
see her and Skip this evening," Melissa said.

"Well, you better answer it, then. I'm so glad the
two of you have struck up a friendship."

"Me, too. I've never had a real close girlfriend before," Melissa said as she pushed back her chair and
hurried into the house. She grabbed the phone on the
last ring. When she heard David's voice responding to
her hurried, "Hello," she caught her breath.

"You sound out of breath," he said lightly.
"What's happening?"

It took Melissa a second to handle the surprise, and
the sudden joy that shot through her. "I was out on
the deck and ran inside to catch the phone before the
answering machine clicked on."

"That's what I got when I called before."

"But…you didn't leave a message."

"No, I just wanted to know if everything was all right, and your recording said, 'All is well,' so I didn't want to bother you."

His silence had bothered her more than a dozen calls would have. For the first few days, every time the phone rang, she leaped at it. Then she took hold of herself. *Quit being a lovesick fool,* an inner voice had mocked. *Be realistic.* She'd read his silence, loud and clear. He was getting on with his life, and she would have to do the same.

"How are things going in Denver?" she asked evenly, her heart thumping around in her chest like an off-balance gyroscope.

"Hectic, as usual. It hasn't been easy getting back in the groove," he admitted. "How are things with you?"

Melissa hesitated. "I'm afraid things aren't going the way we had hoped."

"What's wrong?" His voice was suddenly filled with concern. "Are you and the boys all right?"

"We're fine. It's Paula, I'm afraid."

"Is she still in the hospital?" he asked anxiously.

"No, she's home and recovering nicely, but I had a startling talk with her doctor when I took her in for a checkup." She told him about what the doctor had said about Paula. "It's a miracle that she's still alive after what happened to her."

There was a heavy silence on his end. "Well, then, I guess we'd better bring them back to Denver and see what can be done from here."

"I think there's another possibility," she said quickly. "When we were at Carol's and Skip's for Sunday dinner, it came to me that they would be a perfect couple to raise Eric and Richie. The boys get along great with their daughters. Skip is tender, caring and supportive, and it's obvious that he would enjoy being a father to two sons. It would be a wonderful Christian home for Eric and Richie."

"Have you said anything to Skip and Carol about all of this?"

"Not yet. I've been waiting for the right time. I can't help but believe that there's some divine reason for us to have made the trip here, and if Paula can't give the boys a home, another one will be provided with God's blessing. You liked them, didn't you?"

"Yes, I did," he answered without hesitation. "And I think it would be great if they took the boys. Wolfton is a nice little town, and the people really seem to care about each other." He'd never forget the way people had gathered at Paula's house after she'd been found, hugging and laughing. He liked Skip's friendliness and sense of humor. "I wish I could be there to talk to them with you."

"I wish you could, too. I don't suppose you could get away again anytime soon."

"I'm afraid not," he said. "We'll have to figure something out when you're ready to come back to Denver. How long do you think you'll stay?"

"It depends. Even if Skip and Carol take the boys, I won't want to leave immediately. I've found some wonderful material for my book." Excitedly, she told him about Paula's great-grandmother. "Can you believe it? Her story is exactly what I've been looking for."

He could picture her blue eyes shining and a smile lighting up her whole face as she talked. Just listening to her touched him in ways he hadn't thought possible. He'd been a fool to wait this long to call her.

She laughed. "Sorry, I didn't mean to bend your ear like that. It's just that I miss not having you here to share all these things with me."

"I miss being there. And I miss having you and the boys here in the house," he confessed. "It's just not the same."

"You mean it's too peaceful without all of Eric's and Richie's shenanigans?" she teased.

"You should hear the way Inga and Hans talk about you and the boys. They think it's my fault that you're not coming back. I was tempted to tell them that I'd proposed to you but you turned me down flat."

"Oh, David, please forgive me if I hurt you. It's just that…that…" She tried to find the right words.

"I know. You don't want to live your life in a three-ring circus. I guess I can't blame you. Sometimes I wonder why I do," he admitted frankly. "Anyway, you're right about one thing. Politically ambitious lawyers make poor husbands. You deserve better."

"And so do you, David." She was glad he couldn't see the tears filling her eyes. "I just couldn't be the kind of wife you want."

Yes, you could! he protested silently. *You're everything I want in a woman. Everything.* Aloud, he said, "I think we've been down this road before. Anyway, I just called to see how things were going, not to try to pressure you into changing your mind—although that's always an option open to you,'' he said as evenly as he could.

''I'll remember that,'' she said, disguising a sudden tightening in her chest.

''Well, then, we'll stay in touch. If you arrange something definite for the boys, let me know. And if you need anything at all, I'll get back to you right away. I promise.'' He almost asked her if he could speak to the boys, but decided against it. There really wasn't anything he could say to them that would help them understand the situation. They probably thought he'd deserted them, and David wasn't up to Eric's point-blank questioning.

After they said goodbye and Melissa hung up the receiver, she stared at it for a long time. Then she went into the bathroom to wash the tears off her face.

The affair at the governor's mansion was like many others that David had attended. A small, select group of guests mingled in first-floor rooms before dinner, while waiting for the governor and the first lady of Colorado to make their appearance from private quarters above.

When he felt a tug on the sleeve of his black jacket, he turned to find Pamela Wainwright smiling up at him. Stella had already alerted him that the senator's daughter was to be one of the guests.

''What was your name again?'' she teased. ''It's been so long since I've seen you, I've forgotten. Someone said you were in Montana.''

''That's right,'' David responded easily, ignoring

the questioning in her tone. It was none of her business where he'd been and why. Only Elsie and Stella had known the reason for his absence.

"Stella said that you might like to tell me all about it over dinner."

"Really?" David kept a practiced smile on his face while he silently fumed. He was sick and tired of Stella trying to manipulate a romantic relationship between him and this social-climbing debutante. Pamela bored him, irritated him and set his teeth on edge with her superficial chatter.

"I rather suspect we'll find our dinner place cards next to each other," she added coyly, as if this were evidence of some kind of intimacy between them.

David silently groaned. If he had a chance, he'd slip into the dining room and switch the place cards. A little of Pamela's company went a long way. Unfortunately, she stayed at his side and hung on him in a way that let everyone in the gathering know that she considered David and her "a couple."

Even the beautifully served dinner couldn't rescue David from total boredom and frustration. He tried to make a good impression on important dignitaries who had been invited to the dinner because they had influence in state affairs, but he wasn't at his best. He was relieved when the evening ended and he could make his escape from the pressure of being politically correct in everything he said and did.

Melissa and the boys were invited to go with Carol and Skip to a potluck dinner at the church. Paula had been included in the invitation, but she said she'd rather go to bed early with a good book.

The church's community room was in the basement, and long tables filled most of the floor space between the kitchen and a small stage at the other end of the room.

"The men are going to serve the meal and the children have been working up skits and songs," Carol told her as they placed their dishes on an already loaded serving table.

"My Sunday School class is going to sing 'Jesus Loves Me,'" Holly said proudly.

"We know that one," Richie said with a broad grin. "Melissa taught it to us—didn't she, Eric?"

"Then, you can sing it with us."

"Can we?" Eric asked in surprise. Both boys shot a look at Melissa.

"Maybe we better ask Nancy. She's in charge of the program," Melissa said, nodding at Jim's wife, Nancy, who was sitting at the table with them. She was a young, sweet, caring woman who obviously loved children.

"Of course. That's a wonderful idea," Nancy agreed. "We could use two more boys in the children's choir."

As Melissa looked around the room, she saw that some of the men wearing aprons were the same ones who had been at Paula's house to help in the search. Skip waved to them from the kitchen, wearing a chef's hat that made him look seven feet tall. Zach and Jim hovered around their table, pouring coffee and lemonade.

"Have you heard from that hero of ours?" Jim asked. "We ought to give him a medal or something."

"He proved himself to be one courageous fellow," Zach agreed. "If it hadn't been for him, we could have lost my sweet Paula."

Melissa would have given anything if David could be there to see the sincere admiration on their faces. Whether he knew it or not, he had made some loyal friends.

"Too bad he couldn't stick around a while. He seems like a regular fellow, all right," Jim said. "He's got plenty of guts, I'll say that for him."

"People can't quit talking about the way he saved Paula," Zach agreed. "He's a hero."

Richie looked puzzled and popped up with "What's a hero?"

"Well, young fellow," Zach said, smiling down at the little boy, "a hero is somebody who risks his own life to save somebody else's. The way David saved your aunt Paula."

"Oh," Richie said thoughtfully.

"He saved our dog, too," Eric boasted.

Zach laughed. "Then, he's a hero two times over."

At that moment, Skip rang a dinner bell and waited until he had everyone's attention. When a hush had fallen on the room, he gave thanks for the food, fellowship and all of God's blessings. A murmur of "amens" was followed by a joyful announcement: "Let's eat!"

"This is wonderful," Melissa told Carol, as they filed through a buffet line with loaded plates and helped the children put something on theirs besides dessert.

"Why don't you stick around? You could work on your book here just as well as in Denver, couldn't you?" Carol asked.

"The reality is that it'll probably take me a year to get my book ready to market," Melissa explained. "And I may be offered an editor's job when I get back."

"Good for you. But you have to promise not to forget us when you and the boys get back to the big city. They're lucky to have someone like you looking after them. It's wonderful you took the time to bring them here to visit their aunt. They're sweet, adorable kids."

When Melissa saw the way Carol's eyes were shining as she looked at Eric and Richie seated next to her own little girls, Melissa decided the time had come to share the hope that had been building inside her. She watched how beautifully Eric and Richie fit into this wonderful Christian family, and she couldn't help but wonder if this could be the loving home that the Lord had planned for the boys all along.

She turned to Carol. "Could we excuse ourselves for a minute? I have something I want to talk to you about."

"Sure." Carol laid down her napkin. "We'll be back in a minute, kids. Don't leave the table."

She led the way upstairs to a small ladies' rest room, complete with vanity table and a couple of upholstered chairs. As soon as Carol closed the door, she raised a questioning eyebrow. "Have you heard from David?"

"Yes, but this isn't about him. It's about the boys."
She told Carol everything about Jolene's note, and David's sense of duty to try to place the boys in a good
home. She admitted that they'd brought them to visit
Paula with the hope that she would grow so fond of
them that she'd agree to keep them.

"But she's not physically able to raise two boys,"
Carol said.

"We know that, now. Of course, Paula keeping
them is out of the question." Melissa took a deep
breath and plunged ahead. "The truth is, we haven't
been able to locate anyone else on either side of the
family who could take them. They need someone to
give them a loving home, and I've watched how beautifully you and Skip are raising your little girls..."

Carol's eyes widened as if she knew what was coming next. "What are you trying to say, Melissa?"

"Wouldn't you love adding two wonderful little
boys to your family?"

Carol gave a surprised laugh. "You mean, you
haven't noticed?" She patted her tummy. "I'm almost
four months pregnant, and the doctor thinks it may be
twins. I'm afraid our little house is already going to
be bulging at the seams with these new arrivals."

"Oh, Carol, that's wonderful." Melissa was torn
between being happy about Carol's news, and devastated by her own disappointment. How could she have
been so wrong? She tried to keep her voice optimistic.
"Of course you're going to have your hands full. Obviously, my idea is not the answer I've been praying
for."

"Sometimes we just have to wait on the Lord to

bring about our highest blessing,'' Carol said as she hugged Melissa. "Keep the faith.''

They went back to their table, and as Melissa watched Eric and Richie standing on the stage happily singing "Jesus Loves Me'' slightly off-key with all the other children, she felt estranged from God. Her faith wavered the way Job's had when he thought the Lord had deserted him. She felt alone, adrift, and without hope.

That night, after putting the boys to bed, she went downstairs and picked up the old Bible that had sustained Paula's great-grandmother through so many uncertain times. Before she had opened it, however, the telephone rang.

She glanced at her watch. Ten o'clock. Who would be calling this late? Then her heart lurched. Could it be?

When she heard his voice, she cried happily, "David, how nice of you to call.''

"I hope it's not too late. I just got home from a miserable evening.''

"Mine wasn't the best,'' she admitted with a catch in her voice.

"What happened? Honey, what's wrong?''

"Carol and Skip are going to have another baby, maybe twins. They can't take Eric and Richie. I can't believe it. It would have been perfect. I had it all planned out.'' If he reminded her that she'd been preaching to him "Let go and let God,'' she'd hang up on him. "It was the answer we've been looking for,'' she stubbornly insisted.

"Apparently not,'' he said gently.

"You know, I'm beginning to think that I've been looking at this in the wrong way."

"What do you mean?"

"Carol asked me tonight why I didn't stay in Wolfton, and I've been tossing the idea around. I'm pretty sure Paula would let the boys and me live here while I hunt for some kind of job. The people I've met have been very kind and supportive, and I love Skip's church. With that kind of support group, I think I could adopt Eric and Richie and do right by them as a single parent. What do you think?"

"What about your writing career?" he asked, not wanting to come right out and say that it was an irrational idea. "Don't you have a future there?"

"Yes, but it's not as important as the boys' future," she said in a tone that offered no room for argument. "I'll let you know when I've decided."

"Melissa, you have your own life to think about and—"

"Don't lecture me," she said shortly.

"I'm not lecturing you. I just don't think you should make life-changing decisions on the basis of emotion."

"What *should* you base them on? Hard, cold empirical facts?" She knew she was being unfair, but disappointment made her less than generous. "I'll let you know what I've decided."

He couldn't believe how effectively she'd slammed the door shut on him and any argument he might offer. When she told him goodbye, there was a finality about it that left him gripping the phone so tightly that his knuckles turned white.

Chapter Fifteen

Melissa didn't say anything to anyone as she began to quietly move forward in her plan to remain in Wolfton with the boys. She prayed and searched her heart, knowing that any sacrifice she made to raise the boys would be more than balanced by the happiness of watching them grow into strong Christian men.

But the job market was not a good one. The only opportunity that presented itself was an assistant's job at the public library. She knew she would love working there—but could she possibly manage on the low salary? She decided it was time to talk to Paula and share her plans.

They were sitting at the kitchen table enjoying a midday cup of coffee, while the boys and Scruffy played on the hill behind the house. Climbing and sliding, they scrambled through the trees in games of hide-and-seek. Melissa had never seen them so carefree and happy. Their squeals of laughter quickened her heart with happiness.

She put down her coffee cup and cleared her throat. Not knowing exactly how to begin, she searched for the right words, but before she could say anything, Paula dropped a surprise package of her own.

With a confidential smile, she leaned toward Melissa. "I want you to be the first to know. I've decided to marry Zachary. Can you believe it?"

Melissa had been so intent on telling Paula about her own plans that she was taken by surprise. She shouldn't have been. It was obvious how the judge felt about Paula. Melissa wondered if Paula ever would have said yes if it hadn't been for the accident. Somehow a near brush with death put things in a different perspective.

Melissa reached over and squeezed her hand. "I think that's wonderful."

"Zach's been asking me for ages, so it isn't anything sudden. We dated quite a lot a few years back, and he even rented a room from me once." Her eyes twinkled. "I think he's been ready to move back in ever since."

"I'm so happy for you," Melissa said sincerely. "You shouldn't live your life alone."

"That's what I decided. All those long hours, lying hurt in that cabin. I kept thinking about Zach and how sad he would be if I died. I don't know how many years I have left, but there are a lot of things we could do together. Having him around the house would be a joy. He's quite a cook, you know." She gave a girlish chuckle. "I'll probably put on ten pounds the first month."

"Have you set a date?"

"Not yet, but soon. We don't want to waste any more time. I hope you and the boys can stay long enough to see us tie the knot. It'll be nice to have some of my own family there."

"Of course we can," she said readily, even as her plans to remain at Paula's for an undetermined time collapsed. With Zach moving in, she and the boys would have to move out. With no job and no place to live, the door slammed shut on the possibility of staying in Wolfton. She shoved away the enveloping clouds of uncertainty and concentrated on Paula's happiness.

"Just tell me how I can help."

"I haven't thought much about the ceremony. I'll probably ask Nancy to be my matron of honor, and Jim can give me away. Both of them have been so good to me. All the time he lived in the house, he was like my son. When he married, Nancy became family, too."

Melissa nodded her approval. She remembered how distraught Jim had been that first day when he'd discovered Paula had not come home.

"We haven't decided about the honeymoon. Maybe Hawaii. I've always wanted to wade in those beautiful ocean waters." She laughed like a young girl. "There are a whole lot of dreams that will be coming true."

Just then, they heard the front door open, and Carol's merry "hello" floated through the house. "Anybody home? I smell coffee and fresh-made muffins," she declared as she came into the kitchen with her usual energetic bounce. "May I join you, ladies?

I've had breakfast, but I'm eating for two—or maybe three,'' she said, winking at Melissa.

Paula's eyes immediately traveled over Carol's roomy pullover. "Are you pregnant?"

"Guilty as charged," she laughed, and patted her rounding tummy.

As Melissa listened to Paula's and Carol's excited chatter, she struggled to come to terms with her own crumbling plans. She was glad she hadn't called and turned down the upcoming editor's job. She didn't know how in the world she would swing moving to a larger place, or absorb the expenses of raising two boys, but at the moment she could see no other path.

David was sitting at his desk reviewing his calendar for the day, when his secretary buzzed him. "Judge Daniels from Wolfton, Montana, is on the line."

Zachary. Why was he calling? David's first thought was that something had happened to Paula. "Hi, Judge. This is a surprise. Is everything all right?"

"Fine. I hope this is a good time to call. I know you're a busy man."

"No problem. Is something wrong?"

"Far from it." Zachary cackled. "I feel like a maverick turned loose in a meadow of green grass. I'm getting married. Paula and I are tying the knot. How about that?"

David laughed in relief. "Congratulations. That's great. When's the happy day?"

"Haven't decided. I've got some things to get settled first, and I've got a proposition for you. I don't want any 'no' answer until you've considered it."

"What kind of a proposition?"

"It's like this. I've been a district judge for the past fifteen years and I'm ready to get off the bench. I'm resigning, and I'm opening up my old law office. I've been making some enquiries about you. Your legal career is impressive, David. For a man your age, your experience is outstanding. You've got a reputation for being a top-notch lawyer, and keeping your head on straight when things get tough. I want to make you an offer. How does a full partnership in my law firm sound to you?"

"Are you serious?"

"Absolutely. What do you say?"

"I'll have to get back to you, of course," David answered, giving Zach his pat answer for delaying a commitment to an unexpected request. "There are a lot of things to consider."

"I'd like to contact a friend of mine in Denver to get him to fly you here in his private plane so we can talk. Can you get away this weekend?"

"I'm not sure." The opportunity to make a quick trip to Montana and check on Melissa and the boys was more on his mind than discussing Zachary's proposition. "Why don't I give you a call this evening, when I've had a chance to mull this over?"

"Good enough." Zachary spent a moment on pleasantries and then signed off with "Talk to you later."

After the judge hung up, David leaned back in his chair and laughed so loudly that Elsie poked her head in his office.

"Are you all right?" She frowned, obviously puzzled by his outburst.

"What would you say if I told you I just might decide to join a law firm in the fair state of Montana?"

"I'd say you've lost your mind. You're not serious?"

He shook his head, still chuckling. "No, of course not. I just think it's a joke on me that after all the work and effort I've put into a Colorado political career, someone wants me to leave it all behind, and move to Montana."

On Saturday afternoon, when Melissa opened the door and saw David standing there, she stared at him as if he were some kind of apparition.

"Just thought I'd drop by and say hello." His grin was disarming. "Surprised?"

"Amazed. What are you doing here?"

"I'm trying to figure that out myself. May I come in?"

She stepped back as he came into the house, her thoughts whirling like dry leaves whipped by the wind. For days, she'd been trying to figure out how she and the boys could get back to Denver without calling him. And now, here he was.

"I've missed you." He searched her face. "Aren't you glad to see me?"

As he reached for her, all her defenses against involving him in her life again were leveled. Her voice was threaded with a sudden emotion that threatened to well up and choke her. She whispered, "Yes, I missed you."

When he kissed her, the warmth of his lips brought back a storm of memories of the tender and tense moments they'd shared on the trip. He let one hand trace the curve of her cheek, and then he rested the side of his face against hers. For a moment, they just stood there without moving, until Scruffy appeared at the top of the stairs.

Recognizing David, he came bounding down the stairs, leaping into the air, woofing and wagging his tail, as if trying to get airborne. Both David and Melissa laughed at the dog's exuberant attack on him.

''Whoa! Whoa!'' David picked up Scruffy and was treated to a barrage of wet, licking kisses. ''Easy, fellow, easy.''

The boys appeared at the top of the stairs, wondering what the commotion was all about. They squealed and bounded down, calling his name.

''Slow down,'' Melissa ordered, laughing, afraid they'd land flat on their faces before they reached the bottom.

''How ya doing, cowpokes?'' David asked, giving them a hug. ''I see you're still wearing your boots.''

They both started talking at once, and Richie grabbed his hand to show him their room. Eric grabbed David's other hand, and the two boys pulled him toward the stairs.

''I guess I don't have a choice,'' he said, smiling at Melissa over their heads. ''Don't go away. We need to talk.''

''Yes, we do,'' she said as steadily as she could, considering that her pulse was racing wildly from the unexpected warmth of his embrace and kiss.

As she watched the three of them climb the stairs and disappear into the hallway, her emotions were suddenly under siege. Was she strong enough to stay the course of her convictions and turn away from a love that promised nothing but conflict for both of them? He had pulled her into his arms before she'd had a chance to think. It scared her to realize how much she loved him.

She walked slowly through the house and out to the patio, where Paula was sunning herself.

Paula opened her eyes and asked, "Was someone at the door? I heard Scruffy making a ruckus."

"A real surprise. David's here. He's upstairs with the boys, looking over their posters."

"How wonderful. I've been wanting to meet him and thank him personally for all he did for me. Everyone's been telling me what a terrific guy he is, and I've noticed a special sparkle in your eyes when his name is mentioned." Her smile faded as she noticed Melissa's face. "What's the matter? From your expression, I'd guess you're not feeling very happy about his visit."

"I don't know how I feel." She plopped down in a chair and took a couple of deep breaths. "When he's around, it's hard to keep my head on straight. Why does life have to be so complicated?"

"I don't know, but it just seems to be human nature to make it that way." Paula smiled. "Why don't you just relax and see what happens? Somebody said that worrying is the wrong kind of praying."

Melissa chuckled. "That sounds like something my grandmother would have said."

When David joined them, Eric and Richie were hanging onto him as if they were determined not to let him get away again. The way he was laughing and joking with them made Melissa wonder if he had any idea what he was doing to them. Didn't he realize that he was just setting them up for more disappointment and rejection?

Paula asked David polite questions about his work and how long he planned to stay in Wolfton.

"Until Monday. I have the weekend."

"Good, you can go to church with us tomorrow. Skip and Carol will be delighted, and so will all the other folks who would like to meet you."

David didn't know how to politely refuse Paula without causing hard feelings. He just wanted to spend Sunday persuading Melissa that it was time for her and the boys to return to Denver. Zachary had scheduled a meeting with him on Monday, even though David had warned him that he didn't feel that leaving Colorado was in his best interest.

Paula got to her feet. "Why don't I take the boys inside for milk and cookies, and let you two have some privacy? You'll stay for dinner, of course. I believe Zach is bringing some fresh trout. He's quite a fisherman. Nobody can reel in a fighting fish the way he can," she said proudly.

As soon as Paula had disappeared into the kitchen with the boys, Melissa turned to David. "She and Zachary are getting married."

He started to tell her that he already knew, but changed his mind. "How soon?"

"I don't know, but the boys and I can't stay here as I had hoped. And I don't see any alternative other than to go back to Denver."

He nodded, relieved. Good, that was settled. He was afraid that she'd come up with another plan for her and boys to stay in Wolfton. Once he got her back to Denver, he'd have a chance to change her mind about a lot of things.

"I don't understand how you got here," she said, puzzled, suddenly realizing she hadn't seen any car parked in front of the house.

He told her then about the private plane that had brought him. "I took a taxi from the airstrip. Can you and the boys be ready to fly back with me on Monday afternoon?"

Melissa shook her head. "No, I've promised to help Paula with wedding preparations. And she wants the boys, as part of her family, to be here."

"How long will that be?"

"They haven't set a date yet, but I'm sure it will be soon. Now that Paula's made up her mind, she won't want to wait."

David wasn't happy about the delay, but there was little he could do about it. He'd have to fly back on Monday without her. He hoped that she would never know about the opportunity that Zachary Daniels was offering him. She'd never understand why he couldn't spend his life in a small pond when he had been raised to swim with big fish in the political world. He intended to thank Zachary for his offer of a law partnership, and be on his way.

He was grateful that the subject wasn't mentioned at dinner. Apparently Zachary hadn't said anything to Paula, and the conversation remained general. David had little time for any private conversation with Melissa that evening, but he was glad that he would have all day Sunday to be with her. He decided that Zachary and Paula had done him a big favor by deciding to get married. Melissa ought to know by now that there wasn't any future for her or the boys in Wolfton.

Chapter Sixteen

"**W**onderful to see you again," Carol greeted David at the front door of the church. "It's perfect that you should be here today of all days."

David shot a look at Melissa. Was this some kind of special day that he should know about? Her expression was as blank as his.

As they walked toward the front door, Carol scooted the boys on ahead. "I'll bet your Sunday School teacher is waiting for you. You know where to go, don't you?"

Both Eric and Richie nodded and bounded up the front steps, racing to see who'd be first. "Slow down," Melissa ordered in a motherly fashion. She hoped they didn't burst into their classroom like a couple of wild animals.

Carol turned to Melissa and David. "Let's go into Skip's study. I have some great news for you."

"What kind of news?" Melissa prodded as they followed Carol into a room lined with bookshelves and furnished with an old-fashioned desk and comfortable armchairs.

"Have a seat." Carol waved to the chairs but remained standing, hugging herself as if she couldn't bear to sit quietly for even a minute.

"What is it, Carol?" Melissa couldn't imagine what kind of news had put that twinkle in her bright eyes. "You look ready to burst."

"I have a wonderful surprise. Truly. Truly."

"And we would love to hear it," David said with a smile.

"All right." She took a deep breath. "Are you ready for this? Jim and Nancy Becker have generously agreed to adopt Eric and Richie. They know what it would mean to Paula to keep the boys here, and they're willing to take them."

The ticking of an old-fashioned clock was the only sound in the pastor's study for several seconds. Melissa looked at Carol, uncertain whether she had heard correctly.

"Jim Becker?" David repeated, frowning.

"Are you sure?" Melissa prodded.

"Yes, I'm sure. What's the matter with you two?" Carol looked puzzled. "Don't you understand? I give you the answer you've been looking for, and you act like a couple of sleepwalkers." She looked from one to the other in amazement.

"I'm just stunned, that's all," Melissa said quickly.

"You've been looking for a loving Christian home for the boys, and you won't find any better than Nancy and Jim's," Carol insisted.

"When did all this happen?" David asked, as if he was going to need a lot more information about these two people before giving his approval.

"Jim and Nancy came over to the house last night and told us what they were thinking," Carol said. "A few days ago I shared with Nancy the fact that you'd brought Eric and Richie to visit Paula with the hope that she would be able to keep them. Since Jim really feels close to Paula and Nancy loves children, they decided that raising her great-nephews instead of turning them over to strangers was the right thing to do."

"And they're financially able to assume the added expense of raising them?" David asked bluntly.

"Of course. Jim has a secure job with the fire department," Carol assured him.

David searched Melissa's face. "You like Jim and Nancy, don't you?"

"I really don't know them all that well," she answered hesitantly. "Jim seems like a nice fellow, and Nancy is very sweet. I guess they're old enough to handle the demands of two active boys," she said as if trying to convince herself.

"I've only talked to Jim a couple of times, and our conversation was nothing personal," David said.

"Trust me. You won't find a better home for the boys," Carol said, obviously surprised that her good news had met with such reservations.

"We probably need a little time to think about this," Melissa said, forcing a smile.

"Yes, of course." Carol looked at both of them as if she didn't have a clue as to what was going on. "You'll join us for Sunday dinner, won't you. We can talk more then. It's a little late for Sunday School. Why don't you stay here until it's time for church service?"

Melissa nodded, and Carol slipped out of the study and closed the door behind her.

David searched Melissa's face and hated the empty look in her eyes. When he reached over and took her hand, it was cold to the touch. "What is it?"

"I'm not sure," she admitted. "Maybe I'm just stunned. I don't know why I have reservations about this. Could be that I'm letting my personal feelings cloud my judgment. Come on, let's go sit in the sanctuary. It'll be empty for another half-hour while everyone is in the classrooms." She needed to let her thoughts settle in prayerful silence, and ask for some divine guidance.

A few minutes later, as they sat together in the sanctuary, Melissa bent her head in quiet contemplation, and David tried to think about the situation in a detached, rational manner. For some reason he was as negative about the Beckers taking the boys as Melissa was. Maybe he felt that the young couple were just doing it out of their affection for Paula, and not because they were really taken with Eric and Richie.

As the church began filling up with Sunday worshipers, David was surprised how many people nodded and smiled at him. He recognized some of the men who had been in the search party, and several of the women who had brought food for the celebration at Paula's house. They seemed genuinely happy to see him, and he enjoyed the comfortable feeling of belonging that comes to people who have shared a traumatic experience.

When the organ music began, Skip appeared, solemnly dressed in his clerical robe. He smiled broadly at David. A few minutes later, when the children filed in and sat in the front pews for a short Bible story, Eric and Richie kept twisting around and waving at Melissa and David.

Their eyes were bright and their mouths spread in wide grins as they filed out with the others to go downstairs for the children's service.

As David sat in the radius of sunlight pouring through multi-stained windows, he sensed a oneness with those around him. He experienced a sense of wholeness and completeness that he'd never felt before. At first he didn't know how to handle it, this knowledge that he was not alone or separated as he had believed all his life. He didn't know how it had happened, but he realized that is wasn't power and prestige that were important in life. Melissa's God of Love had reached out to him, and as the swell of organ music poured over him, he gave Melissa a knowing smile and saw her eyes suddenly mist with tears.

The Reverend Skip Carlson based his sermon on Mark 8:36. "For what does it profit a man to gain the whole world and forfeit his life?"

In a nonjudgmental way, Skip challenged his congregation to consider the choices in their lives, and to look to the Lord for the courage to change that which was keeping them from the abundant lives that the Bible promised.

Melissa tried to guess what David might be thinking. Was he even listening, or was he just worried about the time he was wasting spending this Sunday morning in church? His expression didn't reveal anything about his reaction to the service or Skip's sermon.

After the closing hymn, they joined other worshipers moving toward the open doors, and were stopped repeatedly by people who introduced themselves and shook David's hand. When Melissa deserted him to get the boys, he was left to handle all the attention as best he could.

Finally, at the door, Skip shook hands with him and smiled broadly. "Great to have you with us this morning, David."

"You really hit me between the eyes with some of the things you had to say," David admitted. "I took a good look at my life in a way I never have before, and a couple of lightbulbs went on."

"We call them 'God moments,'" Skip said. "It's amazing how suddenly things make more sense if you see them with God's truth."

"I haven't had any practice looking at life that way," David confessed. "But I know that something is missing."

"All the Lord needs is a willing heart," Skip assured him. "And the courage of a man to follow him."

At that moment Zachary joined them, smiling broadly. "Well, now, I'd say you're a pretty popular fellow around here, David. Just the kind of partner that could make our firm the best in the state. After our meeting tomorrow, I hope you'll have a positive answer for me.''

"You don't have to wait until tomorrow, Zachary. I can give you my decision now." He took a deep breath. "If things go the way I hope with Melissa, yes, I would like very much to accept your offer of partnership."

"I knew you were one smart fellow." Zachary grinned.

Skip put his hand on David's shoulder. "Wonderful! It's amazing how things fall into place when the good Lord gets involved."

"I'm going to be needing some heavenly help when I talk with Melissa."

"You'll have it," Skip promised.

Melissa was openly puzzled when David arranged for the boys to go home with the Carlsons, and suggested that they leave the Jeep in the church parking lot and walk the few blocks to Skip and Carol's house. But she was relieved to have the extra time to get her thoughts in order. Her prayers for understanding had not brought the kind of peace she needed.

"I have something to tell you." David took her hand as they walked slowly along the tree-shaded street.

She could see that he was struggling to find the right words, and this hesitant manner was not like him. "What is it?"

"I had a call from Zachary last week. He's retiring from the bench and asked me if I'd be interested in a full partnership in his law firm."

"Here in Wolfton?" Her eyes widened. "Why would he think you'd even consider it?"

"If you want to know the truth, I came here with every intention of turning it down, but I've decided to accept his offer."

She stared at him as if the whole thing was too preposterous to be taken seriously. "Is this some kind of bad joke?"

"It's no joke. I'm serious."

"You can't mean it." She shook her head in disbelief. "Why would you give up everything—?"

"That's the point exactly," he interrupted. "I don't want to give up everything. I almost realized too late that everything that really matters to me is here." He stopped in the middle of the sidewalk and gently turned her around to face him. "Skip's message this morning was like a strong lens that put everything in my life into focus. Now, I know what has been missing, and I'm ready to accept a whole different view of spiritual values. I know I can't rearrange all my thinking and beliefs overnight, but I'm ready to try. I don't want to give up you and the boys. Not now, not ever."

"What about your political ambitions?"

"I want to quit marching to the world's drummer and find a deeper meaning for my life. I've been slow to realize that it's my love for you and the boys that is really important. Skip told me that all the Lord wants is for me to follow my heart—and that leads me straight to you."

She was suddenly so full of happiness that she had trouble breathing. She had prayed for a moment like this, but listening to him say the words that she'd been longing to hear was truly a miracle.

"I'll do my best to be the kind of husband and father that will make you happy. I'm asking you again, Melissa, and this time, please, say yes. Will you marry me?"

Without hesitation, she lifted her face to his. "Yes, I will."

He kissed her tenderly as they sealed their commitment in the middle of the sidewalk on a lovely Sunday afternoon. When someone in a car honked, they looked up and saw Paula grinning at them, as she and Zach drove by.

Laughing, David put his arm around Melissa's waist and they walked happily together, just smiling and feeling in harmony.

About a block away from the Carlson's house, a moving van was pulling away from a beautifully restored Victorian house, and they saw a couple with three children loading belongings into a van parked in the driveway.

Melissa slowed her steps as she gazed at the Queen Anne-style house that was nestled in a frame of tall trees. She was startled by how much the white house reminded her of a picture that her grandmother had always had on her bedroom wall. A wide, old-fashioned veranda circled the ground floor of the two-story house, intricate lacy bargeboards had been freshly painted white, and several brick chimneys rose from the mansard roof. There was even a round turret room with picturesque dormer windows.

David could tell from the rapt expression on her

face that she was taken with the house. "Want to take a look inside?"

"Do you think we should?"

"Why not? There's a Realtor's sign on the lawn."

"But we're not potential buyers."

"Who says we're not? We're going to need a house to live in, aren't we? You just agreed to marry me, remember?"

"Yes, but this house is way too big and expensive."

He just laughed and guided her down the sidewalk. When they asked the young couple moving out of the house if they could look around, the woman looked a little hesitant. "It's really in a mess. I mean, the cleaning people are coming tomorrow. I think the Realtor is going to have an open house in a few days."

Her husband only laughed. "It's all right, honey. They're not here to see how clean we're leaving the place." He motioned them into the house. "Take a look. If you like it, you can come back for a second look."

Arm-in-arm they walked through the rooms. The first floor had a large entry hall, a large parlor with a bay window and marble fireplace, a sitting room, dining room, kitchen, pantry, maid's room, closets and a bathroom. A handsome oak staircase let to the second floor, and four bedrooms, two bathrooms and a sitting room.

Melissa seemed to love everything about the house, and her appreciation of its historical heritage was evident to David in the way she pointed out all the intricate woodwork, embossed ceilings and vintage details.

David just smiled and nodded, enjoying her enthusiasm. When they'd completed their tour of the entire house, he asked, "Well, what do you think? Should we buy it?"

"You mean...to live in?"

"Isn't that what people do with a house they buy?" he teased.

The wonder she felt that this beautiful old house might actually become the home she had always dreamed about was almost too much to handle. "Do you really mean it?"

He just laughed and kissed the tip of her nose. "Yes, I really mean it."

The man greeted them hopefully at the front door. "Well, what do you think? It's a great house for a family. Do you have children?"

"Yes, we have two sons," David said readily. "Two wonderful little boys. Their names are Eric and Richie."

At that moment, Melissa knew what it was like to experience happiness "pressed down, shaken together and overflowing."

*   *   *   *   *

Dear Reader,

I am delighted to share with you the tender story of Melissa and David as they experience the truth of God's promise, "I will lead you in the path that you should go." Melissa and David had their own ideas about handling the situation facing them, and the lesson of "letting go, and letting God" was not an easy one for either of them to learn.

Melissa's faith and confidence wavered when her plans didn't work out. Thwarted at every turn, she found her impatience put her at odds with God's divine timing. Only when all her efforts failed and she released the outcome to God was He able to open the windows of heaven and pour out an unexpected blessing upon her.

Although David was a generous person at heart, his political ambitions blinded him to the real treasures in life. He allowed the world's pressures, his parents' expectations and his own willfulness to control his life. Only when the love in his heart became more important than his ego was he able to turn his life in the direction that God had planned for him, and realize the true meaning of spiritual happiness.

I enjoy hearing from readers of my books. You can reach me c/o Steeple Hill Books, 233 Broadway, Ste. 1001, New York, NY 10279.

Leona Karr

HIDDEN BLESSING

I will give you a new heart
and put a new spirit within you.
—*Ezekiel* 36:26

With love to Debbie, Charlotte, Kay and Vivian.
My special family, and loyal fans.

Chapter One

"I will give you a new heart and put a new spirit within you."

Ezekiel 36:26

The last thing that Shannon Hensley expected when she rented a summer cottage near Beaver Junction, Colorado, was to be confronted with a life-threatening forest fire.

"They're bringing in firefighters from all over," Isabel Watkins, the owner of the town's one grocery store, told Shannon as she quickly sacked her purchases. "This place is going to be worse than a beehive turned upside down."

Shannon's gray-blue eyes widened. "The report I heard said the fire was somewhere in the high country."

"That's us," Isabel replied with a nod. "The fire started up on the north ridge. They don't know if it was started by careless campers or lightning. Everyone was hoping that it would burn itself out, but the winds have spread the blaze downward.''

''But it's still miles away, isn't it?'' Shannon asked, feeling an unbidden quiver of nervousness. She'd rented a summer cottage in a deeply wooded area about fifteen miles from this small settlement and had only been settled a short time.

''Not many miles as the crow flies. It's unbelievable how fast a wildfire can spread,'' Isabel answered, shaking her head. ''They're hoping to get a fire line set up before the flames crest Prospect Ridge. Once it jumps into those thick drifts on the downhill slopes, it could make its way into this valley.''

Great, just great! Shannon thought, and filled with all kinds of misgivings, she left the store and started driving down the two-block Main Street. She'd driven to Colorado, looking for a quiet retreat where she could try to make some sense out of the shambles of her life. She had wanted to leave all the drama and trauma behind in Los Angeles. Even now she couldn't believe that she was jobless, friendless and facing another uphill battle to secure a prosperous future for herself.

It wasn't fair, but then she reminded herself that she'd never expected life to be fair. She'd fought tooth and nail for everything she'd ever gotten. Her parents had believed that looking out for number one was what life was all about and had taught their daughter well. Shannon's focus had been on climbing the corporate ladder since college, and there had been little time in her life for anything or anyone else. She was well on her way to achieving her high goals when, almost overnight, her high-paying position was eliminated because of a corporate takeover, and she was tossed out by new management as easily as they were replacing old office furnishings with new.

Now it seemed that her hopes of spending some relaxing downtime in Colorado were threatening to go up in smoke. Maybe she should pack up her things and get out of the area. Better to forgo a month's rent than put herself under more tension worrying about a forest fire driving her out. But where would she go? Her finances were tight at the moment, and the added expense of seeking out another retreat wasn't something she had planned on. Besides, she told herself firmly, the fire might never get within miles of her rented place. She decided that it wouldn't hurt to hang around for a couple of days even though this mountain valley was isolated with only one two-lane road leading from the Junction to a major highway in Elkhorn, a town about fifty miles away.

As Shannon turned onto the narrow road snaking up to her mountain cottage and other dwellings built on the slopes of Rampart Mountain, she braked to a sudden stop.

"What in the world?" She couldn't believe it. A wooden barricade was stretched across the road, and a man wearing a cowboy hat and Western clothes moved quickly to her car window. Under different circumstances she might have appreciated his strong masculine features and the way his brown eyes reflected a smile as he waited for her to lower the window on the driver's side. She guessed him to be somewhere in his early thirties as he gave a polite tip to his broad-brimmed Stetson and acknowledged her with a polite hello.

"What's going on?" she asked without returning his smile. Used to big city runaround, she was ready to summon any argument necessary to avoid wasting time at a roadblock.

"We have to keep all traffic off this road," he replied in an easy, conversational tone, holding his smile.

"Why?"

"To keep it clear for the emergency vehicles."

That slow easy smile of his was getting on her nerves, and she resented a deep, stroking voice that undoubtedly could play havoc with most females—but not her. She wasn't some backwoods gal who was used to taking orders from any smiling man who happened to be around, nor about to meekly accept this inconvenience without a firm protest.

"I don't see any traffic," she said firmly, as if that should settle the matter.

"You will in just a few minutes. The first caravan of forest fighters will be here shortly with trucks and all kinds of fire-fighting equipment. They're going to establish a base camp just a couple of miles from here. This whole area is going to be under siege before long."

"Does that mean the road is going to be closed indefinitely?" Shannon's sharp mind suddenly shifted into gear. What would this mean to her? She'd been a successful businesswoman because of her ability to handle unexpected situations. With dogged determination she had always made certain that she didn't come out the loser.

"I couldn't say how long it will be closed. It depends upon how fast the fire moves up the other side of Prospect Mountain." His slow, unruffled tone increased her irritation.

"I don't see why you can't let me drive quickly up to my place."

"Because I have my orders not to let anyone up this road."

"Then you're some kind of officer?" Her skepticism was obvious in her tone as she glanced over his Western shirt as if looking for a badge.

"No, just an ordinary citizen doing my duty," he answered smoothly. "Ward Dawson's the name. Now if you'll back up to that wide spot and turn around, you can wait out the road closures in town."

She glared at him. "How long will that be?"

"Well, let's see." He shoved his cowboy hat back far enough for her to see shocks of cinnamon brown hair framing his nicely tanned face. "Not more than a month, I reckon."

"A month!" She echoed, horrified. Then she saw the twinkle in his eyes and gave him a glare that told him she didn't appreciate his humor.

Ward silently chuckled. She was a testy one, all right, and he couldn't help kidding her a little. The California license plates on her fancy sports car had told him a lot. She was a city gal, all right, and a downright attractive one with wavy hair the color of corn silk, petite features and flashing gray-blue eyes that snapped at him. He didn't know who she was, but she sure wasn't going to drive anywhere up this road if he had anything to do with it.

"Surely, you have to allow people to get back to their homes," she insisted, not willing to accept his authority. She'd had plenty of practice confronting male superiors when they'd tried to tell her she couldn't do something and had learned there were always ways to get around rules. "It doesn't make sense to shut down a road when it's the only one in the area."

"I'm sorry," he said, firmly. "But that's the way it is."

"Why all this inconvenience when the fire is miles away? If you want everyone to stay out of the way, just tell them to stay in their houses and off the roads until the firefighters are finished." She mellowed her tone as if she was just offering a helpful suggestion. "That makes a lot more sense, doesn't it?"

Ward searched her face, almost sure she was putting him on, but her steady gaze was clear. Didn't she realize that it was anybody's guess whether they could get a handle on the fire before it crested the ridge and threatened this hillside and all the scattered homes on it? The fire was moving at an alarming rate in three different directions. He was tempted to set her straight that there might not be any homes to return to if the worst scenario came to pass. He decided that frightening her wasn't going to help anyone.

"They're setting up some accommodations at the school gym for people evicted from their homes," he told her with a firmness in his tone that didn't invite any further argument. "Do you know where the high school is? You can't miss it. It's a redbrick building—''

''With a sign that says Beaver High School? I think I can manage to find it,'' she said sarcastically. The small settlement of Beaver Junction would scarcely take up a three-block area in Los Angeles.

''Well, if you get lost you can always flag somebody down.''

Pulling her car in reverse, the woman made a quick turn and headed toward Beaver Junction.

Watching her car disappear down the narrow road, Ward let out a deep laugh. She was a fiery one, all right, might be worth getting to know if things were different. But in the developing emergency, he'd be surprised if he ever saw her again.

As Shannon drove to the Junction, she mentally rehearsed all the things she'd say to him if she ever got the chance. When she reached the high school, she saw with a sinking heart that the parking lot was nearly full. All kinds of vehicles were vying for parking spaces. She was lucky to find an end spot for her small car.

After turning off the engine, Shannon sat for several minutes, listening to a Denver radio news station giving details of the rapidly moving wildfire. She searched the sky and could see a haze of smoke beyond the front range of mountains that cupped the valley. The radio report affirmed that all mountain roads in the threatened areas were restricted to emergency vehicles.

After hearing the news broadcast, Shannon decided

the irritating Ward Dawson policing the road had only been following instructions. She felt a little ashamed of her assumption that he was just some local throwing his weight around. She could even forgive him his little joke of telling her it might be a month before the road was open.

Surely, with a statewide alert, enough knowledgable firefighters would be able to put the fire out as quickly as it had begun. There was no reason to panic, she told herself. Sighing, she realized that she would just have to be patient and wait with the rest of these strangers.

Collecting her purse and bag of groceries, she left the car and followed the crowd inside the building. The Red Cross had arrived. Tables had been set up in the front hall with a cardboard sign that read, Register Here If You Are An Evacuee.

Am I? Shannon asked herself. She wasn't sure just what the identification implied. As far as she was concerned, she was someone waiting for the road to clear so she could get back to her rented cottage.

When Shannon explained her circumstances, a pleasant, ruddy-faced woman handed her a form to fill out. "Your friends and relatives can contact us to know you're safe," the volunteer explained.

For the first time, Shannon felt a quiver of foreboding that the situation might not be as quickly resolved as she had assumed. She wrote her name on the form and handed it to the woman without filling it out.

The lady volunteer raised an eyebrow. "Isn't there someone who needs to be notified about your safety?"

Shannon shook her head and walked away. Her insistence on independence and total privacy suddenly had a hollow ring to it. Even her closest former co-workers had no idea she had taken off for Colorado. She felt it was none of their business. No one would be waiting to hear from her. No friends or relatives would be inquiring after her safety.

Reluctantly, she joined the milling crowd in the gym where clusters of people were busily talking, looking out windows, trying to placate crying children or sitting silently on cots that were being set up as quickly as they were delivered.

A tall, angular woman wearing a Red Cross pin spied Shannon carrying her small sack of groceries. She hurried over to her and gave Shannon a grateful smile.

"Oh, good, donated food. Here, let me take that sack to the cafeteria for you. God knows, every little bit will help. We have no idea how many will need to be fed tonight."

Shannon readily handed over the sack and watched the woman scurry away as if she held a treasure in her hand instead of a quart of milk, three bananas, a box of crackers and a six-pack of a diet drink. The idea of feeding all these men, women and children was more than Shannon could contemplate.

All over the crowded gym, people were talking quietly together. Others were fighting back tears or sitting silently as if in a state of shock. Most of the men were wearing work clothes, as if they'd been suddenly taken off some job, and the women wore casual summer tops with their slacks or jeans. Shannon felt more out of place than ever in her pale-yellow linen dress and matching designer sandals. Several puzzled glances came her way as she headed to a corner of the gym to sit down in a folding chair.

Announcements over the school's public address system blared in her ears, but most of the information had no relevance for her since she was unfamiliar with the names of places and people. Although she had a detached sympathy for the milling townspeople around her, she felt alien to them. As the hours passed, she decided that as soon as the roads opened to general traffic, she'd leave the area and forget about losing her three weeks rent on the mountain cottage.

Ward had forgotten all about the attractive blonde in the fancy sports car until later that evening when he brought some supplies to the high school. The place was a madhouse. Growing numbers of evacuated families from threatened and closed areas had poured into Beaver Junction all afternoon, seeking refuge at the school.

A call had gone out for cots, food and supplies, and Ward had made a quick trip to his ranch, located twenty miles up the mountain valley. He and his young ranch hand, Ted Thompson, had stripped the house of some extra cots and brought them to the school.

"You're God's own angel, Ward Dawson," the preacher's wife, Laura Cozzins, told him with a broad grin on her round face as she accepted his donations.

"That's what my mother always used to say." Ward nodded solemnly.

Laura laughed heartily. She was a small woman with greying short hair and a ready twinkle in her hazel eyes. "Glory, glory, we must not be thinking of the same God-loving woman. As much as your parents adored you, Ward, I don't ever remember them calling you an angel."

"Ah, come on, now, I wasn't that bad."

"No, you weren't." She grinned at him. "Just heading down the wrong road. It was a miracle, for sure, the way you made a U-turn when you came back to the ranch to live." Her smile faded a little. "I know it wasn't easy for you, but the Lord wasn't about to cut you free."

"Yep, He had a lasso on me, for sure," Ward admitted, remembering how hard he'd fought, trying to follow his destructive godless path in the college town where he'd been working. Both Laura and her husband had been there for him when he'd passed through his Gethsemane three years ago. After his wife, Valerie, had died and left him with an infant daughter to raise, he'd moved with Tara to the family ranch so that his older sister, Beth, could help raise his little girl. Since then, he'd learned to live in the moment and trust divine guidance to take care of the rest.

Ward gave Laura's plump shoulders a quick hug. "You're the prettiest gal around. If you weren't already taken, I'd throw my hat in the ring."

Laughing, she gave him a playful shove. "Your sweet talking is wasted on me. Now, you and Ted get busy setting up these cots before I think of some more work to keep the two of you out of trouble."

They had just finished that job when Ward spied the California woman sitting all by herself. Her apparent indifference to the plight of others around her was disappointing but not unfamiliar. When he'd gone off to college, he couldn't wait to leave home. Like the prodigal son, he'd thrown off all restraints and concern about others. Living campus life to the fullest, he forgot about the firm Christian values in which he'd been raised, and when he'd married his last year in college, it had been without any consideration except that he liked Valerie more than any girl he'd met, and they had a good time together. Her death when Tara was only two had left him emotionally bankrupt, and he'd come home to find himself. He didn't know what the emptiness in the pretty stranger's life might be, but he recognized the sign of a soul shut off from its source of peace and happiness.

"Do you know who that young woman is?" he asked his eighteen-year-old ranch hand, who usually had an eye out for any attractive female who wandered into town.

"Nope." Ted shook his curly black head. "Haven't seen her before. She must be new around here."

"I know she's staying at one of those summer homes on the north ridge," Ward offered. "She drives a fancy sports car with a California license, but that's all I know about her."

Ted grinned. "Well, if you're interested, boss, there's only one remedy for that. Go talk to her."

Ward wasn't sure that interested was the right word. Curious, perhaps. Responding to Ted's knowing grin, he took up the challenge. "You know something? I think I will."

Shannon had stayed pretty much to herself during the long hours of waiting, wandering aimlessly around the school or sitting in a corner of the gym. When she saw Ward coming in her direction, she instantly recognized him. Oh, no, she thought, silently, as he wove his way through the crowd toward her. Now that she understood the scope of the emergency, she was a little ashamed of herself for challenging his authority. Not that she was about to apologize. He'd been secretly laughing at her all the time, and she knew it.

He seemed to know just about everyone. She watched him scoop up a little girl for a quick hug, and a moment later he planted a kiss on the forehead of a grandmotherly lady. An attractive young woman dressed in western pants, a plaid shirt and cowboy boots pushed toward him and said something that made them both laugh. As Ward tweaked her chin in a playful fashion, she looked at him with a soft expression that betrayed a strong affection.

Watching them, Shannon was filled with an emotion she refused to identify as strangely akin to envy. Jerking her eyes in another direction, she scolded herself for being interested in this cowboy's personal life.

So he had a sweetheart or wife, so what?

"Hello, again." He greeted her with a warm familiarity as he suddenly stood in front of her. "I see you found the school all right."

Looking into his tanned face with its high cheekbones, firm straight nose and strong jawline, she was terribly aware of how much she wanted to mend fences with him. But she was equally determined to show him she wasn't some whimpering damsel in distress.

"It was a challenge," she answered lightly. "But I managed not to get lost."

"I suspect you always know where you're going."

"Yes, I do," she answered. If he was trying to get a rise out of her, she wasn't going for the bait. "I've heard rumors that the wind has shifted, and the roads might be opened in the morning."

He nodded. "Could be. I guess it depends on whether things stay the same during the night."

"And if they do?" she asked hopefully.

"Well, I reckon that they'll give the okay for people who live in the area to pay a quick visit to their homes. Most of them didn't have time to bring very much with them when they were ordered to vacate." He sobered. "It's not easy to decide what's important when you're under that kind of pressure."

"Are you one of the displaced?" she asked, wondering if he was personally involved or just volunteering to police the road.

"Nope, I'm one of the lucky ones. My ranch is farther up the valley. God willing, we'll be spared."

When he said, *we,* she glanced at his ring finger. No gold band. Feminine curiosity made her wonder who the young woman was who had hugged him with such ardor.

"Have you met any of the other folks?" he asked. Something about her obvious withdrawal from everyone around her challenged Ward to do something about it. "Why don't you let me introduce you around, Miss—"

"Shannon Hensley. Thanks, but I've decided to leave as soon as the main road opens, whether I can get my belongings from the rented cottage or not.'' Where she would go was another question, but she knew she wanted to see the last of Beaver Junction as quickly as possible.

''And you'll be heading back to California?''

''No. Not right away,'' she said, smothering a sigh. It was ironic, really, that she was sitting in a crowded gym with a bunch of homeless people and had no idea what she should do next. She'd spent a month applying to every high-tech company on the West Coast without even getting a nibble for a new position. She'd temporarily rented her expensive beachfront apartment, left her résumé with several employment agencies and made arrangements to come to Colorado to spend some quiet time. She wasn't about to admit to this stranger that she was without home, family or close friends. ''I haven't made up my mind exactly where I'll go.''

Her voice was firm enough, but Ward could see the shadow of worry in her attractive eyes, which seemed to constantly change colours from gray to smoky blue. She was wearing a dress in a shade of yellow that brought out sun-bleached highlights in her hair, and in his opinion, her figure was as eye-catching as any pictured on the cover of a woman's magazine. Why would such a California beauty end up alone in a place like Beaver Junction, he asked himself? He would have thought that fancy resorts in Aspen or Vail would be more her style.

''Do you need to let your family or anyone know that you're all right?'' he asked, in an obvious attempt to learn more about her personal background.

"No, there's no one," she replied quickly. "Since my parents died, I only have one aunt I communicate with once in a while. Thank you, but I can handle this situation nicely by myself."

Her lovely chin jutted out at a belligerent angle, and he hid a smile. There was something of a stubborn child about her that both appealed to him and irritated him. "There's no need to be afraid—"

"I'm not afraid." She flared at the insinuation. "I just want to get out of this place as quickly as I can. One night cooped up here with all these people will be all I can take."

"I see. Well, good night then," he said politely. Her apparent indifference to the plight of others around her sparked the urge to handle her the way he would a stubborn mare. It was a good thing she wasn't going to be around long enough for a battle of wills.

Left alone, Shannon had a moment of regret that she hadn't kept him talking to her. Nobody else had tried to strike up a conversation with her all afternoon. She knew they were caught up in the perils of their situation, and even though she sympathized with their worries and anguish, she wasn't up to all the commotion and crush of humanity crowded together, breathing the same air and having no privacy. The whole situation was some kind of unbelievable nightmare.

As Shannon's eyes followed Ward's tall figure across the gym, she saw him stop to talk to a plump, gray-haired woman. During their conversation, the woman nodded, and her gaze darted in Shannon's direction. Shannon was positive they were talking about her.

She stiffened. What was Ward Dawson telling the woman? How dare he repeat any of their conversation? She knew then that she shouldn't have revealed so much about her family situation and indefinite plans. Shannon began simmering. She was an outsider, and fair game for the rumor mills. She could imagine what fun the small-town gossips would have speculating about her private affairs.

Shannon braced herself when Ward left the gym, and the woman to whom he'd been talking made her way purposefully toward her. Shannon knew then that her suspicions had been right.

"Hi, I'm Laura Cozzins, the reverend's wife," the woman said, introducing herself in a friendly, breezy manner that matched the smile on her broad face. "Sorry I haven't had time to say hello before now. Ward told me he's a friend of yours and that you'd love to help us in the cafeteria. We'll be setting out some food pretty soon now, and I'm grateful that you've volunteered to help."

Volunteered to help? Shannon was speechless and utterly aghast at the number of lies Ward Dawson had squeezed into one sentence. He wasn't a friend, nothing had been said about her helping, and she hadn't volunteered for anything.

"Come on, dear, and I'll show where the kitchen is." Laura smiled at Shannon. "We've really got our hands full. The Red Cross ladies are doing all they can, but more displaced families are arriving all the time. Two more hands will be a great help, and God bless you for offering to help.''

Shannon managed a weak smile. Telling the preacher's wife the truth would have been too embarrassing under the circumstances. She rose to her feet and followed the preacher's wife into a hot, crowded kitchen.

For the next two hours, Shannon cut up a gigantic mound of potatoes for French fries, cooked them in boiling oil, then served them to a seemingly never-ending line of refugees.

She was hot, sweating and had aching muscles by the time all the stranded families had finished eating. When it was time for the volunteer help to sit down at the tables, Shannon had little appetite left. Ignoring the food that had been prepared, she searched the kitchen and found one of the bananas that had been in her confiscated grocery sack.

Like a fugitive escaping, she slipped out the kitchen door. Outside the building, a night breeze bathed her perspiring face with blessed relief. A faint glow on the far horizon marred the dark night sky, and the cool air was tinged with the odor of burned wood. As she walked around the building, eating her banana and enjoying the blessing of being alone, she prayed that the wind was blowing the fire back on itself.

She didn't see the small figure on the sidewalk ahead of her until she heard a childish voice calling in a whisper.

"Pokey! Pokey, where are you?"

As she came closer she saw a little boy about four years old standing in the middle of the walk. When he heard Shannon's footsteps, he turned quickly and came running up to her.

"What's the matter?" she asked, seeing his tear-streaked face.

"Have you seen my puppy dog? His name is Pokey. He's black with white paws, and not very big."

"No, I'm sorry, I haven't," she said gently. "Did he get loose?"

"We left him behind. He didn't come when Mama called. She said we couldn't wait to find him."

"Oh, I'm sorry," Shannon said. Pokey must have lived up to his name one too many times, and had been left behind. Even though she'd never had any pets of her own, she could certainly sympathize with the loss of one. She felt the youngster's anguish and tried to console him as best she could.

"I'm sure he'll be all right," Shannon said, not really being sure about anything at the moment.

"I know Pokey would find me if...if he knew where I was."

"He's probably just waiting for you to come back home."

"When can we go home?" the child sobbed, asking the question that was in both their minds. "I want to go home now."

"I know." She brushed a shock of brown hair from his forehead.

"I don't like it here."

Me, neither, Shannon added silently.

She spoke with more conviction than she felt. "I'm sure they'll have the fire put out soon. Now, we'd better go inside. Your mother will be looking for you.''

Even as she spoke, they could hear a woman's strident voice calling, ''Kenny. Kenny. Where are you?''

Shannon took the child's hand and led him to a worried and anxious young mother.

''Oh, thank God,'' she breathed. ''You scared the living daylights out of me, Kenny. I've been hunting everywhere for you. You know you're supposed to stay inside unless we're with you.''

''He was looking for his dog,'' Shannon said quickly, trying to help the little boy out. ''He's worried about Pokey being left behind.''

''I know,'' the mother said wearily. ''The dog didn't come when we called and called, so we had no choice but to leave without him. Our home is one of the highest on the mountain.'' Her lips trembled. ''We couldn't take time to hunt for Pokey. We barely had time to collect Kenny, the baby and pack a few belongings. The road is still closed, and we can't go back until they say so.''

''Maybe tomorrow they'll open it, at least for a little while,'' Shannon offered hopefully. ''I guess it depends upon the wind.''

Kenny's mother nodded. ''I'm Alice Gordon.'' She smiled when Shannon introduced herself. ''I'm glad to meet you, Shannon. We're all praying they'll get the fire out before it makes it over Prospect Ridge.'' Shannon could see her lips quiver as she took her son's hand. ''Thank the Lord, we're all safe here.''

She disappeared inside the building, leaving Shannon alone. Not wanting to go inside, Shannon continued along the sidewalk that led to the parking lot at the far side of the school.

She slowed her steps when she reached the lot and was about to turn around when she saw Ward heading for a pickup truck parked nearby.

Shannon was debating whether to call to him and give him a piece of her mind when he glanced back and saw her in the glow of one of the high arc lights.

He waved, then came quickly over to where she was standing. "I wondered where you'd gone. Hiding out, are you?" he chided with that easy teasing smile of his.

"Should I be?" she countered, still debating how she wanted to handle this infuriating man. "Have you decided to volunteer me for something else?"

He raised an eyebrow. "Not a good idea, huh?"

"Frankly, I don't appreciate someone manipulating me like that."

"Sorry, I thought that it would do you good just to mix a little bit with the others."

"Thank you for your concern, but I'm perfectly capable of looking out for myself. Good night, Mr. Dawson."

"Wait a minute." Her cool and dismissing manner was a new experience for him. Ward wasn't used to having any female, young or old, treat him with such cold indifference. None of the women he'd dated since Valerie's death had come close to leading him to the altar. He'd given the reins of his life over to God, and so far, he hadn't found anyone who held to the same spiritual values. A deep Christian dedication had been absent in his first marriage, and he wouldn't make that mistake again. He didn't know why he felt the need to challenge this stubborn, self-assured woman, but he did. Even though she'd made it plain that she didn't appreciate his interference, he couldn't help chipping away at her crisp edges.

"Laura said she appreciated the help and told me to thank you. You know, it's going to take all of us pulling together to get through this thing."

His clothes were dusty and wrinkled. Fatigue had deepened the strong lines in his face. Shannon wondered how many jobs he'd taken on.

"I really didn't mind all that much," she admitted. "But you would never have volunteered me for kitchen work if you knew what a disaster I am when it comes to cooking."

"I guess that was pretty nervy of me," he admitted with a wry smile. "I just thought things might be easier for you if you mixed a little bit with the others."

"No harm done," she said, suddenly contrite. She was ashamed for misjudging him. "What do you think my chances are of getting back to my place tomorrow to pack up my things?"

He surprised her by answering, "Actually, I think there's a good chance. The weathermen are predicting that the wind shift is going to last until at least tomorrow night."

"Really? That's wonderful." She almost clapped her hands.

Ward was stunned at how lovely and suddenly alive and beautiful she was. In the shadow of the building, she seemed like some kind of heavenly specter in her soft yellow dress and shiny hair. An undefined jolt shot through him as she smiled broadly at him for the first time, and something deep inside responded on a level that made no earthly sense at all.

Chapter Two

A ripple of excitement and relief moved through the cafeteria the next morning when a fire chief stood in front of the refugees and announced, "All of you who have homes below Prospect Ridge will be allowed back in the area for a two-hour period." He emphasized the time limit. "Two hours only. You got that?" His steely eyes dragged around the room. "The wind could shift at any time, and anyone still on the mountain could be caught in a fiery downdraft. Concentrate on speedily collecting the necessities, and let the rest go. Understand?"

There was a murmur of agreement from the crowd, and as Shannon bounded out of the building with the other evacuees, her mind raced. Two hours! That was enough time to get herself cleaned up with a quick shower and a change of clothes, with time left over to pack all her belongings in the car. Once the highway was open to general traffic, she'd leave Beaver Junction as fast as she could. Just where she would go to find the quiet retreat she needed was something she'd have to decide later. Right now, her pressing need was to get out of the present situation as soon as she could.

As she drove away from the school, she felt a pang of sympathy for those who would have to remain and endure a heartrending vigil, not knowing if their homes would be spared. She already felt drained and off balance.

A line of cars trailing out of town and up the side of the mountain moved at a snail's pace, and Shannon's agitation grew as precious time slipped away. A heavy haze of smoke billowed into the sky from some point hidden beyond Prospect Ridge, and her nostrils quivered with the pungent odor of burning wood. Her chest tightened as she realized that thick drifts of aspen and pine trees on each side of the road promised more fuel for the greedy fire if it topped the ridge and came racing downward. She clutched the steering wheel with nervous hands as she drove up the side of the mountain, forced to take the serpentine curves slowly instead of with her usual speed.

By the time she pulled into the driveway of the rented mountain cottage, she had lost more than a half hour of her precious time limit. She raced into the small house, and before she did anything else, she went directly to the telephone and dialed the employment agency that had sent out her applications. She had tried to use her cell phone, but it had kept fading out on her.

Her mouth went dry as she waited for someone to answer. Common sense told her it was too soon to expect any results, but she might get lucky, and if anyone was interested in interviewing her this soon, she could immediately head to California. Her pragmatic nature desperately needed a definite course of action. She had never been able to stand not having a specific agenda, and her present situation had heightened a need to get back in charge of her life.

"I'm sorry, Miss Hensley, we don't have anything right now, but I'm sure it's just a matter of time," a pleasant woman advised her after Shannon had made her inquiry.

Time. Shannon bit her lip. Patience had never been one of her most admirable qualities. In fact, she knew that impatience with herself, others and the world in general had been a driving force in her life, but she also knew she hadn't accomplished her climb in the business world by wasting time. She was proud of her reputation as a hardheaded businesswoman, and at the moment, she felt even more driven because her life was at a standstill.

"I would appreciate your doing everything you can to facilitate my applications," Shannon said as calmly as she could. She wasn't about to reveal the anxious tremors she felt inside.

"I can reach you at this number, can't I? If something should develop?" asked the lady in her professional, optimistic voice.

Shannon hesitated. Rather than go into the long explanation of the fire and her predicament, she answered, "I'm not sure, but I'll call you frequently and keep in touch."

When Shannon hung up, she sat for a long minute.

Maybe she should start concentrating on finding a position in another part of the country. She hated to leave the Los Angeles area, but if nothing developed in the next few weeks, she'd have to relocate and find a position elsewhere, anyway. She'd only rented her apartment on a temporary basis, but the couple who had taken it would probably sign an extended lease, or maybe even buy it. She ran a tired hand through her hair. Just thinking about giving up all that she'd struggled to create for herself brought a bone-deep weariness and anger. It wasn't fair.

She glanced at her watch, then stood up with a jerk. She couldn't believe how fast the time was going. Hurriedly, she stripped off her wrinkled clothes and dived into the shower, delighting in the cleansing sprays of warm water. Although they had opened the gym showers at the school to the displaced refugees, Shannon had declined to push her way into the line of people waiting to use them. Personal privacy had always been important to her, and having been raised in an affluent family as the only child, she'd always enjoyed her own things and her own space.

She sighed with utter contentment as she bathed with her favorite scented soap and shampooed her hair. She stepped out of the shower, refreshed, and quickly dressed in tailored slacks and a matching soft blue knit top. She towel-dried her shoulder-length hair and secured it in a clip at the back of her head.

She deliberately ignored the moving hands on her watch as she began packing her suitcases, giving careful attention to a small canvas overnight bag that she would keep with her. She hadn't unpacked the boxes that had held her books and laptop computer. She took them out to the car and stowed them in the trunk, along with her suitcases. She made one last trip to fill some kitchen sacks with foodstuff she didn't want to leave behind.

When she was ready to lock the front door of the cottage, she dared a look at her watch. She couldn't believe it! Already a half hour past the two-hour limit. Lifting her head, she quickly searched the mountain skyline. There seemed to be more dark smoke thickening on the horizon.

She bounded down the front steps, opened the door to her car and was about to climb in when she heard some commotion behind her. She swung around. A small black dog with white feet scurried toward her, his tail wagging furiously as he greeted her enthusiastically with a friendly, puppy-size bark.

There was no doubt in Shannon's mind that he was Pokey. She laughed as the puppy danced around her feet and put his paws on her legs. As she picked the fellow up, his little legs shot out in all directions, and his pink tongue was like windshield wipers gone berserk as he washed her face with jubilant kisses.

"I know someone who's going to be glad to see you," she said, chuckling as she opened the back door of the car and put him inside. "Lie down, Pokey," she ordered, but the puppy stood on the back seat, his head cocked to one side and his tail wagging as fiercely as ever.

She tossed her shoulder purse on top of her small overnight bag and hurriedly backed out of the gravel driveway.

There was no sign of other cars on the narrow winding road ahead, and she kept glancing in the mirror to see if there were any stragglers behind her. The road was pointedly empty. She couldn't believe everyone else had observed the time limit. Well, it didn't matter. Once traffic was allowed on the highway to Elkhorn, she'd be on her way out of here.

She was lost in thought when suddenly, without warning, Pokey suddenly leaped from the back seat into the front, sending her purse and the small canvas overnight bag flying.

"No, Pokey, no!" she protested as the dog tried to scramble into her arms. In her effort to shove him away, she turned the steering wheel too sharply.

The car left the pavement.

Frantically she tried to bring it back on the road, but the wheels failed to gain any traction on the narrow dirt shoulder. The car began to slowly slide downward.

Panic-stricken, she fumbled with her seat belt. Before she could get it unfastened, the car sounded as if its insides were being torn out, and it stopped with a jolt that threw her forward. Only her seat belt kept her from crashing her head against the dashboard.

What was happening? The back end of the car slanted downward, and the road lay about fifty yards above. Any moment she expected the car to start sliding again.

The dog was dancing all over the seat, trying to get into her arms. "No, Pokey, we have to get out."

The door wouldn't open. She shoved as hard as she could, but it was wedged shut. She saw then that none of the doors would open wide enough for her to get out. All were jammed against huge boulders that had momentarily snagged the car.

She was trapped, and even the slightest movement seemed to rock the car on its precarious perch.

Ward glanced at his watch for the tenth time in less than five minutes. He was positioned at the bottom of the mountain road, checking off the names of residents who had homes in that area. Every name had been crossed off his list but one, Shannon Hensley.

"Why am I not surprised?" he asked himself. She was already an hour late. As he waited at the checkpoint, his irritation and disappointment over her disregard for instructions turned into just plain anger.

Knowing he was needed in a dozen different places, he answered his cell phone curtly when it rang, "Dawson, here."

"Everybody off the mountain, Ward?" asked one of the fire chiefs watching Prospect Ridge.

"Not quite. We've got one left. A woman."

The chief muttered something under his breath. "We've got trouble up here. The wind's shifting, and our fire line on the ridge may not hold. If the sparks jump across the ridge, the whole mountain could be threatened. Get her out of there if you have to drag her."

"Right. I'll get on it."

"I'll bring her down kicking and screaming if I have to," Ward said under his breath as he climbed into his pickup truck and headed up the mountain, driving at a speed only someone who knew the road would dare.

As Ward silently rehearsed all the sharp things he was going to say to her, he was suddenly filled with a strange impulse to slow down. He'd learned to trust an inner voice that often guided him when he needed it most, and paying heed to it at that moment proved to be a blessing once again. If he'd been driving at his former speed, he would have whipped right by the white car that was off the road without even seeing it. As it was, he glanced down the slope of the rocky hillside and did a double take.

"What in the—" He slammed on his brakes. He couldn't believe what he was seeing. The fancy white sports car was precariously hung up on a shelf of large boulders a good distance below the road. Only rocks and low shrubs dotted the hillside.

Bounding from the truck, he started down the steep slope, slipping and sliding all the way. He fought to keep his balance as he scrambled over loose rocks and thickets of scrub oak.

The closer he came to the car, the tighter his chest got. He saw that by some miracle, it was caught precariously in the midst of some large boulders. If the boulders hadn't been there, there would have been nothing to stop the car's plunge into the deep ravine below.

"Thank you, Lord," he breathed.

Even before he reached the car, he began to weigh the situation. How deeply were the rocks rooted in the ground? How long would they hold against the heavy downward pull of the car? Could he get Shannon out without disturbing the precarious balance that held the automobile? As these questions flashed through his mind, he saw another complication. Huge rocks hugged the sides of the car.

Shannon's stricken pale face was clearly visible through the windshield. As he neared the car, she waved frantically to him as if he might suddenly decide to go away.

He was sure his eyes were deceiving him when he saw what looked like a dog in the seat with her. She hadn't said anything about having a pet.

As he peered through the driver's window, he gave her as much of a reassuring smile as he could manage and said loudly, "It's going to be okay. I'll get you out as fast as I can."

He didn't have an answer for the question he saw in her eyes. He surveyed the car. He knew at any moment the whole shelf of rocks could pull out from the ground, and everything would start sliding. One thing was certain. There wasn't any time to waste.

He was concerned that shifting even one of the boulders could affect the balance of the others. Very gingerly, he began putting his weight against one of the rocks pinning the front door shut.

Lord, lend me Your strength and wisdom. And I could even use an angel or two, right now.

After painstaking effort, only one large boulder remained against the front door on the driver's side. Ward breathed another prayer as he put his full weight against it. Slowly the rock began to move, and then, with one momentous shove, he sent it rolling with a crash down the slope. Afraid that the movement could have loosened the other rocks, he jerked open the door.

"Get out quickly," he ordered. He knew that they had to get away from the car as soon as possible, in case the shelf of rocks broke away under their feet.

The dog scrambled out first, leaping over Shannon. When Ward saw that she was getting out, hanging onto her purse and a small suitcase, he barked, "Drop everything and climb as fast as you can."

In Shannon's shaken state, leaving all her belongings in the car and trunk was devastating. She ignored his order to drop her purse and overnight bag.

When Ward saw the stubborn set of her mouth, he grabbed the suitcase from her. "Move." He gave her a not-too-gentle shove forward. With the dog bounding ahead of them, they scrambled up the steep slope.

Shannon was breathing heavily when they reached the shoulder of the road. Her whole body shook when she looked at the car, which so easily could have been a heap of crushed metal at the bottom of the ravine— with her in it! Tears flooded her eyes, and her lips trembled. She'd never had a brush with death before, and when she felt Ward's arm go around her shoulder, she leaned into him, grateful for the warmth of his strong body that lessened a threatening hysteria within her.

"It's all right," he soothed. "You're okay." *Thank you, Lord,* Ward prayed. He gently stroked her back, and a swelling of tenderness took him totally by surprise. He didn't understand why this woman he scarcely knew could create such a deep stirring in him. They had no common ground to build even a slight friendship, and he was certain that in any other situation, she would only be slightly amused by his presence. And yet, as she trembled in his arms, he wanted more than anything to kiss away the tears on her cheeks and bring a smile to her.

"I'm sorry," she murmured, drawing away and swiping at her tears. Shannon kept her head lowered and didn't look at him. Anybody with eyes in their head ought to be able to drive down an empty road without running off it. She'd always prided herself on her perfect driving record, and now this!

"Nothing to be sorry about," he reassured her. "You're safe—that's all that matters. I think we ought to get going. I don't like the looks of that sky."

Pokey had been bouncing around at their feet, woofing excitedly as if the world was a wonderful place when people were around to keep him company.

"Come on, pup," Ward said as he and Shannon moved toward the pickup. Without waiting for an invitation, Pokey jumped in and settled happily on Shannon's lap.

Ward held his curiosity about the dog in check until he saw Shannon lightly petting him with soft, tender strokes. Then he asked with his usual smile, "Where did the pup come from?"

She told him about Kenny looking for Pokey last evening. "Somehow Pokey made his way to my cottage, and I put him in the back seat. I'd only driven a short distance when all of a sudden he jumped into the front seat and startled me." Her voice faltered.

He could guess the rest of the story. She'd inadvertently turned the steering wheel, and the car dropped off the road.

"It was stupid," she said in a tone that was edged with disgust for herself.

He was surprised she'd bothered with the dog in the first place. He suspected that underneath that polished exterior of hers, there might be a deep, caring nature.

"Things like that happen to everyone," he assured her.

"Not to me," she said firmly. "I should have made sure that the dog stayed in the back."

"Well, no harm done," he said.

Her eyes rounded as she stared at him. "How can you say that? No harm done? My car will probably end up smashed to smithereens and my belongings burned to a crisp."

"True. I guess it's just the way you look at it. Since you escaped without being smashed to smithereens and burned with the rest of it, I'd say no real harm was done." He shot her a quick glance. Didn't she realize how blessed she was that she'd run off the road in that exact spot? There were a hundred other places where there were no rock ledges to halt a sheer drop into the canyon below. "It's all a matter of perspective, isn't it?"

Shannon tightened her jaw and didn't answer. What she didn't need was someone reminding her that she should be grateful instead of resentful about the whole thing. If he started lecturing her about families who had lost everything, she silently vowed she'd get out and walk.

Ward knew she was shaken up and still scared by

what had happened. He could appreciate the toll the experience had taken on her nerves, because his own were still on edge from the ordeal. Even now he could feel sweat beading on the back of his neck if he thought about what could have happened.

They drove in silence until they reached the school parking lot. As soon as Ward turned off the engine, a man with a clipboard came over to the pickup's window.

"Is she the one not accounted for?" he asked Ward as he shot a quick look at Shannon.

"Yes. She had a little accident that delayed her."

The man grunted as if he thought one feeble excuse was as good as another. "The wind is kicking up. They've called in some more tankers. Hot flames could crest the ridge by nightfall."

"Or the fire could burn back on itself," Ward countered, believing that positive and negative thoughts created their own energy.

"Well, you're about the only one who thinks so," the man said flatly and walked away.

Shannon swallowed hard. How much time left before the whole mountain went up in flames? "What are the chances of getting a wrecker to pull my car back on the road?"

"Under normal conditions, Ed's Towing Service could give it a try. If the car stays hung up on those rocks, a pulley and cable could probably bring it up without too much trouble."

She felt a spurt of hope. "So if they put out the fire before it reaches the ridge, and it's safe to go back up the mountain, they could do it pretty fast?"

"Yes, they could—under normal conditions." He hated to douse the sudden spark in her lovely wide eyes as he added, "But I'm afraid as long as the whole area is in a fire zone and restricted to official personnel, the car will have to stay where it is."

"I see." She turned away so he couldn't see her face. Above everything else, she wasn't going to give into any feminine weakness that would add to her humiliation.

Shannon clutched the small dog in her arms as they made their way into the gym, and she searched the crowd for a glimpse of Kenny. Putting Pokey into the child's arms was suddenly more important than anything else.

Kenny saw her before she saw him. His childish cry of joy was unmistakable as he bounded across the floor. "You found Pokey."

"Here he is. Safe and sound." She smiled as she set the dog down, and Kenny fell on his knees, giggling as the pup washed his face with kisses.

"I love you, Pokey," he blubbered. "Where were you? I couldn't find you anywhere."

Shannon's eyes were suddenly misty as she saw the joyful reunion. She wasn't aware that Ward's hand had slipped into hers until she realized she was squeezing it. When she looked at him, she saw a warmth in his eyes that took her completely by surprise. Her defenses against allowing anyone to come too close emotionally shot into play, and she quickly withdrew her hand.

"She found Pokey. She found Pokey," Kenny shouted to everyone.

All Shannon's efforts to stay removed from everyone's notice were wiped out in that happy moment. She felt horribly on display as Alice Gordon loudly thanked her over and over again, and other people, young and old, gathered around her, smiling broadly.

Laura Cozzins's round face beamed at Shannon. "Bless you. That little tyke has been pining away for his dog. It's a good deed you've done this day."

"You don't know what that good deed cost her. Maybe Shannon will tell you about it sometime," Ward said. His smile wavered. "Then again, maybe she won't. She's a very private person," he added, smarting a little at the way she had quickly dropped his hand.

Laura nodded in a knowing way. As a minister's wife, she was obviously adept at reading emotions that lay beneath the surface. "How about a glass of lemonade and maybe a doughnut to refresh the two of you?" she suggested as if she were dedicated to feeding the body, as well as the soul at every opportunity.

"Thanks, but I've promised to deliver some supplies to the base camp," Ward said, "I'm already late by a couple of hours."

Shannon silently winced. They both knew it was her fault he'd been delayed. She quickly took her overnight bag from him and apologized, "I'm sorry I held you up. Thank you for…for everything."

"Rescuing damsels in distress is one of my special talents," he assured her solemnly as his eyes twinkled at her, and his mouth eased into a soft smile. "Call on me anytime."

She wanted to say something lightly back, but she couldn't. Her heart was too heavy.

"It's going to be okay." He gave her shoulder a light squeeze. Ward wanted to suggest that she join the others in prayer and meditation. Maybe, instead of shutting out God, she would gain assurance that she wasn't ever alone, no matter what the circumstances. He'd come to his faith the hard way, and he knew Shannon was on the same kind of path. "I'll try to come back this evening before I head to the ranch."

She watched as his broad back and muscular body disappeared out the door. Laura had been watching the exchange between them. With a knowing smile, she slipped her arm through Shannon's. "Come on, you can help me make some sandwiches for lunch."

The day was long and trying, and only the hope that Ward would come back kept Shannon's spirits from scraping bottom. The danger of firefighting became personal when Laura told her a story about a teenage Ward trying to handle a meadow fire all by himself and nearly getting trapped by the blaze before help got there.

Her heart contracted with a sudden jolt. Surely, Ward had enough sense to leave the fighting to the professionals. He was just delivering supplies, she reassured herself, but how well she knew that he wouldn't think of his safety in a time of danger.

All afternoon and evening, she kept an eye out for him, but he didn't show. It was Ted who came in late that evening and told her Ward had already gone to the ranch.

She wasn't surprised. No doubt he'd had enough of her trauma and drama. Remembering the way she had gone into his arms and accepted his tender caresses, she chided herself for letting her emotions play her for a fool. As she lay stiffly on her sagging cot, she firmly resolved she wouldn't make that mistake again. She knew better than to give her emotions free rein. There was always a price to pay for letting anyone too close. She had plenty of scars to prove it.

Chapter Three

Shannon slept very little that night. About two o'clock in the morning, fifty firefighters from a unit in Idaho arrived at the school. Since it was too late to make it to the base camp, they crowded into the gym with the rest of the refugees.

Shannon was up early and helped serve breakfast. Being in the midst of these brave young people who were willing to put their lives in danger was a startling revelation to her. Many times she had watched television coverage of California wildfires or heard about some fighter losing his or her life, but she had only been touched on a superficial level. Now that detachment disappeared, and her heart was filled with personal concern as she moved among these dedicated men who were going to battle a fierce, monstrous wildfire that was out of control.

When Reverend Cozzins said a prayer for their safety, Shannon bowed her head with everyone else and murmured a fervent amen. Even though she wanted to believe in some kind of heavenly protection, she knew it would take a faith stronger than hers to rely on any divine miracles.

The crew of firefighters left the school right after breakfast, leaving behind a mounting tension and anxiety in the crowded school. A briefing bulletin posted on the bulletin board later that morning was not encouraging. The prediction was for strong winds and high temperatures. Numerous infrared photos taken of the fire's boundary showed an ever widening area of destruction.

"We have to do something to keep the children occupied," declared Laura. In her usual energetic manner, she immediately started enlisting help to get some activities going. She organized several groups to play some outdoor games on the school grounds and sent some of the youngest children into the library to listen to stories.

Shannon had no intention of volunteering for anything or calling attention to herself in any way, but Kenny had different ideas. With childish pride, he pointed her out to all the kids.

"She's the one who found Pokey. He was lost, and the fire almost got him. But she saved him, didn't you, Shannon?"

The cluster of grinning children beamed at Shannon in a way that made her want to sink into the floor. What could she say without taking away Kenny's moment in the limelight? "I didn't exactly find him—he found me."

Laura Cozzins suddenly appeared at Shannon's side, saving her from having to say anything more about Kenny's dog. "Well, now, I see you've already made friends with Kenny and his pals. Wonderful, Shannon." She beamed. "Why don't you take them into the art room and let them draw and color and make all kinds of wonderful things?" She smiled broadly as she elicited nodding approval from the kids. "Doesn't that sound like fun, children?"

Shannon could have summoned a hundred reasons why she was the last person in the world to be put in charge of a bunch of kids, but she didn't have a chance.

Kenny grabbed her hand. "You can be our teacher."

The rest of children nodded and crowded around her with smiles and beaming faces, effectively eliminating any chance she had for refusal. As the children began to pull Shannon toward the classroom Laura completely ignored her frantic plea for help.

"You'll have fun," Laura promised with a chuckle, and quickly turned away to draft someone else for one of her projects.

How in the world did I get myself into this? Shannon would have rather faced a roomful of hostile executives than a roomful of squirrelly youngsters. Raised as an only child by parents who never stayed in one city very long, she had always been the new kid in school, and being around younger children had never been a part of her upbringing. She grew up in an adult world where achievement and success were the driving goals. As a result, Shannon was competitive, motivated and competent when it came to the business world, but it only took ten minutes in the art classroom with a cluster of scattering children to discover that her people-management skills were sadly lacking in the present situation.

"Everyone sit down," she said in a normal voice, which had little impact in the noise level of excited kids darting about the room, handling everything that wasn't tacked or glued down.

Boxes of donated supplies were on the tables. She knew that if she didn't do something, impatient children would be diving into them, and the chaos would grow worse by the minute. It didn't help her confidence to realize no one in the room was paying any attention to her.

She had to take charge, and quickly. Remembering that one of the first rules of a successful business leader was to command attention, she clapped her hands loudly and raised her voice above the bedlam. "Listen to me! I want everyone to sit down now! And be quiet!"

Later Shannon wondered what she would have done if the kids had ignored her, but to her relief, they quickly filled the chairs at two long tables and fixed their grinning smiles on her. She guessed that their ages ranged from kindergarten to second or third grades. Now that she had their attention she didn't know what to do with it.

She walked over to a table and looked at the boxes of pencils, crayons, paper and a few coloring books. She cleared her throat, hoping she would sound steadier than she felt. "All right, we're going to draw and color pictures."

"I want a picture to color," a curly-headed girl named Heather howled when Shannon gave the last coloring book page to someone else.

"I bet you can draw a nice picture of your own to color," Shannon coaxed.

Heather set her lips in a pugnacious line. "I want a real picture."

"Sorry. I'm afraid that there aren't any coloring book pictures left," Shannon said flatly.

"Then you draw me one," Heather ordered with pouting lips, and shoved her plain sheet of paper toward Shannon.

Fuming silently, Shannon grabbed a pencil, and as quickly as she could she sketched a house with a flower garden and tall tree with a child's swing in it. "There. Color that."

Heather looked at it, then gave Shannon a broad smile of approval. "It's nice."

"I'm glad you like it," Shannon said in relief as the little girl picked out some crayons and began to color the picture.

Shannon dropped down in the teacher's chair and wondered how long it would be before she could send all the kids back to the gym.

When Heather finished coloring her picture, she started showing everyone and bragging, "See the picture teacher drew for me."

"I want one, too." The children began to line up at her desk, all of them wanting a special picture of their own. "Draw me something, teacher."

Shannon's first reaction was to refuse, but somewhere at the back of her memory was a remembered pleasure in what her parents had called her doodling. Even though an art teacher had told Shannon once that she had an artistic flair, she'd had never had time or the inclination to foster it. Giving a soft laugh, she said, "All right, let's see what I can do."

Quickly she sketched some simple scenes, then some cartoon figures that seemed to come easily to her. As she handed each drawing to a child, she was rewarded with a broad grin and a thank-you.

"Do one for me," Kenny begged.

"Well, let's see." Shannon pretended to think. "I bet I know one you'd like."

She was drawing a cute puppy with ears and a tail just like Pokey when she was startled by someone leaning over her shoulder. "Very good," Ward said, as his warm breath bathed her ear.

Startled and instantly embarrassed, Shannon almost covered the sketch of the puppy with her hand so he couldn't see. A deep conditioning from her childhood had made her instinctively want to hide what she had been doing. She could almost hear her father's voice. *Wasting your time again, Shannon!*

As Ward saw the muscles in Shannon's cheek tighten, he reassured her. "I mean it. It's very good."

"It's Pokey," Kenny said happily. "I'm going to color him black and white. And I'll stay in the lines," he promised solemnly, as if someone had pointed out this little goal to him once or twice. He proudly took the picture to his table.

Ward eased down on the corner of her desk, lightly

swinging one leg as he looked around the room. "I didn't know you were a teacher in the making."

"I'm not."

"You could have fooled me."

He grinned at her, and she didn't know if he was secretly amused or impressed that the children weren't climbing the walls.

"What brings you back to the school this morning?" she asked lightly. She wasn't going to let him know that she'd been disappointed when he hadn't come to the school at all yesterday.

"I had a little time between chores and helping out the fire wardens this afternoon. When I came in, Laura asked me to deliver a message to you."

"And what was that?" Shannon stiffened, wondering if the preacher's wife had come up with another volunteer job for her.

"It's time to let the kids go to lunch."

She looked at her watch in surprise It was almost noon. She couldn't believe the morning had passed so quickly. When she announced that it was time for lunch, there were some protests from those who wanted to finish their pictures.

Shannon vaguely promised they could finish their pictures some other time or take them with them. Ward sat on the edge of the desk watching Shannon while she collected crayons, pencils and paper. For some reason, his smiling approval was irritating.

"Well?" she demanded, challenging him to say something. "You don't have to look so smug. Laura caught me at a time when I had no chance to refuse."

"It looks like she drafted the right person, all right."

"At least it's better than peeling potatoes, thank you."

Ward laughed, secretly relieved to find her spitting words at him instead of curled up somewhere battling fear. He had some bad news for her. Flying sparks carried by the wind had ignited the tops of tall ponderosa pines on the other side of the high-ridge fire line. Ground crews were scrambling to clear brush in the area, and airplane tankers were dropping fire retardant chemicals in an effort to control the blaze before it became full-blown and started down the mountainside. A dozen homes were in danger of being lost—as well as a white sports car still perched precariously on a rugged rocky slope.

"What is it?" Shannon asked as his smile faded and his forehead furrowed in a frown. Her hands tightened on the piece of paper she was holding, crushing it. "My car's gone, isn't it?"

"No, it's still there."

"But?" she prodded.

"The fire is threatening to start down this side of the mountain. New fire lines are being set up, and crews are cutting down brush and trees around some of the high mountain homes in an effort to save them."

"And if they don't stop it?" Even as she asked, she knew the answer.

"It could sweep down the mountain to the river and spread along the valley below." He didn't add that his ranch would be vulnerable to any fire sweeping up the canyon toward his pastureland. "We're all praying that that doesn't happen. Which reminds me, we're going to have church services here at the school on Sunday. Our little church won't hold this crowd, and I'm sure there'll be a lot more worshipers than usual." He gave her a wry smile. "Lots of people wait to make a 911 call to the Lord, you know, instead of keeping prayed up."

Shannon refrained from commenting. She hadn't seen any evidence that churchgoing people had it any easier in life than anybody else. The only time she was ever in a church was for weddings and her parents' funeral. Neither her mother nor her father had held to any religious faith, and she had been brought up to believe that being a "good" person was all that was necessary.

Ward could tell from her expression that worship was not a part of her life, and for some reason, he felt challenged by her lack of spiritual awareness.

"What do you say to lunch at Bette's Diner?" he asked impulsively. "It's only a short walk from here, and I bet getting out of here for even an hour would do you good."

Shannon searched his face. Was it pity that prompted the invitation? Or did he need an hour away from the heavy pressures as much as she did? There were shadows under his dark-brown eyes and visible lines in his forehead and around his mouth. She wondered how much sleep he was getting these nights.

"Sounds great," she said honestly.

As they left the school, they passed a roped-off area where anxious pet owners were milling around kennels and cages lined up by the building. Shannon couldn't believe the menagerie of animals—cats, rabbits, dogs and other furry creatures—that had been brought to the school for safekeeping. When Shannon spied Kenny running across the playground with Pokey on a leash, she waved and smiled at him.

"You ought to do that more often," Ward told her.

"Do what?"

"Smile instead of frown."

"Oh, is that your way of saying I look like a sour-puss?"

"Yep."

They both laughed, and he took her hand with a playful swing. As his long fingers gently closed around hers, she felt a kind of peace and harmony that denied the biting odor of smoke and the wailing of emergency vehicles.

Neither spoke as they walked slowly away from the school. Shannon was surprised at her sudden sense of freedom from the pressures that had been weighing her down. Nothing had changed. Nothing at all. Her life was still in the pits, but somehow, walking hand-in-hand with him, she felt in a world apart from the shambles of her life. She'd never allowed her feelings to dominate her rational thoughts before, and every ounce of common sense told her to shut down this emotional reaction before she lost her mind completely, but she kept her hand in his, drawing warmth and reassurance from the touch.

They strolled down the hill until they reached Main

Street—two blocks of clustered rustic buildings that housed one gas station, a small mercantile store, a feed store, several small businesses and one restaurant named Bette's Diner.

Schoolchildren were bused into Beaver Junction from the whole county, since most of the population lived on ranches and scattered mountain homes. At the moment, the influx of outsiders was ten times the normal population, and the tiny network of roads around the Junction was snarled with emergency vehicles.

Bette's Diner was crowded from one end to the other, and Ward and Shannon were lucky to squeeze into a booth just as a couple of men vacated it. They didn't have to wait long for service. They had barely seated themselves when a waitress breezed over to them with a welcoming smile aimed at Ward.

"Hi, there. I was wondering if you were going to make it for lunch today. Somebody told me you were up at the base camp shortly after dawn."

Shannon recognized the attractive brunette who had hugged and laughed with Ward in the gym that first afternoon. She was still dressed in Western pants and shirt, and a small apron encircled her waist. Shannon guessed she was probably in her late twenties, and the way her eyes lit on Ward made it easy to tell how she felt about the rancher.

"Judy, this is Shannon Hensley," Ward said, quickly introducing her. "She's waiting out the fire at the school."

"Yes, I know," Judy said as she darted a quick glance at Shannon. "From Hollywood, someone told me. Of course, you can't believe everything you hear.''

"It's true. Would you like her autograph?'' Ward asked with mock solemnity.

"Are you...somebody?'' Judy's eyes widened as she stared at Shannon.

"Of course, she is. Would I bring a nobody to Bette's Diner for lunch?'' Ward asked facetiously.

"Don't pay any attention to him,'' Shannon said with a laugh. "I'm a working girl from Los Angeles.'' And out of a job, she could have added.

A faint color rose in Judy's cheeks. "I should know better than to fall for his joshing.'' As she readied her pad and pencil for their order, she became all business. "What can I bring you?''

Shannon followed Ward's suggestion and ordered baked trout, which he promised was caught fresh daily. After Judy disappeared into the kitchen with their orders, Shannon chided Ward, "Shame on you. You shouldn't tease her like that. She likes you.''

"I know, but humor is the best defense for a lot of things, like letting friendship get out of hand.''

The way he said it made Shannon wonder if he kept all the women at arm's length. And she remembered what Laura Cozzins had told her.

"Well, what's your verdict?'' he asked with a raised eyebrow as he leaned back in the booth.

"What do you mean?''

"I'll tell you a little secret. Your eyes deepen into a startling gray-blue when you're doing some heavy thinking.'' His smile challenged her. "Now, don't lie and tell me you were thinking about what kind of pie to order for dessert.''

"All right," she said, resting her elbows on the table. "I was indulging in curiosity about some things Laura shared with me."

He chuckled. "Well, then, I suppose I should start to deny everything just on principle."

"Oh, she was very complimentary. She bragged about your ranch and explained that you specialize in raising Appaloosa horses. Frankly, I have no idea what makes one horse different from any other horse."

"A real city slicker, eh? Well, you've come to the right place to get a little equine education." There was an unmistakable lift of happiness to his voice as he began to tell her about his stable of Appaloosa horses. "They have beautiful markings. Brown and black spots, with white or black tails and mane, are the most common coloring. A wonderful saddle horse, and one of the best mounts for working cattle. The best thing that ever happened to me was coming back to the ranch to devote myself to raising and breeding them."

"What were you doing with your life before that?"

"Nothing I'm proud of," his said flatly. "My daughter was only two when my wife died, so I decided to move back to the homestead so my sister could raise her. You'll have to come out to the ranch and meet them."

"I'm really hoping to get out of here the first chance I get," she responded quickly. For some reason, she didn't want to commit herself to any personal involvement with his family. It was enough of a strain to try to adjust to a bunch of strangers. The less she knew about anyone, especially this very attractive man, the easier it would be to maintain her distance and not get emotionally involved. What a mistake it had been coming to Colorado in the first place. She'd been running away, she could admit that now. Afraid and scared, she'd thought of a mountain cottage as a sanctuary. What a laugh that was!

Ward didn't know why the barriers had gone up. Probably she was bored to tears with all his horse talk. He wondered why he was so intent upon impressing her. Anyone with a lick of sense could see that his lackluster life wouldn't hold any charm for her. They were from different worlds, and only a crisis like this fire would have put the two of them together in the first place. It bothered him that he couldn't figure her out. Spoiled? Certainly. Vain? Probably. Hurting? Definitely.

When Judy served their orders, she made light conversation with Ward and then lowered her voice in a personal tone. "Am I going to see you tonight?"

"Afraid not," Ward answered readily, giving her his easy smile. "Chores at the ranch have gotten ahead of me. I have to head back as early this afternoon as I can."

Judy looked ready to protest and shot a quick look at Shannon as she turned away.

Was he breaking a date with her, Shannon wondered. It was obvious that the waitress thought she was going to see him tonight. Were they more than just friends? If Judy was his sweetheart, Shannon didn't approve of the way he might be standing her up. Was this his usual way of toying with the opposite sex?

Her earlier warm and comfortable feeling about him was gone. They finished their meal with only sporadic, desultory conversation.

As they came out of the café, Shannon decided she wanted to pick up a few things at the mercantile store. "I'd like to buy some more coloring books. I don't want a repeat of this morning."

"Why not? I'd say you are really talented, drawing all those pictures. Are you an artist in the making?"

"Me?" Shannon protested quickly. "Heavens, no. That's just doodling—at least that's what my mother called it. She used to get furious with me for wasting my time, drawing pictures all over my notebooks and scratch pads. Believe me, I haven't done anything like that for years."

"That's too bad. You looked as if you were enjoying it."

"I was just relieved to find something that would keep the children quiet. It's worth buying some coloring books to keep them busy."

There was a crowd in the small, old-fashioned store. Long counters were piled high with a variety of merchandise, and Isabel Watkins and another clerk were kept busy waiting on the customers. Shannon and Ward went their separate ways for a few minutes, and she found a half dozen coloring books, which could be torn apart. She also purchased several children's card games, which she intended to donate to Laura's recreational activities.

Ward was waiting at the checkout counter with a small sack of his own when she finished shopping. If another day or two went by without her belongings, she knew she'd have to spend some money to replace a good many things. As it was, she was already over the weekly budget she'd set for herself.

"Would you mind waiting while I make a telephone call?" she asked Ward when she spied a phone booth a short distance down the street. The telephone number she'd given the employment agency was useless—she had packed her cell phone in her cosmetic case when her purse had been too full to hold it. "It'll just take a moment."

"Sure thing." He took all the sacks and leaned against the corner of the booth as she closed the door and made her call. It didn't take long to hear the same disappointing story. No response on her résumés yet.

"Keep in touch," the artificial, upbeat voice of the employment lady told her.

Ward refrained from asking any questions as they walked in silence to the school, but he could tell from the flickering tightness in the muscles around her mouth that the telephone call had not been a happy one.

Reverend Cozzins was coming out of the door of the school when they reached it. The minister was as tall and gangly as his wife was short and rounded, but both exuded the same small-town friendliness. "Ward, will we see you at the church meeting tonight?"

"Sorry, Reverend." Ward shook his head. "It's like I told Judy. I've got to catch up on my chores. Just sign me up for whatever needs doing, and I'll try to squeeze it in."

So he didn't have a romantic date with Judy. Shannon didn't know what she felt, but it seemed to be an undefinable sense of satisfaction.

"You're a good man." Paul Cozzins gave Ward a healthy pat on the shoulder. Then he smiled at Shannon. "My wife tells me you did a great job with the children this morning. Some of the kids were so proud of the pictures you drew for them that they posted them on one of the bulletin boards."

"What?" stammered Shannon. "You have to be kidding."

He smiled and shook his head.

"But I didn't draw them for display."

"You've got a God-given talent, young lady. No need to be hiding it."

Ward chuckled. "Some people seek glory and others have glory thrust upon them," he quoted, his eyes twinkling.

Cozzins looked at a piece of paper he held in his hand. "Well, now. I'd best get along. That woman of mine gave me a foot-long list of things to do. See you later." With a wave of his hand, he hurried off.

Shannon saw Ward's mouth quirking with a grin, and she warned him, "Don't you dare laugh. It's not funny. You don't know how horrified my mother would be to have my doodling exhibited like that for all to see."

"Are you sure? I don't see how giving pleasure to other people could upset anyone. Of course, if you want to insist, I'm sure the kids will take their colored drawings down."

"You know I can't do that."

He nodded, smiling smugly. "Yep."

She quickly put on her protective armor of pretend indifference as they went into the school. "It isn't as if anyone really knows me. I guess there's no harm done."

Ward carried her things to her cot in one corner of the gym. "I probably won't be back for a day or two. We have to move some horses into a far pasture, because they get antsy when they smell the thickening smoke haze even though it's miles away, thank God."

She tried to hide her disappointment. His company was the only bright spot in a long, boring day. "Thanks for lunch," she managed. "And the chance to do a little shopping. Oh, this sack is yours," she said, picking up the bag he'd laid on her cot.

"No, it isn't. It's something especially for you."

Before she could respond, he turned and disappeared in a crowd moving out the front door. Slowly she opened the sack and peered inside.

What in the—

With an uncertain laugh that had an edge of tears in it, she pulled out the contents—an artist's drawing pad and a box of colored pencils. She couldn't believe how special this simple gift made her feel. It honored a part of herself that she'd tried to keep hidden. For the first time, she held the drawing pencils with a sense of excitement and delight.

Chapter Four

The next morning, Shannon gathered with the other refugees in the gym to hear the latest update on the situation. Despite the call for more and more firefighters and equipment, the wildfire kept spreading like the tentacles of a greedy octopus. It consumed the southern side of the mountain where it had started, but the good news was that the blaze hadn't crowned any of the tall trees on Prospect Ridge. If the fire burned itself out before cresting the ridge, scattered mountain homes and Shannon's car on the northern side would be saved.

A hopeful murmur ran through the crowded school. "Maybe we'll be getting back into our homes soon, after all."

And maybe I can get someone to pull my car back onto the road, Shannon silently added, suddenly filled with hope that there might be a quick end to this nightmare. She was clinging to this optimistic possibility when her morning walk took her around the school, where she spied a tow truck in the parking lot. The painted sign on the side read Pete's Gas Station, and a husky, middle-aged man was busy hooking an old station wagon to a cable.

Shannon remembered Ward saying something about the possibility that a tow truck might be able to pull her car on the road. Hope sprang like a geyser as she hurried to the tow truck.

"Pardon me," she said to the man who was bent over the front of the station wagon. Either he didn't hear her, or he was concentrating too hard on fastening the tow chain to pay any attention to her.

She waited impatiently for a moment, then raised her voice. "Pardon me, I'm sorry to interrupt you, but I want to talk to you about towing my car."

He finished locking a cable before straightening up.

"Just point it out," he said as he looked around the parking lot. "Which one is it?"

"Oh, it's not here." She searched for an explanation that would best explain the situation, and at the back of her mind was a nagging concern about how much he would charge. "I'm afraid I had a little accident." She turned and pointed. "It's on the side of that mountain. About halfway down, I think. It got hung up on some rocks and—"

"Oh, you're the one." His mouth spread in a broad, tobacco-stained grin. "The city gal."

Shannon could feel heat surging to her face. Did everyone know about her mishap? The way the man was grinning made it plain she'd been the topic of some belly laughs. No doubt she had been the butt of a lot of jokes about California drivers.

"Yes, I'm the city gal," Shannon admitted, forcing a smile. Somehow, she knew this was not the time to demand service in a brisk, businesslike way. "Apparently you've heard about my little accident."

"Yep, Ward Dawson was in the station, talking to me about it." Peering at her from under his bushy eyebrows, he said, "He was saying that you must have had an angel riding with you, for sure."

"He already asked you to take care of it?" Shannon didn't know whether she was pleased or irritated. "He didn't say a word to me about it."

"Ward knows that Pete Shornberger is darn good at pulling cars back on the road," he bragged, chewing on a toothpick as he talked. "Ward's family and mine go way back. He's one fine fellow. We all missed the guy when he went off for a few years. We're mighty glad he's back—to stay." He gave her a brisk nod. "This is where he belongs."

Was there a warning in his tone? It was almost as if somebody had been trying to make something out of the time she and Ward had spent together. She bristled. Small-town gossip had already probably cast her in the role of a big-city man catcher. "He certainly has been helpful to everyone," Shannon said with a deliberate emphasis on the *everyone*.

"Ward's a good man. His mom and pa were good Christian folks. They'd be proud of the way Ward and his sister turned out." He said it in a tone that made her think he'd already heard she hadn't joined any of the prayer groups or lined up with any of the church folk.

"Well, I'm glad he has already talked to you about recovering the car as soon as possible," she said, side-stepping any personal observations about Ward.

"Yep, as soon as the road is open, we'll give it a try—if the car's still there." The way he said it, Shannon knew he fully expected the car to be at the bottom of the canyon by then.

"This morning's report on the fire looked good. Maybe they'd let you get at it sometime today," she said hopefully.

He took the toothpick out of his mouth and threw it away. Without commenting on her suggestion, he climbed into his truck and towed the station wagon out of the parking lot.

Dispirited, Shannon went into the building, and once again, Laura asked her to take the same group of children into the art room.

"Isn't there someone else?" she begged. Every time she passed the large bulletin board where the children had posted all the pictures she had drawn for them, she experienced a mixture of feelings. Her sketches were as good as those in the coloring books. In fact, some of them were better because they contained more detail, she admitted secretly. And her cartoon figures had a happy, whimsical air to them that surprised her.

"You have a God-given talent, Shannon. Why are you afraid to use it?"

"I'm not afraid," she protested. "It's just that I haven't had any reason to spend time that way—"

"Until now," Laura finished for her.

Shannon didn't know how she could argue that she didn't have time for such "doodling." There were no telephones ringing, no meetings to attend, no baskets of reports to fill out. All she had at the moment was time.

She gave Laura a surrendering smile. "All right, I'll go draw pictures."

As she sketched pictures for the children to color, a remembered joy in drawing came back, and she began to think about making some sketches for her own pleasure. She knew that Ward would be pleased if she made use of the drawing pad and pencils he'd given her.

Later she moved quietly around the gym, careful not to draw attention to herself as she sought to catch in pencil drawings the essence of some of the things around her. At first the pencils felt awkward in her hand, but she couldn't believe how soon the harmony of her eye and hand began to create a variety of shaded figures and simple backgrounds. Long-forgotten compliments from her school art teachers came back as she instinctively responded to the need for balance and perspective.

She sketched an old man sitting in a rocking chair, reading his Bible. As the drawing took shape, she couldn't help but wonder how many things he'd left behind to make room to bring that old chair.

In another corner of the school, a circle of older women was busily doing handwork as if they belonged to some impromptu sewing bee. She didn't try to do portraits but sought to catch the essence, expressions and body forms of the individuals she was sketching.

Her best effort was a young mother holding a sleeping baby while another child played at her feet, and she was startled when a young man approached her. As he glanced quickly at the sketch pad in her hand, she quickly closed it, instantly guarded. It was almost as if someone had caught her doodling—again.

"I don't mean to intrude," he said quickly. "I'm Kenny's father, Tom, and I want to thank you for rescuing his dog the way you did."

"Oh," she said, feeling foolish because she'd let his casual glance at the drawing pad make her feel defensive. Kenny had inherited the same thatch of blond hair and sun-freckled face as his father.

"It's nice to meet you," she said, holding out her hand. "You have a wonderful little boy."

"He thinks you're pretty special, too. He never gets tired of telling everyone how Miss Shannon saved Pokey." Tom Gordon hesitated. "I hope you won't think me too forward, but I saw you sketching my wife's grandfather. I wonder if you'd let me see it. I know you're a talented artist—"

Shannon's mouth fell open, and she couldn't hold back a laugh. "I'm not an artist. Far from it."

He shook his head. "Call it what you will, the kids are crazy about the pictures you draw for them to color."

"And that's about the height and breadth of my talent. I'm just amusing myself by making some simple line drawings. The sketch I made of your wife's grandfather is an impression of an old man sitting in a rocking chair, reading a Bible. It's not any kind of portrait.''

"May I see it?''

Even as a deep instinct to flatly refuse him flared, a warning was also there that she'd come off as some ridiculous temperamental adolescent if she refused. She didn't want the small community to have any more ammunition for their talk about the city woman.

"All right.'' She quickly flipped open the drawing pad. "See, it's just a sketch of no one in particular. It's not Kenny's grandfather or anyone else.''

"But it could be,'' he said thoughtfully. "It could be.''

The way he said it was like a healing balm to her spirit. None of her professional achievements had given her more satisfaction than she felt at the moment. She couldn't believe how much peace and joy flooded through her, and when he asked if he could have it, she readily removed the sketch from the drawing pad and gave it to him.

A whole day passed without any sign of Ward. Even though he had warned her that he would be working at the ranch, her eyes still kept roving around the crowded gym, hoping to see him.

In the early evening, she took several walks around the school, searching for a glimpse of his pickup. Maybe, just maybe, she would spy his reddish-brown hair and broad shoulders moving toward her with that winning grin of his, but night came and there was no sign of him.

Shannon was irritated with herself for indulging in

such adolescent behavior, and when Laura asked her if she'd seen Ward, she answered vaguely, "No, I don't believe I have."

"Well, I'm sure he'll be here tomorrow," Laura said with a knowing nod of her gray head.

"I wouldn't plan on it," Shannon answered, surprised at the crispness of her tone. She knew then that she was speaking as much to herself as to the reverend's wife.

"Oh? Why not?"

"He'll probably be working," Shannon said vaguely. "I think he said he had to catch up on chores at the ranch."

"But tomorrow's Sunday," Laura protested, as if she couldn't believe Shannon had forgotten. "He knows we're holding church service here, and I don't think chores are going to keep him from honoring the Lord's day. When his wife died and Ward brought his little daughter back home to raise, he decided to put God first in his life. I can't imagine anything or anyone strong enough to make him ignore the Sabbath."

Shannon fell silent because she didn't know what the proper response should be. Maybe it was her imagination, but she had the impression there seemed to be a subtle warning in Laura's words. Surely the woman didn't think it would be Shannon's fault if Ward didn't show up for Sunday services. Shannon silently fumed. Were people jumping to a lot of stupid conclusions about her pairing up with Ward just because they'd spent a little time together?

"You'll join us, of course," Laura said as if there wasn't any question about Shannon ignoring worship services.

The next morning, Shannon changed her mind a dozen times about whether or not she would go into the small auditorium with the others. As the time came for services to start, the gym emptied, and she was one of a few remaining behind. In spite of herself, she kept an eye on the front door, but there was no sign of Ward. Apparently the preacher's wife was wrong about his dedication to attending church services.

Disappointed, she finally wandered down the hall to the auditorium and sat in the back row where there were a few vacant seats. She didn't know the hymn they were singing, and there were no hymnals, but most of the gathering seemed to know the song. It was a rollicking song about a little church in the wildwood, which Shannon thought was a strange selection for this makeshift worship service in a school gym. She didn't understand the joyful lilt in their voices and the relaxed expressions on their faces. When a deep masculine voice joined in, she turned her head with a start.

"No place is so dear to my childhood," Ward sang as he slipped into a seat beside her and finished the lyrics to the song. Then he leaned over and whispered, "Thanks for saving me a place."

Her first impulse was to protest that she wasn't even thinking about him, but it didn't seem the right time or place to lie. A masculine, spicy scent from his morning shave teased her nostrils, and his crisply ironed shirt and newly creased pants had a fresh scent of their own. All her senses seemed to vibrate with the awareness of his presence. Sitting beside him, listening to his deep, resonant voice as he repeated prayers and sang with great feeling, she felt like an intruder and a fraud.

The worship service poured over Shannon, making only a ripple in her consciousness. She wasn't familiar with any of the scripture readings or the selections sung by the small choir. Reverend Cozzins's message left her unmoved. Surrounded by people who had lost their homes or were in danger of everything they had going up in smoke at any hour, it seemed utter folly for any of them to believe that "All things work to the good to those who love the Lord."

How could any good or blessing come out of this devastating situation? She didn't want to challenge what anyone believed, but as far as she was concerned, trying to justify everything as God's will was totally illogical.

She envied Ward's tranquillity, his worshipful, peaceful demeanor as he closed his eyes, bowed his head and let his large hands rest quietly on his lap. In spite of the physical and emotional demands that had been made upon him since the fire began, he never seemed to lose his easygoing, confident manner.

When the service was over, Laura Cozzins bustled up to them as they were leaving the auditorium. "I saw you sneaking in." She teased Ward with a broad smile.

"Sorry, I was late. It took me a little longer to get chores done this morning because Ted spent the night at his grandmother's place. He wants to be ready to evacuate her if the fire heads down that canyon."

"Oh, my goodness. Is Rachel's place in danger?"

Ward nodded. "He would like to move her now before there's an emergency, but she's a stubborn old gal and won't budge."

"Where are Beth and Tara?" Laura Cozzins frowned. "I was hoping to talk to your sister this morning. She's such a help organizing everything, and we've got plenty of challenges ahead of us."

"Beth insisted on my coming to church while she and Tara stayed and kept an eye on Calico—that's Tara's mare, and she's about to foal any time. It's going to be Tara's colt to raise, so she's really been taking care of the mare. I think my little daughter may have the makings of a veterinarian."

"She's a smart little thing. Have you met Tara?" Laura asked Shannon.

"No, she hasn't," Ward said quickly. "And I was just about to remedy that by inviting her out to the ranch for Sunday dinner." He gave Shannon that easy-going, engaging smile of his. "How about it? Would a nice ride up the valley and a homecooked meal appeal to you?"

The invitation totally surprised her. If she'd had time to think about it, she probably could have come up with some sensible reasons for refusing. "I would love to escape for a few hours," she surprised herself by saying, and added with a smile, "I think my social calendar is free."

Ward suspected that her acceptance of his invitation had more to do with getting away than an eagerness for his company, but he was still pleased. He liked having her sitting close beside him in the worn seat of his pickup truck, and he was eager to show off his beautiful horses.

The road they traveled was cupped on both sides by wooded mountain slopes and bordered by a rushing white foam creek. Ward drove with the ease of some-one who knew every bump in the road, and Shannon was glad that their direction was leading them away from the threatening fire and the gray haze that had been floating over Beaver Junction.

She kept her window rolled down to enjoy the clean, spicy pine smell. When the road suddenly broke through heavy stands of tall evergreens and a beautiful mountain valley came into view, she caught her breath.

"It's beautiful, isn't it?" Ward said when he saw the rapture on her face. "I never tire of this valley, summer or winter. It's God's own masterpiece."

A rambling, two-story white house stood in the mid-dle of a deep green meadow laced with log fences. A steep-roofed barn and a line of stables, shaded by a cluster of aspen trees, had been built a short distance behind the house.

"Here's home," he said with pride. As they passed under an arched sign, Dawson Ranch, Ward pointed out some beautiful spotted horses grazing in the vari-ous corrals. "Those are three-year-olds. Just about ready for sale."

The graceful horses slowly raised their heads at the sound of the truck. They were sleek and beautiful, and no two were alike in their various spotted patterns of deep mahogany, brown and black.

When Shannon saw the loving pride in Ward's eyes,

she realized that the proud smile on his face spoke of a man content with his life. She couldn't help but wonder what it would feel like to really have a home. She couldn't begin to remember all the rented apartments and leased houses that had been in her past. With every promotion, she'd been moving up the housing scale and had really overextended herself when she bought her last luxurious apartment. Even before six months had passed, she'd had her eye on an oceanside condo.

"I grew up in that house," he told her. "My parents moved in with my grandfather as soon as they were married, and my sister and I were raised here. Beth stayed here after our parents passed away. I went off to college and got married. As a single father, I decided to come back here to raise my little girl and follow my dream of breeding and training saddle horses." He smiled at her. "And the rest is history, so they say."

He drove the pickup to the back of the house and parked at the side of a small vegetable garden. Even before he stepped out of the car, the back screen door flew open, and a small girl with pigtails flying came running out.

"What is it, Tara?" Ward hurriedly got out of the truck. "Is Calico—"

"Nope." She shook her head. "She's not doing anything. Just standing and eating. I keep telling her to hurry up, 'cause I want to see my colt." Her dark-brown eyes flew to Shannon, who was still sitting in the front seat. "Who's she?"

"A friend."

"Is she going to help Calico drop her colt?"

Shannon saw an amused quirking at the corner of his mouth. "No, I think Calico is going to have to do that on her own."

As Shannon stepped out of the car, Tara looked at her curiously, taking in her pale-pink slacks suit, floral scarf and laced white sandals. "Where'd she come from?"

"California," Ward answered, a knowing grin on his face as he watched his daughter's expression change from curiosity to excitement.

"California. She's from Hollywood? Golly, gee, I never thought I'd meet anyone from Disneyland."

Ward laughed as he put an affectionate hand on Tara's brown head. "Say hello to Shannon. Maybe she can explain that California, Hollywood, Disneyland and Sea World are not all the same thing."

"Yes, they are," his little daughter said with a pugnacious lift of her freckled nose. "If we went there, we could see them all."

Shannon chuckled. "That's absolutely true. I think she's got you there, Ward." She winked at Tara. "We'll have to see if we can't educate your dad."

"Do you want to see my tree house?" Tara asked Shannon as if anxious to please.

"Not now, Tara," Ward said quickly. "We better check in with Beth. She'll have all our scalps if she has to wait dinner on us. Shannon will be here all afternoon, so there'll be time to show her around."

"Okay," Tara agreed happily.

Ward beamed proudly as his daughter led them with a kind of hopping skip to the house.

The large modern kitchen was filled with wonderful scents of baking. Shannon could see that dinner was ready. Roasted chicken, seasoned dressing, freshly picked peas and all the fixings for a salad.

"Beth, we're here," called Ward.

A muffled voice from the pantry answered, "In a minute."

"Aunt Beth said we couldn't eat in the kitchen. We have to eat in the dining room," Tara said solemnly as if this change was something worthy of notice. "And I'm supposed to mind my manners. I don't know why she's making such a fuss. We never eat in the dining room except Easter and Christmas."

Shannon realized that Ward had been so sure she would accept his invitation his sister had gone to a lot of extra trouble on her account. What if she had refused? She didn't like the position he had put her in by assuming she would come with him. Even under the circumstances, her independence was important to her.

A tall, rather large woman with reddish-brown hair darker than Ward's emerged from the pantry with a couple of jars of homemade jelly in her hands. Her smile was broad and friendly. She quickly put down the jelly, brushed her hands on her faded jeans and held out one to Shannon.

"Hi, I'm Beth. So glad you could come to dinner. Shannon, is it?"

"Yes, thank you for the invitation."

"Shannon's from Hollywood," Tara said, grinning widely.

"Or there about," Ward added with a chuckle.

Beth laughed. "Tara has her own sense of geography. And it doesn't do any good to straighten her out. In some ways she's like someone else I know," she said, sending her brother an affectionate glance. "How are you making out at the evacuation center, Shannon?"

"As well as everyone else, I guess. It's not easy on anyone. But we're all hopeful that they'll get the fire out any time now and we can all get back to our normal lives."

Shannon was grateful when Beth changed the subject and herded them into a high-ceilinged dining room paneled in warm cherry tones and filled with dappled light slanting through lace-draped windows.

When all the food was on the table, they bowed their heads, and Ward gave thanks for all their blessings in a simple prayer of gratitude. His easy, relaxed manner was in harmony with the feeling of the house, Shannon thought, as she found herself relaxing for the first time in days. She discovered that the appetite she thought she'd lost was back. Beth beamed when she asked for seconds.

Tara chatted about the vigil they were keeping on Calico. She seemed to know a lot more about horses than most adults. It was easy to see that Ward was proud of her, and Shannon suspected they spent a lot of time together, talking, sharing and having fun.

This kind of father-daughter relationship was foreign to Shannon. There had been very little companionship with her father. Grades and achievement had been the icons of his approval, and he'd been too busy to pay much attention to her as a child or successful career woman. The sad truth was that she had missed him very little when he died.

"Can we take Shannon for a horseback ride this afternoon?" Tara asked after dinner was over and Beth was serving a deep-dish strawberry and rhubarb pie for dessert.

"I guess we could arrange that," Ward answered, nodding.

"I think I'm much too full to go horseback riding," Shannon answered smoothly. Riding a horse was certainly not at the top of a list of things Shannon wanted to do now or ever. "Sorry, Tara. Maybe another time," she lied.

There was a teasing glint in Ward's eyes, as if he was about to test her earlier pronouncement.

"Maybe Shannon would just like to take a stroll around the place. Get a closer look at some of our prized saddle horses."

Shannon wished she could mount any horse he picked, sit gracefully in the saddle like a true horsewoman and gallop along beside him, but such a fantasy belied the truth. She wasn't even sure which side of a horse was the proper one to mount.

"Would you like to go see Calico?" the little girl asked eagerly, ready to take over the guide duties from her father.

"Maybe a little later," Ward said smoothly.

"Why not right now?" Tara argued. "You said we could show her around after dinner."

"Tara," Beth intervened. "I think you'd better think about helping me in the kitchen while your dad and Shannon have a little time to themselves."

The way Beth said it made Shannon uncomfortable. It was as if his sister were suggesting there was something romantic going on between her and Ward. Shannon suddenly wished she hadn't come at all. What sense did it make to slip into an intimacy with this inviting man that had no future for either of them?

She'd never been one to run away, but she stiffened as Ward put a gentle hand on her arm and guided her out of the house.

"Let's take a walk. I want to show you a private place of mine."

The way his eyes smiled at her created an intimacy between them that frightened her. As they walked through a green cathedral of tall, majestic trees toward the sound of rushing water, she was aware of an instinctive warning not to let her feelings be swept away into deep waters for this man, but in her heart, she suspected that it might already be too late.

Chapter Five

Ward measured the steps of his long legs as they headed down a narrow well-worn path away from the house through a wooded area cupping the green meadow. It had been a long time since he'd been out on a Sunday walk with a woman companion. Several times, his sister had invited single ladies from the church to come for Sunday dinner, but he'd finally put his foot down about her matchmaking. He knew she liked Judy and approved of her brother dating someone from the church. She'd obviously been surprised, and maybe a little disappointed, that he hadn't followed up on the opportunities the pretty brunette had given him to deepen their friendship.

"I'll get myself a girl when you find yourself a fellow," he had facetiously bargained with her. Although he enjoyed feminine company, his life was so full with the ranch, his daughter and the church that he hadn't gone out of his way for that kind of companionship—until now.

When he told Beth he was bringing a woman home after church service, she had raised an eyebrow but held her curiosity in check. He knew his sister was very perceptive about people, and he was glad she had been her usual friendly self during dinner. Ward suspected she'd seen beneath Shannon's polished exterior to the lonely soul that lay beneath, and he was delighted Tara had taken to Shannon with such enthusiasm.

He smiled at Shannon as they walked. "My family likes you."

"I'm glad," she said simply and truthfully. It was nice to have instant acceptance without straining to do and say the right thing. Most of the time she felt she had to play the role of successful modern woman in the company of others, and it was a rare experience to let down those social barriers.

"You haven't said much about yourself," he said as he studied her face. He couldn't help but notice how totally beautiful she was when she was relaxed. He wished her mouth and eyes would always hold the softness he saw in them at that moment, but even as he watched, his words brought a change in her expression. The muscles in her lovely high cheeks tightened. Guarded. Almost defensive. He'd noticed that reaction before when he'd invited information about herself.

"There's not much to say. My parents are dead. I've been successful in my career, and I value my independence above everything else." She didn't add that the one serious relationship she'd had a few years ago had ended badly and that she had determined then not to make that kind of mistake again.

It was obvious she'd been hurt and didn't trust people.

He replied thoughtfully, "Sometimes when we strive too hard to be independent what we are really doing is avoiding an enriching involvement with people, society and life in general."

"Dependence is weakness," she countered strongly. "I hate it."

"Dependency can be a very nice thing," he argued just as firmly. "None of us are totally sufficient unto ourselves. We need each other and God in our lives."

She set her chin firmly. "If you depend upon yourself, you're never disappointed."

He smiled wanly. "I'm afraid I've disappointed myself a good many times trying to satisfy my own ego."

"A healthy ego can be a good thing," she countered.

Not if ego stands for edging God out, he thought, but didn't pursue the subject. She was like a skittish colt when it came to spiritual beliefs, and he sighed, knowing it would take time and patience to lead her to the Lord. And time with her was something he couldn't count on. She could be out of his life as quickly as she'd entered it. If only— Then he stopped himself from trying to force something that wasn't meant to be. *Thy will, not mine, be done.*

They made their way through thick stands of quivering aspen trees and wild shrubs until they reached a slow-moving mountain stream. The water was clear, and shallow enough for them to see the bottom as it rippled over glistening rocks and made lazy eddies along the bank.

Playfully, Ward took Shannon's hand and pulled her toward the water. "Come on. Let's cross over to the other side."

Her gaze scanned the stream in both directions. "Where's the bridge?"

"Right there." He pointed toward the stream. "We'll hop across on those."

"What?" She stared at glistening wet rocks barely rising above the water. "You have to be kidding."

"Nope." Without waiting for her consent, he knelt in front of her. "You'll have to take those off," he said as he unbuckled her sandals. "The soles on your shoes might cause you to fall."

"Are you sure about this?" She could visualize herself trying to hop across the stream on those rocks and falling facedown in the rushing water. "Is this some kind of initiation?"

"Kinda." He grinned.

"What about your shoes?" she protested as she scrunched her bare toes in the damp ground.

"They've got rubber soles. Come on." He took her hand and led her down the edge of the stream. "Just hop quickly from one rock to the other."

"What if I slip?"

"Oh, you don't want to do that."

"But what if I do?"

"The water will be deliciously cold." He grinned. "Don't worry, I'll keep hold of you." With that, he put his hands on her waist and urged her to step out in front of him on the first stone.

She squealed as the icy water hit her bare feet.

"Go! Go!" he urged.

Lifting her feet high, she stepped quickly from one stone to the next. She almost made it all the way across without mishap, but the very last stone was slippery with moss, and one foot spun out from under her. She would have fallen fanny first into the water if Ward hadn't quickly lifted her up on the bank.

They both laughed as they threw themselves down on some warm sandstone rocks, and she tucked her feet under her to get warm.

She felt strangely exhilarated, almost a stranger to herself.

Sitting beside her, Ward wondered at himself for daring to bring her here to his special place. But the luminous glow on her face and the sparkle in her eyes reassured him that he'd made the right decision.

He often came to this spot to sit quietly on these rocks and mediate while his soul drew in the beauty of God's creations. As sunlight bathed quivering aspen leaves with gold, he watched spears of light dance through branches of tall ponderosa pines and white-trunked aspen. To him, the muted sound of flowing water was like a heavenly chorus that always filled his ears with song. Fragile wild blue flowers grew along the bank and among the scattered stones. Impulsively, he reached over, picked one and slipped it behind one of Shannon's ears.

"A pretty flower for a pretty lady."

She laughed, and for a moment, as she sat there with the blossom in her hair, he glimpsed the vivacious young girl she must have been before the world had

had its way with her. His chest suddenly tightened because he knew there was no way he could hold on to this fleeting moment, but he drew in a thankful breath that he had met her, however briefly, and prayed that someday she might realize she was God's precious child.

With her eyes soft and smiling at him, she touched the blue flower. "What kind is it?"

"It's a forget-me-not."

She didn't know whether he was teasing or telling her the truth, but she wasn't going to go there. It didn't matter.

She drew in a deep breath and leaned back on her arms. "This is nice."

"Was it worth the cold footbath?"

"Absolutely."

Her genuine pleasure shone in the graceful posture of her body and the lift of her head as she let her eyes take in the flight of a blue jay returning to his nest in the needled crown of a blue spruce tree. Maybe she would remember this moment when she got back to the demanding city, he thought, and it would strengthen her to face whatever challenges lay ahead. Even though she was in denial that she needed any-one's help—even the Lord's—he intended to keep praying for her, anyway.

Feeling closer to him than she had to anyone for as long as she could remember, Shannon asked about his childhood and was pleased when he willingly talked about his time away from the ranch.

"I couldn't wait to get away from home. I didn't want to have anything to do with my father's plan to turn the ranch to the breeding and raising of Appaloosa horses. I left him and Beth to manage everything while I attended a small agricultural college in northern Colorado.''

He didn't tell her that he'd drifted away from the teachings of his Christian family, that his life at college was a living example of the prodigal son's parable. While in college he married without any spiritual foundation for the union.

''My parents died while I was in college, and when my wife, Valerie, suddenly passed away from cancer, I brought our daughter back to the ranch to raise.'' He took a deep breath. ''I got my life back on track, thank the Lord. Tara loves it here, and Beth is wonderful with her.''

''She's a lovely little girl and seems to take to people easily.''

''Not all people.'' Ward said with a grin. ''Just those from Hollywood, Disneyland and Sea World. She's really got a thing about California.''

''Then you'll have to bring her out for a visit.''

''Yes, maybe I will,'' he agreed, even though he knew that would never happen. It wasn't likely Shannon Hensley would have time for entertaining a chance acquaintance of a few days when she resumed her normal busy life. ''Well, we'd better head back.''

She nodded. ''I'm sorry you have to make another trip to the school and back.''

''No problem. I need to take in some produce that Beth has collected from the other ranchers. The Red Cross needs all the donations they can get.''

He held out a hand and helped her to her feet. "Are you ready for another footbath?"

She grimaced, looking down. "I think they're still blue."

"Then we'd better do it this way." Before she could react, he'd swung her up in his arms. "I'll carry you across?"

"Can you...can you keep your footing?" she stammered.

"I guess we'll find out," he said as he carefully navigated his way into the water and stepped onto the first stone.

The thought of being dumped into the ice-cold rushing stream was enough to make Shannon close her eyes and rest her head against his chest as he gingerly stepped from one rock to the next. Once he wavered slightly, and she tightened her grip on his neck. The steady rising and falling of his breath was reassuring, and she let herself relax against him.

When he set her down safely on the other side, he laughingly tipped her chin up. "See, sometimes trust and dependence are good things."

As his eyes locked with hers, she was startled by an unfamiliar willingness to agree. "That depends on who's doing the depending on whom."

Impulsively, she raised up on bare feet and kissed his cheek.

He laughed. "Well, that's one way to have the last word."

He kept his arm lightly around her waist as they walked to the house.

Shannon was surprised when both Beth and Ward

invited her to take advantage of their spare room and remain at the ranch instead of returning to the evacuation center.

"Thank you, but I really have to be on the spot when the Chimney Ridge road opens to make sure that Pete's Towing Service goes after my car. I want to be ready to leave as soon as they allow traffic on the main highway."

"That may not be for a few more days," Beth warned her. Shannon noticed Ward had remained silent, and her chest tightened as she realized she might never see him or his family again. At the thought, something close to panic swept through her as she realized she might be falling for this churchgoing, straitlaced rancher. No, that wasn't going to happen. She was no dewy-eyed female who was going to let her emotions become tangled in an impossible relationship. She had enjoyed a pleasant afternoon, and that was that.

As Ward drove her to Beaver Junction, he didn't comment on her refusal to stay at the ranch. It was probably for the best all the way around. Logic told him it was better to keep some distance between them. Putting their basic differences and beliefs aside for a few hours was one thing, but pursuing any kind of a continuing relationship was out of the question. Their approaches to life were at opposite ends of the spectrum.

The easy companionship that had been with them during the afternoon dissipated as soon as they entered the overcrowded school. Once again, Shannon was caught up in the tension of worried adults, fretful children and overworked volunteers. Everyone was showing the strain of the endless waiting and uncertain outcome of a dragon fire that refused to die.

The update was not good. Higher temperatures and low humidity caused the burning acres to expand. A call had gone out for more firefighters. The number of air tankers dropping flame-retardant "slurry" and runs made by helicopters releasing big buckets of water had been increased. Some paratroopers had been dropped in remote areas to begin a backburn so the encroaching fire would run out of fuel when it met the blackened area.

Shannon didn't understand any of the tactics of forest firefighting and was filled with an anger that had its basis in fear. "Can't they do something more? How long is this going to go on?"

Ward's calm assurance when he told her to keep the faith landed on deaf ears and made her realize how worlds apart they were. She wanted to do something, take some action, not depend upon some fickle fate to solve her problems.

Ward saw the fear in her eyes and the stubborn set of her mouth. The tender, laughing young woman who sat beside the creek with him was gone. He wanted to take her in his arms and soothe away her fears, but he knew that she would reject any such action.

As she watched him walk away and disappear into the cafeteria with the donated produce, she almost ran after him. The impulse to ask him to take her to the ranch threatened her common sense, and she stiffened against the temptation. No use going down that road, she told herself.

"Miss Hensley."

She turned and saw Kenny's father with some papers in his hand. Grinning broadly, he held one out to her.

"What is it?" she asked, puzzled. Usually daily printed bulletins were left on a table for people to pick up.

"It's a little newspaper. They let me use the school computer, scanner and printer. I wrote up some stories and news items about some of the people here—and look! Here's the drawing you made. I gave you credit and everything."

It took her by surprise. At first, she stared at the sketch she'd made of the old man in the rocking chair, not knowing whether to be angry, flattered or indifferent.

"You're not mad or anything, are you?"

She was surprised when she found a feeble smile tugging at her lips. "No. It's just unexpected."

"I'm going to put out a second one tomorrow. May I use another one of your sketches? It really adds a lot."

In any other circumstances, she would have instantly refused, but she said uncertainly, "I guess so."

This kind of public exposure to her doodling was both satisfying and a little embarrassing, but if it would help anyone endure this trying situation, she didn't see how she could refuse. She offered him the sketches she'd made of the sewing ladies and the mother with her child.

"These are great," he said with enthusiasm. "Maybe I could do a story on you to go along with the drawings."

"No." She shook her head. "And you don't have to mention my name at all. There's nothing about me that would be of interest to anyone."

"I wouldn't be so sure about that. Everyone knows that it was Pokey who made you lose control of your car. We're all glad that a certain eligible rancher has taken you under his wing."

Shannon instantly stiffened. The word *eligible* put a slant on his remark that made her uncomfortable. Did everyone think she was interested in Ward Dawson in that way? She certainly wasn't—was she?

Ward was asking himself the same kind of question when Laura Cozzins thanked him for the large box of donated goods and said, "Bless you. Tell Beth we'll make good use of everything." Then she gave him a knowing smile. "I know you took Shannon to the ranch to spend the day. Did you have a good time?"

"Yes and no," he said honestly, not knowing exactly how he felt about the afternoon. Sunday dinner was pleasant enough, and he was pleased with the way both Tara and Beth had related to Shannon. What troubled him was how suddenly the intimacy he'd experienced sitting with Shannon had dissipated. She seemed almost impatient to return to the school, as if she couldn't wait to put some distance between them.

"I guess Miss Shannon Hensley found ranch life a little boring," he told Laura with a wry smile. "Or maybe just a few hours with me was enough. She turned down Beth's offer of our spare bedroom, as if being around me and my family was less inviting than returning to the crowded gym.''

"Sounds as if your pride is smarting just a wee bit.''

"I suppose it could be that,'' he admitted. He wasn't about to tell her how close he'd come to taking the city gal in his arms and kissing her. Even now, the memory of her soft smile and the flower in her hair sent a warmth through him.

"I guess I picked up some wrong signals.''

"Could be you just need to give her a little more time to get to know you better.''

"I don't think that sticking around Beaver Junction is in her itinerary,'' Ward said honestly. "I'd have to hog-tie her to keep her one minute longer once the roads are open.''

"Maybe not,'' Laura said with genuine optimism. "But in any case, we'll pray for God's blessing upon her, and know that His plan is the best one, after all.'' She eyed him frankly. "You do believe that He has a plan for each of us, don't you?''

"Yes, I do,'' he answered readily. "But sometimes I wonder why the dear Lord has to take us around the bend in the road before He shows us where we're going.''

She laughed and patted his shoulder. "Just fasten your seat belt and let Him do the driving.''

Ward didn't see Shannon as he made his way out of the school, and he decided it was probably best to leave things the way they were. By the time he got back to the ranch, Ted was in the kitchen having a late dinner. The young man looked tired and worried and shook his head when Ward asked how things were at his grandmother's place.

"Not good. Smoke and ashes are heavy in the air even though the fire is not directly threatening her place—yet. Grams has trouble breathing. I tried to get her to evacuate, but she's a stubborn old gal. Ever since my grandpa died, she'd held the place together with pure grit and nothing else."

"Is there anything I can do?"

"Not at the moment. We'll just have to wait and see." Ted eyed Ward as he sat down at the table. "Beth said you had that pretty California gal out for dinner."

Ward nodded.

"And?" Ted prodded.

"And what?"

"Come on, guy. Give. Did you two hit it off, or what?"

Ward pretended innocence as he answered, "I don't know what you mean."

"Did you like her? Does she like you?" Ted demanded impatiently.

"The answer to both your questions is I don't know. Besides, it doesn't matter. She'll be first in line when they open the Elkhorn road to traffic."

"Not in that fancy sports car, she won't," Ted said flatly. Then seeing Ward's expression, he asked, "Didn't you know? I was talking to a fellow in Beaver Junction a little while ago. He said her car slipped off that rock ledge this afternoon. Nothing left but a pile of twisted metal at the bottom of the canyon."

Ward's heart tightened as a deep compassion for the

vulnerable young woman with the soft blue-gray eyes flooded through him. He could see her ashen face when she heard the news. He wished he could have been the one to tell her. She needed someone to hold her close and tell her it was going to be all right.

Chapter Six

Shannon was in the cafeteria, helping to clear off some of the tables after the breakfast rush, when Ward came in the next morning. As he walked toward her, she thought he was looking at her strangely, as if searching her face for some hint as to what she was thinking. Something about his purposeful manner made her stiffen. The curve of his lips was at odds with the serious, questioning glint in his eyes.

"Good morning." He greeted her in a pleasant enough tone, but she caught the hint of a question in it. She wasn't fooled. He had something on his mind.

"You're here bright and early."

"I finished my chores early and thought we might take a little walk before the day's rush begins."

"A walk?"

"And a little talk," he admitted, a shadow flickering in his dark-brown eyes. He knew from her manner that she hadn't heard the bad news.

Her mouth was suddenly dry. "All right."

As they walked across the school grounds, Ward tried to keep the conversation light. The morning sun was a bright apricot, promising another hot day with no rain in sight. They could hear the protesting barks of pet dogs confined to kennels, and the playground was already filled with children expending their energies on swings and slides.

He pointed out a small football stadium. "The fighting Beavers have played many a tough game on that field."

Shannon only half-listened to his story about the time the Beavers almost won a trophy but lost the game in the last two seconds of play. She was perceptive enough to know that he was stalling. Finally, she faced him squarely and demanded, "What is it, Ward?"

"I have some bad news." He knew there was no way to soften the truth so he took her hand and said, "I'm truly sorry, Shannon. Your car broke free of the rock ledge sometime yesterday afternoon. It crashed and burned at the bottom of the ravine."

"It's…it's gone? Everything's gone?"

"I'm afraid so."

Even though she had tried to prepare herself for such a happening, every fiber of her being fought against an overpowering feeling of helplessness. Now if the roads opened in the next hour, she wouldn't have any transportation out of Beaver Junction or to any other place she might decide to go.

"The great blessing is that you weren't in it," he reminded her. "You could have been, you know."

She nodded and took a deep breath. Maintaining self-control was an ingrained habit from the time she was a little girl. When faced with the frightening news that they were moving again, leaving behind the few friends and a familiar place, she had learned to hide her hurts and fears. She was used to hiding behind the pretense that she could handle anything that came along. "Well, I guess that's that. I'd better find a telephone and see what I can do to solve the problem."

"What can I do to help?"

"Nothing, I'm afraid," she said as she withdrew her hand from his. Keeping her feelings hidden was important in the business world, and though she was in no position to finance another car, she wasn't about to let him know it. "I'd better walk down to the pay phone and make some calls. I'll have to call the insurance company and the bank. I suppose I can find a used car for sale that will get me back to Los Angeles."

"Maybe not in Beaver Junction, but Elkhorn has all kinds of car sale lots."

Ward had expected to see some tears and a need for reassurance when she heard the bad news, but obviously she didn't need his strong shoulder to cry on. He felt a little foolish when he realized that replacing the expensive sports car wasn't going to be a problem for her, and she could hitch a ride into Elkhorn when the road opened and buy another one. He felt foolish for having entertained the idea that she might need him in this situation. He should have remembered that one of the first things she ever said to him was, "I can handle things nicely by myself."

She was silent on the walk down the hill to Main Street, and he decided he'd stick around and make sure she got things settled to her satisfaction. "I'll have a cup of coffee at the diner while you make your calls."

"All right. I shouldn't be long," she said with a confidence that belied the trembling of her hand as she took a small address book out of her purse.

He nodded and disappeared inside the diner.

As she called her bank, she wished she hadn't lived so close to the limits of her paycheck every month. Rent for her leased apartment was only enough to cover her mortgage payment. She had arranged for the rent to be deposited in her account and a draft drawn for the mortgage company. No telling how long it would be before the insurance company settled a claim on her accident. It certainly wouldn't be in the next day or two. They'd have to investigate the accident and make out reports. She was worried that the bank might not be inclined to make a loan to an unemployed woman. Still, she had no choice.

Her call went quickly through on her telephone charge card, and in a few short minutes she was given information on her account. In horror, she learned that the rent on her apartment had not been banked, and since she had arranged for the mortgage company to draw the amount due directly from her account, she was dangerously close to being overdrawn. She barely had money enough in her savings to cover her bills.

She hung up the phone, leaned against the booth and fought a rising nausea. Talking to a loan officer about financing another car in her present financial straits was out of the question. *Broke. Jobless. Trapped.*

She covered her face with her hands, and tears that she had been holding back suddenly began to flow. Like the sudden bursting of a dam, torrents of tears poured down her face, and her shoulders heaved with sobs. The last few days had depleted her physical and emotional reserves.

Ward had been sitting by a front window where he'd been watching her make the call. Judy had brought him a cup of coffee and done her best to engage him in some conversation about the fire, but he only made the expected superficial answers.

Judy followed his gaze out the window, and when she saw Shannon in the phone booth, she said rather peevishly, "I guess you've got something else on your mind. Everyone at the church is talking about it, you know."

"Really? I thought the Bible had something to say about gossiping being the tool of the devil? And I think it also says that we are to help those in need."

"Well, it seems to be a little more than just Christian charity the way you've been looking after Shannon Hensley," Judy snapped and flounced to the kitchen.

Ward glanced out the window again, and saw Shannon still standing in the glass booth, but her shoulders were shaking as she covered her face with her hand. He jerked to his feet, ran out the door and covered the ground with long strides.

He knocked on the glass. "Shannon? What's wrong?"

She lifted her tear-streaked face, opened the booth's door and went into his arms without hesitation. He was taken aback by the way she clung to him. He didn't know what had happened to shatter her protective veneer, but she was like a frightened child, desperately needing love and reassurance.

Her fears poured out like a gusher as she related the details of her phone conversation.

His hands soothed her trembling shoulders, and he bent his head close to hers. "Hey, it's going to be all right. It's going to be all right."

"I don't know what to do." Shannon couldn't believe all this was happening to her. Even when she'd lost her important executive position, she'd refused to accept defeat. All that prideful confidence in herself had been slowly eroding, and her life suddenly seemed out of control. "I just don't know what to do," she repeated in a trembling voice.

"You need time to think things out. You're going home with me." The minute the words were out, Ward knew they were the right ones. In his morning prayers, he always asked for divine guidance for the day, and at that moment, he believed that the Lord was leading him in the way that he should go. He wiped the tears from her wet cheeks. "The ranch is a great place to touch base with yourself." *And God,* he silently added.

Tara was ecstatic when Ward returned to the ranch with Shannon later in the day. The little girl clapped her hands and gave Shannon a big hug. "I prayed to

God that you'd come back," she said. "And here you are!"

Ward suppressed a chuckle. Leave it to his daughter to parade her faith in front of anyone.

"We're happy to have you." Beth smiled at Ward in a knowing way, as if she wasn't surprised to learn that Shannon Hensley wasn't going to disappear from their lives as suddenly as she had appeared. "You're welcome to stay as long as you like."

"I shouldn't have to impose on you for very long," Shannon said quickly, having recovered her usual stubborn willfulness to shape her life the way she wanted it, regardless of the circumstances. "Just a few days."

"Let me show you our spare room. Don't feel that you have to carry out any guest obligations. Join the family when you want to, or just be by yourself. Feel free to enjoy the peace and quiet any way you like. I imagine you could use some of that about now."

Shannon sent Ward a grateful look. Embarrassed by the way she had fallen apart, she didn't know what to say to this sudden outreaching of his family. She'd never been dependent on someone else's generosity before, and their open loving kindness was foreign to her.

"While you settle in, Shannon, I'll head out to the stables. We're still maintaining a vigil on Calico," Ward said.

"Why is she taking so long?" Tara asked in a complaining voice. "I'm getting tired of waiting."

Ward playfully pulled on one of her pigtails. "Not as tired as Calico, I'll bet. You'll have to learn that you can't hurry Mother Nature. When the baby colt is ready, he'll make his appearance.''

"It's not going to be a he," Tara announced with all the conviction of a stubborn child. "It's going to be a she. And her name is going to be Princess."

Ward laughed. "Well, I'd better go check and see if Princess is about to make an appearance. I'll leave you in good hands, Shannon. See you at lunch."

For an absurd moment, she almost asked to go with him. Somehow he had become an anchor in a world that had turned upside down, and there was something about him that reached out to her on levels she didn't understand. Her lost feeling must have shown on her face, because Beth quickly moved to her side.

"It'll be nice to have another woman in the house," she said, smiling. "Come on, I'll show you the upstairs." She eyed Shannon's small overnight bag. "Here, let me carry that for you. Is this everything you brought?"

Shannon swallowed hard and nodded. Replacing everything she'd lost was going to be another draining expense she could ill afford. "Everything else was in the car."

"That's too bad, but things can always be replaced. Ward said when he first saw the car, he wasn't sure he could get you out in time. It was amazing the way it got hung up on those rocks, wasn't it?"

"Yes, I guess I was pretty lucky."

"Maybe it was more than luck," Beth countered.

As they climbed the stairs, Tara grabbed Shannon's hand. "You can borrow any of my stuff," she offered with childish generosity.

"Thank you, Tara. That's very nice of you."

"I'm glad you're going to be next to my room. We can talk at night." Tara said it with such satisfaction that Shannon suspected the little girl probably put up a nightly fuss about going to bed and turning out the light.

"The guest bedroom is at the back of the house," Beth said when they reached the upper hall. "It has a nice large window overlooking the meadow. I know you'll enjoy the view. Watching the young colts scampering beside their mothers is always a joy and a lift to the spirits." She eyed Shannon. "It's different than the city, but in some ways just as exciting."

"I can teach you how to ride a horse," Tara said.

"I don't think there'll be that much time—"

"My dad taught me in only a couple of days," Tara insisted. "Besides, I don't see why you can't stay a long, long time."

"Tara, that's enough," Beth said firmly. "Don't pester. We're just happy Shannon came back to pay us a visit, aren't we?"

Tara nodded, but there was a determined frown on her little forehead that hinted she had more to say on the subject. She pointed out her bedroom as they passed down the hall. It was furnished with pretty maple furniture and decorated with childish clutter. "If you get scared in the night, you can come crawl in bed with me."

"Now, Tara, don't be thinking you can do likewise," Beth warned her, giving Shannon a knowing smile.

She led the way into a small bedroom that was furnished with a single bed and a matching oak chest and dresser. A blue, yellow and pink floral bedspread harmonized with simple cotton curtains hanging at the window. One chair with soft cushions was placed beside a small table that held a reading lamp and a Bible.

"The bathroom is at the end of the hall. I'll put out an extra towel for you."

At any other time in her life, Shannon would have been critical of the hard bed, small quarters and the inconvenience of not having a private bathroom, but compared to the evacuation center, these accommodations were a luxury.

"Do you want to see all the stuff in my room now?" Tara asked eagerly. "And then I'll take you out to the barn and—"

Beth quickly interrupted her with a reminder that morning chores were still waiting, and she suggested that it might be better to save the tour until after lunch.

"You run along, Tara, and collect the eggs in the chicken coop. Maybe we'll bake some cookies later."

"My favorite kind?" Tara coaxed. "I bet Shannon likes peanut butter the best, too."

"Absolutely," Shannon responded, and Tara's eyes glowed.

Beth laughed and scooted Tara out the door. Then she turned to Shannon. "Feel free to rest, join us in the kitchen or just wander around. Ward and Ted will show up at noon and be as hungry as bears. I'd better see to getting some grub ready to put on the table."

Shannon knew she should offer to help, but she couldn't make herself do it. "I think I'll rest."

"Good idea." Beth paused, as if searching for the

right thing to say. "It's been a long time since I've seen my brother with a swing in his step." She eyed Shannon. "I hope I'm not talking out of turn, but I can't help but feel protective."

Protective? Did Beth think Shannon had designs on her brother? Was she warning her to keep hands off? Shannon silently bristled. Getting seriously involved with any man was certainly not on her list of things to do at the moment. True enough, she appreciated Ward's friendliness in this dark moment of her life, and she couldn't deny that she found him attractive, but she wasn't planning on making anything permanent out of his attention to her.

"What do you mean, protective?" Shannon asked pointedly.

"Well, I guess I'm concerned that he may get hurt again. He married impulsively while still in college, and the match wasn't a good one for him or Tara's mother. When he came back to the ranch after her death, he had to find himself again, and with the Lord's help, he has." She smiled at Shannon. "Nothing would please me more if he found the right soul mate for his life, but the Bible warns us not to 'yoke unevenly.' Do you understand what I'm saying?"

"Clearly. And you have nothing to worry about, I assure you. I have no intention of 'yoking,' as you put it, with your brother or anyone else. I like Ward and appreciate his kindness to me, but I'll be gone in a few days and put all this behind me."

Beth nodded. "I'm sorry if I spoke out of turn. This is such a stressful time for everyone that it's easy to say the wrong thing. All of us are glad to have you here. Please rest, and come downstairs whenever you want company.'' She smiled as she left the room and closed the door.

Shannon remained standing in the middle of the floor for a long minute, like a rudderless boat. As she slowly turned, she glimpsed her reflection in the dresser mirror and froze. She stared at the pale face, heavy-lidded eyes and listless hair, searching for some recognition. The woman was a stranger. Where was the successful, well-groomed Shannon Hensley? As she stared at her reflection, a flash of defiance rose within her.

No! She clenched her fists. This defeated, frightened image wasn't her. She'd weathered setbacks and disappointments before. Taking care of herself had been a part of her mind-set from the time she was in grade school and her parents left her for nearly a year at a strict boarding academy. She had looked after herself then, and she would look after herself now. She appreciated the generous help she was getting from Ward and his family, but she wasn't about to accept it any longer than necessary. Maybe her next call to the employment agency would be a positive one, and come hell or high water, she'd get back to California for that interview.

She walked to the window that looked out on the stables and corrals and saw Ward swing up into the saddle of a beautiful dark-brown and white Appaloosa. Something inside her warmed to the beauty of horse and man moving in graceful rhythm across the rich green meadow. Despite her resolve, it was a scene she would hold in her memory always. As she turned away from the window she knew this place, this home and this family would always create a sense of longing for something she had never experienced in her life, and if the pattern held true, she never would.

Chapter Seven

The sun was setting when Shannon awoke from a deep afternoon nap. Her first awareness was the tangy smell of something being barbecued floating up from the yard. As she sat on the edge of the bed, she was disoriented for a moment. Then she remembered where she was. Out of the goodness of his Christian heart, Ward had brought her to his home. She felt somewhat like a fraud, imposing upon him and his sister this way. Because it had always been important for her to pay her own way, she was uncomfortable when others did things for her, secretly feeling that she didn't deserve it.

Hearing muffled voices and laughter, she walked to the window, but she couldn't see anyone. She had missed lunch, and the sun was already disappearing behind high barren peaks. For a moment, she almost gave in to the impulse to crawl back in bed and ignore the tempting odor of cooking and the inviting laughter.

Then she heard Ward's deep laugh, and something inside her instantly responded. She wanted to go downstairs and be with him.

A glance in the mirror told her she wasn't fit company for anyone. After peering down the hall, she stepped out of her room and stealthily made her way to the bathroom. She couldn't believe how large it was, spacious enough to offer a separate shower and large, old-fashioned tub.

She opted for a bath and filled the tub almost to the top. Then she eased down into it and sank up to her neck in warm soapy water scented by a rose bubble bath she found in a large bottle placed by the tub. As she leaned back and closed her eyes, she let her whole body and mind rest in the pleasure of the moment. She had never felt such luxury or entertained this kind of deep appreciation for the simple act of taking a bath. With a new awareness she realized that the simple pleasures of life became invaluable when she was denied them.

As she dressed and plaited her hair in a French braid, she was glad she had packed a second pair of designer jeans and a summer pullover top in her overnight bag. Just thinking about the new clothes, still unpaid for, that were now charred cinders in a wrecked car destroyed her momentary sense of well-being. Even though she told herself everything could be replaced in time, the question of when and how long it might take was enough to dampen her spirits.

Quietly she went downstairs and followed the sound of voices to a wide brick patio stretched across the back of the house. Ward was sitting with Ted at a

picnic table, and he rose to his feet the minute he saw
her, giving her a broad welcoming smile.

"I was hoping you'd feel like joining us."

"I didn't intend to sleep the day away," she apologized. She didn't want him to think she was avoiding
contact with him or his family.

"No problem. I've put some chicken on the grill,
and Beth has baked potatoes and the makings of a
fresh salad from her garden. How does that sound?
She and Tara are busy preparing strawberries for dessert."

"Maybe I should go in the kitchen and help?"
Shannon offered uncertainly.

"Oh, no." Ward laughed and shook his head. "You
don't want to invade Beth's domain without invitation.
She's been known to hang up intruders by their
thumbs." He winked at her. "Better you sit down and
have a glass of lemonade."

Ted had also risen to his feet, looking a little uncomfortable in Shannon's presence. He shot a quick
look at Ward, then looked at her as if he wasn't sure
what to say or do. Shannon had the feeling they might
have been talking about her before she interrupted
them.

Ted mumbled self-consciously, "Nice to see you
again."

"Pour her a glass of lemonade, Ted, while I check
the chicken."

She said thank-you when the young man handed her
a glass, then she casually followed Ward to a large
brick grill at one end of the patio. Sounds of juice

popping in the fire mingled with the sizzle of chicken as he brushed the pieces with a rich barbecue sauce.

"I hope you're hungry," he said. "And rested."

She nodded, but Ward didn't believe her. The nap had done her good, but there were still faint shadows under her eyes and a tightness around her mouth. He had a strong urge to draw her close and assure her once again that everything was going to be all right.

A little earlier, Beth had suggested that having Shannon around for even a short time might not have been such a good idea, after all. "There's some kind of an undercurrent going on between you two."

He had made light of her remark, but he knew Shannon Hensley had challenged him from the first moment he laid eyes on her. There was something about her spunky bravado that appealed to him, and almost immediately he had recognized her tough exterior for the sham it was. Underneath that sophisticated, independent veneer, he glimpsed a child of God who had fought too many lonely battles. He was taken by her soft eyes, her vulnerable smile and the way she held her head up when she was afraid. Yes, there was no doubt about it. He was attracted to her in a way he hadn't been with other female acquaintances. Maybe this was some kind of test to see how dedicated he was to his determination not to marry anyone who didn't believe in the presence of God being as close as one's breath.

At that moment Tara bounded out the door. "You're here, Shannon," she cried. "Aunt Beth said you were probably still sleeping. You should see the strawberry shortcake we made. You can have as big a piece as you like. Even two! And—''

''Whoa, girl.'' Ward laughingly cut her off. ''I bet you're the one hankering for two pieces.''

''Well, maybe,'' she agreed with a sheepish smile. ''I even snuck a taste or two while we were putting on the whipped cream. Just to make sure it was okay for company. Only Shannon isn't company, is she? 'Cause she's staying here, just like family.''

Shannon's chest suddenly felt tight. The little girl's innocent exuberance made her feel more out of place than ever. Had she made some kind of terrible commitment coming here? She could tell from the deepening furrow in Ward's forehead that his daughter's remarks were disturbing him, too. She didn't know how to respond without seeming totally ungrateful for their hospitality.

Fortunately, Beth called both Tara and Ted to come and help bring out some dishes, so Shannon and Ward had a moment alone.

''You'll have to forgive Tara,'' Ward said quietly. ''Never thinks before she speaks. You should be glad she likes you. My daughter always lets everyone know exactly how she feels, and sometimes it can be darn right embarrassing. We've all turned beet red when she shows her lack of judgment about saying certain things even if they're true.''

''You mean she hasn't learned the art of lying?''

''There's a difference between lying and refraining from saying things that hurt someone else.''

Shannon thought for a moment. ''I think I'd rather know the truth and be hurt.''

"Sometimes it's difficult to know the truth," Ward replied honestly. If she was asking how he felt about her, he didn't have the answer. "I guess that's where trust and faith come in."

"I guess I've always had a short supply of both of those."

"That's all right." He touched her arm gently. "Maybe I've got enough for both of us," he surprised himself by saying, and was glad his sister wasn't around to hear the remark. At least, he hoped she hadn't heard, but when Beth came out of the house at that moment, she gave him a searching look.

"The chicken's ready," he told her, as if he thought that would answer the question in her eyes.

When the picnic table was loaded with food, they sat down and held hands while Ward said the blessing. As Shannon listened to him pray, she was struck by the familiar tone he used in talking about the Almighty. If she hadn't known better, she would have thought he was speaking to some close friend sitting at the table with them.

The meal was a pleasant one full of humor, with Ward and Ted exchanging friendly gibes and telling stories on each other. She learned something about the routine at the ranch and was surprised that Ward had more hired hands than Ted. At the moment, they were all helping with the fire, so the burden of the daily chores fell on Ward and Ted's shoulders. From the talk, Shannon could tell that Beth handled all the business end of the family's thriving sale of Appaloosas throughout the whole Rocky Mountain region.

Beth refused Shannon's offer to help with the

cleanup but accepted Ted's offer to carry in the dishes from the table.

"Well, then, Shannon, would you like to go with me and Tara to check on Calico?" Ward asked, delighted with the way Shannon was relaxed and smiling.

When she said yes, Tara grabbed Shannon's hand and skipped along at her side as they walked to the stables. The little girl chatted all the way, and Ward sent Shannon an amused smile that showed the deep affection he had for his outgoing, confident little daughter.

"Did you know a daddy horse is called a stallion? And a mama horse is called a mare. A little girl horse is a filly, and a little boy horse is a colt." She grinned at Shannon, obviously proud as punch to be showing off her knowledge of horses and riding. "Calico is going to have a filly."

"We don't know that," her father cautioned.

"I know it," she answered with the innocent wiseness of a child.

"We'll see," Ward said softly.

"Okay," Tara answered agreeably, "but I already told Calico I'm naming her little filly horse Princess. I think she likes it." The little girl bubbled happily.

"Well, who am I to argue with feminine logic?"

"What's logic?" Tara asked, looking at her father and Shannon with a puzzled expression on her freckled face.

Smiling, Shannon answered, "It's a way of looking at things that most men don't understand."

Ward held up his hands in mock surrender. "No

fair ganging up on me, ladies. I know when I'm licked.''

Laughing, he led the way into the stable where several horses were stalled. Most of them were standing quietly with their heads hanging over the half gate, but the sorrel mare in the largest end stall was moving about restlessly.

''What's the matter, old girl?'' Ward asked as he went into the stall and let his hand move over the pregnant mare's back. He hadn't said anything to Tara, but Calico was almost six weeks over the usual eleven-month gestation period, and he'd been praying that she would deliver without any complications. The mare had been eating very little bran mash, and he was worried that she might be losing weight. If they lost this foal, he knew his daughter would be devastated. Maybe he shouldn't have promised it to her, but the experience of raising her own horse was something he didn't want her to miss.

Tara hung on the gate, chatting away, telling Calico to hurry up and drop the baby. Shannon could tell from Ward's expression that he was concerned about the mare's condition, but he answered his daughter's questions in an upbeat fashion.

''She's getting ready to be a mother,'' he assured Tara, noticing some physical signs that she was getting ready for nursing. ''I'll keep an eye on her, but most mares will foal in the dead of the night without help from anyone,'' he told Shannon as he came out of the stall and locked the gate.

As they left the stable, he glanced at his watch. ''Time for you to start getting ready for bed, Tara.''

He ignored her groans. "Head back to the house, now, and tell Beth that I'm going to show Shannon around the rest of the place before we turn in."

Tara made a feeble protest, but apparently she knew when her father meant what he said. The little girl surprised Shannon by giving her a big hug. "I really like you...bunches."

"And I like you bunches." Shannon leaned down and impulsively kissed her cheek.

As Tara headed toward the house in a childish skip, Shannon wondered if she had ever been that free and spontaneous as a child.

"You've really made a hit with my daughter," Ward said as he took her arm. "It's amazing how perceptive children are, isn't it?"

"What do you mean?"

"She saw through to the real you right away."

"Oh, and what is the real me?" Shannon asked, a little testily.

"I'm not sure. But Tara seems to be. Anyway, I want to walk you out to the pasture. It's beautiful in the twilight when the moon is just rising. Besides, the exercise will help you relax and sleep better." He didn't add that this nightly ritual lent a spiritual benediction to the end of a busy and sometimes disappointing day.

They walked slowly down a footpath that edged one of the lodgepole fences. Several horses raised their heads as they passed, and Shannon thought they looked almost ethereal in the silver touch of moonlight.

Ward opened a gate and closed it after they had

walked through it. Leaving the house, stable and horses behind, they walked into rippling tall grass that held a hushed silence. The shadowy meadow stretched away to darkened peaks that rose in jagged silhouettes against the vaulting night sky.

Shannon said abruptly, "Let's go back."

Ward was startled by the urgency in her voice. Her face looked white and drawn in the moonlight. "What's the matter?"

She bit her lip, not knowing how to explain without sounding like a frightened child. Standing in the middle of an enormous mountain meadow with an endless canopy of a dark sky above was not a pleasant sensation for her. She felt small, insignificant and of little value in this vastness of earth and sky. The endless galaxies that stretched far beyond man's ability to comprehend made a mockery of the importance of one single human life. She tried to express this feeling to Ward.

"It's only a mockery if you don't believe that every breath you draw is important in the divine scheme of things," Ward responded. "One single soul is as important as any of the other wondrous things God has created. When you know that in your heart, Shannon, you'll never feel small and insignificant again."

She shook her head. "I can't believe that anything I do matters to anyone but myself. It would take a miracle for me to feel differently."

"Well, if the good Lord put the stars in heaven and set our little earth spinning in space, I guess He can handle something as challenging as keeping track of Shannon Hensley's precious soul."

"You really believe that, don't you?"

"Yes." He touched her cheek with a fingertip and eased back a strand of hair falling on her forehead. There was so much he wanted to say to her about God's love and the divine plan He had for everyone, but some inner voice cautioned him to move slowly.

Shannon braced herself for a lecture on religious doctrine, but Ward simply smiled at her. "Come on, I want to show you where I sit and commune with God and nature by myself."

Putting a firm arm around her waist, he guided her to a slight rise in the meadow where several trees had been felled. Their trunks were stripped of bark, and three of them had been laid together like a rustic floor.

"It's my outdoor house, without confining walls, windows and a roof to spoil the magnificent view." He sat down, motioned for her to join him and was surprised when she refused.

"This is your private place, and I think you ought to keep it that way." She couldn't share his beliefs, and by inviting her here, he wanted her to be something she wasn't.

He could tell from the set of her chin it was useless to argue, and any hope of making her feel more comfortable in the awesome expanse of sky and earth faded. "All right, I'll walk you back to the house, and then I'll go check on Calico."

They walked in silence as they made their way through the meadow toward the house. Ward was aware of the sharp tingle of smoke in the air and wondered if that meant the fire was moving closer. The canyons behind the ranch, like the one where Ted's mother lived, would be the first to be invaded if the fire wasn't stopped.

As they passed the stables, they heard a faint whinny. Ward stiffened, stopped and listened.

"Wait here," he told Shannon, as he turned and disappeared into the stable.

Shannon's first impulse was to ignore his order and follow him, but if it was Calico delivering her foal, she wasn't sure she was up to viewing the process. Watching television medical dramas was as close as she'd ever come to viewing a birthing.

She sat on a bale of hay outside the barn, waiting for him. As the minutes passed and Ward didn't come out, her chest began to tighten. Was something wrong? She knew how much Tara wanted this colt. The little girl would be devastated if something went wrong.

More and more time went by. He'd been gone a long time. Shannon debated whether she should keep on waiting, go inside the stable or return to the house and tell someone what the situation was.

But what was the situation?

Maybe Ward wasn't tending to Calico at all. Something else could be demanding his attention. She'd feel like a fool if she got everyone excited about the mare when Ward's hasty disappearance might be due to a different problem altogether.

Finally, impatient with herself for being so indecisive, she rose to her feet, firmed her steps and made her way into the dimly lighted stable. The noise of restless horses in the stalls echoed loudly in her ears as she cautiously walked past them. She stopped before she reached the brightest light at the end stall, Calico's.

There was no doubt about it. It was Calico's whinny that had brought Ward racing into the stable. Shannon debated whether she should retrace her steps or see for herself what was happening.

"Ward?" she finally called cautiously.

There was a long silence before he answered, "Yes. It's all right, Shannon. Come here."

Slowly she approached the well-lighted stall but didn't see him or the horse until she was close enough to look over the half gate.

Both man and mare were on the straw-covered floor.

There was something else, too.

A tiny, bright-eyed newborn raised its head as if impatient to get a first look at the world. Filled with an undescribable swell of emotion, Shannon stared speechless at the beautiful brown-spotted baby horse.

Ward grinned at Shannon from ear to ear. "Say hello to Princess."

"Is she okay?"

"Perfect." He gently stroked the newborn foal with a warm cloth. "Princess is perfect in every way." His eyes suddenly brimmed. "I'll never get used to the miracle of birth. It's the perfect expression of God's magnificence."

Shannon's throat was tight with emotion as the mare rose to her feet. In a few minutes, Princess tried her long wobbly legs without success. Minutes passed, but she couldn't get up and maintain her balance.

"Is something wrong?" Shannon asked worriedly

when Ward came out of the stall and stood beside her at the gate.

He shook his head.

"Then why don't you help her up?" Shannon asked him impatiently.

"She'll do it herself when she's ready."

"Are you sure?" How could he just stand there and watch the little creature struggling to get up?

"That's the wonderful thing about letting nature have its way. Everything has perfect timing if we will just keep the faith. If we try to force things, we end up in trouble."

The way he said it, Shannon wondered if there was more than a surface meaning to his words. Patience, certainly, was not one of her strong suits. She preferred to make things happen, but a few moments later, she realized he had spoken wisely. Princess stood on wobbly legs. Calico moved closer to her and, protecting her with the warmth of her body, she allowed her baby to nurse.

The touching scene brought tears to Shannon's eyes. Never had she experienced such a moving, tender scene.

"I know, it's beautiful." Ward's voice was husky, and his eyes were misty.

"Yes, beautiful," she echoed softly.

The moment was a precious one, and as Ward looked at Shannon's rapturous expression, he knew with a strange sense of certainty there was no woman in the world with whom he'd rather share it.

Chapter Eight

Ward knew his daughter would never get back to sleep if he woke her up with the good news, so he waited until breakfast to tell her about Princess's arrival.

With a shriek, the little girl left the table with her pigtails flapping as she bounded out of the house. Since Beth had been out to see the new arrival earlier, she laughed, poured herself another cup of coffee and let Ward and Shannon follow the little girl to the stable.

"Isn't she the most gorgeous thing in all the world?" Tara hung over the stall gate, bubbling with excitement as she viewed the perfect baby horse. "Can I pet her?" she asked eagerly.

"Maybe later today," Ward said, his eyes twinkling at his young daughter's enthusiasm. "We want to let mother and baby get used to each other first. Calico is going to be very protective of Princess, and we don't want to make her nervous by getting too close."

"I'm not going to hurt Princess," Tara protested.

"I know that, sweetie, but you'll have to be patient. You'll have plenty of chances to show her how much you love her."

"I'm going to bring her treats every day."

"Not a good idea," Ward warned her gently. "If you do that, she'll expect a treat every time she sees you and she'll develop a bad habit of nipping."

As Shannon listened to his gentle instructions, she was struck by the way he was ready to take the time to talk with his daughter. Even on the rare occasions when Shannon's father wasn't consumed with business, he'd never spent time with her, and there had never been any companionship between them. Not like Ward and his daughter, she thought with undisguised envy. It wasn't as if Ward had time on his hands. Shannon knew he'd been up at dawn, getting his chores out of the way so he could help wherever he was needed during the forest fire.

"Remember, Tara," he said tenderly, "Princess won't learn how to be a perfect little saddle horse for you if you don't train her properly. You'll need to give her water, the right feed and make sure that she has a mineral-and-salt block to lick." He pointed to a hard square brownish cube sitting just inside the gate. "That's like daily vitamins for Princess."

"Well, I can come to see her any time I want, can't I?" Tara protested, unwilling to give up all the fun things about having her own horse.

Ward tugged playfully at one of her pigtails. "I guess a couple of dozen times wouldn't hurt. And maybe tonight you could help me clean out her stall."

Tara clapped her hands and turned to Shannon. "You can help, too, if you want to."

As Ward tried to picture Shannon mucking out a horse stall, he muffled a chuckle. "I think the two of us can manage, honey."

Shannon heard the amusement in his tone, and it spoke volumes about the way he thought about her.

Now she had her answer. Tara's childish invitation and his reaction made it clear that he must be laughing to himself at the very thought of her trying to fit in with his lifestyle. She shouldn't have been surprised. His kindness and attention to her were just a part of his generous heart. He'd been honest about the importance faith in God played in his life. She wasn't anything close to the kind of woman with whom he would be willing to share his life.

Her head came up. "Well, I think I'll head back to the house and help Beth. I should be able to handle some dirty dishes without any problem."

Ouch, thought Ward. She was obviously offended by his quick response to Tara's suggestion. "I was thinking that you might ride out with me to check one of the water troughs before I leave for the Junction," he said quickly.

"I told you I don't ride."

"No, what you said was that you haven't ridden up to now," Ward corrected her, smiling.

"It's easy, Shannon," said Tara. "You don't do anything but sit there. Daddy, she can ride old Betsy and I'll ride Harvey. I'll show you, Shannon. It'll be fun. Okay?"

While common sense warned her about setting herself up to look like a fool, an inner voice asked her what she had to lose. Ward already had pegged her as someone who could never fit into his way of life. "Okay. It sounds like fun." She lied with a straight face.

"Well, I guess that settles that," Ward said, hiding his surprise. He hadn't intended for Tara to come along, but he knew that Shannon would have turned his invitation down flat without his daughter's help. "Come on, ladies. Let's saddle up."

Shannon managed to mount a gentle brown speckled horse with comparable ease, and she was a little surprised to find herself riding between Tara and Ward with some degree of pleasure as the three mounts moved across the ground in a slow walk.

"See? It's fun, isn't it?" Tara said, happily. "But it's more fun if you let the horse gallop."

"Oh, I don't think I'm ready for that," Shannon said quickly and searched Ward's face for reassurance. "This nice easy walk is just fine."

"You'd love racing across the meadow with the wind blowing in your hair. There's a total freedom about it that takes away your breath," he said, and then, seeing her worried expression, he added quickly, "But not on your first lesson. Maybe later."

Maybe later. The words had the ring of a false promise in them. They both knew the moment the main highway was open to traffic and she solved her transportation problem, she'd be gone. All this would only be something that had briefly touched her. She would remember it, of course, but only as a water color memory that would fade in the bustle of her life.

By the time Ward checked the water tanks, and they returned to the stable, Shannon was ready to get back on firm ground.

"Wasn't that fun?" Tara asked. "Maybe we can go riding all by ourselves. Ted can saddle up for us."

"No, Tara," Ward said firmly. "You know better than that. You stay out of the stalls and corrals when I'm not around."

His daughter gave him a pouting frown, but by the time they reached the house, she was smiling again. "Anyway, Shannon and I can find something to do."

When he saw Beth waving at them from the back door, he quickened his step. "What is it?"

"The Red Cross called," she said hurriedly. "They need more shelter for people fleeing from some of the threatened canyons. The school is overloaded, and they are trying to find housing even this far away. I told them we could take two or three small families." She shook her head. "I don't know exactly where we'll put them. Anyway, they'll be here this afternoon."

"We'll manage somehow," Ward assured her.

"Of course, we will," she answered briskly as if there never had been a question about it. Without another word, she disappeared into the kitchen and began making plans for feeding the new arrivals.

Shannon felt a sudden tightening in her stomach. More people. More tension. No longer would the ranch provide peace and quiet. She hated the thought of being engulfed in a mass of frightened strangers, enduring the same kind of crowded, tense atmosphere as at the school. She caught Ward's searching eyes on her, as if he was reading her thoughts and emotions.

"It's going to be all right," he assured her. "We have to try to take care of anyone who needs our help. We can't cross on the other side of the road." Ward knew from her puzzled expression that she missed his reference to the parable of the good Samaritan. Obviously Biblical teachings were not familiar to her, and he was saddened by the great spiritual gulf between them.

Shannon could tell he was disappointed in her response to this latest crisis. Apparently he didn't mind having his home turned into public housing at a moment's notice. An inner voice reminded her that she couldn't very well fault his generosity when she had been a beneficiary of it.

Feeling a little ashamed, she asked, "What do you want me to do?"

"Just help wherever you can. I know Beth will appreciate any suggestions you have for handling our unexpected guests."

"This kind of thing is a little out of my line," Shannon protested. Her privacy had always been important to her. She'd never offered to share her home with anyone, let alone a bunch of total strangers. "I'm afraid you've got the wrong gal."

The lines in his face softened. "Maybe not. Somehow, I sense that you're going to be a great blessing in this situation."

"Blessing?" She looked at him with open astonishment. "What kind of blessing?"

He smiled. "That remains to be seen, doesn't it?"

"Well, you have more confidence in me than I do."

"To tell the truth, I have an idea that just keeping a rein on Tara may earn you a halo."

"I'm not sure I'm up to that challenge," Shannon admitted with a wan smile. "Your daughter seems to have her own ideas about a lot of things."

"I know. And if Tara can show off for some youngsters, she may be hard to hold down." He sobered. "Living on a ranch can be great for kids, but it can hold a lot of dangers, too. Someone will need to look after them."

She stiffened. Was he setting her up to be the unofficial volunteer baby-sitter for all the children? Before she could protest, he gave her that winning smile of his and headed for the telephone.

A little later, he tried to reassure her that there were a lot of nice people in the world. "I wouldn't be surprised if some of them turn out to be close friends."

That'll be the day, she thought. If all of them felt as displaced as she did, the whole atmosphere of the house would take a plunging drop downward.

The next few hours passed in a blur as they readied the house for the arrival of the evacuated families. When they heard the cars coming, Ward, Shannon and Tara went out on the front porch to greet them, but Shannon held back and let Ward and Tara greet the new arrivals pouring out of two vans. She counted four men, three women, a baby, two children and a dog.

"Shannon. Shannon." A childish voice squealed her name.

She was totally unprepared for the little boy and the black-and-white dog who bounded up the porch steps to greet her. "Kenny. Pokey," she gasped.

Kenny gave her a hug around the knees, and Pokey bounded around her, jumping and barking as he demanded his share of attention.

"I don't believe it." Laughing, she hugged Kenny and tried to keep the exuberant pup from knocking her over. "I wasn't expecting to see you."

"The school got too crowded. And my dad said Mr. Dawson asked for us specially."

"He did?" Shannon rounded her eyes in disbelief. How could that be? Ward only knew this morning that they were going to have people coming to the ranch. He must have requested Kenny's family when he returned the call to the evacuation center.

He had done this for her, she was sure of it. Knowing that she was anxious about being surrounded by total strangers again, he was trying to make the situation as pleasant for her as possible. She'd never had anyone look after her or care about her feelings before. She felt totally ashamed of herself.

"Pokey hated that old kennel. Now he can run all over the place. Mama says this will be a much better place for my baby sister, and Grandpa came, too. Isn't that great?"

"Yes," she said huskily. "Just great."

Beth came out of the house with a broad smile of welcome on her face. "So they're here."

Shannon watched her greet everyone as if it would be no trouble at all to furnish room and board for three more families. Tara was ecstatic because there was a little girl, Gloria, about her own age, and the two of them immediately skipped off to Tara's room as if they were longtime friends instead of strangers.

The men carried Grandpa in his wheelchair up the porch steps and settled him in a small room off the kitchen. A double bed had been moved into the front parlor for Mr. and Mrs. Winters, a retired couple in their sixties. Ward gave up his bedroom to Kenny's parents and provided a pad and sleeping bag for Kenny. The guest room Shannon had occupied was given to Gloria's family, with a small air mattress for the little girl. Ward was going to sleep on a cot in the tack room in the stable, and Shannon was to share Beth's bedroom. The gratitude of the three evacuated families made Shannon feel doubly guilty about her earlier dread.

As soon as she had a moment alone with Ward, she said, "Thank you for inviting Kenny's family to the ranch."

"Well, I knew that you're very special to them, and it's a good thing to be around people who make you feel good."

"That was very thoughtful of you. You make me feel ashamed sometimes."

"I don't want you to feel ashamed, Shannon. What I want you to feel is worthy of love." His tender gaze studied her face. "You are, you know. Shannon, if you don't love yourself, you won't have any to give to someone else."

"Isn't loving yourself being narcissistic?"

"Selfish love, yes, but not love that comes from knowing you are a beloved child of God. That kind of caring spills out to everyone. I suspect that you've put a tight cap on the well of love within you, but some day it will burst free, and when it does, there'll be some very lucky people standing in that shower.''

The way he was looking at her made her wonder if he was hoping he might be around to see it. Then she chided herself for trying to read something into his kind generosity and general concern.

''I think Reverend Cozzins should be careful about holding onto his job. Have you ever thought about being a preacher?'' she asked with a teasing grin.

He chuckled. ''Nope. But thanks. I don't think anyone else has ever taken me for a man of the cloth. Quite the contrary, in fact. But that's another story.''

''Well, since Beth and I are rooming together, maybe I'll have the chance to hear it from her.''

He made light of the idea but silently wished there had been time for him to tell her himself how he'd come to recognize that all things work to the good of those that love the Lord.

As the wildfire continued into the second week, daily anxiety about the spreading devastation lay heavily on the hearts of the displaced families. The small television in the sitting room kept them abreast of the growing number of acres being lost every day. They collected each evening to pray and listen to Beth read from her well-worn Bible.

Shannon felt at peace during the evening devotions but failed to summon any kind of miraculous conversion. She wished somehow she could tap into Ward's strong faith. He seemed to have enough to uplift everybody in the house.

All the men except Grandpa left the ranch each morning after chores so they could help out in the threatened areas. The women shared the cooking and household chores with Beth—all but Shannon. As she had suspected, her job was watching the two girls and Kenny.

"She draws great pictures," the little boy told Tara and Gloria as they walked to the stable to check on Calico and Princess.

Tara proudly led the way to Calico's stall. As the three children hung on the stall gate, the little girl gave them an enthusiastic lecture on the caring and raising of young horses. Shannon hid a smile, wishing Ward could have been there to hear his daughter repeat his teachings.

When Tara noticed the water bucket was half empty, she said, "We have to fill it up."

"No, we don't," Shannon said firmly. There was no way she was going to let the little girl open the stall to fill the water bucket or anything else. "Your father will take care of it when he gets home."

"Calico is thirsty," she said, setting her mouth in a stubborn line. "And I know how to carry water to the stalls."

"I'm sure you do. And when your father does the chores tonight, you can help him. There's still plenty of water in the bucket." Shannon ignored her pugnacious scowl.

Kenny wanted to know all about the other horses.

"Maybe there's one I could ride," he suggested hopefully.

"I guess old slowpoke Betsy would be all right for you," Tara said, obviously still out of sorts. "Shannon rode her, and she doesn't know anything about horses."

Shannon hid a smile. Obviously, Tara was no longer her champion because she wouldn't let the little girl have her way. When they got to the house, Shannon agreed to draw some pictures for them to color. She sat with the children outside at the picnic table, and she appeased Tara by sketching a young horse in a nearby corral.

"I'll do one of Princess and Calico later on," she promised, secretly pleased at the way she was able to capture the essence of the sleek, graceful Appaloosa.

The afternoon passed pleasantly, but Shannon was relieved when it was time to collect their things and go inside. Kenny and Gloria bounded upstairs, and Tara disappeared into the kitchen. Shannon decided to join the Winterses in the sitting room to watch the latest report on the fire.

As the horrible orange and red inferno blazed on the screen, the thought of Ward being anywhere near the fire line brought a cold sweat into the palms of her hands. Already there had been a tragic loss of life fighting the fire, and she knew that he wouldn't hesitate to put himself in danger. He would be the first to volunteer anywhere they needed him.

Shannon left the older couple watching a game show and was leaving the sitting room when Beth poked her head out of the kitchen. "Have you seen

Tara? I sent her out to the garden for some lettuce a half hour ago.''

"I'll go check on her."

"Thanks, Shannon. That child can find more ways to dawdle over the simplest task."

When Shannon reached the garden, she didn't see any sign of the little girl. Remembering the stubborn thrust of Tara's chin when she wanted to enter Calico's stall and fill the water container, Shannon was willing to bet the little girl had decided to do it anyway. She must have gone to the stable.

Shannon hurriedly left the garden and headed in that direction.

The door to the stable was ajar, confirming Shannon's suspicion that Tara was there instead of in the garden, as she was supposed to be.

"Tara," she called as she headed down the row of stalls toward Calico's. No answer, nor any sign of the little girl hanging on the stall gate. Maybe she'd been wrong thinking that Tara had run off to see her new horse. Maybe Tara was busy getting water. Shannon wondered if there was an outside pump. The rear door to the stable was closed. She couldn't think where the child might be.

As she approached the half gate, she saw that Calico was standing quietly near the back of her stall with the colt. Everything seemed serene, but when Shannon looked over the gate to see if the water container had been filled, she froze in horror and cried, "Tara!"

The little girl's crumpled body lay unconscious on the floor of the stall. Blood stained the edge of the rocklike mineral and salt block, and Shannon knew with sickening horror that Tara must have lost her balance climbing over the gate, trying to get the water bucket, and had struck her head on the block when she fell.

Chapter Nine

Shannon threw open the stall gate and knelt by the unconscious child, calling her name, but Tara did not respond. There was a frightening whiteness in her face. The horses were still standing quietly at the back of the stall, even though the gate was open. Shannon knew Tara was too heavy for her to carry to the house. Hurriedly, she shut the gate, raced the length of stable and burst out the door, yelling for help as she ran.

Beth heard Shannon's frantic call from the kitchen and ran out of the house. "What's happened? What's the matter?"

"It's Tara. She's hurt."

"Where?"

"In Calico's stall."

The two women ran as fast as they could to the stable, and Beth quickly knelt beside the unconscious child. "Tara, baby. Oh, dear God."

When the little girl didn't respond, Beth picked her

up in her strong arms and rushed out of the stall, yelling at Shannon to shut the gate.

Before Shannon could respond, Calico started moving toward the open gate with the little colt wobbling close beside her. The mare looked enormous coming at her, and Shannon's instinct to get out of the way fought with her determination not to let them out.

"Back, back," Shannon ordered, waving her arms. Calico tossed her head, but she stopped just short of the open gate, and Shannon managed to get it shut.

She raced out of the stable and caught up with Beth.

"We'll have to call 911, and they'll send an ambulance from Elkhorn," Beth said, her face creased with worry. She laid Tara on the living room couch, then raced to the phone while Shannon stayed by the little girl's side.

The emergency operator informed Beth that because of the fire, there was an overload on ambulance services. She wasn't certain that one would be immediately available, but she would alert the authorities to the emergency so they would allow the Dawson vehicle through the Beaver Junction roadblock to Elkhorn. "If there's an ambulance available at the Junction, I'll have them meet you at the roadblock, and they can take the child from there into Elkhorn."

Beth said, "We'll leave immediately. Can you locate Ward Dawson and tell him that we're taking his injured daughter to the hospital?"

"I'll do my best. Good luck."

By this time the whole house was alerted to the emergency, and Kenny's mother insisted they take their new van instead of Beth's old model car.

''There's room for the child to lie down in the back. If I didn't have the baby to tend I'd drive you.''

''Shannon can do that,'' Beth said crisply, and handed her the car keys. ''If Ward calls, tell him to get to the Elkhorn hospital as quickly as possible.''

''We'll be holding a prayer vigil for Tara,'' Mrs. Winters promised. The other two women nodded. As they hurried out of the house, Shannon heard Kenny ask, ''God will make her well, won't He?''

Beth sat in the back with Tara, holding her gently but firmly in her arms. The little girl's breathing was raspy, but the bleeding from her head wound had stopped.

Shannon drove the speed limit all the way to Beaver Junction. Her experience driving mountain roads was negligible, and the pressure of precious minutes slipping by brought a cold sweat to her forehead. Her hands had a clammy wetness as they tightly gripped the steering wheel.

She could hear Beth praying over the unconscious child and trying to rouse her with tender and loving murmurs. Shannon wanted to pray, but she wasn't sure that the lines of communication were open between her and any divine spirit. Nevertheless, she found herself praying, ''Please let there be an ambulance in Beaver Junction to take Tara to the hospital.''

When they reached the roadblock, Shannon wasn't surprised that her prayer wasn't answered. She really hadn't expected that it would be. She did the best she could to make time on the double-lane highway. Fortunately Beth seemed to know every turn and curve in the road.

When they finally reached the hospital, Shannon was not prepared for the snarl of traffic going in and out. Even the emergency entrance was crowded with vehicles, and scurrying hospital personnel were trying to assess the priorities of those needing attention.

A male intern came out to the van, took one look at Tara and whisked her away into the ER on a stretcher.

Beth and Shannon kept a silent vigil in the midst of organized chaos in the waiting room. It was nearly thirty minutes before a nurse approached them. She glanced uncertainly at Shannon and then Beth. "Who is the mother of the little girl?"

"Her mother is deceased. I'm her aunt," Beth said quickly. "How is she? She's going to be all right, isn't she?"

"The doctor is still doing tests," she replied with practiced calmness. "It may be a couple of hours before they are finished. Is there a father—"

"Yes, my brother. He's a volunteer, helping out some of the firefighters. We've left word for him to come here as soon as possible."

"Good. Try not to worry. We're doing everything we can for your little girl."

She started to turn away, but Beth stopped her. "Is there a chapel?"

"Yes, on the second floor."

"Thank you." Beth rose to her feet, and Shannon didn't know whether to go with her or stay in the waiting room. She didn't want to intrude if Beth wanted to be alone in this moment of crisis.

"Shall I wait for you here?" she asked.

"No." Beth looked surprised at the question, and as if Shannon's prayers were as important as her own, she added, "This is a time to call upon our Heavenly Father for Tara's healing. I'll leave word at the desk so Ward will know where to find us."

Meekly, Shannon followed Beth into the softly lit small chapel, wondering if someone would challenge her right to be there. A few people sat quietly in the pews, bowing their heads or staring at a simple altar holding two lighted candles.

Beth slipped into one of the pews, then quickly knelt on the knee bench, folding her hands as her lips began to move in prayer.

Shannon sat stiffly in the pew, her eyes fixed on some unseen point in front of her. She knew Beth expected her to pray, but she didn't know any of the right words. Fear and anxiety dominated her thoughts. Why had this happened? Ward had trusted her to watch his daughter. And she had failed him. If Tara didn't recover, it would be her fault. How could she ever live with herself? She wanted to run away and hide.

When they left the chapel and returned to the waiting room, there still was no news about Tara's condition. Beth couldn't sit still. "I'm going to see if I can find the cafeteria and get a cup of coffee."

"I'll stay here just in case they tell us something," Shannon said, her stomach in knots from the long hours of waiting. She covered her face with her hands, and silent tears streamed down her face.

When someone gently pulled her hands away from her face, she stared in disbelief. "Ward!" With a whimper, she turned and buried her face in his shoulder. "I'm sorry...I'm so sorry."

"How is she?"

"They haven't told us anything," she said tearfully.

"Where's Beth?"

"She went for coffee." Shannon pulled away and faced him. "It's all my fault. She wanted to fill the water bucket, and I wouldn't let her. Calico still had water, and I didn't think it was important to get her any more. I told her to wait until you got home." She'd turned a deaf ear to the child's concern, and with her stubborn willfulness, Tara had decided to take care of the matter herself.

Ward brushed a lock of hair on Shannon's forehead. "Then it's not your fault. That was the right thing to tell her. Tara knows she's not to open any stall—"

"She didn't." Shannon's lower lip trembled. "Tara must have been climbing over the gate to get the water bucket and lost her balance. There was blood on the mineral block. Oh, Ward, what'll we do?"

Ward didn't answer her, but bowed his head. From the moment he'd learned about his daughter's accident, prayers for her well-being had been on his lips and in his heart. Quietly, he prayed, "Father, You have all the power in heaven and earth, and I know that when I call upon Your name, You hear me. I ask that You touch Tara with Your healing power, and I know that You will because You have promised that all things are possible to those who believe. She is in Your hands, Lord, and I thank You for Your loving kindness. Amen."

Shannon remained silent, and when Beth came

back, she asked Ward if he would like to spend a few minutes in the chapel. He nodded, and Beth told him where it was located. He glanced at Shannon, silently asking if she wanted to accompany him, but she shook her head.

It was another hour before a nurse led the three of them into a private consultation office. A middle-aged doctor with thinning sandy-colored hair and gold-rimmed spectacles turned and introduced himself. "I'm Dr. McGrail."

Ward quickly introduced himself. "I'm Tara's father. This is my sister, Beth, and this is Shannon Hensley, a friend of the family."

The doctor acknowledged the introductions and motioned to some chairs in front of a desk. "Please have a seat." Then he sat down and picked up some papers. "I know that you're anxious to hear what our tests have shown about your little girl's injury. We've done a CT scan and a complete battery of X rays."

He paused for a moment, and Shannon's heart lunged in her throat. Then he gave them a faint smile. "Under the circumstances, the news is good. She has suffered a concussion, but there is no internal bleeding. We are hopeful that the swelling caused by the blow will recede without any complications."

There was a moment of breathless silence, and then Beth said, prayerfully, "Thank you, dear Lord."

"Amen," echoed Ward, letting out a deep breath of relief. "She's going to be okay." Unexpectedly, he took Shannon's hand and squeezed it.

"Your daughter has regained consciousness, and you may see her, Mr. Dawson, but only for a few minutes. We'll keep her in intensive care overnight. A family member may visit for five minutes every hour. Tomorrow we'll see about moving her to a private room.''

Shannon knew that Beth was disappointed not to be allowed in the ICU for the first visit, but as they waited for Ward to see Tara, the lines in Beth's face eased.

''We need to call home and thank everyone for their prayers.'' Then she hugged Shannon. ''If you hadn't found her when you did and driven us here so quickly through all that traffic mess, she might have been a lot worse.''

Shannon's feelings of guilt overrode Beth's expression of gratitude. None of this would have happened if she hadn't ignored Tara's strong feelings.

When Ward came back, the lines in his face had eased. ''She's alert and asking questions. I told her as much as I knew about what had happened. She asked about you, Shannon. She seems worried that you're going to be mad at her.''

The pain in Shannon's eyes and sad face touched him, and Ward would have drawn her close if Beth hadn't been there. He regretted that she lacked the faith and the spiritual strength to call upon the Lord in a time like this. He wanted to assure her that God had answered his prayers and share with her the thanksgiving that was in his heart. It saddened him to know that even in this crisis, they didn't share a common gratitude for the heavenly Father's blessings. The situation had highlighted more than ever how far apart they were in ways that mattered to him most.

Shannon saw the regret in his expression and knew

she had failed to measure up. He had wanted her to go with him to the chapel and pray with him. Her unbelief obviously weighed heavily on him, and she wished things were different between them. She knew that her lack of faith had not only disappointed him, but had made it clear that he would never commit himself to any kind of serious bond between them.

"What are we going to do about all those people at our house?" Beth asked.

Now that the crisis seemed to be over, Beth had started worrying about the stranded families. Her caretaking nature immediately shifted into high gear.

"They'll take care of themselves," Ward reassured his sister. "And Ted will tend to the chores. It's better that we wait and see how Tara is in the morning. No use all three of us staying here at the hospital all night, though. I'll make some calls and see if I can find a motel room. With all the extra people in town because of the fires, we may be out of luck."

His words were prophetic. There wasn't an empty room to be found. Ward was resigned that all three of them would be spending the night in the waiting room when a middle-aged woman who seemed familiar approached him. She was wearing a volunteer smock and badge.

"Aren't you Ward Dawson?" She held out her hand. "I'm Sue Williams. You probably don't remember me, I'm Laura Cozzins's sister. I was widowed a couple of years ago, and I've seen you at church a couple of times when I was visiting. Do you have someone in the hospital?"

Ward explained the situation. After a short conversation, and a generous offer from Sue Williams, Shannon and Beth left to spend the night at the widow's spacious home. Ward would be keeping the vigil at the hospital.

Thankful that Christian charity had answered their needs, Ward settled himself in the waiting room, glad to be able to make short visits to the ICU to hold his daughter's hand while she slept.

Shannon had wanted to be alone with him before leaving, but there hadn't been an opportunity. A friend of the family was all she was in this situation, and she left the hospital with Beth, feeling displaced and empty.

"I'll be home after my shift ends," Sue had told them. "Here's the address and a key to the front door."

They drove to the address the widow had given them and gratefully accepted her hospitality.

In spite of Shannon's physical and emotional exhaustion, she spent a restless night in a strange bed and borrowed nightgown. In a chilling nightmare, the distance between Ward and herself stretched and stretched until she couldn't see him anymore. When Ward's accusing voice resounded in her ears, she awoke with a cry and his name on her lips.

As she lay there, feeling emotionally depleted and empty, she realized for the first time how much his approval had come to mean to her, an approval that she would never have.

By the time she'd showered and dressed in the wrinkled outfit of the day before, she had decided to take charge of her life the only way she knew how—making her own decisions and carrying them out by herself. Now that she was in Elkhorn, she would find a way to leave the area. There was nothing to keep her there. Her growing feelings for Ward were a mockery of the truth that even though he liked her and might be attracted to her, he was committed to a strong religious faith that she couldn't share. The regretful way he had looked at her last night had spoken volumes. There was no reason for her to return to the ranch. No reason at all.

She pleaded a headache and let Beth and Mrs. Williams go to the hospital without her. Then she put a ten-dollar bill under the bedroom phone and made a couple of long distance calls. The first was to the Los Angles employment agency.

"Oh, I'm so glad you called, Miss Hensley," the woman said with obvious relief. "You really should have kept in close touch with us. Good news. We've lined up two very promising interviews for you, and if you will give me the date of your return, I'll schedule them."

When she mentioned the names of the companies, Shannon felt a quiver of excitement and answered firmly. "I'm sure that I can make arrangements to be in Los Angles within the week, but I'll have to let you know for sure."

She hung up and immediately called her bank. The money on her rented apartment had come in. Her finances had improved, and she had the option of using her credit cards to get to Los Angeles.

When the doorbell rang, Shannon hurried downstairs to open the door, ready to say that Mrs. Williams wasn't home. Her breath suddenly caught when she saw Ward standing there.

"Good morning," he said, a weak smile on his tired, unshaven face. "How's the headache?"

"It's better," she said, remembering in time the excuse she'd given for not going to the hospital. "You don't look so good. How's Tara?"

"She made it through the night in good shape." He rubbed his eyes as if struggling to keep them open. "They'll be doing more tests this morning. I thought I'd catch a couple hours sleep while Beth takes over."

"I'll show you where you can crash." As they walked up the stairs together, he smiled at her, and she let herself enjoy his masculine closeness. Nothing about him brought out her fierce competitive nature or distrust. It was a unique experience for her, and one she would not soon forget.

She showed him the bedroom where she had slept. She hadn't gotten around to stripping the sheets from her bed like a good houseguest, and it was obvious from the rumpled covers that she'd had a bad night. She smoothed them as quickly as she could.

"The bathroom is across the hall. Have a nice sleep." She paused in the doorway, wanting to tell him about her decision to fly to Los Angles as soon as possible, but the weary slump of his shoulders held her back. She'd tell him when he woke up.

"Shannon, wait a minute. You aren't still blaming yourself for all of this, are you?"

She avoided answering his question. "Can't we talk about this later?"

The way she caught her lower lip and avoided looking at him was answer enough for Ward. If he hadn't been so blasted tired, he would have settled the matter right then and there. Later he realized he shouldn't have let the moment pass without confronting her sense of guilt.

While he slept, Shannon skimmed through the yellow pages of the telephone directory and began her search for transportation that would get her to Denver's international airport. Buying a car and driving to Los Angeles was out of the question. The lack of daily bus and train service to the small mountain community and her limited funds narrowed her options considerably. An expensive shuttle service that made a daily run into Denver seemed to be her best bet. If she imposed on Mrs. Williams one more night, she could use her credit card and make a reservation on a red-eye flight to Los Angeles the next night.

She was on the phone most of the morning, sitting at a kitchen counter making her calls. She had just hung up from talking to the employment agency again when she realized Ward had come into the room. One look at his questioning expression told her he'd overheard her discussing her plans.

"You're leaving?" Ward asked with a stab of disbelief. She couldn't go. Not yet. He'd seen a marked change in her in the few days that she'd been at the school and ranch, a softening of her defenses, a growing willingness to allow other people into her life. He'd been encouraged that with a little more time to find herself, she'd experience the right relationship with the Lord.

"I'm going tomorrow," she told him. "I've found transportation to Denver."

He eased down on a stool beside her and resisted the temptation to reach over and take her hand in a gesture of persuasion. "Why do you have to go? Why can't you stay?"

The answer was so simple, she wondered why he had to ask. "Because I don't belong here."

"Maybe you would if you didn't rush off like this."

"Stay and cause everyone more trouble? No, thank you. If I had only helped Tara with refilling a simple bucket of water for the horses, none of this would have happened."

"And you didn't help her because?"

"Because I don't know anything about taking care of horses," she answered defensively. "And I was trying not to do anything wrong or stupid."

"Doesn't that seem like a pretty good reason to refuse her? You were being cautious and had no reason to think Tara would sneak back and do something so foolish and dangerous."

She shook her head.

"I saw that she was concerned about Princess, and I turned a deaf ear to her. You asked me to look after your daughter, and I let you down, pure and simple."

"Is this why you're leaving? You believe all of us are blaming you? And you're running away?"

"That's part of it," she admitted. "But it's time I got my life back. At the moment I don't know what's going to happen or if I'm going to be able to handle all the challenges, but the sooner I start, the better. I can't stay here."

He searched her deepening gray-blue eyes. "Why not?"

"Because...because..." Because I'm in love with you. In horror, she wondered if she had spoken the words aloud. They seemed to come from nowhere. Clear. Honest. Shattering. In spite of herself, she'd fallen in love with a man who lived the convictions of his heart. He had made it clear what kind of a woman he wanted to share his life. And it wasn't her.

"Are you running away from me? Yourself?" God? Her chest was suddenly tight as she slipped off her stool and walked to a kitchen counter where Mrs. Williams had left a pot of coffee brewing. With trembling hands she took down two cups and filled them.

"Are you hungry? I can see what's in the fridge. You'll need to eat something before you go back to the hospital."

When his warm breath brushed her neck, she knew he had come up behind her. She stiffened, not wanting to turn and look into those arresting eyes of his or be tempted by the inviting curve of his lips. She needed to put some distance between them before she made a fool of herself.

"What is it, Shannon? Why are you running away?" he asked quietly, as he put his hands on her shoulders and gently turned her.

Her chin came up. "I'm not running away. I've got to get back to Los Angeles. It's time, don't you think?" she said with a rueful smile. "I've lost my car and all my belongings." And my heart.

"Maybe you haven't lost as much as you think.

There may be a hidden blessing in all of this that you're overlooking.''

''I don't know what it could be.'' After tomorrow she would probably never see him again. The memories she would be taking back to the city would only make her aware of being alone and rejected. ''I really can't wait to put this all behind me,'' she lied. ''I hope I can see Tara before I go.''

''The doctor said they would probably be moving her into a private room later today.''

''I want to stop at the hospital gift shop and buy her something to remember me by.''

''I don't think any of us will need a reminder of your time with us,'' he said, trying to still a silent rebellion in his heart. He didn't want to let her go. If there had been any argument that would have convinced her to stay, he might have been tempted to use it. Only a deeply rooted belief that the matter was out of his hands, and in God's, kept him silent.

Chapter Ten

Beth called Ward from the hospital to tell him that Tara's morning tests had been positive and that they were going to move her to a private room after lunch.

"The doctor wants to keep her twenty-four hours for observation. He confessed that he'd never seen someone recover so quickly from such a hard bump on the head. I just smiled. The Bible tells us that it is done unto us as we believe. We believed that God would work a miracle for us, and He did. Tara is sleeping now, and I was thinking that you might want to do the shopping and pick up the supplies we need before you come back to the hospital. Maybe by then she'll be out of ICU and in her own room."

"Yes, that sounds like a good idea. That list you gave me will likely fill up the whole back of the pickup," he teased, and added, "Shannon will probably want to pick up a few things for her trip. She's leaving for Denver tomorrow."

"Tomorrow," Beth echoed. "You mean she's not going back to the ranch?"

He tried to ignore the dead feeling in his chest. "Shannon's made arrangements to catch a flight to Los Angeles, but I'm sure she'll want to say goodbye to you and Tara."

Beth sighed. "Maybe it's for the best, Ward. I don't want you hurt, and anyone around the two of you for two minutes can see how you feel about her. I know what you were hoping, we both were, but you can't make someone change just because you want them to. Oh, maybe on the surface, but not deep down. They have to find the Lord themselves."

"I know." Ward didn't need his sister to tell him how difficult it was to change and find a relationship with God. He'd been there himself.

After he hung up the kitchen phone, he turned to Shannon, who was still sitting at the counter. "I need to pick up some supplies for Beth and stop by the vet's to get some medicine for one of my horses. Was I right in telling Beth you might want to stop in town?"

She nodded. "I'm down to the clothes on my back and the personal items in my purse. I'll want to stop at a bank and use my ATM card." She was thankful that the rent money had come in the nick of time to get her back to California.

"All right, let's go. I'll show you the bustling town of Elkhorn." Now that the hours in Shannon's company were numbered, Ward intended to spend as many of them with her as he could.

"What about your breakfast? All you've had is toast

and coffee.'' She knew he was used to the big breakfasts Beth prepared every morning.

''We'll stop somewhere. It's almost time for lunch, anyway. Somehow I don't feel like a crowded café. Is fast-food all right by you?''

''Fine.''

They took his pickup and headed toward the business district. Ward obviously knew his way around town and pointed out some interesting landmarks. When he pulled up to a drive-through window at a popular fast-food place and they gave their orders, Shannon expected to eat in the car, but he surprised her by driving away from the parking lot.

''There are some picnic tables in a small park down by the river. Let's take our lunch and eat there.''

A picnic? Today of all days?

''Is that okay?'' he asked, seeing her surprise.

''Yes, fine.'' He never ceased to surprise her. No matter what the world threw at him, he seemed to find ways to make life a pleasure instead of something to be endured. She was envious of the quiet corner within him that remained sure and unchanging and was amazed at how being with him eased the tension that had been building all morning.

''Here we are,'' he said as he turned into a parking space that bordered a small park close to a wide, slow-moving river. Several picnic tables were scattered under huge oak trees, and they walked down a grassy slope to one near the river. ''I like being near moving water.''

''I know,'' she said, and her chest was suddenly

tight as she remembered the day he had picked her up in his arms and carried her across the mountain stream.

"It's great fun rafting on this river," he told her as they ate, entertaining her with stories about riding rubber tubes down the river and fishing along its banks. As he talked, Shannon smiled, picturing the energetic and adventuresome boy who had probably sat under this very tree many times. Maybe he'd even brought a teenage sweetheart here to sit and watch the water while they held hands or stole an adolescent kiss. In one way, she wanted to ask him about the girls and women who'd been a part of his life, but in another way, she didn't want to know.

"Laura told me you'd been a handful when you were growing up," Shannon said, wanting to keep him talking about himself and all the things that made him who he was.

He laughed, a deep rich sound that she'd come to love.

"I guess there are plenty of folks around who'll bear witness to that, all right. In a way you get your just desserts when you spend your life around people who knew you when. Just this morning I ran into Samuel Shornberger when I was putting gas in the truck." He chuckled. "I could tell from his frosty greeting that he hasn't forgotten me after all these years."

"And who is Samuel Shornberger?"

"He was an Elkhorn high school coach when I was a student there. Before they built the consolidated school at Beaver Junction, we were bused into Elkhorn for high school. We didn't have much of a football team, and Coach Shornberger wasn't exactly on any of the players' good fellow list. One time a couple of us managed to get hold of a pair of red sweatpants he always wore, and we hooked them to the flagpole so the next morning when he drove up, they were flying over the school as pretty as you please.''

Shannon laughed with him, visualizing the prank and wishing her school days had been filled with friends and fun times. She had missed all that. This moment of sharing created a poignant longing in her for what might have been if they'd met earlier. She shoved the fantasy aside. What was, was.

Ward watched the laughter fade from her lips and eyes, and as dappled sunlight moved over her fair hair, touching the sweet lines of her face, he couldn't stop himself from asking, ''Why don't you stay a little longer, Shannon?''

''I can't. I've got to get my life back on track as soon as possible. I'll be interviewing for a couple of positions with companies that will give me a chance for advancement.''

As she talked about the prospect of new employment, he was reminded of the first time he'd met her. Even then he'd glimpsed a softness under that brisk demeanor. He silently sighed. If only there were more time to show her a different way of life than the one she knew. He was certain she would be successful in securing the kind of position she wanted, and the vulnerable part of her that needed love would once again be deeply buried in the world's pressures. He had prayed for her, for himself and for guidance and he knew there was nothing he could do now but let go, and let God.

Sighing, he glanced at his watch. "Well, I guess we better get a move on. While you go to the bank and do your shopping, I'll stop at the vet's and feed store."

"All right. It won't take me long." Shannon had already decided on the few things she needed to buy. She'd asked Ward to mail her the items she'd left at the ranch. "Will you be going back to the ranch tonight?" she asked, hoping he would say no. If he stayed in town, they might have some time together. Now that time was short, she was guilty of wanting to delay their parting for as long as possible.

"If Tara is doing okay, I really have to get back. Ted needs help keeping everything going at the ranch, and I don't know how soon my other ranch hands will be free from their volunteer duties. This wildfire has played heck with everyone's life."

"Hasn't it?" she replied dryly as she nodded in agreement.

"I was gone all day yesterday, and I'll need to run these supplies home," he told her, reluctantly. "Beth can stay with Tara until she's released, and then I'll come back. We'll caravan to the ranch."

Shannon shoved away a tinge of guilt about leaving, telling herself there was no need for her to stick around. Tara was in good hands. The little girl had a loving family to take care of her. Shannon decided she'd be more in the way than anything.

They finished their lunch and gathered the trash. Ward suggested, "Why don't we meet at the grocery store and you can help me shop for the things Beth wants?"

"You might be better off by yourself," Shannon

warned with a smile. "Buying groceries for one person doesn't exactly provide a lot of experience in wise shopping."

Ward grinned. "Well, then, I'll just have to put the blame on you if I get the wrong brand or size this time."

"Maybe it's a good thing I won't be there when you unload them at the ranch," she said, trying for the same light tone.

"Yes, you'll be gone," he said quietly, his smile fading. The truth of the words created a strained silence as they walked to the pickup.

Everything went smoothly at the bank, and Shannon breathed a sigh of relief as she left the building with money in her pocket. Using her charge card, she made several purchases at a nearby boutique, including a small suitcase. She chose a pair of tailored mint-green slacks, a short-sleeve blouse and a matching summer jacket for traveling. In addition to a nightgown and short robe, she bought several sets of lingerie. Weary of her limited wardrobe, Shannon had expected to feel good about having something new to wear, but she didn't. She left the store with numerous packages but with little joy.

Every place she went people were talking about the forest wildfire, and televisions were tuned to the latest news—which wasn't good. Thousands of acres had already been burned, and every time the fighters put out one hot spot, another would develop. The weather forecast was the worst, dry and windy.

Shannon wished she could get on a plane that very moment and get away. It would be a relief to get back into her old reassuring patterns. Even though her life was extremely stressful at times, she'd proven that she was capable of handling demanding responsibilities and holding her own in the corporate world. Ever since she'd become a refugee from the forest wildfire, she had lost the security of being in command. She was tired of feeling off balance, adrift and confronted with challenges that seemed to have no solutions. Admitting to herself how she felt about Ward only compounded the need to leave as soon as possible.

His pickup was already in the parking lot of the supermarket when she got there. It took her a few minutes, wandering through different aisles, before she found him at the meat counter. His grocery basket had some meat packages in it, and he was staring at his list with such a furrowed brow that Shannon had to smile.

"Problems?"

He pointed at a couple of hastily written words. "What does that say? I can read pork chops, but not the other words."

"Herb stuffing. Apparently Beth is going to bake some stuffed pork chops."

"Oh." His brow smoothed. "Thanks. Where do we find herb stuffing?"

She laughed. "We hunt. Every grocery store is different."

Walking beside Ward as he pushed the cart, Shannon checked Beth's list and read the posted signs hanging from the ceiling. Finding the exact item and brand became kind of a treasure hunt as they went from one end of the store to the other.

"I found it." Ward triumphantly held up a particular brand of starch that had been shelved in an inconspicuous place.

Shannon wasn't aware of anyone noticing their laughter and amusement until one woman customer said enviously, "I wish I could get my husband to have that much fun shopping with me."

Husband. Shannon was too startled to correct her, but the fun she'd been having suddenly left. Ward was not her husband. He would never be her husband. She was glad he hadn't heard the remark, and when he came back to the cart, she asked rather curtly, "Are we about through?"

The change in her voice and expression startled him. He gave her a quick look. "What's the matter?"

"Nothing."

"Something has upset you," he insisted. "What?"

She pretended to rearrange the crowded grocery cart while she got her feelings under control. Then she looked up and said evenly, "People are getting the wrong impression, seeing us shopping together. They think we're a couple. You may have a lot of explaining to do when this gets on the grapevine."

"And that should worry me?" He frowned. "Why?"

"Because we're not a couple. We never will be." She faced him steadily. "In less than twenty-four hours I'll be gone. And whatever might have been between us will be another casualty of a Colorado forest fire."

"It doesn't have to be that way," he argued. "Lots of things take time and patience."

"I know what you're hoping—that I'll change. But the truth is, I can't help but be skeptical about the Christian beliefs that are so important to you. I've never experienced anything in my life that makes me think there's a Supreme Being the least bit interested in me. I can't pretend to be something I'm not."

"Why are you so ready to shut down on yourself—and me?"

"Because I know what I want out of life. Success. Freedom. Independence." She squared her shoulders.

"Really? Are you trying to convince me or yourself?"

"There are a lot more important things than love."

Ward didn't believe for one minute that she spoke the truth that was in her heart. If there was anyone who desperately needed to be nurtured, loved and cared for it was Shannon Hensley. That brisk, I-don't-need-anyone veneer of hers didn't fool him. "Why don't you quit lying to yourself?" he asked gently.

She turned away without giving him an answer. They returned to the pickup in silence. On the drive to the hospital, she was defensive and rigid on her side of the seat. Finally, he decided to speak his mind. This might be the last time they would be alone together.

"I know this experience has been rough on you, and it's made you angry and frightened, but if you were honest with yourself, you might find that all in all, you've grown in this experience. It's been good for you."

"How can you say that?" She looked at him in utter amazement.

"Whenever something happens that causes us to

change and grow, it's for our own good. That's what this earth school is all about, Shannon,'' he explained patiently. ''We are put here to learn and discover the divine nature in each of us. You may think you are the same person you were before this experience, but you're not. You've grown a lot. Just look at the way working with the children has made you a gentler person. Look at the way your creative talent has brought new pleasure.''

She choked back an angry reply. And look at the way falling in love with you has brought new misery into my life. He might think she had lowered her defenses against being hurt by him or anyone else, but he was wrong. She hadn't changed. More than ever she felt alone, vulnerable and unwanted. The whole experience had reinforced what she already knew. Life was one long, heartbreaking challenge.

Ward saw her closed expression and was saddened by the truth.

There are none so blind that will not see, and none so deaf that will not hear.

When they arrived at the hospital, they were told that Tara was just being moved to a private room and they would have to wait until the nurses were finished getting her settled.

''I want to stop at the gift shop, anyway,'' Shannon told Ward.

''Okay, I'll go ahead and find Beth. If I know my sister, she's probably waiting in the chapel.''

As Shannon watched him walk down the corridor in that easy, confident way of his, an overwhelming sense of loss created a tightening in her chest. She leaned against a wall, struggling with a wave of emotion that made her breath short.

"Are you all right?" asked a young woman in a volunteer's uniform who was passing with a cart loaded with flowers and books.

"Yes…I'm fine," Shannon stammered.

"You look a little peaked."

"Just something I ate," Shannon lied, feeling foolish. She gave the young woman a false smile. "Where's the gift shop?"

The volunteer motioned in the direction from which she had come. "Just around the corner."

"Thank you." Shannon waited for a moment until the weak sensation in her legs passed, then she walked slowly down the corridor. She was bewildered by the strong physical reaction she'd had watching Ward disappear from sight. What on earth was the matter with her? She felt as if she were perched on a precipice, about to fall off.

By the time she reached the gift shop, she was in control again. The physical and emotional upheaval had passed, her breathing was steady, and she chided herself for giving way to such feminine hysterics.

The gift shop was small, and the choices were limited, but she found a Dr. Seuss book for Tara and a large stuffed Cat In The Hat to match. She was sure the little girl would enjoy having her daddy read the book to her while she hugged the silly happy cat.

Her arms filled with the floppy stuffed toy, she made her way to the second floor, where Ward and Beth were waiting.

"What on earth have you got there?" Ward asked, chuckling, when he saw her.

"It's a cat," she answered, showing them the long-legged creature with the sloppy smile and tall black-and-white hat.

Beth laughed. "Not like any cat I've ever seen."

Shannon replied a little defensively, "Well, I think Tara will like it, and there's a book to go with it."

"I think it's great," Ward assured her, loving the way her cool professionalism gave way at times to an appealing, innocent, girlish charm. The way she was holding the stuffed animal hinted at an early childhood void of such comforting toys. He knew his daughter would treasure the gift because it came from Shannon. She had captured his daughter's heart as deeply as his own, and he wondered how he was going to explain Shannon's disappearance from their lives.

"*Our* little girl is doing wonderfully," Beth told Shannon. "They expect to release her tomorrow."

Our little girl. The possessive noun only highlighted the sudden emptiness Shannon felt, knowing she was going to miss Tara's childish exuberance and love of life.

Dr. McGrail stopped at the waiting room and verified that they could take Tara home in the morning. "She's one spunky little girl," he said, smiling. "I'd keep her off a horse for a week or two, but I don't see any problems ahead."

"Bless you, Doctor, for all that you did," Beth told him gratefully.

"I did very little besides watch a healing take place that went beyond our expectations," he said honestly.

"Somebody up there is watching out for her, that's for sure."

"Yes, and we're grateful to the Lord," Ward said readily.

"Well, your little girl is waiting to see you." The doctor smiled. "She's a talker, that one."

Ward laughed. Tara must be back to normal if she was entertaining everyone with her usual nonstop chatter.

Shannon hesitated about going into the room with Ward and Beth. "Maybe she shouldn't have this much company all at once. I can wait until later."

"No, she'll want to see you." Ward declared and put a guiding hand on her arm. A nurse was leaving as they entered, and she warned, "Don't stay too long."

"Hi, sweetness," Ward greeted Tara as he went to her bed. "Are you ready for company?"

She laughed and held up her arms for a hug and a kiss from her daddy. Shannon's breath caught when she saw how tiny and fragile the little girl looked in the hospital bed. A small bandage clung to the left side of her small head, and a section of her hair had been shaved.

When Tara saw Shannon standing near the foot of the bed, she grinned, and her bright eyes widened when she saw what Shannon had in her arms.

"Is that for me?" she squealed.

"No, it's for me," Ward teased. "But I'll let you play with him once in a while."

Shannon moved to the side of the bed and put the

stuffed toy in Tara's arms. "This is the Cat in the Hat, and here's a book to tell you all about him."

"Thank you," the little girl said, hugging the toy.

"You're very welcome," Shannon said and placed a kiss on Tara's forehead. The child's skin felt soft and sweet under her lips, and when Tara's arms went around her neck in a hug, Shannon blinked back some unexpected tears. She quickly stepped to the foot of the bed.

As she watched Ward smooth his daughter's hair away from her cheek and pat her shoulder lovingly, she fought a sudden urge to flee from the room. That peculiar weakness and tightness in her chest was back again. She must have made some kind of sound, because Ward turned and looked at her.

"Are you all right?" he asked, frowning. She looked pale and had a hand pressed against her chest. "What's the matter? Are you sick?"

She tried for a light laugh. "Of course not."

Ward quickly moved a chair to one side of the bed for her. "Come sit down. You look a little tired."

"When we get home, Shannon, we can read my book," Tara said happily. "And you can draw the silly old cat doing all kinds of crazy things. It'll be fun. I bet Kenny and Gloria have been missing us."

Ward and Beth exchanged glances as they waited for Shannon to tell Tara that she wouldn't be going back to the ranch. When she sent a beseeching glance at him, he ignored her silent plea that he do the explaining. He was afraid the words would catch in his throat.

Shannon swallowed hard. "Tara, honey, I won't be going back to the ranch."

Tara's little face instantly clouded, and she burst into tears. "I'm sorry. I'm sorry I was bad. Please, Shannon, don't go. I'll behave. I'll never, never do anything bad again. I promise. I promise. You can't go," she sobbed. "Please don't go."

"Honey, you don't understand." Shannon quickly stood up and gathered the little girl in her arms, horrified that the child thought she was to blame for Shannon's decision to leave. "Please don't cry. You haven't done anything wrong. You're a wonderful, beautiful little girl, and I love you."

Tara pressed her wet cheek against Shannon's. "You do? And I love you, too." She gulped. "And so does Daddy. And Aunt Beth. And Kenny, and—" She hesitated as she raised her tear-streaked face to Shannon. "Maybe even Calico and Princess. I could show you how to ride better, so you won't bounce all over the place like a city dude."

Ward chuckled. "How can you refuse an offer like that, Shannon?"

"I guess I can't," she answered slowly as she realized why she was feeling ill. Even though it didn't make sense to prolong the inevitable, something deep inside was telling her to delay her return to California. She couldn't get on with her life until she was free of the loving claims a persuasive little girl and her handsome father had put on her.

Chapter Eleven

When Shannon and Beth drove Tara to the ranch the next afternoon, a large paper banner with childish printing was hung over the front door. Welcome Home, Tara.

The little girl clapped her hands when Shannon read it to her.

Kenny and Gloria rushed out of the house ahead of the adults and circled Tara as she got out of the car.

"Oh, no, they shaved part of your head," Gloria wailed.

"Did it get bashed in?" Kenny asked, peering at the bandage with large curious eyes.

Beth opened her mouth to halt the flood of questions, but Tara, obviously pleased by all the attention, began weaving a tale that skirted the truth enough to make her stay in the hospital sound like an exciting adventure.

Ward arrived a few minutes later, having followed

them in the pickup. He expected to find his daughter upstairs in her bed, and he frowned when he saw that Tara had gathered all the well-wishers around her and set up court in the sitting room.

"You should be resting, young lady."

"Daddy—"

"No argument." He picked her up in his arms and passed Beth and Shannon without a glance.

His sister shrugged. "Well, I have work to do."

She disappeared into the kitchen with the three women guests, and Kenny and Gloria raced off to finish a game of horseshoes they'd been playing. Kenny's grandfather wheeled to his room for a nap, and Shannon was left alone in the sitting room.

What am I doing here?

Restless, she walked to the window and stared at a dark swath of smoke swirling above the wooded mountains cupping the valley. By now she could have been on a shuttle bus to Denver, putting a widening distance between her and this whole nightmare. The feelings that had accompanied her decision to return were gone. She couldn't remember why she thought Tara needed her or why she wanted to bring more pain into her life by spending time with Ward. His life was full with his daughter and his horses, and she had little to offer him on any level. If he'd been serious about any kind of a commitment between them, he would have spoken up before now. She'd sabotaged her future by failing to honor the interviews that had been set up for her, and for what?

* * *

When Ward came down from Tara's room, he didn't see Shannon and asked Beth where she was.

"Maybe upstairs," his sister answered uncertainly. "I told her we didn't need any help in the kitchen."

"I think she said that she was going for a walk," offered Kenny's mother, who was busy fixing a bottle for the baby.

"Did she take Kenny and Gloria with her?"

"No. They're still playing horseshoes. Gloria's mother is watching them."

"So she went alone?"

Beth chided her brother. "Shannon's a big girl. She can take care of herself."

"In the city, maybe, but she doesn't know beans about rough country like this."

"She'll learn quick enough if she sticks around awhile." She eyed her brother as if asking, Is she sticking around?

Ward ignored the unanswered question, mainly because he didn't know the answer. He didn't know what had happened to Shannon in that hospital room to make her change her mind. Why had she put aside her plans to return to a situation that had challenged her in every possible way? Was it divine guidance that had kept her in his life?

As he left the house by the back door, he let his gaze rove over the open meadow where they had walked under the stars, but he didn't see her small figure anywhere in the wide expanse of wild grasses. Maybe she was walking around the corrals, looking at the horses who were being groomed for sale, or had gone to the stable to see how Calico and Princess were doing.

He asked the two ranch hands who had shown up for a couple days work if they'd seen her, but they shook their heads.

"No, boss. We've been busy unloading the pickup. We'll keep an eye out and tell her you're looking for her." They exchanged glances as if Ted had already filled them in on the news that the boss had a pretty lady on his mind.

If Shannon wasn't in the meadow, around the corrals or in the stable, where had she gone? The only hike they'd taken together was down to the stream. He stopped short. She wouldn't hike through the thick stands of aspen and pines trying to find her way to the stream, would she? He knew the answer even as the question crossed his mind. Shannon would do anything she put her mind to. Getting lost in the thick stand of timber between here and the stream would be easy for someone who didn't know the way. What if she tried to cross the stream by herself? Or got hurt trying to find her way down some of the rocky bluffs that bordered the water?

These thoughts quickened his long stride, and he began calling her name when he reached the dense forest edging the far pasture, but his voice was swallowed up in the infinity of tree trunks and heavy vegetation. The path was almost invisible, and there were a hundred places where the rising and falling ground would challenge the most seasoned hiker.

He was angry that she would put herself in danger. What was she trying to prove? When he heard the muffled sound of the stream, he rushed forward, breaking through a band of trees and rocks edging the water.

For a minute his eyes didn't register the black-and-white dog who came splashing out of the water with a stick in his mouth.

Then he heard Shannon squeal and saw her sitting on the ground, trying to ward off the dripping wet dog who was determined to deposit the stick in her lap.

"Pokey, no." Laughing, she grabbed the stick and threw it into the shallow eddy swirling along the bank.

At first, Ward's emotions were too muddled to separate. Relief, annoyance, amusement and bewilderment all vied for expression, but thankfulness won out. She was safe. He felt foolish for jumping to conclusions.

Pokey greeted him with wet paws and a wagging tail spraying droplets of cold water. As Ward dropped on the ground beside Shannon, she looked at him in surprise. "How did you find me?"

"My great grandfather was a scout."

"Really?"

"Yes, really." His smile faded. "But you shouldn't take off by yourself like that. It's easy to get disoriented and end up miles from where you think you are."

"I'm not as inept as you think I am," she retorted. "Believe it or not, I didn't have any trouble finding my way to the stream. And you didn't have to come looking for me. I'm sure you have more pressing things to do."

Ouch. Her tone was as sharp as a cactus barb. "Do

you want to tell me what's the matter, or shall we play twenty questions?''

She ignored his teasing grin. ''It shouldn't take twenty. One ought to do. What in blazes am I doing back here?''

He ignored her accusing tone. ''You're here because you made that choice,'' he answered evenly.

''I'm not sure I did,'' she argued. ''I think it just happened.''

''Nobody lives a choiceless life, Shannon. Sometimes we make a decision not to make a choice, and that in itself is a choice. Sometimes we let others make choices for us, but that's not you, Shannon. You're here because that's what you decided to do.''

''Well, it was a mistake…a terrible mistake.'' She glared at him as if she dared him to deny it.

Obviously, she wanted him to argue that she'd made the right choice or admit that he was responsible for it. He wasn't going to go there. The truth was that he'd been totally surprised by her sudden decision. At the time, he had truly believed there had been some kind of divine intervention in answer to his prayers for her well being, but he knew if he offered such a possibility, she would scoff at him. They couldn't even talk about the situation in terms of where the good Lord might be leading them.

''Why do you think it was a mistake?'' he asked, searching her eyes for some glimpse of insight that he needed to understand where she was coming from.

''It's obvious, isn't it? I've put my life on hold—and for what?''

''To be of help?''

"Who needs me? Not anyone, that's pretty obvious. It took me about fifteen minutes back here to figure that out. Not Tara. She has you and Beth to love and care for her. And you have a family and a ranch to run and dreams to realize. There's nothing I can add by being here. Nothing. It's a waste of my time."

"Are you sure? What about this moment? Drawing in the freshness of pine-scented air. Listening to the soothing water. How many hours in a crowded office are worth this peace and quiet?"

"More than I can afford."

"Are you sure? Why not take this opportunity to let yourself enjoy a different pace and—"

"Don't you understand? I have to be doing something about my finances, my future, instead of pretending that all is well when it isn't."

He reached for her hand, but she stood up, ignoring the gesture. "Do you want to see if I can find my way back?"

"I'd rather sit here for a few minutes and figure this thing out."

"There's nothing to figure out. I made a mistake, and it only took me an hour to find it out."

She started through the trees, not even looking to see if he and Pokey were coming. What in the world had set her off like that, Ward wondered as he followed her. He could have overtaken her, but he decided to treat her like a stubborn horse, let her have her head and see where she ended up. If she started moving too far in the wrong direction, he'd stop her before she got into trouble.

Shannon turned her head once to see if he and the

pup were following, then she increased her pace. Much to his surprise, she slipped through the grove of trees and brush without difficulty and came out of the wooded area almost where the shortest way to the ranch house began.

At the edge of the meadow, she stopped. What's the matter with you? she asked herself. She was suddenly ashamed of her childish tantrum. Taking out her mistake on him wasn't fair. He hadn't put any pressure on her. The decision had been hers. It wasn't his fault she had given in to some irrational impulse. He didn't deserve to have any added responsibilities, and she had seen a concerned tightness in his expression when he sat down beside her.

"I'm sorry if I caused you any worry," she said when he caught up with her. "I just thought a walk might clear my head, and Pokey needed a run."

"It's all right. Just tell someone next time where you're going. I know you're used to being independent, but in this part of the country, we depend upon each other. None of us can do our own thing without it affecting everyone else."

"I'm not used to thinking in those terms. I'm used to going my own way."

He turned her around to face him. "I want to take care of you, Shannon. Not because it's a responsibility. Not because it's a duty. I just want to take care of you."

"I don't need—"

"I know." He sighed. "You don't need anyone." Just you, she admitted silently.

He searched her expression, and as he tightened his arms around her, she let herself be drawn into the warmth of his embrace. She waited for him to speak of the building attraction between them. If he would compromise and set aside the issue of her spiritual beliefs or lack of them, maybe, they could find a solution to their other differences. Even as she longed for him to speak some words of love to her, he slowly set her away from him.

''We'd better get back to the house before they send out someone to look for us,'' he said gently.

She managed to cover her disappointment with a bright smile and a nod. Once again, she'd let her guard down, desperately wanting him to declare himself, but he had sidestepped any commitment. Was she completely misreading his attentions to her? She had the feeling he was waiting for some miraculous conversion that would change her into the kind of woman he wanted in his life. She was hurt, disappointed and angry, but she wasn't about to pretend to be something she wasn't for any man. What you see is what you get, Ward Dawson.

When they came into the kitchen, Beth was talking earnestly to Ted. ''Well, now, that's a worry, isn't it?''

''What's a worry?'' Ward asked.

''The wildfire,'' Ted answered, a deep frown on his young face. ''It's moving toward Box Canyon. If they don't get it stopped before it starts down that draw, it'll hit my grandma's place, for sure.''

''Maybe it's time you moved Rachel out of there. You don't want to wait until the last minute,'' Ward warned.

"That's what we were talking about," Beth said. "What are you going to do with a stubborn woman like Rachel, hog-tie her and carry her bodily out of her home?"

"If necessary," Ward answered firmly.

"She's agreed to start packing some things, just in case," Ted said. "The problem is, she's moving kinda slow these days." He hesitated and then added, "I was wondering if one of the women could go and help her."

Ward frowned. "I don't know. Beth's got her hands full, and the other women have children—"

"I could go."

There was a pointed silence while everyone looked at Shannon as if they'd forgotten she was even there. The skepticism on their faces sparked her indignation.

"I'm perfectly capable of helping Ted's grandmother pack up some of her things," she insisted.

"Sure you are," Beth said, nodding her head in approval. "It's kind of you to offer."

"Her place is pretty isolated," Ted warned.

That's not the half of it, Ward thought. Ted's grandmother lived in a tiny three-room log house that had been on the homestead property for years. No electricity. No heating. Only well water for the kitchen and other uses. No modern conveniences. No neighbors for miles.

"Gram's place is pretty rustic," Ted said, as if his thoughts were running along the same line.

"You might call it ramshackle," Ward offered bluntly. All the surrounding land had been leased out for grazing, providing Rachel with her only income except what Ted's wages added. By the wildest stretch of his imagination, Ward could not picture Shannon spending even a couple of hours in such primitive surroundings. She could get hurt and create more problems for Rachel without realizing it.

"No, Shannon. It's out of the question," he said flatly.

"I beg your pardon." Her temper flared, and her eyes shot fire at him. "If Ted needs someone to help his grandmother, and I volunteered, I fail to see why you even need to offer your opinion on the matter." She used the same brisk tone and unyielding eye contact that she employed when challenged by some belligerent adversary in a board meeting.

The only sound in the kitchen was a teakettle making a merry whistle on the stove. Both Ted and Beth lowered their eyes and didn't say anything.

"All right, Shannon," Ward said with reluctance, knowing that anything he said she would brush aside as interference. "I withdraw my objections. I know that Rachel will be happy to see you." *Forgive me, Lord, for the lie.* Ward knew the crusty old lady would delight in putting a city girl through a briar patch of demands and embarrassments.

Shannon ignored Ward's warning frown as she turned to Ted. "When do we leave, Ted?"

"We could go right now. It's about an hour's drive. I'll drop you off and then head back for the evening chores." He looked at Ward for approval. "Okay, boss?"

"Fine," he said, even though he wanted to suggest that Shannon wait until morning. That way he could drive her to Rachel's and bring her back when she had a look at the place and met Ted's grandmother, but Shannon's hands-off attitude toward him rang loud and clear.

"I'll fix up a basket to send with you," Beth said. "I don't think Rachel cooks much anymore."

"I'll pack up my few things and be ready to go when you are, Ted," Shannon said, but her stubborn bravado was for nothing.

The telephone rang, and Ward answered it. "Yes, he's here." He handed the receiver to Ted.

He listened, then quickly answered, "Yes, sir. I understand. Thanks for the warning. Yes, I'll tell Ward." He hung up and said anxiously, "I've got to get Grams out of there tonight. The fire's broken over the ridge and is heading down Box Canyon."

"I'll go with you."

"No, you're to call Chief McGrady right away," Ted told him. "Something about a helicopter going down on Silver Mountain." Ted hesitated. "Can I borrow your truck? I'll need it to bring down Gram's stuff. I'll leave my Jeep."

"Sure. Good enough," Ward agreed. They exchanged keys.

"Tell Rachel that she can stay with us. We've got plenty of room," Beth lied.

Ted nodded. "I'm out of here."

Beth shook her head as he disappeared out the back door. "I'll wager he'll have to carry Rachel out kicking and screaming. She won't leave willingly even if the roof's falling in on her."

Shannon felt completely at a loss to keep up with

what was happening. Once again she felt like excess baggage, and her stomach tightened as Ward made his call. From his side of the conversation, she knew that one of the aircraft dropping water had gone down and that air reconnaissance had failed to spot the wreckage. They had called on Ward because he knew the area and had experience with a rescue unit.

"Well, if the copter went down in that thick timber on this side of the mountain, it'll take a ground search to find it," Ward said, frowning. "Yes, sir, I probably know that old mountain as well as anyone. There's an old Jeep trail up to those old mine diggings." He listened for a long moment. "Yes, sir, as soon as it's daylight, I'll head up that way and radio you if I see anything." He thoughtfully hung up the phone, then turned to the two women staring at him. "Well, I guess it's a good thing Ted left me his Jeep. I'm going to take a little ride up Silver Mountain in the morning."

"Too bad Ted isn't here to go with you," Beth said, shaking her head. "Why does everything happen at once?"

"I'll go with you."

"What?" Ward looked at Shannon with an expression he might have used for one of Tara's foolish pronouncements.

"I said that I'll go with you. My offer to help Rachel has gone down the tube, so I'm available."

"I really don't think that's a good idea—"

"You can't use a second pair of eyes?"

"It isn't that," he answered quickly, both amused and irritated by her insistence. "I haven't taken that

Jeep road for a couple of years. I don't know what condition it's in, and I may have to leave the Jeep and do some demanding hiking.''

"So—"

He stared at her as if he couldn't believe he was having this conversation. "For starters, there's the matter of hiking shoes, and some serviceable clothing for this kind of outing.''

Beth cleared her throat. "I believe Kenny's mom wears the same size shoe. Shannon, wasn't Alice trying on one of your summer sandals? I'll bet she'd willingly make a temporary loan of her hiking boots and maybe a heavy jacket. Your blue jeans ought to do fine with a couple of sweaters. Don't you think so, Ward?''

Ward stared at his sister. There was no doubt about whose side she was suddenly on.

"This could turn out to be a very demanding search,'' he argued.

"Then I would think you could use an extra body along,'' Beth answered flatly. "You were going to let Shannon go off by herself. Wouldn't you'd rather have her along with you?'' She eyed him frankly. "Maybe the two of you ought to share a few experiences together.''

Shannon sent her a grateful look. "Let's take a vote,'' she suggested factiously.

Ward was smart enough to know the odds were stacked against him. He decided it was no use wasting his breath, trying to argue with a couple of hardheaded women.

He still had reservations about taking Shannon

along, but suddenly the idea of being with her began to outweigh his reluctance.

"All right, but you may end up sitting in the Jeep," he warned. "There's not even daylight left to start up that mountain now. We'll head out as soon as it's dawn."

"Yes, sir." She gave him a mock salute, and she could hear Beth chuckling as she hurried upstairs to get ready.

She collected what she needed from Alice Gordon, then peeked in Tara's room. She wanted to tell her that she wouldn't be seeing her the next day, but the little girl was sound asleep. She was obviously tired from the excitement of coming home.

Tara looked so small and fragile that Shannon wanted to take her in her arms and just hold her. A strange kind of ache suddenly made Shannon realize that somehow the little girl had slipped through the protective guard she had placed around herself. She turned away quickly, knowing in her heart that it was too late to deny the deep need to belong to someone— even to a child and a dedicated man who found her wanting.

Chapter Twelve

Ward and Shannon left the ranch the next morning just as the night sky was giving way to a gunmetal gray. The condition of the Jeep road would determine how quickly they could reach the old mining ruins near the crest of the mountain. Ward hoped they would sight the downed plane before nightfall or assure themselves it had not gone down on the southern slope of Silver Mountain.

He glanced at Shannon, sitting beside him, and couldn't tell if the early morning rising was responsible for her silent behavior or if she was having second thoughts about insisting she go with him. He was certainly having second thoughts. In the cold light of morning, the decision seemed ridiculous. What was he thinking? He had no idea what the day would bring. He'd been swept along by her forceful insistence that she help Ted's grandmother, and when that didn't work out, she'd turned that into a determination to go with him. His sister's remarks hadn't helped at all.

"We should reach the base of the mountain just about the time the sun comes up," he said over the roar of the engine. "Beth packed a thermos and some egg sandwiches for breakfast."

"Sounds delicious."

He silently chuckled. She lied beautifully. That strong independent stubborn streak of hers would never let her admit she'd made one heck of a mistake by insisting that she come along. He bet there'd be no whining from her. She was wearing an unbecoming too-large jacket, a flannel plaid shirt, jeans and borrowed hiking boots. And yet she had never looked more feminine or appealing. It was as if she belonged beside him in an old Jeep, bumping over a rough road at the breaking of a new day. An emotion he was startled to recognize as pure contentment surged through him.

"Why are you smiling?" she asked in a slightly defensive tone. She was aware of his clear brown eyes appraising her even though the brim of his tan cowboy hat put his face in shadow. "Don't you think I look like the well-dressed woman ready for a rescue mission?"

"Absolutely."

"I can do this, Ward. You have to give me a chance. I know I haven't exactly demonstrated that I'm the strong, outdoor type, but all my life, I've been able to learn what I need to know and made a success of it. I want to be a help, not a tagalong. Do you understand?"

He nodded. He understood, all right, but the truth was that she didn't have a glimmer of an idea what was involved. Once the Jeep road ran out without any sign of the wreckage, a climb would have to be made to reach the rocky promontory giving an overview of the southern slope of the mountain. She'd never be able to keep up with him. He was used to the high altitude and oxygen-thin air, but she would need repeated rest stops to make it. He had already decided she would stay with the Jeep.

"What are you thinking?" she demanded, her eyes fixed on his face.

"About having a cup of that coffee," he lied. "How about pouring me one? We'd better have breakfast before we reach the base of the mountain." He knew she'd need something in her stomach before they started the harrowing climb. He just prayed that sections of the road hadn't been washed out since he'd last driven it. "I think Beth put in some cinnamon rolls, too. And who knows what else? That sister of mine knows how to fill a food hamper."

"She's a wonderful cook," Shannon said, with a hint of envy in her tone.

As they ate breakfast in the jolting Jeep, the rising sun spread a tapestry of orange, pink and red across the eastern horizon.

"Wow. Isn't God magnificent?" Ward breathed reverently, gazing at it. "He gives us a masterpiece like that every morning and evening. Just looking at it creates a sense of the divine, doesn't it?"

She responded honestly. "I've never looked at a sunrise in that way."

"It's simple. When you start looking for God's miracles, they're all over the place." He chuckled. "Tara and I made a list of God's miracles one day, starting with the seeds for Beth's garden. At first, Tara wouldn't believe that each tiny seed knew the exact kind and number of leaves to grow and what color each flower should be, but as Beth's garden grew, she witnessed the miracle." He glanced at Shannon. "It's the same with people, you know. We're all programmed for a miracle."

"Oh, really?" she answered with obvious disbelief.

"Yep. There's a divine plan for our lives. Ready and waiting when we're born."

"Are you talking about fate?"

"Nope, I'm talking about the choice we have to follow our own desires or give ourselves up to the plan God has for each of us." He waited to see what her response was going to be. If only she would lower her defenses, he thought hopefully, and trust that God was not going to disappoint her the way other people in her life had. He knew she was afraid to take that step and he didn't know how to convince her to make it.

She stared out the window for a long moment without answering. Then she leaned her head back against the seat rest and closed her eyes. "It's too early in the morning for a theological debate."

He sighed, knowing that the religious gulf between them was still as wide as ever.

When they reached the base of Silver Mountain, Ward tightened his grip on the steering wheel. "Well, here we go."

Shannon sat up straight. This was a road? Surely, Ward had made a mistake. He didn't intend to drive up the side of the mountain on this narrow crumbling shelf, did he? One glance at the way he'd set his strong chin told her he intended to do exactly that. When he had mentioned a Jeep trail, she had thought he was using a western euphemism for a scenic western drive.

As they began to climb, she could hear loose rocks spitting out from under the wheels and feel the Jeep sliding in the loose earth. Her mouth went dry. She'd already had one experience going over the side of a mountain road. She might not be as lucky this time.

"How far?" she managed to ask, trying to keep from looking out the window as the ground fell away below them.

"The trail is about ten miles," Ward answered evenly, silently adding, If it hasn't washed out or fallen away. The road had certainly deteriorated a lot since he'd driven it. Once this Jeep trail had been listed in a Colorado guide to old mining camps, but it was obvious that was no longer the case. He doubted if there was much left on the mountain except mine tailings and gaping tunnel holes left by disappointed prospectors.

Leaning forward over the wheel, he searched for ways to avoid dangerous rocks and washouts in the narrow trail. The engine was straining in the higher elevation, and Ward wished Ted had kept the Jeep in better condition. What if one of the old tires blew? What if— He cut off that train of thought and in his mind substituted a favorite scripture.

He will give His angels charge over thee to keep thee in all thy ways. They shall bear thee up in their hands, lest they dash thy foot against a stone.

"Amen," he murmured.

Shannon shot a quick glance at him. Things must really be bad if Ward was praying. Her stomach took a sickening plunge. She swallowed to get some moisture in her dry mouth.

The rough trail twisted back on itself like a thin serpent.

Sometimes it looked as if a part of it had fallen away and was too narrow for the Jeep's wheels. In these places, Ward braked, eyed the passage ahead, then eased the Jeep forward, almost scraping the side of the mountain on his side. When they came to a passage wide enough to get his door open, he got out and surveyed the wooded areas above and below.

"See anything?" Shannon asked hopefully, and every time, he shook his head as he got back in.

"It's likely the helicopter went down at a much higher elevation than this. We don't even know if it's on this side of the mountain. Chief McGrady has another scout combing the north side, and they'll radio me if they find anything." He smiled at Shannon. "I bet you'd be real disappointed to cut our Jeep ride short."

"Try me," she answered dryly.

"Believe it or not, some people pay good money for a trip like this."

"Some people have a suicide complex, too, but I'm not one of them," she assured him, trying to return his smile. The fact that she had insisted on coming was not lost on either of them. She silently vowed she'd do her best not to let him see how terrified she was. "If you say this is fun, I'll try to believe it."

Despite her attempt at levity, he could see her hands clenched so tightly her fingernails were biting into her soft flesh. Impulsively, he stopped the Jeep and pulled her close.

"It's going to be all right. I'm going to take good care of you," he whispered as his lips touched her soft cheek. "I'm glad you're here," he murmured with an honesty that didn't make any sense at all.

"Me, too," she said honestly. Even as they were precariously perched on the side of a mountain cliff, she was glad she was there with him.

He lightly kissed the tip of her nose, pulled away and started driving again. Looking back, they could see the dark haze rising on the far horizon where the wildfires were raging. Ward thought about Ted and his grandmother and silently prayed they would get safely out of the canyon. He glanced at Shannon, thankful she was here beside him instead of at Rachel's place. "We're almost there," he assured her as they took the last switchback.

"So soon?" Shannon quipped. Each hour had seemed like ten. She couldn't bear to think about the paralyzing return trip.

"This is it," he said as the road ended abruptly in an open area. "End of the line."

Gaping black holes and mounds of tailings dotted the nearby slopes. Weathered piles of wood hinted at a bygone prospecting frenzy.

As they got out of the Jeep, he said, "We'll hike a short distance in both directions. Chief McGrady said that last communication they had from the missing helicopter could have been in this area. If we don't see anything at this elevation, I'll take a look from that crest up there.'' He pointed to a rocky bluff high above the place where they stood.

Shannon was aware he had used the pronoun *I,* but she didn't argue. At the moment, she was too grateful to have solid earth under her feet. She followed him as he led the way along a rocky shelf that gave a good view of the wooded slopes below. He had given her a small pair of binoculars that belonged to Beth.

"Look for any sign of damaged treetops, a glint of metal, anything that stands out as unusual and unnatural," he instructed.

They pushed through scratchy thickets and climbed on top of large boulders to get a better view. She was grateful for borrowed hiking boots and the long-sleeved flannel shirt. After searching the landscape in every direction in vain, they returned to the Jeep.

"Let's grab a bite of lunch," Ward said, peering at the sky. He didn't like the way darkening clouds were gathering on the western horizon. Everyone had been praying for rain, but it would certainly play havoc with their ground search if it arrived in the next few hours.

"Why are you frowning?" Shannon asked as she swallowed a bite of egg sandwich, which to her surprise tasted wonderful.

"Was I?" he asked in mock innocence. He brushed a crumb from his mouth. Took a swallow of water from his canteen, then stood up. "While you settle comfy in the Jeep for a spell, I reckon I'll take a little stroll."

She wasn't fooled by his good ol' boy jargon. He

was telling her to stay put while he continued the search. "And if you see something?"

"I'll radio McGrady, come back to the Jeep, and we'll wait for a rescue team. They'll have medics and personnel to handle any victims. I should be able to make it to the rim in a couple of hours, have a look and be back before dusk." He strapped on his back-pack, made sure the radio was fastened to his belt, then bent and kissed her lightly. "Stay put."

She nodded, clinging to his hand an extra second. "You be careful," she ordered.

"Yes, ma'am." He gave her that winning grin of his, turned away and in a long, purposeful stride headed up the ravine that cut into the mountain as it rose toward the crest of the mountain.

Shannon fully intended to do as he ordered, but as soon as Ward disappeared from view, her imagination fired all kinds of images of him in trouble. Slipping. Falling. Getting hurt with no one around to see it.

Her thoughts whirled. If she hadn't insisted on coming, he could have brought one of his ranch hands, and Shannon knew Ward wouldn't have ordered him to stay behind. Guilt stabbed at her. He'd given in to her stubborn determination to come at the cost of his safety.

Grabbing her borrowed jacket, she took off after him. She was confident she could overtake him without any trouble because he'd only had a few minutes' head start. She soon discovered she had miscalculated two things—the swiftness of his long stride and the demands of the increased altitude on her breathing and energy.

Every time she stopped to catch her breath, she knew he was getting farther and farther ahead. As the stands of trees and undergrowth became thicker, a quiver of panic set in. He could have veered off in any direction. She saw nothing but thick stands of trees, tumbled rocks and decaying logs. As she turned to look in every direction, she suddenly wasn't sure which way she'd come.

I can't be lost.

"Ward. Ward? Where are you?"

Her voice bounced right back at her. She strained to hear something besides the loud thumping of her heart. Nothing.

She called his name again.

Suddenly he was there, standing at the top of a mound of boulders just beyond the place where she had stopped.

"There you are," she gasped.

A flood of relief surged through her body. But when she saw his expression, she wished with all her heart she could disappear. She had never seen him angry. His usually soft brown eyes were hard as steel, and his mouth was rigid with controlled fury. Instantly, her rationale for disobeying his orders seemed terribly shallow and without merit. She swallowed hard and braced herself for his fury.

"What part of stay in the Jeep didn't you understand, Shannon?" he asked coldly.

"None of it," she answered with her usual stubbornness. She forced herself to meet his angry gaze squarely. She'd been on the hot seat plenty of times in her job and had decided that leading with her chin was the only way to handle a foul-up—especially one of her own making. "I was worried about you. You said the other searchers are on the far side of the mountain." She hoped the nervous tremor in the pit of her stomach didn't show. "So I decided to come along—whether you like it or not."

At first she thought he was going to turn and leave her standing there, breathless, frightened and ashamed of herself. "I don't have time to take you back," he said shortly. She was relieved when she saw the stiffness around his mouth ease slightly. "I guess you win—for now."

"I'll keep up, I promise."

He nodded, held out his hand and helped her over the mound of boulders. With grim determination, she did her best not to lag too far behind as he led the way up the rugged slope. They skirted narrow ledges, crawled on all fours and fought through thick drifts of trees and bushes.

Because going straight up was impossible in the craggy terrain, they hiked in zigzag patterns around rock ledges, steep inclines and cliffs. There were still mounds of tailings and mining tunnels, and Shannon marveled at the tenacity of men searching for a fortune on this craggy hillside.

What a waste, she thought. What people wouldn't do for money. Quickly she shoved away the truth that she was the one who had been struggling all her adult life to find success in a world where money was the driving force.

"You okay?" Ward asked as he looked back to check on her.

She nodded, hoping he wouldn't notice that she was limping slightly. Her borrowed hiking boots had begun to rub a blister on her right heel.

They stopped repeatedly to survey their surroundings in every direction. The hope was always there that they would spot the wreckage and could radio the location to a rescue team searching the other side, but each time they were disappointed.

It became clear to Ward that Shannon was drawing on every bit of endurance she could summon. He wished there was some way to make things easier for her. Even though she'd asked for the grueling climb, he knew misguided concern over his welfare was responsible for her stubborn determination to come with him. Unfortunately her good intentions could very well be an additional burden he could ill afford. She had slowed him down, and time was of the essence.

The wind had quickened, and he kept looking at the darkening sky. He knew how quickly a summer storm could form in these mountains, and climbing would be more perilous than ever when the ground was wet and slippery. *Lord, I don't know how this is going to turn out, but I trust that You do.*

"What do you think?" Shannon asked, searching his face.

"It could blow over," he said. "Sometimes we don't get more than a sprinkle from clouds like that." He prayed that this was one of those times.

When they reached a small waterfall trickling down from the rocks above, both of them were ready for a break. Shannon's chest was burning more than she was willing to admit. She eased down on a patch of green near the pool of water and resisted the urge to take off her boot.

Ward quickly filled his canteen and handed it to Shannon. He was about to sit down beside her when he heard something.

"What was that sound?"

Shannon looked at him, puzzled. "The water falling?"

He shook his head. Not water. More of a thrashing noise. He swung his eyes in the direction of a nearby grove of trees.

"What's the matter?" Shannon asked, watching his face as his eyes narrowed.

"I'm not sure," he answered. The pool could be a watering hole for wild animals. There were plenty of black bears and wildcats in these mountain forests. Several times he'd seen mountain goats scampering over rocky cliffs at lower elevations. It could be that they were coming this way for water.

"I don't hear anything." She strained to listen, but couldn't hear anything besides the gurgling, tumbling water.

He waved his hand. "Get behind those rocks and stay out of sight."

She started to argue, but for once in her life, she did as she was told—well, almost. She didn't stay out of sight. She couldn't keep from peering around the large boulders. What was out there? She couldn't even begin to imagine what kind of danger might be just a few feet away.

Ward moved slowly forward, holding his head in a listening position. He still couldn't identify the sound, but no animal he knew about made that much noise. Very slowly, Ward walked away from the waterfall toward the heavy stand of trees.

Shannon wanted to scream at him to come back. He didn't carry a gun. What if some wild creature attacked him? She lurched to her feet. Stay out of sight. His order vibrated in her ears, and only the thought of his anger kept her from bolting after him.

Ward made his way into a dense stand of evergreens. Now that he was away from the rushing water, the thrashing sound grew louder.

What was it?

He could hear the snap of broken twigs and the crunch of ground cover. He pressed up behind a large tree. Something was coming right toward him.

What was it?

His breath caught as the heavy undergrowth parted, and he saw what was making the noise.

"Dear God," Ward breathed as a man dressed in a blood-splattered pilot's uniform staggered into view and nearly fell at his feet.

Chapter Thirteen

Ward bolted forward and caught the man before his knees gave out. "I've got you. Take it easy."

He was a small man with graying dark hair.

His face was scratched and bruised. One eye was nearly swollen shut. His uniform was torn and covered with stickers from wild mountain shrubs. "I—I— we—" he stammered.

"We've been looking for you." Ward raised his voice and called, "Shannon."

When she heard him calling her name, she lurched to her feet. What was wrong? What had happened to him? Not hesitating for even a split second, she ran toward his voice. The horror of his struggling in the savage grip of a wild beast was in her mind's eye as she bolted through the trees.

When she saw him half carrying a blood-covered man, she had trouble registering the truth. She gasped in disbelief. "Is it…"

"One of the flyers. Get the first aid kit out of my pack." He eased the man down on a green patch near the waterfall. "You're okay now."

"Pete," he croaked.

"That's your name?" Ward asked kneeling beside him.

"No… Pete is still in the plane." He gasped for breath. "Hurt. Needs help," he mumbled in a hoarse, exhausted voice.

"All right, we'll get him help. Here, take a drink. Not too much."

Ward put the canteen to the man's trembling lips, and a flood of questions instantly swarmed in his head. How far had the man walked? He needed information to relay to McGrady as soon as possible. Where had the helicopter gone down? Ward forced himself to wait for answers.

Shannon opened the small first aid kit and eased down beside the injured man. There were several cuts on the pilot's face, crusted with blood, but none of them seemed to be still bleeding. Shannon knew nothing about nursing, but there were no signs of broken bones. Several times she'd passed up the chance to take first aid classes that the Red Cross offered. She had asked herself, When will I ever need those? Never in a dozen lifetimes would she have imagined that the answer to that question was a situation like this.

A warning rumble of thunder jerked their eyes upward. Ward groaned as fast-moving dark thunderhead clouds blanketed nearby craggy peaks.

"We've got to find shelter."

"Where?" Did Ward know of a mountain cabin some place close?

"Help me get him to his feet," he ordered, ignoring her question. He motioned her to take one side while he took the other. He knew these mountain storms. In a matter of minutes they could be caught in a blinding downpour. With the exhausted man stumbling between them, they headed down the slope they had climbed a few minutes earlier.

Shannon choked back a protest. Why were they retracing their steps? What was he thinking? They couldn't possibly make it to the Jeep before the storm hit.

When Ward veered off in an unfamiliar area, she became completely disoriented. In the darkening forest, she couldn't see what direction they were heading.

Where was Ward taking them?

Vibrating thunder sounded like heavenly artillery drawn across the skies. Almost immediately the gentle spray of cool drops thickened. Ward urged them forward, moving as fast as the exhausted man stumbling between them would allow.

"We're almost there," he shouted over the pounding rain.

Almost where? Shannon squinted ahead. Then she knew.

Through the thickening rain, she could see a gaping black hole in the side of the mountain. They were headed for an abandoned mine tunnel.

Oh, no! A surge of panic whipped through her. She couldn't do it. She'd never been able to stand confining, dark spaces. Cowering in a dank, dark mine was as terrifying as the thought of being buried alive. She would rather stay out in the drowning rain. When they were just a few feet away from the mine's entrance, the exhausted man's legs gave out.

"I've got you," Ward said, lifting him on his shoulders, carrying him the rest of the way.

Shannon watched as they disappeared into the depths of the black tunnel. As sliding mud and gushing water poured down, she couldn't make herself follow Ward into that dark abyss. Visions of earth tumbling down on her kept her rooted in the driving rain. She closed her eyes against the spears of lightning and the cannonlike booms of thunder.

"Shannon," Ward barked as he dashed into the rain.

"No, I can't—"

He ignored her sobbing. With one swift movement, he lifted her in his arms and carried her into the black hole.

He set her on the ground, and she bit her lip, struggling to hold back a rising hysteria. "I...I can't stay here."

"Yes, you can," he said firmly as if he were talking to his five-year-old daughter instead of a twenty-eight-year-old adult. He lifted her chin so she had to look directly into his eyes. "It's safe."

Safe? The word was a mockery. Echoing thunder vibrated from the walls, and the dark passage looked ready to let tons of dirt slide down upon them at any moment. It must have been years since anyone had been inside the dark, crumbling mine tunnel. It was filled with tumbled rocks and rotted wood, and it had a penetrating dank smell. Even in the dim light, she could see where the earth and timber had fallen away from the dirt walls.

"We can't stay here," she protested vehemently.

"We have to," he answered firmly. "And I need your help. That's why you tagged along, remember?"

But I didn't bargain for this, she raged silently, swallowing hard against a rising quivering in her stomach. She hated the way he was reminding her it was her fault she was here—even if it was true.

"You're not going to faint on me, are you?" he asked anxiously as she wavered.

"No, I'm not going to faint," she answered as firmly as she could, silently hoping it was true.

"Good," Ward said. He knew how hard she'd tried to measure up to the demands she had invited by coming with him. And he understood and sympathized with her feelings about the mine.

The first time his father had taken him into one, he'd wanted to run shrieking out of the horrid place. He couldn't breathe. The darkness seemed to claw at him. His eyes were blinded by the lack of light. Those feelings had never quite gone away, and if it hadn't been for the injured man, he would have taken his chances in the forest, lightning or no lightning.

"It's going to be all right, Shannon," he said gently as he brushed a damp strand of hair from her face. "Trust me. Okay?"

"Okay," she echoed, drawing on his warm breath touching her cheek and the gentle stroke of his hand. This was no time to exert her stubborn independence.

"Right now, we need to keep this fellow warm."

"How do we do that?" she asked, struggling to focus on something besides the echoing sounds of their voices and the dripping of water seeping down the dirt walls.

"I've got a poncho in my backpack. Let's get it on him right away. I'll try to make radio contact with McGrady as soon as the electrical interference from the storm will let me. Right now, I need to get all the information I can about where the helicopter went down."

As he bent over the man, Ward was relieved to see his eyes still open and tracking. His breathing was rapid, but Ward thought he looked fairly alert for someone who was soaking wet and exhausted.

"We're waiting out the storm here," Ward told him.

He gave a faint nod to show he understood.

"I'm Ward Dawson. I'm one of the people sent out to look for you. From your last transmission, they thought you might have made it to this side of the mountain. What's your name?"

"Ross Johnson," he whispered with blue lips.

"Okay, Ross, we're going to try and get you warm," Ward said, and covered him with his heavy poncho. He never went out riding without it, and more than once he'd been grateful for its warmth.

"Do you feel like talking a little, Ross?" Ward asked, knowing the man might pass out on him any time. If the storm hadn't come up, he would have quizzed the man as soon as he'd found him. There was a rising urgency to get as much information as quickly as possible about the location of the downed craft so he could get that information to McGrady right away. "Just take your time."

With halting, labored breaths, Ross told what had happened. The helicopter had developed mechanical problems. Ross had tried to set it down on the high bluff, but it had slid off into a deep ravine.

"I blacked out...stayed there all night. Pete was hurt bad, but he was still breathing." His cold lips quivered. "When it got light, I crawled out of the wreckage."

"Where was the sun?"

"In front of me...east."

Slowly, Ward was able to get answers to some pointed questions that gave him a good idea of the general location of the downed craft. From Ross's description of the terrain, Ward was pretty sure the aircraft had slid into the deep draw in the mountain just west of the waterfall. Ross couldn't have hiked very far in his condition.

"I was trying to climb where I might be seen if a rescue copter came over. But I had to keep stopping...not enough strength."

"You did great," Ward assured him. He knew that, despite Ross's valiant effort, making it up the steep incline to any place he might be seen would have been unlikely in his condition.

The pilot must have realized it, too. "It was pure luck that you found me."

"It wasn't luck," Ward corrected gently. "It was divine guidance." *Thank you, Lord.*

The man closed his eyes without answering.

Shannon's heart missed a beat. "Is he—"

Ward felt for a pulse. "His heartbeat is steady. I think he's just fallen into an exhausted sleep. He's pushed himself too hard. We've got to keep him dry and warm."

"How are we going to do that?"

Shannon hugged herself against a rising wave of shivers. Her hair lay plastered against her head. Although her borrowed jacket and her jeans had shed some of the rain, they were still damp. Fortunately the plaid shirt was still dry, and the heavy boots had kept her feet warm.

Ward glanced out the mine opening. No sign that the storm was passing over. In fact, if anything, the wind had shifted and was stronger than before. If the storm clouds got hung up on these mountains, the rain could settle in for hours. A downpour like this one would put out the wildfire, and the scorched hillsides would give off smoldering whiffs of smoke. He could imagine the jubilation of the evacuated families. The crisis would be over in a matter of hours if the sky kept dumping sheets of rain in the area.

"A good storm for ending the wildfires," he said, knowing it was the worst kind of weather for a rescue. His immediate concern was bringing two injured pilots to safety. "We just have to wait and see if the storm clouds are going to lift. In the meantime, we need to handle things as best we can."

She nodded, but at the moment, she didn't see a glimmer of best in the situation. He rose to his feet, reached into his backpack and took out a small flashlight.

"Where are you going?" A sudden panic shot through her as she realized he was going to walk into the tunnel.

"I'll be back in a minute. You stay here."

As he disappeared into the engulfing darkness, she couldn't have forced herself to follow him. Where had he gone? She needed his presence to ease her raw-edged nerves. Why had he left so abruptly? Was he aware of a new danger? Her sense of claustrophobia mingled with a new rising fear.

When she saw the bobbing flashlight coming toward her in the dark tunnel, she jerked to her feet. As his shadowy figure came into view, she saw that he was carrying something.

"What is it?" she asked, unable to make out what he was clutching in his arms.

"Dry timber."

"Timber?" she echoed.

"We need to make a fire as soon as the rain stops." He walked to the mouth of the tunnel and dropped the splintered dry wood in a pile just short of the entrance.

"Do we have to wait until then?" she protested, hugging herself against a wave of shivers.

"Yep, I'm afraid so. A fire burns up oxygen, so we can't build one in an enclosed passage," he explained. "In any case the smoke would drive us out...so we'll wait." He eased down on the ground beside her, and put an arm around her shoulders. "At least there's plenty of dry timber lying around for fuel."

Shannon failed to find comfort in the reassurance. It was all she could do to keep her teeth from chattering.

"Once I got caught out in a storm like this," Ward told her. "I was so cold I thought my blood was turning into red icicles, but I kept thinking about how warm I was going to be when the sun came out and the shivers went away. Strange, isn't it, how our mind can control our body?"

"Are you telling me that if I think I'm sitting here getting a sunburn, my body will believe it?"

He chuckled. "Well, I couldn't guarantee it, but keep that thought, and see what happens."

She gratefully pressed her chilled face against his chest. The strong rhythm of his breathing settled the wild flutter of her heart and the warmth of his strong, muscular body seemed miraculously to seep into hers. She'd never felt this kind of close bonding with anyone. In fact, she'd never been comfortable being too physically close to anyone. She'd always insisted on her own space and made sure no one violated it by getting too close. She stiffened when someone tried to hug her, but being in Ward's arms was different. She welcomed his physical closeness with a bliss she wouldn't have thought possible.

"Better?" Ward asked as the shivering of her body began to ease.

"Yes. Much better."

He rested his head against Shannon's, dismayed by the depths of the feelings he had for her. Many times in his life he had been confused and uncertain, but never as much as from the moment he'd met her. Nothing about their relationship made sense. He'd been determined not to make a mistake when he married again, and Shannon Hensley was nothing like the mate he thought he was looking for. The kind of life she led was completely foreign to him. Her ambitions had led her down a completely different path. Living on a ranch would probably drive her crazy in short order.

As he huddled in the dank cave, filled with tenderness and love for the woman in his arms, the same question kept taunting him.

Why, Lord, why have You brought her into my life?

Shannon had fallen asleep, and he was grateful for it. The responsibility of keeping her safe was a heavy one. She had risen with unbelievable determination to every challenge the hard climb had thrown at her. A woman conditioned to the altitude and vigorous physical demands couldn't have done any better. He hated to think of leaving her here alone, but he had to get a radio message to McGrady and check on the crash site. There was no question about it. Getting to the injured Pete as soon as possible was imperative.

Adding up all the information Ross had told him, Ward was pretty sure he had mentally zeroed in on the likely place where the helicopter had gone down. Ward reasoned that all he had to do was retrace his steps to the place where they had found Ross, then head for the deep ravine that lay almost in a direct line with the waterfall.

From time to time he glanced out the mine's entrance. Was the rain slacking off? Was it just hopeful thinking? He waited a few minutes more, then was sure—the echo of thunder was getting fainter. Good. That meant that interference from lightning might have lessened enough for him to make a radio transmission. He gently removed his arms from around Shannon.

She woke up with a start. For a moment, her eyes rounded in confusion. Where am I? Then she remembered. "What's the matter? What's happened?"

"Nothing. It's okay. You've been sleeping." He brushed a kiss on top of her damp head. "Sorry to wake you up, but I think the storm may be about over."

"It's still raining," she protested as she glanced out the tunnel's opening.

"I know, but it's slacking off. Listen. You can tell the thunder is moving farther away. Maybe I can get a radio transmission through now." He eased away from her, stood up and took the radio from the case fastened to his belt.

Hope spurted through her as he stepped outside into a light rain shower. Shielding the radio with his face and cowboy hat, he turned one way and then another. She couldn't tell whether he was talking because she couldn't see his lips clearly.

Maybe…maybe…?

She held her breath. If he could report where they were, all they had to do was sit and wait for a rescue team. When he strode into the tunnel, her hopes were dashed.

He shook his head. "The transmission keeps breaking up. There's still too much electrical interference. I'll have to keep trying, but before I leave—?"

"Leave? What do you mean, leave?" She jerked to her feet.

He put his hands on her shoulders looked straight into her frightened eyes and explained that he wanted to resume his search for the helicopter.

"But it's still raining! It's insanity for you to even think about going out in this weather." Her voice trembled in utter disbelief.

"The storm is moving on, and the rain is slacking off. I'm hoping it will stop altogether before night sets in."

"You don't even know where the copter went down."

"I have a pretty good idea. There are a few hours of daylight left. I'm going to check it out, and I'll keep trying to contact McGrady."

You can't leave me here alone!

Even as the frantic plea crossed her mind, she knew it was exactly what he intended to do. She also knew that pleading with him would be a waste of breath. One thing she knew without any doubt, Ward Dawson was his own man, and he wouldn't be swayed from doing what he thought was right. She wanted to insist on going with him, but that was out of the question. She knew it, and so did he.

He started unloading his backpack. "I'll leave the sandwiches I packed, the canteen, a couple of apples, a flashlight and matches. Once the rain stops, you can build a fire." He started to ask if she'd ever built a bonfire, but he knew the answer from her expression. "Here's a map to use as paper. Just make sure the fire is close enough to the entrance to let the smoke out. Understand?" She nodded, but she really wasn't taking in any of what he was saying. The thought of being left alone in this abandoned mine was bad enough, but what about the injured pilot?

"What about...about Ross?" she stammered anxiously. What if he gets worse? What if he dies?

"His breathing and heartbeat are still regular," Ward reassured her. "He'll probably stay asleep, for a while at least. When he wakes up, give him some water and see if he wants to eat anything. There's a little of our lunch left."

"When will you be back?"

"I don't know. But you can handle this, Shannon. I know you can."

She knew it was useless to argue. Her head came up. "Please, take care of yourself. I don't want to have to come looking for you."

He chuckled and gave her a tender look as if he were going to say something more, then he turned and was gone.

Weird shadows that seemed alive began to invade the mine tunnel as it became darker outside. At first, as the hours crept by, she kept her eyes on the mine's entrance, wanting to see Ward's returning figure. Surely, he would decide he'd been wrong about the storm blowing over. He would come back, and they would wait for morning together.

The fantasy faded as the rain slowed to a trickle and night shadows crept into the already dark abyss of the mine. She steeled herself to wait out the night in silence alone when suddenly Ross moaned and started thrashing out at the poncho that covered him. Shannon quickly bent over him, using the flashlight to see his face.

"Ross, are you awake?" His eyes were open, but they had a frightened glazed look about them. With her free hand, she felt his forehead. She silently groaned. No wonder he was flinging off everything. He had a fever.

"Water," he croaked.

"Yes, water." She grabbed the canteen, lifted his head and let him take a deep swallow. Her mind raced. What should she do? What did she know about fevers? She'd had the flu a couple of winters ago. What had she done for the fever? Aspirin and plenty of water.

She grabbed the first aid kit Ward had left and was all thumbs as she gave him two of the pills and enough water to swallow them.

"You'll feel better now," she promised him with false bravado in her voice.

"Pete?" He tried to sit up.

"Ward is looking for him now. We just have to wait." She bit her lip as she added silently, And wait, and wait.

As the hours passed, strange noises from the depths of the mine brought a new fear. As she huddled in the darkness with the injured man, her imagination taunted her. Was some wild night creature beginning to move? Maybe the mine was filled with bats. The thought sent a cold prickling up her spine.

As a young child she'd been frightened many times when her parents left her alone for most of the night while they partied with friends in another apartment. She'd wake up in the middle of the night, listening to the frightening noises and knowing they hadn't come home.

Maybe they wouldn't. Maybe she'd be all alone forever. She'd lay awake for hours, stiff and frightened, waiting to hear the sound of their muffled laughter as they passed her room. She never called out to them, fearing they would chide her for being a baby. Above everything else, she wanted their approval, and the fear had never left her that they wouldn't love her if she didn't measure up.

As she sat there alone, childish memories she had buried deep became real again. The light of her flashlight began to dim, and in a few minutes the batteries went dead. As the darkness closed in, she fought the driving need to get to her feet and run. She felt all alone again. Uncertain and fearful. The strong confidence she'd struggled to maintain all her life deserted her. She felt totally helpless. The driving forces in her life, prestige and money, were valueless in the circumstances. There was nothing she could do for the man who might be dying just feet away. Nothing, she could do for herself.

You could pray. Ward's voice was as clear as if he'd been whispering in her ear.

She jerked her head up and searched the empty shadowy darkness.

"I don't know how," she answered, as if he were there to hear.

Yes, you do.

"No, I don't."

Try.

She'd listened to the prayers others had spoken during the evening prayer gatherings at the ranch, but she had always remained silent. Ward had assured her that prayers were just like communicating with a beloved friend. As she sat there, cold and fearful, she knew she'd never needed a friend more.

She moistened her lips. Not knowing how to start, she repeated one of the verses that seemed to be a favorite with everyone.

Call upon the Lord and He will give you the desires of your heart.

Drawing upon that promise, she began to put into words all the feelings that were swelling up inside her. "I thought I could handle anything, but now I know I can't. Please help me get through this. I've never thought I needed to believe in anything but my own determination and my own strong will." For the first time, she admitted an honesty that stripped away the worldly pretenses that had been the guiding force in her life. Her driving ambition seemed hollow and barren. "I need to change. I know that," she whispered. "God, please help me. Don't let Ross die. Bring Ward back safely." Not knowing what to do or say next, she whispered a faint, "Amen."

Putting her head against her drawn-up knees, she fell silent. She didn't feel any different after offering her stumbling prayer. In fact there was a faint mockery deep inside that she'd offered up her fears to a God she'd never known before.

"Water," Ross croaked in a dry voice.

She fumbled in the shadowy darkness until she found the canteen. Then she helped him sit up while he drank. She couldn't see his face well enough to know if he was fully conscious, but she was relieved when he remained seated.

"Feeling better?" she asked hopefully.

"I don't hear any thunder," he mumbled.

"The storm is just about over. It's stopped raining."

"That's good. They'll find Pete now."

"Yes," she replied in a positive tone that didn't match her apprehension.

Where was Ward? Had he reached the helicopter safely? And what had he found?

"I'm sorry," he said as they sat in the dark.

"Nothing to be sorry about," she reassured him. "You've shown a lot of courage, Ross. You could have stayed in the helicopter, but you didn't. You went for help."

"And ended up here?" he asked, as if he was trying to reassure himself that this dark hole in the ground was for real.

"It was the only place out of the rain. I just wish there was something I could do to make you more comfortable." She was relieved that he seemed stronger and more lucid than before. Having someone to talk with made all the difference in the world in her feelings. The sound of their voices echoing in the tunnel was reassuring and comforting.

"You're a brave lady, Miss—"

"Shannon."

"Why don't you take this?" He started to give her the poncho. "I'm not very cold. I was just dreaming that I was sitting in front of a fire."

Shannon smiled, wondering if Ross had overheard what Ward had told her about using her imagination to keep warm. "No, you keep it around you." She felt his forehead. "I do think your fever has gone down."

She glanced out the mine opening. Was it safe to have a fire? The next question was, could she build one? Her expertise in this area was sadly lacking. Gas fireplaces didn't require anything more than turning a switch. She'd never laid a fire.

So what? some inner voice chided her. You've done a lot of things in your life for the first time. Shannon tried to remember what instructions Ward had given her. At the time, her thoughts had been reeling with the shock that he was going to leave her, and she hadn't focused on what he was saying.

Close to the entrance. Use the map for paper.

"Yes, I think I'll build us a nice, warm fire," she said with more confidence than she felt. "Ward collected some wood and left some matches. It shouldn't be that hard." She was talking to herself more than to Ross.

"It isn't," Ross said in a stronger voice than she'd heard before. "You just have to start out right. That's what I tell my Cub Scouts. You need to use small pieces of wood at first."

"All right. Let's give it a try."

Ward had left the pile of wood just inside the mouth of the tunnel. Shannon lingered for a moment at the entrance, gratefully breathing in the fresh night air. Everything glistened with droplets of water, and in the shimmering patina of moonlight, the landscape looked like a painting dipped in silver. She had never seen anything so beautiful. Never again would she take the spacious out-of-doors for granted.

Ross suddenly came up behind her with shuffling

labored steps, then eased down on the ground. "Let's build that fire, Shannon."

Following his instructions, she used the map and small pieces of wood to form a kind of teepee. Then she carefully lit a match. Her hand was so shaky the first two matches went out before she could light the paper. The third try was a success.

"That's it," Ross said. "Now feed more wood to the blaze when it gets a little bigger. Don't put on too much wood too fast or you'll suffocate it. Good job, Shannon," Ross said a little while later when dancing flames licked at the old dry wood and gave out a blessed circle of warmth.

"Maybe I could get the hang of this camping thing, after all," Shannon said, surprised at the satisfaction she felt sitting beside a fire she'd built with her own hands. Her spirits were almost light as she looked at the heavens, where stars twinkled at her through thinning clouds.

"Ward was right, you know," Ross said thoughtfully.

"About what?"

"When I said that it was luck that led me to that exact spot where you found me, Ward corrected me. Not luck, but divine guidance." Ross was silent for a moment, then added, "The good Lord answers our prayers in strange ways sometimes."

"He certainly does," she answered thoughtfully. She no longer felt alone and was strangely at peace.

Was God answering her prayers?

Chapter Fourteen

Shannon and Ross passed the night talking and confessing things about themselves they probably wouldn't have under any other conditions. From time to time, they dozed off as they sat leaning against the outside of the tunnel.

When dawn came, Shannon fed the last piece of wood to the fire. For breakfast, they shared the apple and sandwich Ward had left, and finished the last of the water in the canteen. Shannon didn't trust herself to find her way to the waterfall because she had become disoriented in the rain. She regretted not taking any food from the hamper when she had dashed after Ward.

"They should be coming after us before long," Ross sighed as they watched the sun getting higher and higher.

"Yes," Shannon hopefully agreed. If Ward got through to McGrady last night, the rescue team could be on its way by now.

She knew Ross was hurting. He looked awful in the daylight with matted blood on his face and clothes.

"Are you all right? Do you hurt anywhere?"

"Only all over," he answered with a wry grin. "Nothing serious."

She knew he was making light of his condition. His courage and companionship had give her the strength she needed to get through the night, and she was deeply grateful to him.

Hurry, Ward, please hurry.

As the morning hours passed, Ross sat quietly in the warming sun, but Shannon's restlessness grew. She began walking back and forth in front of the mine, her eyes searching the surrounding terrain. Several times she stopped and listened.

Nothing.

When her ears picked up the faint sound of men's voices, she was afraid to believe it was true. She froze like a statue, waiting, holding her breath until three men came into view a short distance below the mine.

Ross saw them at the same time, and he gave a weak shout, "Hurrah."

Shannon's eyes instantly flew to the figure walking behind the two uniformed men. Ward! With a joyful cry, she darted forward, slipping and sliding all the way down the muddy incline. When she reached him, she threw herself in his arms and unabashedly hugged and kissed him.

"Wow." One of the young men laughed. "What I wouldn't do for a greeting like that."

Ward responded to her welcome with a fervor of his own. His hands pressed her close, and he let his mouth trail from her mouth to the sweet softness of her cheek. The torment of leaving her alone instantly faded. She radiated a new confidence. Even with her hair hanging listless around her smudged face, her clothes soiled and wrinkled, she was beautiful. And the way her shining eyes were looking at him filled him with incredible happiness. She had been in his prayers during the long night he had held his vigil in the wreckage of the helicopter. He didn't know what had happened while he'd been gone, but there was something different about the way she was keeping her arm possessively around him.

She was all right! *Thank you, Lord.* And from the way Ross was standing waiting for them to reach him, he was all right, too.

Ross called out before they reached him. "Pete? What about Pete?"

"The rescue helicopter lifted him off about an hour ago. I spent the night with him. He's got some broken bones, but they say his vital signs are good."

"What about you, fellow?" asked one of the paramedics as they stopped beside Ross.

"I'm okay."

"You two guys are one lucky pair of dudes," a young, curly-haired paramedic told Ross. "How either of you survived that crash is a miracle."

"We sure didn't expect to find you looking this good," the older attendant added.

"I had a good nurse." Ross smiled at Shannon.

"Well, we need to give you the once-over. Make sure we don't need a stretcher to get back to where the helicopter can pick you up later."

While the two attendants bent over Ross, Shannon and Ward walked a little distance away. They still had their arms around each other as if afraid to let go.

"I don't believe it," Ward said, smiling at her. "What kind of nursing went on while I was gone? I expected to find Ross flat out, unconscious. What happened?"

For some reason, she wasn't ready to confess her feeble attempt to pray. She didn't want him to jump to the conclusion that she had become something she wasn't. One prayer didn't make her a devout Christian. Certainly not the dedicated kind of woman he was looking for. "I don't know."

He knew she was holding something back, but he didn't press her. He'd wait for a better time to share the long tedious night that had just passed. They both were exhausted, mentally and physically.

After the paramedics examined Ross, they were satisfied he had not suffered any broken bones or internal injuries and were prepared to take him to the place where the returning helicopter would set down. A portable stretcher was ready if the hike proved too much.

Impulsively, Shannon gave Ross a hug as they were ready to leave the mine. "Thank you. Take care," she whispered as a hint of tears collected in her eyes.

"You, too." His eyes were misty.

Ward and Shannon watched them leave, then he asked, "Ready for a hike back to the Jeep?"

"I've never been more ready," she answered. As they walked away from the mine, she took a deep breath of the fresh pine-scented air and lifted her face to the warmth of the sun. "It's a beautiful day."

"The day after a storm is always uplifting. Everything looks fresh and new. Makes you feel great to be alive, doesn't it?"

"Yes, but I'm not sure I'm ready to face a long hike," she admitted honestly. Already the blister on her heel was beginning to hurt. Thankfully, she soon discovered that going down the mountainside was certainly less demanding than climbing up the rocky slopes.

"We can take our time," Ward assured her. "When I finally got through to Chief McGrady last night, I asked him to get a message to Beth that we were spending the night. I didn't want her and Tara to worry."

The Jeep was just where they had left it, and so was the hamper of food Beth had packed. Although eating had not been at the front of Shannon's mind during the last twenty-four hours, as they sat in the Jeep, her appetite came back.

"Feeling better?" he asked, secretly amused at her obvious enjoyment of the day-old food.

"Much."

"Nothing like food, sunshine and a successful mission to put the world right."

She didn't answer, and he could see her forehead furrowed in thought. Suddenly she turned in the seat to face him. "Last night, Ross said you were right...about it not being luck that we found him. He also said that sometimes God doesn't answer our prayers the way we expect. Is that right?"

He nodded and smiled. "Do you want to hear a story that makes that point? There was this guy who got lost in Alaska. He was all alone, didn't know where he was, nothing but ice and snow stretching out in every direction, and he prayed to God to save him. The poor guy was about to freeze to death when an Inuit showed up and took him back to civilization.''

Shannon looked at him, puzzled. ''So?''

''Well, when someone asked the man what had happened, he told them how he'd been lost and almost died. 'I prayed to God to save me,' he said indignantly, 'but He didn't do anything. If that Inuit hadn't shown up, I'd have frozen to death.''' Ward chuckled. ''God uses anyone or anything that's handy to perform His blessings.''

''I see,'' she said thoughtfully. She hesitated to tell him about asking for God's help last night. She needed time to understand what had happened—if anything. Certainly, no Inuit had showed up to offer her help.

What about Ross?

Ward's story suddenly put everything in a different light as she thought about what had happened last night. When Ross got better and began to interact with her, her panic at being alone had almost instantly dissipated. She'd never expected the injured pilot to recover so quickly and become a companion in the terrifying situation—but he had! A comradeship had developed between them, and his presence had strengthened her through the long night hours.

Had the injured Ross been her Inuit? God's answer to her prayer?

Ward watched her, not knowing why she was worrying her lip as she seemed to be fighting some invisible challenge. ''Do you want to tell me about it?''

She shook her head.

He stifled his disappointment. Every time he thought they were getting closer to sharing soul-searching feelings with each other, she backed off.

"I need to do some thinking first," she said. Above everything else, she wanted to be honest with Ward and herself. She didn't want to make promises she might not be able to keep.

As they headed to the ranch, the narrow Jeep road was even more treacherous than before. The drive up the mountain had been grueling, but coming down was worse. Yesterday's heavy rain had washed earth and rocks down the mountain slopes, and in some spots Ward had to maneuver the Jeep's wheels cautiously over the accumulated mud and rocks.

When they finally reached the paved road running along the river, Ward loosened the knuckle-white grip he had on the steering wheel. "We're almost home."

Home. The word had a nice sound to it, Shannon thought, even though it didn't quite seem to apply in the present situation. She was too weary at the moment to handle any emotional analysis.

Ward sounded the horn as he stopped the Jeep at the back of the house. The kitchen door flew open. Wiping her hands on her apron, Beth hurried out.

As Ward and Shannon wearily climbed out, she gasped, "Heaven help us. You two look like death warmed over."

"I guess we feel like it, too," Ward admitted with a tired grin as Tara bounded out of the house with Pokey at her heels.

"Daddy, Daddy. You're back." She threw herself

at him. "Where did you go? Why didn't you take me?"

As he lifted his daughter up for a big hug, weariness eased out of him, and he felt renewed. The demanding experience he'd been through made him realize once again how precious life is. Not one minute of love should be wasted.

"Yes, I'm back." He laughed. "And how's my little cowpoke?"

"I'm all better now," Tara said. "And my hair is going to grow back. Aunt Beth said so."

Shannon could see that one of Tara's pigtails was a little thin, and she still wore a small bandage on her head, but her dancing eyes and broad grin were the same. Warm feelings spilled through Shannon as she watched Ward unabashedly show his deep love for his daughter. That's what fathers and daughters should feel for each other, she thought. Unconditional love wasn't about money or pride.

As soon as Ward put Tara down, she ran to Shannon, and grabbed her hand. "Come see Princess. She's all bigger."

"In one day?" Shannon teased. "That's all I've been gone."

"It seems longer," Tara insisted.

"Yes, it does." How wise children were, Shannon thought. Sometimes time couldn't be measured in minutes. A lifetime could pass in a few hours—or in one long night.

"Tara, can't you see these two are dead on their feet?" Beth chided. "Goodness gracious, I've seen half-plucked chickens in better shape."

Ward laughed. "That's what I like about you, Sis. You're not a bit shy about calling things as you see them."

"Well, anyone with eyes in their head can tell you're both on your last legs." She sobered. "We were all worried about you being out in that thunderstorm. It hit here with the force of a gale. The whole house shook as if it might be lifted off its rock foundation. The windows rattled, loose tiles flew off the roof, and the trees in the yard were almost bent double."

"You should have been here," Tara said with childlike enthusiasm. "Kenny and I ran around the house, singing, 'It's raining, it's pouring, the old man is snoring.' But Kenny's grandpa laughed and shook his finger at us. 'I am not snoring.'" She giggled. "We kept singing, anyway."

"That's enough, Tara," Beth said briskly. "You can tell them your stories later, and from what Chief McGrady said to me, these two have a few to tell us."

"Is Ted still at his grandmother's place?" Ward asked.

Beth nodded. "As far as I know."

"Then I'd better check on the horses and the ranch hands." With Tara tagging along, he headed toward the stables.

Beth motioned to Shannon. "Come on, honey, let's get you cleaned up and into a nice warm bed."

It was heavenly having someone take charge. Shannon meekly let Beth run a bath, then settle her in her own bed instead of the cot Shannon had been using.

Having someone fuss over her had been a rare experience, even as a child.

"Have a nice long nap. I'll have a nice meal ready for you when you wake up."

"You're too good to everyone, Beth," Shannon told her, marveling at the way Beth gave of herself in so many ways.

"Nonsense," Beth scoffed with her usual briskness. "I haven't seen any sign of a halo the last time I looked in the mirror."

Shannon moistened her lips. "Do you...do you think God always answers prayers?"

"Yes," Beth nodded readily. "Why are you smiling?"

Shannon was too tired to explain about Inuits. She closed her eyes and was hardly aware of the bedroom door quietly closing.

When Shannon awoke five hours later, it was dark. She could hear muffled sounds in the house, and smelled tantalizing smells wafting from the kitchen. Suddenly she was ravenous and filled with a sense of excitement. How wonderful to be part of a bustling household!

Quickly dressing in the new outfit she'd bought in Elkhorn, she hurried downstairs. The television was blaring, and people had collected in the small sitting room, listening to a newscaster.

"Only a few warm spots remain after the deluge of rain," he reported. "Most of the firefighters and National Guard are pulling out, leaving only a small number of men to clean up. The crisis is over."

"Yahoo."

"Hurrah!"

"Praise God."

"The fire's over. The fire's over." Tara, Kenny and Gloria grabbed hands and began dancing around the room. Pokey bounded at their heels, barking.

The adults hugged each other.

Ward reached for Shannon, and she leaned into the length of his strong body with a joy she wouldn't have thought possible. His lips lightly touched her ear. "Time to celebrate."

She closed her eyes and shoved away all unanswered questions about her future. All that mattered at the moment was that the nightmare was over.

"All persons evacuated from their homes are asked to report to the center tomorrow morning," the newscaster continued. "Arrangements will be made to conduct groups into the affected areas for an assessment of property damage."

"Does that mean we'll be going back home?" Kenny asked eagerly.

His parents looked at each other, and his father answered cautiously, "We'll have to wait and see, Kenny. They're saying that some of the homes in our area have been spared. Maybe ours is one of them."

Mr. Winters spoke. "Hazel and I have decided that no matter what we find, we'll move to Arizona to be close to our daughter and grandchildren. An experience like this makes us realize that family is the most important thing in life." The gray-haired couple smiled at each other. "We've not seen nearly enough of ours in the last few years. It's time to make up for lost time."

Gloria's parents were pointedly quiet, and Shannon suspected they were putting off making any decisions until they knew whether their home had been reduced to smoldering rubble or was still standing.

All of them thanked Ward and Beth for their hospitality, and there were a few tears shed as they expressed their gratitude.

"Come on, everybody. Into the dining room," Beth ordered with a wave of her hand. "We're going to have ourselves a thanksgiving feast."

In a matter of minutes, the dining room table was loaded. Shannon couldn't believe how much food Beth had set out. Everyone teased her about having a magic wand to produce such a feast on short notice.

Beth laughed and admitted she had raided her freezer. "What better time to enjoy God's bounty?" Then she added with her usual practical honesty, "It was getting too full anyway. My garden will be going crazy with all this rain."

There was room for everyone around the large oval table, and even Kenny's grandfather parked his wheelchair with the others. Ward made sure Shannon sat next to him.

After he gave a sincere lengthy blessing, the level of talk and laughter rose like helium balloons. The tension of the last weeks gave way to a thankful joy.

Ward teased Shannon about preferring egg sandwiches to fried chicken. As they laughed at their private joke, Ward couldn't believe how much she had changed from the woman he had met. Gone was the chilly, stuck-up manner that had challenged him the first time he stopped her car. Her whole demeanor had softened. Her eyes had lost their hard glint and her lovely mouth its rigidity.

As he watched Shannon laugh and joke with the others, he knew she was looking at people and life in a different way than before. On the ride back, he had sensed a tenuous surrender to a belief in God, and he wanted to think her priorities had changed.

But had they?

Because of the traumatic events that had affected her life, she seemed to be content to sit at his table and enjoy the simple food, talk and laughter. But would it last? How could the humdrum of a rancher's life compete with the excitement of being a career woman in a big city? She had changed—but maybe not that much.

She was obviously embarrassed when Kenny's grandfather leaned toward her and asked in his cracking voice, "Don't you want to draw another picture of me? My son says you're wasting good talent."

"Dad!" Tom Gordon protested. "I just said she had a lot of ability she wasn't using."

"Isn't that the same thing?" the old man muttered. Then he turned his attention to his glass of milk, as if bored with the conversation.

"Have you done any more sketches while you've been here?" Tom asked, trying to cover for his father.

"A few. Mostly just sketches to entertain the children."

"Some of these mountain scenes would look great

on greeting cards. And horses are always a good subject.''

"You could draw Princess and Calico," Tara offered, jumping into the conversation.

"I'll think about it," Shannon said, surprised when she felt a quiver of excitement talking about the possibility that maybe, just maybe, she might take up drawing in earnest sometime.

"You could give me a picture of Princess for my birthday," Tara said with a bright smile.

"Oh, and when is that?" When Tara told her the date, she smiled. "That's not very far away."

"I know. You can come to my birthday party and everything. I'm wishing for something special for my birthday," Tara said, her eyes glistening. "Do you want to know what it is?"

"If you want to tell me."

"I'm wishing for a new mommy." The little girl grinned at Shannon with a knowing far beyond her years. "Do you think my daddy will get me one?"

All the table conversation came to an abrupt stop as everyone's eyes fell on Shannon and Ward. For a brief moment, the silence was deafening. Then everyone started speaking at once as if trying to cover up the embarrassment.

Beth pushed back her chair. "Anyone for dessert?"

Shannon kept her eyes lowered. She couldn't bear to look at Ward. There were too many things unsettled between them.

Chapter Fifteen

Although Ward had tried to make light of Tara's announcement, the flush on his face made it clear that he was embarrassed by it.

When everyone began to collect in the sitting room for evening prayers, Shannon quietly excused herself. Ward walked with her to the bottom of the stairs.

"I'm terribly sorry. Not for the world would I have had you embarrassed like that," he apologized.

"You can't fault Tara for being up-front and speaking her mind." She hadn't intended for it to sound like a criticism, but it came out that way.

"You're right. We need to talk about this."

"Yes, but not tonight."

"The timing isn't good is it?"

"No, it isn't," she said firmly. She didn't like the idea that he was being forced into declaring his intentions by the innocent remarks of a little girl. "Now that the emergency is over, we all need to look at things more clearly."

More clearly. Her brisk, businesslike tone was not lost on Ward. Her protective barriers had gone up again, and he upbraided himself for letting it happen. They had been drawing closer every day they spent together, and now all that was being lost because of bad timing on his part for not speaking sooner.

At that inopportune moment, Beth poked her head out of the sitting room. "We're waiting, Ward. Aren't you two coming?"

"In a minute."

Shannon quickly said good-night and didn't look at him as she mounted the stairs. She prepared for bed as if she wasn't slowly breaking to pieces inside.

Where was this attraction between them going to lead? Why didn't he declare himself?

All her life she'd made plans and meticulous preparations for what lay ahead, but at the moment she was floundering like a boat without a rudder. How could she plan a future when she didn't even understand the present?

As she lay rigid in her tiny bed, something Beth had said came back to her. "Trust in the Lord and He will direct your path."

Trust. Shannon had turned the word over in her mind, and then had shaken her head. "I'm not sure I'm ready to give up my driver's seat, Beth."

I'm still not sure, Shannon admitted as she lay awake despite a lingering bone-deep weariness. She knew she loved Ward with a depth that she'd never felt for anyone, but she had only dipped her toes in the waters of becoming a Christian. For good reason, Ward might not believe it was lasting. A lot of people made promises to God under stress, then slipped back into their own way of thinking. How could she be sure she wasn't one of them? It wasn't fair to Ward to pretend she had experienced a deep conversion when her faith was about as solid as a soap bubble.

She pretended to be asleep when Beth came to bed, but she could hear the soft whisper of her nightly prayers, and somehow, even secondhand, they had a soothing effect. Silently, Shannon said her own, amen and fell asleep.

Breakfast was a hurried affair. A hopeful excitement put a smile on everyone's face. There were plenty of hugs and thank-yous to go around as the families made preparations to leave the ranch and return to the evacuation center.

Ward was pleased when Shannon smiled at him without any hint of last night's unpleasantness. She looked relaxed and rested. He couldn't keep his eyes off her. He impulsively put his arm around her waist and kissed her cheek. She smelled wonderful, and the softness of her skin stayed on his lips as he looked at her. If there had been any music at all, he would have danced her right around the kitchen floor.

"Sleep well?" he asked, locking his eyes with hers.

"Actually, I did."

"Good. Ted brought the truck back last night, so you and Tara can ride with me into the Junction."

"I hadn't planned on going. I'll stay here and help Beth straighten up."

"You'll do nothing of the sort," Beth intervened in her no-nonsense voice. "I'm looking forward to having the place all to myself. Besides, they'll be needing some extra hands at the school. I'm thinking there's going to be plenty of heartaches and disappointments when some folks get bad news.''

''I'm afraid you're right,'' Ward agreed. Who knew what the families would find left on the scorched mountainsides? ''Well, let's get going, folks.''

After all the others had left in their cars, Ward and Shannon climbed in the truck Ted had exchanged for his Jeep. Ted's grandmother had decided to stay in her home since the fire danger was over.

Shannon was thankful for Tara sitting between them, chatting away with her usual exuberance. ''Kenny said he'd bring Pokey back to see me, Daddy. And I told him he could come and pet Princess any time he wanted. Isn't that super-duper?''

Ward smiled at his daughter. ''Sounds super-duper to me.''

''Why did it take so long for God to make it rain?'' Tara asked, her mind hopping to another subject.

''His time is not our time,'' Ward answered easily. ''And maybe there were lessons to be learned.''

''And some of us are slow learners,'' Shannon offered with a rueful smile as her eyes connected with Ward's.

''Not me,'' Tara said. ''I learn quickly, don't I, Daddy?''

''Sometimes too quick.'' Ward gave Shannon a conspirator's wink over the little girl's head that drew them together in a strange way—like an intimate bond between the three of them.

As they drove into Beaver Junction, an air of excitement was everywhere in the small community. Streets and sidewalks were filled with people moving about with new energy and optimism. Although the main road out of the Junction was still closed to general traffic, numerous fire units had already left their fighting positions, and convoys were moving out of the area.

The area around the school resembled the bustle of an anthill. Several television crews were busily panning the crowd and looking for stories. At the entrance to the school, Red Cross workers were on full alert, acting as dispatchers for the vans arriving at the school to drive families into the burned-out areas. A loudspeaker announced that after surveying their property, the families would be brought back to the evacuation center until emergency traffic was thin enough to allow personal cars on the narrow roads.

''I'll take Beth's garden produce to the kitchen,'' Shannon offered as they joined the crowd pushing into the school. ''Tara can go with me.''

Ward nodded. ''I'm going to see if they need more drivers. Will you be all right if I get tied up for a few hours?''

''We'll be fine, won't we, Tara?''

''Hunky-dorky.'' She giggled. ''That's what Kenny always says.'' Ward sent her a warning look. ''Just make sure that everything stays hunky-dorky. Don't give Shannon any trouble.''

''I won't, Daddy. I'll be real good.''

Ward watched as Tara took Shannon's free hand and hugged her side as they walked away.

If she leaves us, Tara, what will we do?

* * *

As Shannon and Tara made their way across the crowded gym, a rush of memories came to Shannon. Memories that clashed with the present moment. She remembered how she sat in the corner, alone, resentful and angry at the inconvenience the wildfire had caused. As far as she was concerned the whole situation had been simply something to be endured. How could she have known the experience was going to change her whole life? She looked at Tara holding her hand and she was grateful her life had been touched by this child's love. All the discomfort she had experienced these past weeks was worth one smile from this little girl.

When they reached the kitchen, Laura was there, as usual, busy as three people. It seemed to Shannon that the cafeteria was more crowded and hectic than ever.

"Well, look who's here." Laura gave Shannon and Tara her usual ready smile. "What's this I hear, Shannon, about you and Ward rescuing a couple of pilots? Word is that they both owe their lives to you."

"Not me. It was Ward who did the rescuing." Shannon quickly corrected Laura.

"Well, I want to hear all about it some time. I'm betting you have a story of your own to tell."

The invitation to share her frightened surrender to prayer with Laura was tempting, but Shannon was afraid Laura would read too much into it. "Maybe sometime," she said vaguely.

"Good. We're having a short worship service in a few minutes. I was just about ready to head in that direction." With her usual easy commanding manner, she took Shannon and Tara in tow, and they made their way through the crowded gym.

She gave Shannon a promising smile when they reached the auditorium. "See you after service. I've got a few things to tend to. Preacher's wife, you know."

Almost immediately, Tara saw Kenny and Gloria near the front and bounded over to sit with them. Shannon hesitated to join them. Instead she took a seat near the back. Familiar sights, smells and sounds triggered a flood of memories of that Sunday morning she'd been there with Ward. How vividly she remembered the way he had smiled at her, ignoring how she shifted uncomfortably in her seat during the service. Even now, she could hear his deep clear voice raised in song and feel the warmth of his large hand as it tenderly engulfed hers, giving her reassurance.

Every time someone came through the door behind her, she turned hopefully. Maybe... But she was disappointed. Obviously there had been a need for Ward's services somewhere else, or he would have been back.

She was ashamed when she remembered how she had behaved toward him in the beginning. Why had he bothered to befriend her? What had he seen in her that made him willing to take her into his home? Would it be enough for any future they might have together?

The worship service was one of jubilation and thanksgiving. Reverend Cozzins's message reminded them of the good things that had happened in the midst of the tragedy—people had been drawn closer together, there were more displays of kindness and generosity than before, there was a realization of what was important in life.

''All of us have been changed by this experience. We need to look ahead, not back.''

Shannon bowed her head as Reverend Cozzins prayed that the lessons of the wildfires would not be forgotten, and in her heart she echoed that prayer. She was surprised by the feeling of surrender that came over her. When the minister read Jeremiah 29:11, it seemed that the scripture was directed right at her.

'' 'For I know the plans I have for you,' declares the Lord. 'Plans to prosper you, and not to harm you. Plans to give you a hope and a future.' ''

The words echoed in her heart. *A future and a hope.* Ward had told her there was a divine plan for every child of God, and now she believed him. Why else was she sitting in this place feeling totally complete for the first time in her life?

After the service was over, people hugged and smiled at each other, and differences that might have been between them before the wildfire had faded in the life-and-death situation they had faced. Why did it take a catastrophe to bring out the best in human nature? Shannon wondered.

She collected Tara, and they made their way out of the auditorium with the rest of the crowd. Shannon was surprised when Judy came up to her and asked about Ward.

''He's helping out somewhere,'' Shannon told her.

''I've been worried about him,'' she said. ''He doesn't use good judgment sometimes.''

"I'm sure he can take care of himself," Shannon answered, wondering where this conversation was going.

"He always has, up until now. But sometimes men get a little off balance, you know what I mean?"

"No, I'm not sure that I do," Shannon answered. "Ward seems to be about the most balanced man I've ever met."

"Really. I would have thought you'd be bored to death with a plain old cowboy. It's too bad your vacation turned out to be such a bummer. I guess you'll be leaving soon?"

"No," Tara said, glaring at Judy. "Shannon's not leaving. She's staying."

"Not even to go back to California where she lives?" Judy asked in the patronizing tone adults often use with children. "I bet she's ready to get out of here and get back to where all the action is."

"My daddy isn't going to let Shannon go away," Tara declared, giving a pugnacious lift to her little chin. "Besides, we're all going there to see Disneyland, Hollywood and Sea World. Aren't we, Shannon?"

The lie was a whopper, but Shannon wasn't about to let Tara down. "Yes, we are."

"Well, I guess that answers my question."

Shannon knew Judy's assumption was premature. No matter how much Tara liked her, Ward would never allow himself to be manipulated by his daughter.

Judy turned her back on them and walked away with a decided slump to her slender shoulders.

Tara kept close to Shannon's side as they made their

way to the cafeteria. Lunch was a hurried affair with people coming and going as if the school had suddenly turned into a bus station.

Evacuated families anxiously waited for their scheduled time slot to tour their home. The vans began leaving the school. Mr. and Mrs. Winters and Gloria's parents were in the first group. Shannon could tell from their worried expressions that they feared the worst.

Shannon was surprised when a Red Cross volunteer came up to her. "Miss Hensley?" At Shannon's nod, the woman studied her clipboard. "Your name is on the list of people living on Prospect Mountain."

"I was renting a place there," Shannon acknowledged.

"We have a van going to that area at two o'clock. You will be able to view the damage, but you will not be allowed to stay in the area until the okay is given for you to return."

Shannon's first impulse was to decline the offer to see whether or not the rented cottage still stood. She wasn't quite sure why she nodded at the lady and said, "Thank you." Perhaps she needed some kind of closure to the events that had stripped her of car and possessions, her false pride and even her direction in life.

As Shannon and Tara waited for their ride, they were surprised to find that Kenny and his parents were going in the same group. When the van pulled up in front of the school, Shannon had an even bigger surprise. Ward was the driver.

Tara squealed, dashed into the van, and gave him a

hug. "I'm going to sit with Kenny," she announced, and bounded toward the back of the van.

"Never saw a bus driver in a cowboy hat before," Shannon teased as she took a front seat.

"Yep, we're pretty versatile, ma'am." The corners of his mouth quirked with a grin. "Come rain or shine, I'm your man."

The double meaning brought a warmth to her face. "But can you drive these mountain roads?" she asked with mock seriousness.

"I reckon I can give it a try. I've had a little experience."

"Really? I never would have guessed."

His smile faded a little. "It may not be a very pretty ride. Are you sure you want to go?"

"Yes," she said firmly. "I need to see it."

He nodded. "I understand."

Shannon wasn't sure she did, but she wanted to witness the devastation with her own eyes. In some strange way she needed to see the charred trees and scorched earth and smell the lingering acrid smoke. There was an undefined need to find assurance in her heart that in time the mountain would heal itself. It surprised her how deeply she had come to love these rugged surroundings. If she'd been born here, being the kind of wife Ward deserved would have come naturally to her.

They left the school, drove through Beaver Junction and headed up the mountain road that had been opened to official travel. Ward chuckled when they passed the place he had stopped Shannon's car that first day.

She'd been as feisty as a wild colt, and just as challenging.

As they traveled upward, they began to see more and more blackened trees where tongues of the fire had surged downward. Some areas remained untouched even though sections of the mountain on both sides had been ravaged. When they reached the spot where her car had gone off the road, he shot a quick look at her. A surge of thankfulness swept through him that she was here with him, safe and well. There had been many blessings in their short time together.

Shannon was thinking along the same lines as she viewed the rocky slope where she had nearly lost her life. A crumpled heap of blackened metal was all that remained of her expensive white sports car. She remembered how devastated she had been. How angry. How resentful that such a thing had happened to her.

"What do you see?" Alice Gordon called from her seat across the aisle.

"Nothing important. Nothing at all," she said when Ward slowed the van at the place where her rented cottage had stood. Only tumbled timbers and charred remains were left to mark the spot. She shivered, remembering her stubbornness in wanting to stay there. When the Gordons' property came into view, there was a collective holding of breath in the van. Then a loud cheer went up from Kenny's parents.

"Praise God."

"Hallelujah."

Their house still stood, untouched by the wildfire. Blackened trees on the slope behind the house showed how close the flames had come. They could see where firemen had cleared all shrubs and wild grass around the house. Evidence of a backburn had left a barren, six-foot-wide strip that had stopped the fire before it reached the house.

"Do you want to take a look around?" Ward asked.

"No. I'm sure they'll let us return before long. Now that we know everything is safe, our worries are over."

Ward turned the van, and they returned to the school. The Gordons were sharing their good news when Gloria and her parents returned from their surveillance trip. They had lost everything.

"We're leaving as soon as the highway is open," Gloria's father said. "My wife's parents live in Denver. We'll stay with them until we decide what to do. You're welcome to come with us, Shannon. We can have you in Denver in a couple of hours."

"Thank you, but I'm staying...at least for a little while."

Ward didn't know what he would have done if she had readily accepted the offer. He'd never thought of himself as a caveman, but he might have thrown her over his shoulder and carried her home.

The ride to the ranch was a silent one. The sun slipped behind the high mountain peaks, and a dusky twilight was settling over the valley. Tired from the exciting outing, Tara had curled up between them and fallen asleep with her head on Shannon's lap. From time to time, Ward and Shannon glanced at each other, waiting for the other to speak.

When the ranch came into view, Ward suddenly pulled over to the side of the road. Lights from the house and stable were like yellow beacons guiding the way home. They could see a scattering of horses slowly moving about in the grassy meadow.

"This is my life, Shannon," Ward said quietly to her. "I left it once, but I'll not leave it again. It's not an easy life. It's not glamorous. It's not even all that profitable as businesses go," he admitted wryly. "Just a lot of hard work. I can't promise you anything more than what I am and what I have. I know you're used to a lot more, and I've tried to tell myself that it wouldn't be fair to…to…" He hesitated.

"To ask me to marry you?"

"Yes. Will you? I love you, Shannon, more than I ever thought possible. Would you make me and my little girl the happiest two people in the world?"

She hesitated, knowing that she had to be honest with him. "I know how much your faith means to you. I've only taken baby steps toward the kind of commitment that is important to you. What about all the warnings you gave me that you would never marry anyone who didn't have faith in God as strong as yours? Wasn't that a criteria for choosing a wife and mother for your child?"

"I was wrong," he answered readily. "None of us have a full measure of faith. We are all on the same path in different places. You can help me grow, and I can help you. That's what we're here for—not to judge each other. I can tell you're seeking the Lord, and that's all that matters." His eyes softened. "I know I'm asking you to give up a lot to marry a cowboy rancher."

"Yes, you are," she agreed, smiling. "I would have

to give up things like being lonely, frightened, and trapped. But I think I could get used to having a family who loves me, and a strong, loving man to protect me. In case you haven't guessed, I'm deeply in love with you, Ward Dawson.''

He leaned across and kissed her. ''Is that a yes?''

''Yes!'' Tara answered loudly as she lifted her head and her wide-awake eyes snapped with happiness. ''Yes, yes, yes.''

''I guess that's definite enough,'' Shannon said, laughing. ''I couldn't have said it better.''

Ward leaned over, kissed her and whispered how happy she'd made him. Then he chuckled and said, ''Let's go home and tell Beth what Tara's getting for her birthday.''

Epilogue

One year later

"Whose idea was it to have a big shindig like this?" Ward teased Shannon as the cars pulled into the ranch driveway.

"Yours," Shannon said smugly, lifting her face for a quick kiss.

"Come on, you lovebirds," Beth chided as she joined them and Tara on the patio, setting down more dishes on the picnic table already loaded with food. "Don't you know the honeymoon is supposed to be over after a year?"

"Not ours," Ward answered. "We're going to set a record, aren't we, darling?"

"Absolutely." Shannon smiled, feeling like a bride all over again. They'd been married on this very patio, and the same people who had been invited for that happy occasion were soon to arrive to celebrate their anniversary. She couldn't believe how totally happy she was, how completely head over heels in love with her husband.

As a familiar van pulled into the driveway, Tara shrieked, "Kenny's here." Her ponytail danced in the wind as she raced across the yard.

Shannon smiled at Ward. "Do you think Kenny is bringing her the puppy he promised?"

He chuckled. "I certainly hope so. If he doesn't, she'll raise such a fuss that we'll all have to leave home."

Beth nodded. "That's all Tara's talked about since she heard that Pokey was the proud papa of five puppies."

As Kenny got out of the car, they saw he had something in his arms. Shannon laughed. "He brought it."

Alice and Tom Gordon joined them on the patio, giving hugs all around. The wiggly black-and-white puppy was the image of Pokey, and Kenny smiled proudly as he showed it off.

Remembering the night the little boy had tearfully been hunting for Pokey, Shannon gave him a big hug and petted the tiny pup. "He's almost as nice as Pokey."

"It's a she," Kenny corrected her solemnly. "My dad says she can have puppies when she's bigger."

"Oh, goody," Tara exclaimed. "Now we can raise puppies and horses, too."

Ward was saved from commenting on his daughter's enthusiastic remark by the arrival of Reverend and Laura Cozzins.

The minister and his wife had been frequent visitors

at the ranch during the year, and Ward and Shannon had become a mainstay in the church.

"I brought you something," Laura said in her usual bustling manner. "No, not an anniversary gift," she said, as she handed Shannon a large box.

Shannon looked frankly puzzled, and Ward raised a questioning eyebrow.

"You agreed to be secretary of our women's service group, didn't you?"

Shannon nodded. "Yes, I did."

"Well, here's all the recording books, papers and records of the last five years. We've been passing it around every election, hoping someone would have the know-how to get it organized."

"Well, this little lady is the angel you've been looking for," Ward said proudly. "She's worked miracles with our record keeping. For the first time, we really have a handle on the business end of the ranch."

With her usual frankness, Beth said, "I swear that Ward never really knew how much money was coming in and going out until he married Shannon."

"Guilty as charged," Ward readily admitted. His eyes held a loving glow as he looked at Shannon. "She's a woman of many talents, and I thank the Lord every day for bringing her into my life."

"We all do," his sister agreed.

Tom Gordon cleared his throat. "Well, I have a little surprise for her."

Shannon's breath caught. "Is it—"

"Sure is. Want to take a look?"

"I'm not sure," she said honestly as she held the packet he gave her without opening it.

"Go ahead, honey," Ward urged.

"Maybe I should wait." Shannon hedged.

Kenny's father laughed. "You might as well get used to people looking at your work. In another month, it's going to be all over the place."

His words were not reassuring as she opened the packet and saw her drawings printed on cream-colored stationery. She looked at each sketch with a kind of wonder. Pride mingled with amazement. They were really good.

"Let me see, let me see," begged Tara.

With a self-conscious smile, Shannon passed the stationery around. She had denied her talent for so long that none of this seemed real.

Ward whispered in her ear, "Pretty good doodling."

Tom bragged that he'd been the first one to recognize the commercial value of her sketches and had persuaded her to find a publisher who agreed.

"I guess you'll be pretty busy from now on," Laura said, eyeing Shannon's figure with a speculative eye. "You two wouldn't have some more good news for us, would you?"

Shannon tried not to blush. They had intended to wait until later in the evening to share with everyone their latest blessing. Beth was the only one who knew.

Ward sent Shannon a questioning look, and she nodded. "Tell them."

He really didn't have to say anything. Everybody knew just by looking at them. Teasing and smiling, they clapped Ward on the back and hugged Shannon.

"We're going to have a baby?" Tara gasped.

Shannon sent Ward a worried glance. She couldn't tell from the look on Tara's face how she was reacting to the news. They should have prepared her, but it was too late now.

Ward knelt and took her hand. "Yes, Shannon's going to have a baby. God is sending you a little sister or brother."

The little girl looked at Ward and at Shannon. Then she smiled and said with childish wonder, "We really are a family now, aren't we?"

* * * * *

Dear Reader,

I chose to set *Hidden Blessing* against the backdrop of a Colorado forest fire, because it is in times of crisis that we examine our spiritual beliefs and are open to change.

The hard shell of ambition and pride that my heroine, Shannon, has placed around herself begins to crack when she finds herself a refugee in an evacuation center without any worldly possessions. The hero, Ward Dawson, is challenged to bring Shannon into a relationship with God, but like so many of us, he has come to his faith the hard way, and he suspects that Shannon is on the same path. When he tells her that growing in spiritual faith is not a sprint but a marathon, I believe that he speaks a truth for all of us.

Please enjoy the excitement, drama and tenderness in this love story. Letters of sharing are truly welcome.

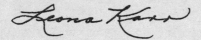

2 Love Inspired novels and a mystery gift... Absolutely FREE!

Visit
www.LoveInspiredBooks.com
for your two FREE books, sent directly to you!

BONUS: Choose between regular print or our NEW larger print format!

There's no catch! You're under no obligation to buy anything. We charge nothing—ZERO—for your first shipment. And you don't have to make any minimum number of purchases.

You'll like the convenience of home delivery at our special discount prices, and you'll love your free subscription to Steeple Hill News, our members-only newsletter.

We hope that after receiving your free books, you'll want to remain a subscriber. But the choice is yours—to continue or cancel, anytime at all! So why not take us up on our invitation, with no risk of any kind!

Love Inspired.
CLASSICS

TITLES AVAILABLE NEXT MONTH

Don't miss these stories in August

A BRIDE AT LAST
AND
A MOTHER AT HEART
by Carolyne Aarsen

Two couples share their journeys of love and
homecoming in the Canadian heartland.

THE FORGIVING HEART
AND
A DADDY AT HEART
by Deb Kastner

A pair of single dads each get a second chance
at love in two unforgettable stories.

LICLASSCNM0706